Errol Hall

Order this book online at www.trafford.com
or email orders@trafford.com

Most Trafford titles are also available at major online book retailers.

Printed in the United States of America.

ISBN: 978-1-4907-4774-3 (sc)
ISBN: 978-1-4907-4773-6 (hc)
ISBN: 978-1-4907-4775-0 (e)

Library of Congress Control Number: 2014917461

Trafford rev. 10/09/2014

 www.trafford.com
North America & international
toll-free: 1 888 232 4444 (USA & Canada)
fax: 812 355 4082

Chapter 1

⸺⁍◦⁖♥♥◦⁖⁌⸺

The last thing I wanted to do was lie to Liseth about anything. We had a great relationship, and had always been honest with each other. We always told each other the truth and never kept secrets from each other. It was the backbone of our relationship. Saturday, I told her I was going to meet a client. She said she would try to finish the living room decorations, and then visit her mother, and that I should pick her up there when I was finished. She walked me to the car and kissed me good-bye, and watched as I headed out of the dead-end street toward the main street leading to Montauk Highway. I watched her in the rear-view mirror as I accelerated the Jag. The July afternoon sun shone through the Victoria's Secret robe she had, on revealing her braless and pantyless body. For a girl whose only workout, other than having sex, was lifting a bottle of beer to her mouth, she always managed to keep her five-feet-seven-inch body under 125 pounds. Her long blonde mane was all over the place. And even though she had just gotten out of bed and had no makeup on, she was a sight to behold; but then what would you expect from a twenty-two–year-old? She sipped her coffee as she retrieved the mail from the mailbox. It was a little after two. She waved as I turned the corner, and we lost sight of each other.

1

I could have told Liseth I was going to be at my office working on a brief or something, or doing research. It would not have been unusual. Big-firm lawyers are not nine-to-fivers, and Saturdays, and even Sundays, were not off limits. But had I told her that I was going to the office, she would have wanted to come with me, or joined me later on. There was no way I could have kept my date with Connie without lying.

It was not unusual for traffic to be backed up on the Long Island Expressway on a Saturday afternoon, or anytime for that matter. The LIE is unpredictable. There could be traffic jams in either direction even in the middle of the night. When traffic is moving, the way I drive, it takes about forty-five minutes to get to the Bronx from my house in Bay Shore. That day it took me the same amount of time to get from Exit 33 to 32. As I sat there waiting for the traffic to move, I thought of calling Connie and canceling our date. It wasn't too late to break it off. We were supposed to meet at six. Even though I'd stopped at the service station up the street from my house to fill my tank, check my engine oil and transmission fluid, and even small-talk a little with the men, there was still plenty of time. It was close to four.

Connie and I had broken up about three and a half years before, because I had insisted on us getting married. She wanted us to live together. I told her, "If you're good enough to sleep with, then you're good enough to live with, and if you're good enough to live with, then you're good enough to be my wife." She said she didn't want to get married again. Connie was married once, when she was only nineteen. She has a daughter, Nicole. The marriage fell apart by the time she was twenty. She was divorced by the time she was twenty-one. I had never been married. When we broke up, she was three months shy of her twenty-ninth birthday. I was closing in on forty-one.

The last time I saw Connie had been two years before. She was with her sister Greta; they were visiting Greta's husband, Victor, who was my barber. Connie was still single, but I had heard she was dating some doctor she met on the job. Connie is a nurse. I was going out with Carmen Grant, among other women, and I had just renewed my vow of bachelorhood. After Connie, being a bachelor was the one thing I was faithful to, until I met Liseth eleven months earlier. For seven of those months, Liseth had practically been living with me.

About six or seven months after I saw Connie, Greta told me Connie and the doctor were getting married. She'd been against marriage, and now she was about to get married again. This was hard for me to understand. I was sure the fact that she was pregnant with twins had something to do with it. So, if she was married with children, why did she want to see me? Especially since she knew I was living with someone.

I leaned on my horn, knowing full well it wouldn't help the situation. But what the fuck, it's one of the things we New Yorkers do best. The traffic was still moving at the same pace, if you could call it moving. I switched off the CD player and tuned in to KISS FM to see if there was any news of the traffic jam. Instead, I got Puff Daddy. WBLS was not any better; they had Busta Rhymes. I quickly changed to HOT 97.1, but it was not any better either. Must have been a rap music weekend. I'm a jazzman. Give me some Miles, Coltrane, or Cannonball; and I am in musical heaven. All right, so I am also a big fan of Luther Vandross and Teena Marie, but rap music? Please, I'd rather confess to killing Jimmy Hoffa. Had it not been for WQCD 101.9, it would have been worth tuning in to one of those crazy rock n roll stations. I was ready to listen to Kid Rock. Kid Rock? I don't even know what the fuck he sings. Can he sing?

As traffic inched slowly along, a Miles Davis song filled the Jag and saved me from calling the local FBI and confessed to the Jimmy Hoffa killing and where he's burried. Across from me, to my right, a couple in a silver BMW 7 series was having an argument, and the woman, whom I presumed was the driver's wife (there was a baby seat in the back) was doing most of the talking. She looked to be in her midtwenties. The man was possibly a year or two older. He could have been the same age. They were dressed casually, as though they were coming from the beach, or going (she still had on a bikini top). The man would occasionally answer as though he was trying to explain something.

There is something unique about traffic jams. It's like sitting through a Ronald Reagan movie on an airplane flight. You're stuck. You can't walk away. Which explains why the man in the BMW was forced to take the shit his wife was dishing out.

The Bimmer's windows were up, as were my Jag's; and even if I'd put mine down, it was unlikely they were going to cooperate by putting theirs down just for me to hear what they were saying. But even without the volume, I could tell he was in a spot. The woman was turned sideways in her seat, facing him, and was waving her hands as she talked, I was certain, at the top of her voice. Every now and then, she would pause to let him say something; but before he could get two words out, she would cut him off. This went on for more than half an hour, before the traffic started to move again. There was a gap of at least three cars' length in front of me, but I was not about to give up this sideshow for love or money. Horns started to blare, but I said, "Fuck you. This is a once-in-a-lifetime event, and it's free."

I wished I could hear what they were saying, because I would have paid any amount of money to hear him try to talk his way out of the mess I was sure he had created. If there is one thing us men are good at, it's getting ourselves into shit. Hey, that's why we are men. It's our nature. Every now and then, the man in the BMW would look in my direction, as if to solicit my help or sympathy, maybe both. But the look on my face, I was sure, told him I was enjoying his pain, not feeling it. Even though I couldn't hear what they were saying, I found it funny. I'd started to laugh when my phone rang. It was Liseth.

"What's so funny?" she said.

I told her about the couple in the Bimmer. "She must have caught him in a position he can't explain," she said.

"I'm sure you would think that," I said, although that's what I thought too.

"If he's doing most of the talking, he's guilty of something," she replied.

I didn't tell her it was the other way around. I switched the subject. "Miss me already?"

"Of course I do."

"I miss you too."

"I just wanted you to know we received an invitation to my aunt's wedding. Do you want to go? It's for both of us."

"Knowing how she feels about me, why would she invite me?"

"I would love to go. You should too."

"OK. I gotta go. Traffic is moving."

"Maybe the girl needs a lawyer. Give her your card."

"Only if she kills him. I don't do divorces."

"Bye, darling. I love you."

"Me too."

Finally, traffic started to move faster. Any attempt on my part to stay with the couple in the BMW would have only caused further delay. In any case, I had a feeling I knew how the argument would end. My money was on the woman.

Ever since New York State introduced the E-Z pass on all the toll bridges and tunnels, it has become nothing less than a nightmare for those who failed to get one. Lucky for me I have one, and it made the trip over the Throgs Neck Bridge easy. I got to the Holiday Inn in New Rochelle a little after five. I had called Connie on her cell phone and explained the problem with traffic. She was waiting for me in the lounge, and was two drinks ahead of me. I apologized for being late. She said it was OK, that she was enjoying the piano player, and that I was worth waiting for. If I didn't agree with her on anything, I had to agree with her on that. She was about to order her third drink. We embraced, and it felt like old times.

"How are you?" she said.

"I'm fine," I said, even though, I must admit, I felt a little nervous being there with her. I felt as though I was cheating on Liseth. Not that I expected anything to happen. But even if nothing happened, I was still cheating on Liseth, because I had lied to her about where I would be, and what I would be doing.

I ordered a brandy. My favorite drink is a gin and tonic, but with brandy, you can sip it slowly. At least I do. Connie's third white wine was served with my brandy. She had been there more than an hour, she said.

Two years, two more children, and five or seven pounds hadn't changed anything about Connie: at thirty-two, she still looked ravishing. She was tanned and relaxed, and her brown hair was longer than I'd ever seen it. It fell unruly down to her shoulders and down the sides of her face, softly framing her cherubic face. Intermittently, and in slow motion, she would use her index finger and her thumb to guide her hair to the back of her head. But as if to please me, the unruly hair would return to where I liked it. It gave me a hard-on.

The extra weight was not obvious, but I knew her; I could tell. I remarked on how good she looked. She returned the compliment. She was dressed for the weather and the occasion: faded blue jeans, a multicolored short-sleeved silk shirt, and open-toed sandals. The shirt was tied high enough to show her midsection. Her belly was still flat. I, as usual, was overdressed: suit and tie. She looked happy, as though she was enjoying life to the hilt. This made me feel good about being there, because if she was happily married, then by now, she would have gotten over me.

I sat across from her and watched as she sipped her wine. There were some specks of gray in her hair. Not enough to be noticed by anyone, but I was not just anyone. I was, after all, the man who went shopping for a 2-karat diamond ring. The man who had been willing to stand before a priest even though I passionately loathe all religions. I'm the same man who had promised her that on her thirtieth birthday I would buy her the house of her choice anywhere she wanted. I was the man who took great pleasure in noticing everything about her. I knew every last inch of her body, down to the little birthmark she had on the entrance to her vagina, which would be unnoticed even if she shaved off all her pubic hair. The only way to see it is if you're face-to-face with it. A position I'd relished.

And yes, I'm the idiot who gave her an ultimatum when she turned down my marriage proposal. Looking back, I know it was a decision I wished I could have reversed. I should have jumped at the chance to live with her. What was the big fucking deal anyhow? We wouldn't have been the first people to have lived together without being married. But the rest of the world didn't have my parents. I should have stood up for what I thought would have made us happy. But no, I had to behave holier than thou; and other than the exclusive prize for being the noble idiot, what the fuck did I gain? I had lost her forever. She was married, and I had Liseth, who was the prize of all prizes, and who I hoped would be the mother of my children. I took a sip of my brandy and said, "I almost didn't come, you know."

"I'm glad you did," she said.

"Now that I'm here, I'm glad I did."

She asked again how I was doing. I gave her the same answer. She asked if I was still running five miles a day, and if I still didn't eat meat. She asked about my parents and about my job. I asked about the twins, and how her daughter, Nicole, was doing in school, particularly in math. She was terrible at math. I used to tutor her.

"Nicole must be . . . what, fourteen on her next birthday, if I'm not mistaken?"

"Yes, in December. The twins just made one two months ago."

"Nicole must be speaking fluent French by now. If not, you wasted your money."

"That girl, let me tell you, you can't shut her up. You know how she loves to talk from the moment she gets up in the morning. Well now, love, she still talks like she swallowed a radio, except now all she does is talk in French. You ask her something, and she answers in French. If she asks you something, she asks it in French. Then to top it off, she has a friend—let me tell you something else, when she and that girl gets on the phone, all you can hear is 'Oui, je comprends, excusez-moi,' and a lot of laughing, and you just know they have to be talking about boys. I swear to God I'm thinking of learning French just to communicate with that girl and to know what she and her friend talk about."

We both cracked up laughing. I'd almost forgotten what that laugh used to do to me. And believe me, it did things to me. Things that came rushing back as I looked at her. Have you ever felt hungry? Really hungry? I mean like you haven't had anything to eat for ages, and you start to think of your favorite dish? You just can't wait to sink your teeth into it, and then you see the woman you love, and she smiles and breaks out into laughter, and right then you forget how hungry you are. That's what Connie's laughter does to me. She had a sexy laughter. Not to mention those lips, and how she'd run her tongue across them when she stopped laughing. It was so sexy. She did it again, and I swear I felt something wet on the tip of my hard-on.

Connie's eyes lit up when she talked about Nicole. "I'm so proud of her. She is a good kid," she said, as she knocked on wood. "But I gave up any hope of her ever being a mathematician. She said she won't need math because she is going to be a lawyer like you. She misses you a lot, Delroy."

I was not surprised to hear that Nicole missed me. We had been close. I was like a father to her. I knew her since before her fourth birthday. Connie pulled a mini photo album out of her handbag. She showed me pictures of her twin sons, of Nicole, and of her husband. Nicole was almost as tall as Connie. She was five three. Connie was five six, four inches shorter than me. Her sons were beautiful boys. A streak of envy ran through me. I had always wanted her to have my child. If the boys were any older, given that her husband and I were black, I would have been suspicious; but the last time we made love was far too long ago for me to make any claim. I held the boys' picture in my hands for some time and stared at them. I wondered what it would have been like to have fathered twins. I asked her their names. Kevin and Francis. Kevin I could understand, but when she told me the reason she named the other one Francis, I was moved. Imagine that: one with his father's name, and the other with my middle name. Had they been mine, I would have named them Delroy and Francis. Delroy Lloyd and Francis Lloyd Bradshaw. Sounded good to me. *Lloyd* was my father's name.

I asked her about the relationship between her husband and Nicole. She said it was good. She said he took them to France for a two-week vacation last summer. Nicole, she said, was ecstatic. The pictures Connie showed me of her family showed a happy and loving family who seemed to enjoy a lot of things together. "You look like such a happy family," I said, and I meant it.

"That's the magic word," she said. "We look *happy*."

"You're not happy?"

"I remember something you told me years ago."

"What was that?"

"That there are degrees of happiness."

"Yes, I remember."

"So there are degrees of happiness.

"What's your point?"

"What was that phrase? That you would rather be 'an unhappy Socrates than a happy pig.'"

"Connie, if pigs look like you, I'd start eating pork. What's your point? You're not saying you'd be happier divorced, are you?" I don't know why I said that. It just came out.

"Maybe I would, but I don't want a divorce—at least not right now."

She waved for the waiter to come over, and she ordered another white wine. It could have been her fourth or fifth. I'd lost count. After two brandies, I ordered an iced tea and tonic and asked the waiter if he had any cheesecake. I ordered a slice. Connie finished her glass as the waiter returned with the drinks and the cheesecake. She took a sip of the cold wine and then leaned back in her seat as she reached over and put her hand on mine and gently curled her fingers around the back of my hand. She avoided eye contact with me.

She said, "The two times I got married, I got married for the same reason: I was pregnant. With Nicholas, I was a kid and was just learning about sex. I can't say I really loved him. At seventeen, eighteen, we all think we are in love. After my divorce, I promised myself I would never ever get married again, and that was why

9

I said no to your proposal. I didn't want to spoil what we had, because what we had was special. With you, I knew I had found true love for the first time in my life, and I didn't need a piece of paper to validate it."

She flipped her hair from her face, and as usual, the hair returned to where I wanted it. I said a silent *Thank you*. Her hand on mine, the hair thing—the setting added up to a harder hard-on.

"When I got pregnant with Nicole, I was a little over seventeen. Nicholas was twenty-three and was in his last year of college. Both our parents wanted this marriage, so we went along. We knew it wouldn't last. By the time I was twenty-one I was divorced, with a two-year-old child, and a year of college. I made two promises to my daughter and my family, but most of all to myself: I would finish college and never get married again. I was determined to get an education. Even when I was pregnant with Nicole, I knew I had to get an education if I wanted to be somebody. You remember I told you that I went to my high school graduation pregnant, and that after Nicole was born, I wasted no time, I went straight to college? You remember I also told you that right after the divorce I said 'fuck it, life goes on, you remember?"

I didn't say a word. I remembered, but I just listened and nodded my head to everything she said. She continued: "You know, every day I thank God for the supportive parents I had. Without them, I don't know if I would have been able to finish college and do what I always wanted to do—be a nurse."

The positions of our hands had changed by now. We were pressing our palms together, fingers intertwined. Dick still hard. I could imagine what was going on between her legs. If I'd say let's get a room, no way she'd say no. I said, "And I have firsthand knowledge of your determination in keeping the second promise." Her hand was as soft as I remembered it.

"You know, Delroy, I was a little disappointed in you. A grown man, and a lawyer, and you let your parents tell you how to live your life. I said to myself, *If this man can't stand up to his parents at his age, when will he ever?* You know, I resisted getting involved with you, because at the time, I had a young child and school to finish, but you were persistent, and just wouldn't take no for an answer. But I liked the fact that you wouldn't give up. It showed a man of character, and I fell in love with you, just for that. Because somehow, I saw in you a man I could depend on, who would fight for me in every way possible. But when you gave in to your parents, somehow I lost a little respect for you. Not that I ever stopped loving you, I don't think I ever could, but you should have—oh shit, forget it."

I took a sip of the iced tea. I took a deep breath afterward and took in what she just said. I had no idea she had so much on her chest, but I was glad she'd decided to unload it. I started to say something when she excused herself to go to the bathroom. I watched her as she walked away. As pretty as Connie was, and as beautiful as her body was, she never had the greatest ass. Oh, don't get me wrong, there was nothing bad about it, and I loved it. It was just that it was a little flat. Firm, but flat. No rise to it. It was not like—well, Liseth, whose ass was so firm and was right there. You know. And those legs of hers—made me want to say "My God." And I'm an atheist. Just goes to show what those legs can do to a man. What legs! Well, let's put it this way: you remember that James Bond movie *For Your Eyes Only* and the picture of the girl on the poster, shown from her backside in a bikini and holding a crossbow, and Bond standing from afar between her legs? Well, Liseth was too young then, but that could have been her ass and legs. I always teased Liseth that her behind was a cross between a black and a white woman's, and that for a white girl, she had a great butt. She hated it when you called her a white girl. "I'm not white, I'm Puerto Rican," she would say. Connie, from any angle, was just white.

I'd almost finished the iced tea and was sucking on the lemon wedge that came with it as Connie reentered the room. There were three black girls sitting across from us, and as soon as Connie left, one of them came over and asked me if I had a cigarette. I told her I didn't smoke and pointed to the cigarette machine across from the bar. She would have had to be blind not to see it. "Oh," she said. And then she asked me how much the machine took.

"I have no idea. I don't smoke," I said. I was sure she sensed the displeasure in my voice. And in anticipation of her next question, I said, "Yes, she's my wife."

She got defensive and said she didn't care. "Nice meeting you." She went back to join her friends, and they then engaged in seeing which of them could give me the dirtiest look.

While I waited for Connie, I took the opportunity to check out the lounge. We were on the third floor, seated in one of those curved booths, with really soft leather seats—the kind that sinks when you sit. Complete soporific comfort. Our booth was at an angle, half looking out the window onto Highway 195 and the other half facing the bar. My back was to the highway. To the left of me was a small dance floor, and behind it on a platform was the piano player. The piano was a black baby grand set against the backdrop of dark red drapes and carpet to match. There must have been thirty people or so scattered about the place. Unfortunately, the silly black girl was one of them. The lights were soft, and the music soothing. The piano player not only showed he knew how to play a piano, but that he had respect for it. To hear his rendition of "Satin Doll" was to witness a man having a love affair with a piano. He would have made Duke Ellington proud.

I drained the remainder of the iced tea and took one of the ice cubes in my mouth. I bit on it and chewed the pieces, crunching them in my jaw. It felt good, and I took another and repeated the process. Connie looked at me and smiled. She finished the rest of her drink. We both smiled at each other. Her makeup was fresh, and she obviously had done something to her hair. It was pulled back and held in place with the hair band that was on her wrist. Her beauty was magnified. If I was a religious man, I would have thought God had singled me out for special blessings. There I was, in the company of a thirty-two-year-old woman who looked twenty-two, and with a body that three children had not damaged, and I must admit, I had no idea how the night would end. At the same time, in Manhattan, there was a real twenty-two-year-old who should be happy that I'm a lawyer, and a darn good one to boot, because if for some reason they ever pass a law against beautiful women, she's going to need all the legal help in the world.

I could smell Connie's replenished perfume when she sat down. I asked her if she wanted another drink. She said no. "Before you went to the bathroom, you accused me of everything short of being a bitch. Maybe somewhere in there you said it, and I missed it."

She interrupted me. "I would never use that word to describe you. What I was saying was—"

"Never mind what you were saying. Hear me out for a minute. I let you have your moment."

"OK, I'm sorry. Go ahead." Her voice was barely audible, but the childlike quality in which she spoke lent credence to her sincerity.

"Thank you. Let me agree with you on one thing: you had every right to be disappointed in me for being guided by my parents' principles and not my own. I was disappointed in myself too. But you were wrong about one thing."

"What?"

"Will you please let me finish?"

She mouthed *I'm sorry*.

I inhaled and exhaled. I remembered how vulnerable she was when she was childlike, and how easily I always fell under that spell. I continued. "Connie, I did fight for you. I had a big argument with my parents about them not interfering in my life when it came to matters of the heart. I told them that who I lived with was none of their business. It was the first time I ever went up against them. I told them I was a good son, who had done everything to make them proud, and if all I did wrong was live with some woman I loved more than anything in the world, next to them, then they had nothing to be ashamed of.

"But, Connie, even if I had lived with you, and we had a child, wouldn't you have insisted on us getting married? Weren't you the one who didn't want a child out of wedlock? Isn't that the reason why you married Kevin? Correct me if I'm wrong. Am I missing something here? How do we solve that dilemma?"

She was silent. I repeated the questions. Still no response. I added, "Now, I wouldn't have a problem marrying you if you were pregnant, because that's what I wanted in the first place. But you still haven't answered my questions."

She sort of sighed, bit her bottom lip, crossed her legs, and then said, "I don't know. Maybe I wouldn't have had to worry about anything if you were the father of my children. I don't have the answer for everything, Delroy. That was why I . . . you're the lawyer. You're the smart one. You were supposed to be my knight in shining armor. You're supposed to . . . I don't know what I know. All I know is that I miss you very much. That I'm miserable, that I never stopped loving you, and that I've not been held and touched by a man in close to seven months. Delroy, tell me you feel the same way about me that I feel about you. You can't tell me you don't feel something for me."

With the glass at my lips and a cube of ice and liquid in my mouth, I almost choked when I heard her say those words. Did I hear her right? Did she really say that? No, she didn't say that. Please tell me she didn't say that. But she did. The waiter was clearing the table next to ours when I almost choked. The black girls across from us would have been happy if I had choked to death, because whether they know you or not, any white woman with a black man is with their man.

The waiter asked me if I was all right. I told him I was fine. He asked me if he could get me anything. I said no, and I asked Connie if she wanted anything. She said no again. I still had some of the brandy left. Suddenly I wished that traffic jam had lasted longer. Long enough for her to call me and say she couldn't wait any longer. That she had to go home to her husband and children. Instead, there I was, wondering why she hadn't had sex with her husband for close to seven months, and whether she was still in love with me, and was it the wine talking, and was she for real? Whatever it was, we were in a hotel lounge holding hands. Holy fuck! What did I get myself into? And if I remember right, she had said she didn't want a divorce—at least not yet. What the fuck did

14

she mean by that? Suddenly I was the one without answers. "Can I ask you a question, Connie?" I said.

"Sure," she said.

"What is going on between you and your husband that you guys haven't had sex in close to seven months?"

"Besides me not loving him?"

"It's obvious you don't love him, but there is a bigger problem. What is it?"

"He wants a housewife. He doesn't want me to work. I have to stay home, keep the house looking beautiful, have his dinner ready on time, and be a good hostess when he invites his friends over, which is often enough. And God forbid I should have dinner late, and I'm reminded that I don't have a job and he has to work hard to save people's lives, and the least I could do is have his fuckin' food ready."

"Did he say it exactly like that?"

"Not the fuckin' part. The jerk thinks he's too good to curse, so when we get into an argument, I'd let loose and say whatever I feel like. It has gotten to the point when sometimes I purposely don't have dinner ready just to annoy the fuck out of the little prick, and I mean a little prick in more ways than one." She laughed when she said that. I couldn't help but laugh too. She can be a spiteful little bitch when she wants to be.

"So how often do you get into this mood?" I asked.

"When I feel like fuckin' with his head, which is becoming frequent."

I was a little confused. Earlier, she had said he had a good relationship with Nicole, but now she was painting a picture of a dominating, possessive wacko. I had to ask.

"You know," she said, "that's the problem. On the one hand, he's great with the children. I suppose some people could describe him as a good father. He's a good father, but on the other hand, he wants the dutiful little wife, to keep house, entertain his friends, and spread my fuckin' legs when he wants me to."

I looked at my watch. We had been there a little over four hours. I asked her where the children were and what time she was expected home. She said they were at Greta's. She was spending the weekend with Greta because Kevin was out of town at a medical convention. According to Connie, when Kevin was not attending some medical convention or seminar, he had work on weekends. In a sense, she said, she understood that, because as a doctor, he was always on call. But the breaking point, she said, was when it moved from spending weekends alone to spending holidays and his days off alone.

Her voice was breaking with emotion as she turned to face me. There were tears welling up in her eyes. She fought them back, but some escaped and traveled halfway down her cheeks before she dabbed at them with her napkin. I wanted to take her in my arms and hold her. I wanted to kiss her tears away and tell her everything would be all right. I wasn't sure what to say or do.

"About three months ago," she said between blowing her nose and wiping her eyes, "I decided to go back to work. I couldn't take it anymore. It was either that or have an affair."

More tears rolled down her cheeks. And I couldn't help it. I moved to sit beside her. And this time, it was me who dabbed her cheeks. She rested her head on my shoulder, and I, instinctively, put my hand around her and gently stroked her shoulder. I said, "So did you?"

"What?" she said.

"Have an affair?"

"Of course not," she said, rather surprised by the question. "Not that I couldn't."

"Why didn't you?"

"Oh, I could have. I had many opportunities, but I want more than just sex. I want to feel like a woman. I want to be made love to. I miss being talked to. It is so boring to make love in silence. I want a man to talk to me, to tell me what's on his mind, to say just what he feels, and not be afraid to. Someone like you. Oh, I miss that."

I felt sweet memories flowing through my brain, and I must admit it made the erection harder. And it was good. Another time and another place and I might have encouraged it, but with Connie, I knew there is no such thing as a quickie.

She continued, "You know what I loved about you, Delroy?" Before I could answer, she said, "You were spontaneous. You were the kind of guy who would just fuck me in your bathroom with a house full of people outside. He would say, on his way to work, something like 'can we have sex tonight?' Boring."

I remembered full well, and trust me, it was not doing anything for the boner I had underneath the table. I looked at my watch again. She asked me if I had to be somewhere. I told her I had to pick up Liseth at her mother's. She asked what would happen if I didn't. I told her I didn't know, because I'd never stood her up before. Nor had I ever lied to her. She put her arm around my waist and gently tightened it. It felt good. I stroked her shoulder some more, and then kissed her on the forehead. Our embrace reminded me of when we used to cuddle up on the couch in front of the TV. We would hold each other tight, oblivious to what was on the TV, safe in each other's arms. It had felt good.

"Connie," I said.

She answered, "Hmm."

"Connie, I'm a little confused."

"About what?"

"Well, if things are not working out between you and Kevin, I don't understand, why don't you seek a divorce? Don't you think it would be better for everyone in the long run?"

She loosened her hold on me and straightened up a bit. "I don't think so," she said.

"Why not? You know eventually it will come to that, don't you?"

"Yeah, but not right now."

I was careful in what I was about to say, hoping it would not create the wrong impression. "Connie, you shouldn't stay in a relationship where you're unhappy, especially when, by your own admission, you don't love him."

We were now facing each other. She took a sip of my brandy. "This shit is strong," she said, and took another sip. "I agree with you, Delroy, but right now, I can't afford, financially, to be on my own, and I've been away from my parents for too long to move back in, and not with three children. Plus, he would do whatever he could to take my boys away."

"So what are you going to do?"

"I don't know right now, but I know I wished he was dead. If I thought for a moment I could get away with it, I would kill the son of a bitch."

"You don't really mean that, do you?"

"Right now, I'm not really sure what I mean, but I know if I got a call right now telling me he was dead, I'd be a happy, not to mention a rich woman."

"Please, Connie, I hope you don't express these sentiments around anybody else. It could be taken the wrong way."

"Oh, I know that. I'm not a fool. But if that motherfucka ever hits me or rapes me again, I swear to God, there is no tellin' what the fuck I'll do."

For a moment, I was not sure I'd heard what she said, and I didn't want to ask her to repeat it, but the word *rape* resonated in my mind, and somehow, without thinking, I said, "Connie, did you say rape?"

"Well, when he forces himself on me and have sex with me without my consent, isn't that rape?"

"Under the legal definition, yes. But—"

"But what? You're not going to tell me that because we're married it would be hard to prove, are you?"

"In a sense, yes. That was what I was about to say."

"Well, that's bullshit, and you know it. So don't give me that."

"I agree with you, but I have to ask you one question."

"OK, go ahead. Be a lawyer."

"Hey, I'm your friend. I should be able to ask you this."

"Go ahead," she said, taking another sip of what was left of my drink.

"Have you ever told anybody in the past when this alleged rape—forget I said that. Please forget I said that. Have you ever told anybody about any of these rapes? Anybody at all?"

"No, not really."

"What do you mean not really? Either you did or you didn't tell anyone. Which is it?"

"Well, I did tell Greta."

"Is she the only one?"

"Listen, Delroy, you don't just go around telling everybody that your husband slaps you around and rapes you. You know it's hard as it is telling you, and . . . and I really don't want to talk about it. It's embarrassing as it is."

There were tears in her eyes as she said it. That was the one thing about Connie that didn't change: she cries easily. I suddenly disliked her husband, without ever having met the guy.

"Listen, I'm not saying that you couldn't make a case against him, or have a good defense if, God forbid, you . . . I don't even know why I'm going there, but if you should—listen, Connie. Listen to me carefully. Listen to what I'm about to say. Talk to somebody outside of the family. Somebody who is objective. See a counselor. Anybody. Anybody at all. Just in case. Listen, I'm a lawyer, an officer of the court, so all I can tell you is just in case. Talk to somebody. A battered spouse defense needs corroborating evidence. Witnesses who are independent and objective, and that's all I'll say. Let's talk about something else."

"So, Delroy," she said, "Kevin thinks I'm at Greta's, and I don't have to worry because he would never call there. No love lost between him and her. According to your girlfriend, where are you now?"

"Meeting a client."

She laughed, pinched my waist, and said, "Oh, come now, Delroy, you can come up with something more original than that."

Chapter 2

I f there were ever three people in the world that are different, it's me, Connie, and Liseth. I'm from a family of lawyers. Both my parents are lawyers, and both their parents were lawyers. My father's two brothers and his only sister are lawyers who are married to lawyers. My mother's three sisters are all lawyers, and they too are all married to lawyers. All my cousins are lawyers. The one oddball in the family was my father's younger brother's only son, who was a doctor. (Dad was the eldest.) Whenever there are family gatherings, my cousin Teddy, the doctor, would feel as though there was no one to talk shop with. Uncle Theodore would remark about how lucky he was having two daughters who had seen fit to continue the family tradition. Of course, he was kidding, but Teddy could not help feeling as though he had let his father down by not going to law school.

When I was growing up, I thought there were two kinds of people in the world: lawyers and people who needed a lawyer. Although, I supposed, I could have chosen another profession and my parents would have been just as happy if I did, the thought of not going to law school had never crossed my mind. This only-child thing can be a heavy burden.

Connie had a brother and a sister, who were both older. Greta, a public schoolteacher, was three years older than her; and her brother, who was the eldest at thirty-seven and whom I had never met, he was in the army and was always stationed overseas. Her parents were second-generation hardworking Irish Americans from the Bronx. Her mother was a schoolteacher, and her father was retired from the New York City Police Department. Before they moved out of the Bronx to somewhere in Rockland County, they had lived about a mile and a half from where I grew up in Pelham Manor.

Pelham Manor was one of those communities in lower Westchester County sandwiched between New Rochelle on the north and the Bronx on the south. West of Pelham Manor was Mouth Vernon, where we had once lived. To the east of it was the Long Island Sound. Pelham Manor was a community where the houses start at a million dollars. And where the residents could be anything from federal judges to foreign diplomats. Starting from the bridge that connected it to the Bronx and ending at the New Rochelle border, Pelham Manor was about two miles long and about four miles wide, with very little excitement or any form of entertainment to go with it. For that we had to go to New Rochelle or the Bronx. Even for a decent haircut I had to go to the Bronx. Well, in all fairness, there was a good barber up on Main Street, but he was an old white guy, who had been there forever. For a black man's barber, the Bronx was the place to go, which was how I met Connie.

The main street, not to be confused with Main Street, running through Pelham Manor is Boston Road. It runs from New Rochelle through the Bronx, where it meets up with White Plains Road. On the Bronx side of Boston Road, about four miles, was a barbershop, where the owner had been cutting my hair for the past fifteen years. Head Quarters One was owned by a young West Indian named Victor, who was married to Connie's sister. Victor and I met when he was working at another barbershop farther down Boston Road. Two years later, he would opened his own shop up the street from where he worked; and five years later, he opened another, Head

21

Quarters Two, in the shopping center closer to the Pelham Manor border.

Victor was the only one who could cut my hair the way I liked it. Even after I moved out to Long Island and tried a few local barbers, I would always return to the Bronx. I could literally fall asleep in his chair and he would cut it right. Not that I ever fell asleep. I couldn't. The barbershop was always a forum for politics, gossip, the latest news, and, I kid you not, stock tips. Victor believed in the market. He was a devotee. He played the market with as much care and consideration as he cut hair. For a guy who didn't finish high school, he had a great understanding of the stock market and how to analyze stocks. He and several of his customers, many of whom were college graduates, would analyzed stocks and predict their movements. And, apart from his two shops, his skills in playing the market were evident in the house he owned in the New York suburb of Scarsdale, and the new Mercedes Benz he drove every three years.

The modus vivendi of all barbershops is allowing a certain socialization. It makes for good business. Head Quarters was no exception. The shop was twenty by fifteen, with twelve chairs, and one where a woman does women's hair only. In the back, there was a mounted large-screen TV with speakers on the wall at the back and front of the shop. On Saturdays, the customers would start to line up in front of the shop before the 7:00 a.m. opening. When Victor let them in, they would take a ticket, which was done mostly on Saturdays because of the crowd, which by noon would be overwhelming. I usually arrive sometime between two and three. By then, the client list, which included everyone from janitors to doctors and police to drug dealers, would be in deep debate on every social topic imaginable. The floor would be covered with hair, but every now and then, before it got too heavy underfoot, a young man would sweep it up. And while we waited and debated various topics, the consistent aroma from the Jamaican restaurant next door would quietly intrude on our presence. By noon, you could smell the succulent jerk chicken and oxtail fighting for dominance over the curry goat and fried fish. The concrete wall was no match for the addictive smell seeping in.

One Saturday in Head Quarters One, Greta, for the first time, came in with Connie. By this time, Greta and I had known each other for as long as I'd known Victor. Greta is a very warm and friendly person; she had talked about her sister in general and specific terms. I had never actually met Connie, although I had seen her more than once, sitting in her little blue Datsun outside the shop, waiting for Greta. The day she walked in, I was in the middle of a conversation with some guy about how the law works. Head Quarters One, unlike Head Quarters Two, was a smaller shop. It was about half the size and had half the chairs. There was a fish shop next door to Head Quarters One, whose smell permeated the barbershop. Connie walked in to the shop in the middle of me holding the floor. I was saying something—I don't remember exactly how the line of argument went, but I knew one thing: the minute I laid eyes on her, I lost all concentration, which was totally out of character. It was the summer, and she had on a pair of shorts and a top that stopped a little below her breasts. Her stomach was flat and taunt. Her navel looked as though it was artificially put there. It was too cute to be real. Her hair was longer then; it went all the way down her back, and it was unruly. Which was what caught my attention. I tried not to make it too obvious, but I couldn't help it. She was much too beautiful to ignore. Besides the fact she and her sister were the only white people in an all-black barbershop. She stood out. Forget the fact that Greta was Victor's wife; everyone still looked when she entered the shop. And they all froze when Connie walked in.

At the time, I didn't know if it was my oratory or just me that caught her interest, but she was captivated, and stood there looking at me. I could feel her eyes on me, but I tried my best not to make it obvious that I was aware. Years later, she told me that it was a little of both. I watched her out of the corner of my eye as she stood there looking at me. When I finished, I introduced myself. "Hi, you must be Connie," I said. Before she could answer, I told her my name.

She looked sort of surprised that I knew her name. She extended her hand and said, "Pleased to meet you." She looked at Greta as if to say, *Who the hell is this?*

If Greta was about to answer, I didn't give her a chance. I interjected, "I'm sorry if I have you at a disadvantage, but I've heard so much about you. It's a pleasure to finally meet you."

She smiled and said, "Don't believe everything you hear. Greta has a way of being overly dramatic."

Greta interjected, "I didn't tell him anything."

"Well, somebody did," said Connie.

Victor, who could hear everything, said, "Don't look at me."

"Let me assure you," I said, "that everything I heard is all good."

She smiled again and said, "That's nice to know."

Victor and Greta went to his little office in the back and left Connie standing there. I asked her if she would like to sit down. She said they wouldn't be long. They weren't. I handed her one of my business cards as she was about to leave. "It was nice meeting you, Delroy," she said.

"For me, it was a pleasure," I said with a smile that would have rivaled any toothpaste commercial. She smiled back, and that was the end of that.

I didn't see her again for over a month, and neither Victor nor Greta would give out her number. So one Saturday, since I knew Greta would be there, I bought a dozen red and a dozen yellow roses, and on a card, I wrote, "I'm not one who believes that life is fair, because it isn't. But do you think it's fair for you to just walk into my life, say hello, and just disappear? I would certainly like to see you again, and even if it's not possible, I'd like to at least hear from you. Oh, by the way, I couldn't decide if I should send you red or yellow roses, so I got both." I signed the card simply "Delroy" and put another business card in with it. This time I included my home and cell phone numbers.

That Sunday evening, she called me at home. It was after ten. She apologized for calling that late and asked if she was interrupting anything. I told her she wasn't. She thanked me for the flowers and told me yellow roses were her favorite next to tulips. Then she proceeded to tell me how much she was not interested in any relationship at the moment, and that her daughter was her main priority. I told her I understood, but that I would like to see her again, maybe take her out for dinner.

"Listen, Delroy, I'm sure you're a nice a man and everything, but right now, I'm not interested in seeing anybody."

I remained quiet.

"Hello?" she said.

"I'm here."

"Oh."

"It's just that I was thinking, that if I'd wanted to let somebody know that I was not interested in them, the easiest way would be not to call them. What better way to get my message across." She was the one who paused this time. There was silence on the other end.

"Hello?" I said.

"Well, I . . . I thought the polite thing to do was to tell the person that I was not interested. I think that would be better than leaving them wondering, don't you think?"

"I suppose you're right. It can never harm one to have good manners."

"Precisely my point."

"Well, now that you've made your point, do you think it's possible we can go out, maybe to dinner sometime?"

"Tell me, Delroy, are you one of those guys that won't take no for an answer?" she asked.

I was curious to see her face when she said that, because I was quite sure she was not serious when she said it.

"It's not that I can't take no for an answer . . ."

"But?"

I sensed that my answer was important to the continuation of the conversation. "There is really no buts—it's just that I would like to see you again. Is that so bad?"

"Depends on why you want to see me."

"Must there be a reason?"

"There is always a reason."

I chose my words carefully before I answered. I said, "Of course there is a reason. There always is. Whether we know it or not, there is a reason why we do the things we do. This is not to say the reasons are bad."

"And your reason?"

Again, I carefully chose my words. "Other than wanting to know you, I can't think of a better reason." For some reason, I was sure I'd said the right thing, even though I knew she would not have told me. But somehow I just felt it in my heart.

"I'll have to think about that," she said.

She still didn't give me her number, but I was happy that the conversation lasted as long as it did. She never came back to the barbershop again, and it would be a whole month before I saw her again.

It was exactly three weeks later, and I was in a deposition at my office. When we broke for lunch, my secretary handed me a note. It read, "Ms. Darby called. She said she will call back." At first I didn't recognized the last name. It was not until she called back that I realized that Connie's last name was Darby.

"Hello, Mr. Bradshaw," she said. Her voice was soft and enticing. I knew right then that I wanted her. Nothing else mattered. I wanted her, and I was determined to get her.

"Hello," I said. "To what do I owe the pleasure?"

"I was just thinking," she said. "Do you like Aretha Franklin?"

Had I known better, I would have asked her if she was an idiot. Who doesn't like Aretha? "Of course I do," I replied.

"Well, I have two tickets for her show at Radio City next weekend, and since Greta can't make it, I figure I would invite you. I have one confession to make, though," she said.

"And what is that?"

"The idea to invite you was Greta's."

This was where I would have quipped: "I see. And you objected strongly, and she overruled you, and you gave in." But considering how elated I was, I resisted the thought. Instead, I silently said, *Thank you, Greta.* Then I told her I would love to go.

She said she would meet me at Radio City. I said that would be fine, since my offices were practically across the street from the theater.

"I thought so," she said. "That's why I suggested meeting there." Then she said good night, and I didn't hear from her again until the Thursday before the concert.

There is a reason why we all love summers. Women are allowed to dress any way they want to, and get away with it. The concert was scheduled to start at eight that evening. I left my office at seven and walked the three blocks up. The sun had left its residue on the pavement. You could still feel the trapped heat rising from the asphalt. That morning, I wrestled with what to wear, and eventually settled on white pants, a light blue shirt, and a blue single-breasted blazer with a crest, and my English slippers with the crest on the front. No socks. I was not sure what she would be wearing, so I tried to keep it simple.

She was early. She had to be. She was standing at the box office when I approached. She was wearing a short skirt and black shirt to match, which was tied instead of tucked in, with two buttons undone showing just so much of her black bra. Her hair was held back from her face with a large hair clip. Her exotically tanned skin glistened under the lobby lights.

I was not sure if it was appropriate to greet her with a kiss on the cheek, even though I wanted to. Instead, I extended my hand. "So nice of you invite me to the show," I said.

"So nice of you to accept," she said.

"Were you waiting long?"

"Not, but I have been in the city for some time."

I noticed a Victoria's Secret bag. "I see," I said, pointing to it.

"I couldn't resist it," she said as she twirled the little bag around her finger and handed me the tickets. I gently guided her with one hand toward her seat, after we had both got us a beer. The seats were fifteen rows from the stage.

I'd seen Aretha twice before, and as usual, she was in top form. It was Connie's first time, and even though some of the songs were way before her time, being that she was only twenty-two, she and

I were singing along with Aretha. Especially when she sang "I never loved a man the way I love you." This was a sixties song, but Connie knew every word.

After the show, I asked her if she would like to have something to eat. Unfortunately, she said, she couldn't. She said she'd promised her mother she'd pick up her daughter that night.

"I thought you lived with your mother," I said.

"Whatever gave you that idea?" she said incredulously.

"I don't know. I just thought—"

She cut me off. "I have been living on my own for some time."

As I walked her to the garage in the back of Radio City Music Hall, she emphasized how much she enjoyed the show, and that it was very sweet of me to accept her invitation on such short notice. I asked her if we could maybe do it again, possibly go out to dinner.

"Taking me to dinner is important to you, isn't it?" she asked.

"Is this a trick question?"

"No. But I'll tell you what, I'll think about it. Is that good enough?"

"That is very good, indeed."

When the attendant brought her car around, she tipped him what I think was a dollar, kissed me on the cheek, and said good night. I watched the light-blue Datsun pull out of the garage and take off down Fifty-First Street and then make the right up Seventh Avenue.

I tucked both hands in my pants pockets and headed toward Seventh Avenue, made a left, and then headed straight for the garage in my office building.

"Working late as usual, Mr. Bradshaw?" said the parking attendant, a young Jamaican who was working his way through college, and whose ambition was to go to law school.

"Not tonight, Neville," I said. "Tonight I went to see Aretha Franklin with a very special lady."

"I thought they were all special?" Neville said.

I handed him a ten-dollar bill and said, "This one is extra special, my boy." The Jag was parked next to his booth. I got in, clicked on the CD, turned up Miles, and drove off. Even over Miles, I could hear Neville say, "Good night, Mr. Bradshaw."

Connie and I had something that Liseth wished she had. We had what most people would describe as a normal upbringing. Both our parents were still married to each other. Liseth's father left her mother when she was only two. Her mother had to raise her and her sister, who was two years older, and her two brothers, who were five and seven years older, by herself. Liseth grew up without any man in the household, and although her mother dated other men, she would never live with another man. For this, Liseth's approach to relationships was much tarnished. She saw men as unreliable and manipulating, whose only aim was to charm women and then, after they got what they wanted, dump them. She was determined not to fall into that category.

Liseth grew up in what is known as Spanish Harlem. They lived on 118th Street, between Lexington Avenue and Third Avenue. Her mother was a housekeeper at the Plaza Hotel. Ms. Fernandez had worked there since she came to New York as a teenager from Puerto Rico some thirty years ago. She was only sixteen when she met her husband, and was only seventeen when she had her first child. Her husband was three years older. She and I were the same age. Liseth's brothers never went to college. Her oldest brother was a barber. The other one, only God knew what he was. Her sister had an associate's degree from the Borough of Manhattan Community College. She was a secretary in a major law firm. She had one child, and although she was not married to the child's father, they both lived together.

When Liseth was in high school, she was recognized as a gifted student and was awarded a scholarship to the Riverdale Country School. After graduation, she was accepted to Columbia University, where she majored in political science and philosophy. She graduated with straight As. After that she got a mind-blowing 175 on her LSATs, which, coincidently, had something to do with how we met.

It was the first Friday in July of 1998, and I was invited to a birthday party of an old friend from college who was married

29

to another old friend from college, who I'd inadvertently brought together. Ebony Saunders and I were freshmen at Columbia University. She had an apartment on Riverside Drive, while I commuted from Pelham Manor. Ebony was from Jamaica and had lived with her parents in Crown Heights, Brooklyn. She had a twin brother who played cricket in England. For the first year, we went steady; and at times, I would sleep over at her place, especially on weekends.

During our sophomore year, Dalton Gray, who was also from Jamaica, came up to attend Columbia. I met him through some mutual friends, and we became fast chums. Dalton was living on campus. We would hang out together on most weekends, and sometimes he and Ebony would come up to my parents' house. They particularly loved the pool. The three of us were a team. That is, until our junior year, when they found they were attracted to each other. It came to me from out of left field, but the philosopher in me had conditioned me to not be surprised by anything in life. Human beings are susceptible to any behavior. In any case, they were honest about their feelings. Ebony knew the kind of person I was, and that I would not take it personally. It was Dalton who was worried about my reaction.

To his surprise, I was not angry. Instead, I did what any civilized, rational person would have done—let love prevail. After all, what choice did I have? I could have either behaved like a silly child and lost two good friends, or behaved like a mature man and retained two lifelong friends. The latter proved the wiser. The only problem was that Ebony had taken it upon herself to fix me up with every one of her available single friends, as if to make amends or something. The closest she came was with Jasmine Chambers, one of the best legal minds to ever come out of Yale.

Jasmine and I went out for about ten months. Ebony had more hope for the relationship than either Jasmine or I had. Jasmine was a self-centered, ambitious, career-driven nympho who used sex as therapy to relieve work stress. Hey, I'm not complaining. When the chance presented itself for her to be the first black woman, at thirty-one, to head up the civil rights division at the justice department, she was not about to pass it up. I could not have blamed her. We remain friends still.

Dalton and Ebony got married right after she graduated. I was Dalton's best man. Years later, when they would tell anyone how they met, it would always end up being the topic. I stayed on at Columbia Law School while they went on to Harvard—he to medical school, she to law school. After medical school, Dalton did his residency at Beth Israel Medical Center and then settled at Harlem Hospital Center. Ebony got a job at one of New York's top ten law firms as a tax attorney, where she has been ever since, and where she made partner, her first time up, ten years ago.

In the early nineties, a bunch of black professionals decided they wanted to move back to Harlem. I was more partial to the suburb. They were buying up most of the great brownstones north of 110th Street. Dalton and Ebony bought a great brownstone with character (circa 1890) up on Sugar Hill. It was on 148th Street off Saint Nicholas Avenue. I remember when they closed on it. They were so excited. Dalton planned on one day making the step down street level into a doctor's office. The first floor would be their living room and kitchen, and the top floors would have the bedrooms. There was a third floor, and at the time, they were not sure what they would do with it.

The building needed a lot of work, and I mean a lot of work. They had to gut the whole interior. But when they were finished with it, *Architectural Digest* would have been lucky to have had it on their covers. What a beautiful home it was. They put in all new hardwood floors, a new boiler, and central air-conditioning. They put in working fireplaces in the living room and the master bedroom, and painted the walls of the living room yellow and, to frame the view, chose white for the window moldings. The dining room was arranged to allow one to focus on the interior. They put in cove ceilings, from which hung two 1930s Murano glass chandeliers. In the master bedroom, they modified the moldings and installed a limestone mantel over the fireplace. But it was the master bathroom suite that was the killer. They tore out the wall between the dressing room and the bathroom and converted it to a formal bathroom. The central beam couldn't be moved, so they created two interior domes that made the ceiling feel as high as possible and allowed space for an antique French chandelier.

The kitchen was a modern, state-of-the-art affair packed with all the latest appliances—in particular, two stoves. This I couldn't figure out. Why two stoves? Once, Connie asked Ebony if she was Jewish, but she didn't get it. Neither did I until, Connie explained it to us.

As I climbed the steps to the brownstone, I was hit smack in the face by the delicious smell of jerk chicken. My favorite. I had to hold on to the rail. I was only two or three steps up when I was sucker-punched by the aroma of curried goat. I held the rail with both hands and pulled myself up another set of steps. From where I stood, the front door looked like the stairs at the bottom of the Fifty-Ninth Street subway station on the Lexington Avenue line looking up. "Courage," I said to myself as I struggled up the stairs.

By the time I got to the landing at the top of the stairs, I was weak and delirious. I was gasping for air but was determined to walk into the house under my own power. And I might have damn well succeeded had somebody not opened the front door and finished me off with that irresistible smell of ackee and saltfish. I had no idea how I got into the living room, and I really didn't care. All I knew was that I had a Red Stripe beer in one hand and a plate of jerk chicken in the other, and Ma Saunders was standing over me.

By the time I finished the third piece of chicken breast, I'd regained my composure. "Delroy, me son, how yu do," said Ma Saunders in that thick Jamaican accent. It was like heaven to look in those wise old eyes. I stood up and threw my arms around this septuagenarian cuisinier perpetrator. She hugged me back and honored me with a kiss. I was thinking that I should have married Ebony just for Ma Saunders's cooking.

Ebony was in the kitchen. She was on the phone talking to Dalton, who was at work. As head of the trauma center, he can be called to the hospital at any moment. It was one of the reasons he chose to live in Harlem. Luckily, he was on his way home. I snuck up behind her and put my arms around her. "This is why you should have married an attorney," I said. "You always know where they are."

She turned around and faced me, and we gave each other the tightest hug imaginable. "Thanks for coming, Delroy," she said.

"Have I ever missed any of your parties?"

"Should we count the one where you and Connie were too drunk to know where you both were?"

"Hey, I didn't miss the party. I didn't know what was going on, but I was there." I reached into my pocket and pulled out a little gift-wrapped box and handed it to her. "Happy birthday," I said.

She kissed me on the lips and said, "Thank you."

"Before you even open it?"

"I know you, Delroy. You went overboard, as usual." She tore open the little box and took out the pair of diamond earrings. "You should have. Indeed, you should have." We hugged again, and she thanked me again. Two of her friends walked into the kitchen as she was putting on the earrings. One I'd met before but couldn't remember her name, and the other one I'd never met before. Ebony introduced me to them, and I remembered where I had met Nancy before. She was an attorney at Ebony's firm. Married with children. The other girl was too young to be an attorney; she looked no more than nineteen or twenty. But she was tall and strikingly beautiful. She was not the kind of girl one would easily forget.

She had on faded blue jeans, ripped in several places, and a white T-shirt that was obviously too tight but complimented her body. Her long blonde hair was tied back underneath a Yankees baseball cap. "Delroy, meet a friend of mine who works summers in my office. Liseth, this is Delroy." I extended my hand and took hers in mine, and I knew from that moment that I was in love.

"I'm pleased to meet you," I said. "How're you?"

"I'm fine," she said.

"So you work with Ebony?" I said, trying to make small talk. "What do you do there?"

"I'm a paralegal," she said and then took a swig of her beer.

"Is this a precursor to law school?"

33

"Maybe."

"Where do you go to school?"

"Columbia."

"That's my alma mater."

"I know. So it is with half the people here."

"Are you having regrets?"

"About what?"

"About having gone to Columbia?"

She looked at me sort of funny. "No. Why?"

"I don't know."

She took a chicken wing from off the platter. She held it with a napkin. She sank her teeth into it and then wiped her mouth with the back of her hand.

"What was the reason for the napkin?" I said.

"What's the reason for all these questions?" she said.

"What do you study at Columbia?"

She finished the chicken wing, took another swig of her beer, and took another wing, this time with some rice and peas. "Can I ask you something?" she said.

"Sure."

"Don't you think you look silly in that suit and tie? You gotta be uncomfortable."

I could understand her reason for thinking that way. Since the mid-eighties, a new mode of dressing had slowly crept upon us: casual Fridays. By the start of the nineties, it was the rule. Every major corporation had adopted it. Some had even graduated to casual summers. Lawyers were no exception. During the summers, most lawyers would dress in khaki or seersucker suits (how vulgar!), and on Fridays, the office would look like a gathering at a Fourth of July barbecue. Secretaries were the worst offenders. They dressed as though they were going to a tailgate party. Whoever came up with the idea of casual Fridays should be tied to a stake and whipped.

I, as usual, dressed the same way every day. Someone once asked me why I never dressed down on Fridays, to which I replied that it was not my inability to dress down that was the problem but, rather, the inability of others to dress up. Plus, somebody had to uphold the standards. If one is going to charge a client $675 an hour, then for goodness' sake, one should at least dress like he deserves it.

One thing one should never ever do is ask a philosophy student to define anything. The answer will be complex, and possibly elongated. I knew better, but I had to ask her to define *silly*. She looked at me and started to laugh, and then took another swig of her beer, but the bottle was empty.

"Look around the place. This is July, and it's as hot as it'll ever be. And it's not even the middle of summer. Most of the people are in jeans and T-shirts."

I looked at her when she said that and noticed that there was a certain cross between a child and a woman. I wanted to ask her how old she was, but I knew this was not the right time.

She continued. "Some are in sweatsuits, shorts, and what not. You're the only one in a suit and tie—now that's silly, don't you think so?"

"I wouldn't call that silly," I said.

"What would you call silly?" The way she held her beer and took a swig of it, you could tell she was not new to it.

"If you're saying silly in the sense of one being different, as in a person wearing an overcoat at a nude beach, you might be right, since a nude beach would hardly be the place for one to have an overcoat on, or say entering a duck at a cockfight—now that's silly."

"Not if you're Polish or Italian," she said with a slight laugh, and I knew then I was definitely in love.

"How's that?"

"Well, a Pole would be the only one who'd enter a duck at a cockfight."

"And the Italian?"

"He's the only one who'd bet on the duck. And you want to know something? The duck better win, or it's duck for dinner."

We cracked up laughing. I thought that was so funny. She was not only pretty and smart, but she had a sense of humor. How could I not love somebody like that? "If this conversation is going to continue, do you mind if I ask you your last name? I'm Delroy Bradshaw."

"I know," she said.

"You have me at a disadvantage. You seem to know me."

"No, only about you."

"I admit nothing, and if forced to, I'm taking the Fifth."

"You ever stopped being a lawyer for a minute?"

Before I could answer her, Dalton walked into the kitchen; he still had on his scrubs. He took a cold Red Stripe beer out of the freezer, twisted the top, guzzled half of it, let out a sigh, and then finished the rest of the beer—all before saying hello. "What's up, Delroy?" he said as he reached for a drumstick, only to be slapped on the wrist by Ebony, who had walked up behind him.

"Go take a shower and get out of those contaminated clothes," she said.

He obeyed, kissed her, and headed upstairs. "See you later, Delroy. Hi, Liseth."

"What's up, Dalton," she said and then excused herself. I watched her as she headed toward the downstairs bathroom. It gave me an opportunity to ask Ebony about her.

She anticipated my questions. "That's Liseth Fernandez. She is twenty-two. She is single—that is, no boyfriends. She is a straight A student at Columbia, class of '99. She is smart, academically and streetwise. She is Puerto Rican. She is highly motivated, and I'm her mentor. Harvard and Yale would be lucky to get her. What else do you want to know about her?"

"Does she like older men?"

"That you'll have to ask her."

I was not sure how to take that, and whatever Ebony meant, I was not sure I wanted to know. Although I did ask her how Liseth knew as much as she alluded to knowing about me.

"As my best friend, I naturally talked about you, and that we dated in college," Ebony said.

"What else did you tell her about me?"

"Well, I didn't tell her anything about you in the sense of telling her about you. It's not like I was . . . well, there are pictures of me and you and Dalton from our college days in my office, and one with you, me, Dalton, and Connie, and one day she asked why you were in so many photos, and I told her the whole story, and she seemed to be fascinated by your legend."

"So she knows how old I am, then?"

"If you and I went to school together, yes, she knows."

I started by asking her, nervously, "So do you think my age makes a difference?"

Liseth reentered the kitchen just then.

Before she got close enough, Ebony said, "I'll tell you one thing, though: whatever you want to ask her, don't beat around the bush. Ask her. You'll get a straight answer, and don't let that angelic looks fool you. She can cut you down to size. Good luck." She headed toward the living room as Bob Marley vibrated and bounced off the wall.

I took a beer and asked Liseth if she wanted one. She said yes, and said that she was going out in the backyard. I wanted to go out there with her, but I figured I would wait and then go out there later. I had some of the rice and peas and mingled with some of the people in the living room.

There must have been close to twenty-five people at the party. Except for maybe half a dozen or so, I knew them all. One was Ira Goldstein, one of the senior partners in Ebony's firm and one of the leading old-time liberals in the legal establishment, and a political heavyweight in the Democratic Party. He was seventy-five, give or take a year, and was the one who brought her into the firm and made her a partner. He was not only a senior partner, but the firm bore his name as well: Dickens, Gray, Goldstein and Hughes. Ira was the only active and living partner of the four—except for Hubert Hughes, who had retired to Florida.

I said hello to Ira, and he asked how my parents were doing. His and my father's paths crossed when they were on opposing sides of a case. Dad got the best of him and made a lifelong friend. Funny thing what money and a young wife can do to a man. Ira had more money than he could have spent in three lifetimes. Less than a year after his first wife died after close to forty years of marriage, he, at sixty-six, married a thirty-three year-old lawyer, knocked her up two years later, and is in his second stage of youth, enjoying the fuck out of it, no thanks to his three children who are all older than his wife. We've never been sure if it was her age or her being non-Jewish they objected to. And then there's her giving him another son at his age. Or all three. Nonetheless, the man was living his own life and didn't give a fuck what those narrow-minded kids of his thought. He was my kind of man.

I was introduced to some of the people I didn't know. One of them was a major rap artist, who I wouldn't know if I fell over him. Not only was he an artist, but he was also head of his own record company. He was also Ebony's client. He had a major tax problem. What else is new? I said hello and a few insignificant words, but enough for him to remember me when he needed a criminal attorney. Trust me, he will.

After the introductions, I went over to say hello to an old classmate of mine who I hadn't seen in over four years. The last time was when he was leaving the firm he had worked for after twelve years. He was setting up a solo practice. It almost cost him his marriage. His wife thought it was not the prudent thing to have done, not with their second child on the way. I asked how his practice was going. He said it was doing well, that he had brought in a second partner and hired three associates, and that billing was up. I congratulated him and wished him continued success. The only people that were missing from the party were Ebony and Dalton's two children: Dalton Junior and Dante. The boys were with Dalton's parents in Jamaica, where he and Ebony would be joining them the next week.

I wandered out onto the back porch. By now, my jacket was in the downstairs closet, my tie folded in one of its pockets. I stood there and watched Liseth, another girl, and a guy smoking in the garden. I couldn't smell it, but I was certain it was ganja. I stood there for a while before they noticed me. The guy and the girl headed back up the path and into the house. I was sure it was not because they saw me but because they were finished. Liseth remained seated on the garden chair. I proceeded toward her. As I approached her, I could smell the faint smell of the weed.

She said, "You're out of uniform." The bill of her baseball cap was turned to the back of her head. She turned around as I approached her.

"I don't dress like this every day, you know," I said as I sat down across from her.

"No?" she replied.

"I'm serious. I wear jeans sometimes."

"Now why would you want to go and spoil my image of you." She laughed when she said that.

"You want to know something?"

"What?" she said.

"You should definitely go to law school. If not, I'm prepared to offer my service pro bono."

"What're you talking about?"

"If they outlawed beauty, you'll need a good defense." I couldn't believe I said that. What a corny line. I handed her my card. "But even if you don't go to law school, I'm sure you've heard the saying about defending yourself and having a fool for a client."

"Are you flirting with me?"

"And suppose I am?"

"Well, I'm just thinking, you're a successful lawyer; you're a bachelor, although you were turned down once; you're in your forties; you have a house on the beach on Long Island; you drive a Jaguar and a Range Rover; you shop in London; you're an only child, and your parents adore you, especially your mother; and I'm quite sure on the nights you sleep alone, it's only because you want to—"

She would've gone on, but I interrupted her. "Where is this leading to?"

She continued. "Well, you're a man of the world, with very little needs because, let's face it, we all need something. But I'm only twenty-two and still in school. What could you possibly want from me?"

"Do I have to want something from you?"

"Let's not start off being dishonest now. That won't get you anywhere."

Ebony's warning resonated in my mind. This girl would chop down any bush I would try to beat around. There was a pebble in my shoe that was making my right foot very uncomfortable. I asked her if she would mind if I took off my shoe. There was no reason why she should mind, but I thought it would have been impolite and very ungentlemanly to do so without asking.

She said, "Can I ask you an honest question?"

"Of course," I said as I put my shoe back on. She switched her crossed legs, right over left. The jeans were torn at the knees. Her beer bottle was empty. I asked her if I could get her a fresh bottle.

"Maybe later," she said. Then: "Are you looking for a trophy wife?"

"That's a non sequitur question."

"I don't think so. The conclusion follows the premises."

"Only if I agree that your premises are right."

"Am I wrong?"

"Let me put it this way: if you see yourself as a trophy wife, don't you think you're demeaning yourself? Don't you think you're saying that all you have to contribute to a relationship is your beauty? I wouldn't want a woman who has nothing but her beauty to contribute to a relationship." She was flipping my business card like you would a playing card. Then she looked at it and asked me what the *F* stood for.

"*Francis*," I said.

She laughed. "You're kidding, aren't you?"

"No, I'm not. That's my name. You have a middle name?"

"Yes, but I'm not telling you."

"Why?"

"I don't know you well enough."

"I could ask Ebony."

"You wouldn't dare."

"Are you ashamed of your name?"

"No, but I've never used it, and only a few people know it. And they're only people who are close intimates."

At the end of Liseth's first year at Columbia, Ebony taught a course on taxes at the law school. Liseth's professor, who thought she was a student with a promising future, arranged for her to meet Ebony, who invited her to intern at her firm the next summer. She has been returning on every semester break ever since.

Liseth and I sat out in the garden for most of the evening. We talked extensively about everything. Including my proposal to Connie and my short liaison with Jasmine. She asked me if I had been in love with Ebony, and I diplomatically sidestepped the topic. She told me about the two guys she briefly went out with, both in her age range and all too immature for her. That gave me hope. Maybe an older man might stand a better chance, but I wasn't sure if the twenty-odd-years difference wasn't too much.

Our conversation was intermittently interrupted by Ebony to replenish our drinks and to find out how we were. We were oblivious to the time and were surprised when Ebony told us it was after eleven. It was totally the opposite of when I first met Connie.

After two beers, I said to Liseth, "You know what I would love right now?"

"What?" she said.

"A good slice of cheesecake."

She laughed. A loud, outrageous laugh that attracted attention. Ebony and Dalton came out to the back porch to inquire. Liseth said, "Go away, I'm fine. This man is too much."

I looked at her, astonished, not knowing what to say, but she said. "I have to tell you something, Delroy. You have just said the magic word."

"What was that?"

"*Cheesecake*. I love cheesecake."

"You do?"

"I love it so much that I would have to know you very, very much to tell you what ranks up there with cheesecake on my list." She toned down her laughter a bit, and I looked at her, and I could imagine what would rank up there with cheesecake.

"Where is the best place to get cheesecake at this time of night?" I asked.

"The only place I know is in the Bronx, but it is closed now."

"I know a place," I said.

"Where?"

"The Stage Deli."

"On Seventh?"

"Yes, wanna go?"

"OK."

We said good night to Ebony and Dalton. They looked at us, me in particular, as if to say, *Wow, that was fast.* Dalton walked me to the curb while the two women girl-talked. He told me the age thing was insignificant, but not to start anything unless I was serious. He gave me an old Jamaican piece of advice: "If you can't be good, be careful." It was typical Dalton.

Liseth and I walked over to 155th Street and Saint Nicholas Avenue to pick up the Range Rover at the all-night garage. We headed down Adam Clayton Powell Jr. Boulevard and around Central Park, since the park was usually closed to traffic on weekends. I asked her what Ebony said to her. While she checked her makeup in the mirror, she said, "You know something, you have great friends. They care about you a lot."

"Thanks, but what did she said to you?"

"I'll tell you one day."

"Does that mean we're gonna see each other again?"

"It's a figure of speech. What did Dalton say to you?"

"That to make sure I'm in well-lit places with you at all times, where lots of people are around, and that I should call him if you get out of hand."

"I know Dalton well enough, and I can tell you word for word what he told you."

"What did he tell me?"

"I don't have to tell you, because you're a gentleman."

***

We each had a slice of cheesecake. I had tea. She had coffee. Afterward, we took a walk down Times Square. At Forty-Seventh

Street, to avoid a pool of water, I held her hand as she skipped across it. I didn't want to let go, but did. A few more blocks, and I found our hands slowly finding each other's. We didn't resist. In front of the sports cafe, we met a young girl with a basket of roses, pitching her best sale pitch: "Buy a rose for your lovely lady. She deserves it."

How could I have resisted, even at $5 a rose. Gratuitously, Liseth kissed me on my cheek. I told her she was welcome, though I should have been the one to thank her. Her lips felt soft against my unshaven cheek. For the rest of the night, my lips were envious of my right cheek, especially when she repeated the process when I dropped her off at her apartment.

Unlike with Connie, who I went out with for close to nine months before having sex, it took me only a month to consummate the relationship with Liseth. Four months later, she was practically living at my house. Well, she was there often enough she might as well be living there. Not that I was complaining. I loved it. That fall, before she went back to school, I took her on vacation to the Bahamas. Thanksgiving, we had dinner at my parents' house.

I couldn't think of a girl that I'd been out with who made me feel the way Liseth made me feel, that fast. It was love at first sight, and it was mutual, and it was passionate, and most of all, we enjoyed each other's company. For her graduation, I bought her a Geo Tracker and took her to England for two whole weeks. When we came back, we went up to a friend's cabin in Vermont for the weekend. For the first time, I'd found true love, and I was telling everyone who would listen. Not only was I in love with Liseth, but I was having some of the best fucking sex I could remember ever having—well, with all due respect to Jasmine. But Liseth was not even twenty-three yet, at least not until December of 1999. We were in a world of our own—that is, until Connie decided to reenter my life.

Chapter 3

------⚹♥⚹------

I am one of those people who believe that our fortunes or misfortunes are a product of our creation. So the fact that I was getting paranoid every time the phone rang was a result of me not telling Liseth about my meeting with Connie. All I had to do was simple: tell her the truth. What's the worst that could happen? Plus, a friend at work once told me to "always tell your woman the truth." They expect you to lie anyway, so why not just tell them the truth? Had I told Liseth the truth in the first place, even if she didn't believe me, I would have found solace in the fact that I was not lying. And I would not have hesitated in answering the phone that Sunday morning.

Liseth was never one to get up early. The earliest she would get out of bed was noon. And if we went out to a club the night before and came in like five or six in the morning, she would sleep till way past noon. It was not unusual for her to get out of bed at three or four the next evening. Trust me, the girl loved to sleep, and didn't like to be interrupted when she was sleeping. She was also a heavy sleeper. You could pretty much do anything with her when she was asleep. I could have sex with her, and she wouldn't know it. Me, I was always an early riser.

I was going through the entertainment section of the Sunday *New York Times*. As I flipped the pages and sipped my orange juice, the phone rang. Even though I was up, it startled me. I looked over at Liseth, even though I knew the house would have to be on fire to disrupt her sleep. I let the phone ring, hoping that whoever it was would get tired and hang up.

As the phone rang over and over, I looked at Liseth again, and then at the phone, hoping each ring would be the last. Suddenly I heard a voice. "Delroy, get the damn phone."

I picked up the phone and looked over to see what she was doing. She didn't move. "Hello," I said in a low voice. At first I didn't recognize Charles's voice, but the fact that it was a man's voice, any man's, was a delight.

"Hey, Delroy, you going running?"

Charles Grant and his wife, Mildred, lived two houses down from mine. They had been married for close to seven years. He was pushing forty, and she was thirty-six. They were childless and were obsessed with having a baby. They were also one of the only couples who were frequent guests at my house. They were also my running partners, and when they were not at work (he worked for the state, counseling troubled kids; she was a freelance writer and was working on a novel), they spent most of their time working on getting pregnant. So if it was Saturday or Sunday morning, you could bet everything they were working on it.

"I'll be ready in fifteen minutes," I said. "Let me put on my gear."

"OK, see you."

I looked out of my bedroom's French doors, which led to the balcony. I had an unobstructed view of the ocean as far as the eyes could see. My house was a three-bedroom contemporary two-story affair that had been converted to two bedrooms (I wanted bigger rooms). It's situated on a dead-end street, with the beach as part of my backyard. It also had a boat slip, like every house on this side of the street. Of the nine houses on the street, I was among the three people who didn't have a boat tied at my slip. I didn't know the intention of the other one, but I knew Charles and I had no intention of getting a boat. Boats were not my passion. I was not sure if it was the cost that had deterred Charles, even though I was sure he could afford it. Before working for the state, he had worked on Wall Street as a stockbroker, made a little money, and decided to do what he always wanted to do.

I watched the darkness fade, giving way to the Sunday morning light. It was close to six thirty, and I could already feel the July heat struggling with the cool ocean breeze for dominance over my domain. It was great running weather. Liseth was fast asleep. She lay there in her black thong. No bra. *Fuck running*, was the first thought came to mind, but I knew I didn't look the way I look, at almost forty-five, skipping ten-mile runs on weekends.

As I put on my sneakers, still looking at her curled up in that big old bed, one pillow between her legs and another tightly in her embrace, I couldn't help but picture Connie lying there. I could see her lying there fast asleep, stark naked as usual. She was soft, tender, and cuddly. She had that smell of a young baby, as though she had just taken a bath with Pears soap. God, I could smell her breath right then. The freshness of her body was an aphrodisiac. I could feel her warm breath and feel my fingers running through her hair. I kissed her, and she kissed me back, and we kissed again, and although I had kissed her many times before, that moment was like magic. It felt different and so new. It was sweeter than wine, and softer than the summer night. In my head, I could hear the melody of a Drifters song over and over, and when it got to the part at the end when they fade with the line "forever till the end of time," I found myself singing the song.

I turned the stove on, filled the kettle with water, put an Earl Grey tea bag in my mug with two spoons of brown sugar, peeled a banana, and then limbered up. The goddamn Drifters song was still humming in my head. It was amazing. I hadn't heard that song in so long, but it was vivid in my mind. The words were fresh, as though it was being played at that very moment. Again, I started to sing it out loud:

> *This magic moment, so different and so new,*
> *Not like any other, until I met you, and then it happened*
> *It took me by surprise da da da da . . . by the look in your eyes,*
> *Sweeter than wine, softer than the summer night da da da*

But as I continued, I realized I didn't know the words to the song as well as I thought, and I didn't have that CD in my collection. What a pity. But the melody was still there. I stacked six CDs in my player (two Anitas, two Luthers, and two Whitneys), turned the volume up, and went back to the kitchen to make my tea, and started to stretch. The Bose stereo filled the room with sound

As I stretched and limbered up, I looked around the house; and it dawned on me how big the place was: a converted two-bedroom, two and a half baths. And the size of the living room, and that dining room, and that kitchen. My goodness. The kitchen had the range in the center of it with a marble counter. On the opposite side, there were four stools for when I felt like having one of my informal dinners. The formal dining room, which seats eight, was rarely used. The living room (next to the bedroom) was my favorite room. It was expansive, yet it provided a sense of intimacy. It had floor-to-ceiling windows. The ocean was only fifty feet away. It was like being on the prow of a tall ship. The furniture was Old English.

I bent over and grabbed my ankles and held them for what seemed like a minute; but it was only several seconds. I must have been fucking crazy. I had the sexiest and most delicious twenty-two-year-old upstairs in nothing but a black thong, and there I was, thinking about a married woman with three kids. Talk about fucking coincidence. Right then, Anita Baker started to sing: "Been so long / I'm missing you, baby." What was she, some fucking mind reader?

***

"You wouldn't believe who I saw last night," I said, as Charles, Mildred, and I walked to the end of the street before we started our run.

"Who you saw last night?" Charles asked as we trotted.

"You remember that girl I told you I almost married?"

"Connie?"

"Yes."

"Isn't she married to some doctor and have twins or something?"

"Yep."

"So where did you see her?"

"I met her for drinks." By now we were running on the beach.

"Why?" said Mildred.

"Mostly to talk about her failing marriage," I said as we picked up speed.

"You said that as if you're happy," she continued.

"For what?"

"That her marriage is failing."

Charles interrupted. "Come on, Mildred. Delroy is in love with Liseth. Why would he be happy about that?"

"Somehow I don't like this," she said.

"We just had a few drinks and talked," I said. "That's all."

"And you just happened to forget to tell Liseth, I'm sure."

"There was no need to."

"That's what I thought."

Charles again interrupted. "Hey, come on, guys—"

"I'm just saying—"

"I know what you're saying, but I don't want to hear it. OK?" Mildred didn't say anything more, and we finished our run without any further comment. They would be having lunch at my place.

Later, I stood in the middle of the bathroom viewing my naked body in the full-length mirror. For a guy who had just made forty-four, I not only looked good, I looked great. "Damn, I look good," I said as I slapped my firm stomach. I had the body of a guy half my age. He should look this good. And my sex life—he should have it so good. Sex sometimes three times a week, not counting weekends, with a girl half my age. Not bad, Delroy.

The ocean breeze was coming through the French doors, and Luther Vandross was going in circles. What the fuck was his problem? I lathered up my body and let the water slowly pound my head as I stood under the shower. The water felt good—not too hot and not too cold, but a little on the cold side. Just the way Connie loved it, when we made love in the shower. There were times when she would even turn off the hot water, making it really cold. By the time we finished making love, we couldn't tell the difference. She loved doing it in the shower and then finishing up in the bed, still wet, and then I would dry her hair gently with a towel. She hated blow-drying her hair. Then after we made love again, I would get the pralines and cream and two spoons, and we would watch TV as we ate ice cream. And then make love some more.

I closed my eyes and just stood there and let the water cascade down my body. I was lost in the moment as the Bose stereo carried Luther Vandross's velvet voice throughout the house as he sang his sexy ballads. He could sing like a motherfucker. He was putting a hurt on Roberta Flack's "killing me softly with his song." The boy could sing, but he needed to get him some pussy and stop letting that boy kill him softly with his song.

I stepped out of the shower and reached for a towel, which I tied around my waist. I couldn't help looking in the mirror again, still feeling proud of what I saw. Vainly, I searched my hair for any gray ones. They had started showing up when I was about thirty, and each time I saw one, I would reach for the tweezers. I found one all by itself. Too short for anyone to notice, but I would know it was there, so it was tweezer time.

I was combing my hair when Liseth walked into the bathroom in a sort of daze. She mumbled something incoherently and then sat on the toilet seat and took the longest piss I'd ever seen anyone take. She didn't respond to my "Hi baby." She just sat there, even after she finished pissing.

Then she said, "There is no toilet paper. How come you never replace the damn toilet paper?"

I reached under the sink and handed her a roll. She tore the wrapper off, unwound some, put the roll on the floor, wiped herself, and said nothing. Then she got up without flushing the toilet and stumbled back into bed as if sleepwalking.

"How come you never flush the damn toilet when you piss?" I mumbled. I stood at the bathroom door and watched her as she lay across the bed. "Liseth," I said, "Charles and Mildred are coming to lunch."

"What time is it?" she asked. I wasn't sure, but I told her it was about twelve thirty.

. "Wake me at one."

"They'll be here at one thirty."

"That's fine. Wake me at one. It won't take me long to shower and get ready."

When Charles and Mildred arrived, I was in the kitchen making the salad. They came in through the side gate. Mildred had on one of those black leggings and a white tank top that showed off the ring in her navel and revealed her braless nipples. From behind, you could see the butterfly tattoo that rose from the crack of her ass. Her shoulder-length hair complemented her beautiful dark face, which was accentuated by a slight trace of foundation and lipstick. She flopped her lean five-foot-six-inch ex-dancer's body in one of the chaise as Charles came into the kitchen for a beer. If Mildred didn't have the photos to prove it, I would never have pictured her with an Afro. The texture of her hair was too soft and fine. She was a mixture of East Indian and African ancestry. The light wind coming off the ocean was having its way with Mildred's hair, and she ignored it.

Liseth joined us as I was putting the salmon on the grill. She walked out onto the deck and poured herself some iced tea, lit a cigarette, kissed me, and then flopped down in one of the chaise. "Hi, Mildred," she said. Charles had gone down to the beach.

"Hi, Liseth," said Mildred. "You look like shit."

"I feel like shit," she said as she tucked the end of her sarong between her legs to avoid it being flapped about by the breeze.

"Up late last night?"

"It's not even about that," she said between drags on her cigarette. "It's just that I'm so fucking tired."

"You're starting law school this fall, aren't you?"

"Yeah, I'm going to Yale." She took a sip of her iced tea and then called out to me. I looked over at her as I turned the salmon. "Could you put a burger or two on for me, dear? I don't feel like eating fish today."

"Sure, baby," I said. Then she began to tell Mildred how she helped her mother clean her apartment the day before, and how she had planned this great night for us, but that I had to see a client and didn't pick her up till late, and that she was too tired when we got home to even have sex.

Mildred gave a slight chuckle, and without being too obvious, looked at me with that look of *Boy, you're in a mess.*

Liseth poured herself some more iced tea, got up, and undid her sarong, revealing a white thong. The matching bra didn't cover much either. "Maybe the cold sea water will wake me up," she said as she picked up two towels and headed toward the ocean.

"That ought to do it," said Mildred. We watched her as she walked down to the beach, dipped one foot in the water as if to test it, then, with a run, dove in. I watched her as she swam out into the ocean, until the only thing I could see were her hands moving.

The first thing out of Mildred's mouth was, "You're not planning on seeing Connie again, are you?"

I kept my eyes on Liseth as I took a swallow of my iced tea and contemplated my answer.

"You're gonna see her again, aren't you? Please don't tell me you're planning on seeing her again." Mildred kept repeating herself until Charles, who had returned from the beach, answered for me, as if I needed help. "Of course not. Are you crazy?"

Mildred said without acknowledging Charles. "Well?"

"I really don't know. I wish I could honestly tell you I won't, but I don't know. I wish to God I never heard from her, and that I never went to see her last night, but a part of me wanted to go. God, I wish I had enough courage to say no to her."

Mildred refilled her glass with some more iced tea and drank some. She tried to see where Liseth was. She was swimming back to shore.

"I don't want to talk about it right now," I said. "Liseth is coming back."

Mildred turned around to see where she was. She was emerging from the water, slowly. She moved as if in slow motion. I wished I had a movie camera. The water dripped off her as if it was deliberate. With both hands, she smoothed back her hair and squeezed the excess water from it. Then she straightened her thong and shook her body as though she was cold. I could almost hear her utter *Brrrr*, rubbing her shoulders. Then she picked up one of the towels and started to dry her hair. She then wrapped it around her head and then used the other one to dry her body, and then wrapped it around her waist. Then she headed toward us.

As she approached, Mildred said, "You know you'll have to do one of two things."

"What's that?" I said, keeping my eyes on Liseth.

"Either you'll have to not see Connie again or be honest with Liseth. Which will it be?"

"Not now," I said as Liseth came closer.

"That's just what the fuck I needed," Liseth said as she sat down. "That cold water sure woke me up. Shit, that feels good. Where are my burgers?"

I fixed one burger for her and gave her some potato salad. She sank her teeth into the sandwich and asked for a beer. "That water was so fucking good. Millie, you should take a dip. Go on."

"Maybe later," said Mildred.

I was about to tell them that the salmon was ready when my cell phone rang. It was on the charger in the kitchen. I let it ring.

"Delroy, why don't you answer the phone? If I didn't know better, I'd think you're hiding from a bill collector. Damn, this morning you let the phone ring so long the shit woke me."

Mildred gave me another of those looks that only she and I knew why. The phone call was from my mother. It was brief. She wanted to know if Liseth and I would be coming up next weekend.

"Don't I always come up after going to the barber?"

"Yes, you do," Mom said. "But I was just wondering if Liseth would be coming with you."

"If you want her to, I'm sure she would be more than happy to come."

"As a matter of fact, I particularly wanted to see her."

"Want to talk to her?" I gave Liseth the phone. After she said hello and thank you a few times, over some laughter, she said, "I'd love to." Then she said good-bye and hung up.

I was tremendously happy with the relationship between Liseth and my mother. Liseth was like the daughter Mom always wanted. Despite the age difference, Mom thought she was good for me. Dad loved her too, only that he wished we were closer in age. But he got over it quickly. The first time he brought it up, Mom reminded him that Liseth and I were not setting any precedent.

I was taking the salmon off the grill when the phone rang again. Liseth still had the phone with her. With nothing to worry, about I said, "Answer it."

"Hello. Hello. Hello," she said.

Shit. Connie, I said to myself. But to Liseth, I said, "Who is it?"

"I don't know. Whoever it was hung up. And it's from a restricted number."

Definitely Connie. As I transferred the salmon to the platter, Jasper entered through the side gate. Jasper was a sort of handyman who did my garden and washed my cars, and took care of anything else I might needed done.

There was something about Jasper that made you just like him. He was not much older than me, and financially, he was, well, let's just say he had seen better days. But although he cut my lawn and washed my cars every week, he was the epitome of class. You could tell by just looking at him that at one time, he had lived the good life. He would never drink his beer from the bottle, and when he ate, he would spread his napkin in his lap, and between each bite, dab his mouth. I once invited him to dinner, and the way he used his knife and fork was so Victorian. None of that American tradition of putting down the knife and switching the fork to the right hand.

The clothes he wore were old, but they were quality. He was tall and lean and kept his hair short and well combed. He was a proud black man, but I could never get him to talk about his past. Instead, he would quote Shakespeare, Langston Hughes, Marx, Plato, and the like. In the year and a half since I'd first met Jasper,

I'd learned to respect his privacy. I addressed him as Mr. Ricketts, and he would address me as Mr. Bradshaw. He even addressed Liseth as Ms. Fernandez. He was a true gentleman. He could be a little blunt, but he was nonetheless a gentleman.

"Mr. Bradshaw, this is very good salmon, and you did not overcook it," said Jasper. Leave it to him to notice something like that. "I hate when a fish like salmon is not done right. So few people know how to cook salmon. And you did put just a tad of vinegar in the potato salad."

Gee, I would have hated to disappoint you.

Charles broke in and asked Jasper if he had finished some book he lent him. Jasper said he would have, had it not been for his neighbor's dog who kept barking all night. He and Charles had hit it off right after they met, which was about the same time I met him. He thought Charles was modest, and that I was arrogant. And that I should have been dating a woman much closer to my age. He came right out and said it. No beating around the bush.

"Mr. Bradshaw," he said, "can I ask you an honest question?" This was a few months after I had met Liseth, and he'd been sitting right where he was. Liseth was lying in the chaise and heard every word he said. He went on, "Do you honestly think you and Ms. Fernandez have anything in common?"

I wanted to tell him it was none of his fucking business, but the man was so goddamn polite when he said it that I hated to be rude to him.

"We have a lot in common," I said.

"Like what, wanting to satisfy your natural urges? Shouldn't there be more to a relationship than that?" He had that look on his face that said he had heard it all.

I would have loved to have slapped it. Instead, I said, "Well, we were both graduates from Columbia, and we both studied philosophy and politics. I'm a lawyer, and she's going to Yale Law School."

"But don't you think a woman closer to your age with the same credentials would be better suited for you?"

I calmly said to him, "Look, Mr. Ricketts, I come from a long line of lawyers. I'm an only and privileged child. I'm successful and have everything I need." Then I paused, took a sip of my beer, and started to say something, but then changed the subject.

"What's wrong, you finally realize that I'm right?" he said with a smug look on his face that I definitely wanted to slap.

"With all due respect to you, Mr. Ricketts, I don't think I should be discussing my social life with you, if you don't mind."

He shut up, and since that day never said a word about it again.

Despite Jasper's aversion to my relationship with Liseth, there was something peculiar about the way he treated her. Something paternal, which led us to believe he had a daughter somewhere, whom he hadn't seen in some time, or that Liseth was the daughter he wished he had. He would often inquire about her childhood, and other things that a father would normally take an interest in. On her twenty-second birthday, he gave her a gift. It was a simple bracelet, costume jewelry, but it apparently meant a lot to him giving it to her.

Liseth greeted Jasper with her usual hug. He liked that. They had a mutual respect and admiration for each other.

"So you're off to Yale Law School in September?" said Jasper with a well pleased look on his face. If he was thinking that the distance would make any difference in our relationship, he was wrong. If he knew me, he would know that I was the kind of person who would go up to New Haven on a Friday right after work and be back in New York in time for work on Monday morning.

"Yes, Mr. Ricketts, I am. And I'm so excited," she said. "Isn't it wonderful?"

"I'm so happy for you, love. Since you folks are eating and all, I think I'll do the cars first," he said. I could have sworn I saw a tear in his eyes. He headed toward the gate leading to the front of the yard.

"That man is sure one emotional man, if you ask me," said Mildred. "He was acting like his own daughter was going off to college."

"I think he has a daughter about Liseth's age," said Charles.

"What makes you think so?" I said.

Charles paused, walked toward the gate, peeped through the slats, and then said, "I don't know this for sure, but one night, he and I were talking. We were over at his house. We kicked back a few beers, and he opened up." This I would have loved to see: Jasper drinking too much. I've never seen him drink more than one and a half bottle of beer. Charles went on. "I started to tell him how desperately Mildred and I want a child, and how hard we are trying, and then he started to talk about what it was like being a father."

"What exactly did he say?" I asked anxiously.

"Well, at first he was specific, but then he started to talk in general terms, but I knew he was talking about himself."

"The son of a bitch, you can never pin him down. He is so sly. What the fuck is he hiding?"

"Maybe he's in the witness protection program," said Mildred.

"Wouldn't that be dangerous, Delroy?" said Charles.

"Could be."

"You guys are crazy?" said Liseth. "Mr. Ricketts? No way. A sweet man like that. No way."

I assured her that some of the sweetest people were in the witness protection program, and that it wouldn't be far-fetched for Jasper to be one of them. We would have continued talking about him if he hadn't returned to tell me that there was some tar on the bottom of the passenger side of front door of the Jag, and that he needed to get some thinner from the shed to remove it. He assured me it wouldn't damage the original paint. He got the thinner from the shed and returned to the driveway. One thing all of us agreed on was that if Jasper is indeed a father, something very serious had to have happened to separate him from his child, or children.

By four o'clock, the temperature was still high. The sun had passed its zenith, but the rays lingered long enough to keep the heat trapped in the wooden deck. The sand was still too hot to walk barefoot on, and the tide was lapping up on the beach. I could hear my neighbor's boat banging against the slip. Liseth had wanted to undo her top for an even tan on her upper body, but not with Jasper there. It would've pleased me to see her with an even tan, except for the bikini bottom. I loved to see her naked with the white outline of the bikini bottom. I found that sexy.

As I watched her lie on her stomach with that sliver of material running from her waist down the crack of her ass, I wished I'd let her get a tattoo like the one Mildred had. Maybe when she comes home for Christmas I'd surprise her by taking her to a tattoo shop. I looked down at her firm ass. That ass that said so much about her. That ass that had me teasing her that despite her white complexion and her blonde hair, there was still some African blood left in her. And that it might all be where she sat. However slight.

I should not have been thinking about Connie, but I was. Even with Liseth lying there. Even though I knew it would be dangerous to see Connie again. And even though I knew that in all likelihood Liseth would leave me, my feelings were ambivalent.

Chapter 4

O ne of the advantages of being a partner in one of the top law firms in New York City, particularly if you were one of the top-billing partners, was that you could pretty much, within reason, make your own workday. I was not just the only black partner at Bright, Gray, Saxon, Clay & Klein, but I was one of the top money earners. My billing had gone up 20 percent over the last two years, and was expected to top that this year. Over the years, I'd brought in some very impressive clients. With numbers like that, taking off Friday and Monday mornings to spend time with Liseth before she went off to Yale in September was reasonable. On Mondays, I would get to the office about one, work until seven, when she would pick me up at the office and we would drive out to Roosevelt Field, the shopping mall, and have dinner at the California Cafe, her favorite restaurant. We try to go there at least once a week.

Our weekends were pretty much the same, except for yesterday when I lied about meeting a client. Fridays we would drive the Range Rover up to the Hamptons, and maybe book into a hotel for the night. Then we would hit the beach. She would work on her tan, and I would read a book. After that we would stroll in the village, do some window shopping, dine at a fabulous restaurant, and maybe go to a nightclub and rub the proverbial shoulders with the rich and famous and the wannabes. On the occasions we would forgo booking into a hotel, we would come back home late that same night, which was two or three the next morning. We would disconnect the phone, sleep all day Saturday, and pretty much flip a coin on what to do that evening. Sundays we would always invite the Grants over for brunch.

It was late when Charles and Mildred left, maybe nine, or close to. Between the four of us, we must have put away close to twenty bottles of beer. I know I had at least five. Liseth was a big beer drinker, but that evening, for some reason, she only had two, and that included the one she took upstairs with her.

Liseth had just finished taking a shower when I walked into the bathroom. She reached for her half-empty bottle of beer and finished her drink in one gulp. I reached for the towel and wrapped it around her body and held her from behind. I kissed her soft shoulders while she asked me what I wanted to do with the rest of the night. "I'm doing it," I said.

"Sounds good to me," she said.

I turned her around and kissed her lips, then the tip of her nose, and then her left breast, then her right, and then I started to work my way down to her navel, then to her crotch. Instinctively, she put her left leg up on the bathtub while I gently kissed her inner thighs. "Oh, that feels so good," she said.

I was on my knees, with my face buried between her legs and my hands cupping her ass. My tongue was teasing her clit. It was not time to give her the full treatment yet. I could feel her body twitch as I manipulated her clit. Her hands were on the back of my head, pulling it into her warm vagina. I started to say something, but she told me that it was impolite to talk with my mouth full. I teased the clit some more, and her ass tightened a little. I felt it was time to give her the full treatment. I covered the clit with my mouth and sucked on it as she moaned and said something in Spanish. I must admit that I'm not well versed in the idiom, but I knew enough to tell she was telling me to continue doing what I was doing. I didn't have to understand Spanish; her body was saying enough. Her hands tightened on my head, and my hands gripped her ass as she climaxed and slumped against the glass shower compartment. Her body went limp as I continued licking her clit. She pushed me away.

I picked her up, carried her to the bedroom and laid her on the bed. I still had my clothes on. I stood at the foot of the bed and looked down on her, her body tanned to a shade lighter than mine, except for the thong and bra outlines. I unbuckled my belt and let my khaki shorts fall to the floor and pulled my T-shirt over my head. I pulled my boxers off and got into bed. She put a pillow under her ass and pulled me down on top of her. As usual, I never knew where to start. I always regarded Liseth as much too beautiful to just fuck. Just fucking her would be a disservice. I wanted to taste every part of her.

"Hold on a minute," she said. She reached over and took the phone off the hook and said, "In case someone got bad timing."

I didn't say anything but was glad she did it.

"Now where were we?" she added.

"I think one of your legs was up on the bathtub."

"So that's where it was. Well, today you can put it anywhere you want. I'm all yours."

Having always had a great appreciation for her body, and she being too beautiful to just fuck, I returned to giving her oral pleasure. This time I finger-fucked her as my tongue worked her clit. She reciprocated, and then we fucked, and then I got the pralines and cream and two spoons, and then watched TV. Fucked some more, and then we slept.

***

The next morning, a combination of wind and rain coming off the ocean came in through the French doors with no subtlety. The wind let its presence known by greeting my bare ass and showed that the screen door was no match for its might. The rain was coming down as though the sky had been sliced opened. The combination of the banging screen door and the rain beating down on the terrace and the chill on my bare ass was enough to get me out of bed. Liseth didn't stir an inch.

I got up and, without putting anything on, went over to close both doors. The carpet around the door was soaking wet. I climbed back into bed and looked at the clock. It was a little after seven. Since I was an early riser, I couldn't go back to sleep, so I slipped on my robe and went downstairs to retrieve the *New York Times* and make some tea and start the percolator for Liseth.

I switched the TV on in the kitchen and immediately turned to CNN. Then I flipped through the newspaper for nothing in particular, but settled on a piece about Zimbabwe, whose president had decided to return a number of farms owned by white farmers to black ownership. I deliberately use the word *return* in relation to the farms as opposed to the media's more inflammatory use of the word *seized*. If *seized* must be used, it should only be to describe how the white farmers got the farms in the first place, which was illegally. They forcefully removed the original owners off the land. Like the Indians were forced off their land right here in the United States, and the Aboriginals off theirs in Australia.

I was just finishing the piece, and had a newfound respect for Robert Mugabe, when Liseth walked into the kitchen. "Did I hear the screen door banging earlier?" she said as she looked for her mug. It was in the dishwasher. "Did you run the dishwasher last night?" she said, smelling the mug. She started to wash the mug before I could answer.

"No," I said.

She poured some coffee, poured some half-and-half in (no sugar), and then came over and kissed me. "Good morning darling."

"Good morning, babe."

"What you reading?"

I told her.

"Do you think Nelson Mandela will do that in South Africa?"

I laughed. "No."

"Why not?" she said as she took the sports section.

"Because Mandela came to power by the ballot box wanting to be included in the system, not change the system. Mugabe came to power by fighting a bloody war against the white power structure, which was determined to hold on to power at any cost. And, I must say, with our support."

She had on the Victoria's Secret robe she had on the day before. She sat on the chair and put her right foot up on the counter. The robe parted and revealed her crotch. She flipped the pages of the paper and took a sip of her coffee. "That's the difference between South Africa and Zimbabwe. The white minority in South Africa learned from their neighbor. The whites in South Africa were allowed to keep their ill-gotten gains by giving the majority political power while they kept the economic power."

"Exactly. The power structure hasn't changed, only the personnel."

"How long do you think it will take for real change to come to South Africa?"

"At least two or three generations."

"By that time, the money will have ended up in Israel or over here. Hey, look," she said, "the Williams sisters are in the semifinals at Wimbledon."

"Great, now one of them has a chance to win the top prize."

"It's about fuckin' time."

I turned the burner on to make some more tea and pressed the head of the cantaloupe to see if it was ready to eat.

"I think it's ready to eat," Liseth said.

"You think so?"

"I'm sure. Why don't you cut it?"

"So what are your plans for the rest of day after you drop me off?" I said as I inserted the knife in the cantaloupe.

"Well, I was thinking that maybe you could call a car service to take you to work. I have a few things to do: like check on the progress of the drapes, and a few errands I have to run, and they are all out here on the island. So I was thinking instead of driving you into the city and then coming back out here, why don't you just call the car service? You don't mind, do you?"

"Of course not," I said as I removed the middle of the cantaloupe. "You want some of this?"

"Sure. And thanks, baby."

"You're welcome," I said as I made my tea and dug my spoon in the fruit and put some in my mouth. "Damn, this is sweet."

She took a mouthful of hers and asked me to pour her some more coffee. I did and then asked her to call my secretary and have her send a car for me while I go take a shower. I laid out three suits on the bed, along with shirts and ties, not sure of what I wanted to wear. Then I went into the shower. I was lathering up for a second time when she joined me.

"The car will be here at eleven forty-five," she said. I didn't say anything as she soaped my back, and then I did hers.

I washed off and stepped out of the shower before her. I'd almost finished drying myself off when she came out. I handed her a towel. I watched her towel off with her back turned to me. I couldn't resist kissing her neck and started to run my tongue down her back.

"Two things I have to tell you," she said.

"What's that?"

She was giggling as she turned around to face me. "First, that feels fuckin' good."

"And what's the next?"

"That you should not start anything you can't finish."

"I always finish anything I start."

"That's what I'm afraid of. We don't have time for that, and the only thing we can do is a quickie, and you know how much I hate quickies. So why don't you hold that thought for later, big boy."

"It's not going to be easy, but I'll try."

"Well, let's look at it this way: tonight we'll have a bottle of wine with dinner, come home, have a brandy, and fuck till we drop."

"Since you put it that way, how can I argue."

"Now you'll have something to look forward to this evening." She bent down, ran her tongue over my dick, and said, "I love you, darling."

"Of course you do," I said. I went into the bedroom to get dressed. I chose a gray pinstripe double-breasted suit, a bold-checked blue shirt with a solid light-blue tie, and brown suede shoes.

One of the reasons why our firm keeps an account with Big Apple Limousine service is their punctuality. The car was there at eleven thirty. It must have been a driver familiar with my home because he came right up into the driveway. He blew his horn once and then read his copy of the *New York Times* as I finished eating.

"You won't mind if I don't walk you out today, would you, darling?"

I looked at her in her Victoria's Secret robe and said, "I'd rather not. I'd like the driver to keep his mind on the road."

"Maybe I should go out there and flash him just for the fun of it," she said. We both laughed and then had a long passionate kiss. "I love you, darling," she said. "And have a wonderful day."

"I love you too. And you have a wonderful day too." I picked up my briefcase and my laptop case and walked out to the car. The car was backing out of the driveway when she shouted to me from the living room window: "Darling, you forgot your cell phone."

"I'll come and get it."

She was halfway out the door as I came up. "You're determined to kill that poor driver today, aren't you? Don't forget I'll be in the car with him." I took the phone and kissed her again and then headed back to the car. "Hey," she said, "don't forget about tonight."

"If I don't get to work, there might be no tonight."

"I love you," she said.

"I love you too. Good-bye." I tapped the driver on his shoulder and said, "Please get me out of here."

He laughed and said, "Most men would kill to have your problem."

"I'm not complaining," I said.

Except for a slight tie-up at the Queens-Midtown Tunnel, we made it into Manhattan in less than forty minutes. The traffic was very light. On the way in, I checked my mailbox. There were two calls from Connie. One from an adversary requesting time to answer a complaint, and one from an associate telling me he had a first draft of the brief he was working on. I called my adversary first. I told him to draw up a stipulation and send it over. Then I called Connie. I left the associate for when I got to the office. He was a bright young man, with good writing credentials. I was confident that he had done a good job. But since I would have to sign it, I would have to read it.

I got Connie on her cell phone. She answered on the first ring.

"Hi, how are you?" I said.

"I'm fine," she said.

"I got your messages. Is everything all right?"

"Oh yes. I just wanted to know, what are you doing this weekend?"

"Well, as you know, Liseth is going off to Yale this fall, and I'd decided that I would spend all the weekends with her until she goes away."

"Well, I was going to be in the city this Friday, and I was thinking maybe we could have lunch."

"I'm afraid that's not good."

"Actually, it's a dental appointment, so maybe I could change it to Thursday, and maybe we could have lunch or dinner. I really would like to see you. There are a few things I'd like to talk to you about."

"An early dinner would be better," I said as I watched the driver eyeing me through the rearview mirror. I got the feeling that he knew I was not talking to a client.

"Why don't I call my dentist and see if I can change my appointment to Thursday, which I'm sure won't be a problem, and get back to you."

"Do that."

"Talk to you later," she said, and we hung up.

Bright, Gray, Saxon, Clay & Klein was on the fifty-sixth through the sixty-fifth floor of 1245 Avenue of the Americas. The firm also had part of the basement where the mailroom was located. My office was on the sixty-fourth floor. On a clear day,

I could see as far as West Point, southern Connecticut, and the George Washington Bridge.

Bright & Gray, as most people liked to call it, was primarily a New York firm with offices in Washington, Los Angeles, London, Japan, and Germany. The firm had a distinguished background. Among some of the people of distinction who had worked there was a former CIA director, the late Andrew Saxon. Andrew and Wild Bill Donovan were members of the OSS, the World War II spy agency that was the precursor for the CIA. After the war, they helped formed the Central Intelligent Agency, with Wild Bill as its first director. Andrew stayed with the agency for a few years and then went into private practice, joining a young Wall Street firm that was just getting started by Ralston Bright and Jack Gray, two young Yale Law School graduates who wanted to exploit his Washington connections. After getting rich, years later, Andrew was called back to Washington by an actor-turned-president, whose cold war policies were in line with his.

Unless I told my secretary otherwise, she always picks up my phone on the third ring. The young associate was passing my office when I walked in. "Delroy, do you think you might have a chance to look at the first draft of the brief?" he said.

"Of course. When is it due?"

"We have to serve it by Wednesday."

"That's OK. You send it to me, and I'll read it and have it back to you before the end of the day."

"I'll send it right up. Thanks."

Gregory Abrams was a graduate of Harvard Law School. He had clerked for a judge in the Southern District of New York before joining us. Getting a young associate who had clerked for a federal judge is always an asset.

I was putting my coat on a hanger when the phone rang. I let it ring. Bernice picked it up on the third ring. "Ms. Darby is on the phone," she said through the intercom.

"I'll take it," I said. "Connie what's up?"

"I was able to get Thursday at three. I figure I'll be there for about an hour. My doctor is on Central Park West, on

Seventy-Ninth Street. I can grab a cab from there and meet you at the Plaza for dinner."

"I don't think the Plaza is a good idea," I said, hoping to not elaborate.

"Why? I like it there. Some friends and I had dinner there about a month or so ago, and I loved the food, the service, and the whole atmosphere."

"I know. I'm familiar with the place."

"So why can't we have dinner there?"

"Because it's where Liseth's mother works."

Obviously surprised, she said, "Oh. So where do you suggest?"

"There is a good restaurant at Rockefeller Center," I said. "The food is very good."

"How about the Sheraton Hilton on Seventh?"

"On Fifty-Third Street?"

"I think so."

"That's OK. What time?"

"Five too early?"

"No. Five is good." Then we hung up.

Liseth picked me up at about seven fifteen that evening. She was looking radiant and sexy in her white slip dress and gold slippers with matching handbag. Her hair was pinned back. She looked much younger than a woman who would be twenty-two in December. I kissed her before I did my seat belt. Jasper had done an excellent job on the Jag. The British green sparkled even without the sunlight. "Hi, baby," she said as I buckled up.

"We have a reservation for eight." I looked at my watch and at the clock in the car. The car's clock was ten minutes fast.

"I'll make it there by eight," she said.

"I know you will," I said.

"How was your day?" she continued.

"Good. And yours?"

"Terrific."

"Got everything you wanted done?"

"The drapes will be installed in two weeks, and I looked at a gift for my aunt's wedding, that I would like you to see before I pick it up."

"OK. When do you want us to go look at it?"

"Friday would be fine." We exited the Midtown Tunnel. Traffic was light until we got to the entrance to the Grand Central Parkway. It was backed up for about three miles. Before I could say anything, she said, "I'll still make it by eight." Before I could ask how, she rode the soft shoulder and inched back onto the LIE, where traffic was moving freely. From there she made it to Exit 38 in seven minutes, and took less than twenty-five minutes to get to Roosevelt Fields. By the time we pulled up in front of the restaurant's valet parking, it was five after eight. When it came to driving, the woman was a menace. She had her usual filet mignon, and I had the Cornish game hen, with a bottle of burgundy. Since I would be driving, I let her have most of the wine. We left the restaurant about eleven and were home a little after twelve. And as promised, we had a brandy and picked up where we left off that afternoon.

***

For the second time in less than one week, I lied to Liseth. Like a doctor, I had the advantage of using emergencies at random. Patients do get sick every day. And clients need their hand held when it suits then. And it's always billable. But having used up my "have to see a client" just the Saturday before that Thursday, I told Liseth I had to make an emergency motion that must be served and filed the next day. Given that she had worked as a litigation paralegal for the past three summers, I didn't have to do much explaining. She understood full well that these things do happen.

Connie was sitting at the bar that looked out onto Seventh Avenue when I got to the Sheraton. She had only had one glass of white wine by the time I got there. We embraced, and I ordered a gin and tonic. She had on a tailored light blue pantsuit with a white silk shirt. She fitted right in with the afterwork crowd who usually frequented the bar. "Are you hungry?" she asked me.

"I had a salad for lunch," I said.

"I'm starved," she said. "Whatever that dentist cleaned my teeth with has made me very hungry."

Her talking about her teeth reminded me that I was long overdue going to the dentist. My last visit was approaching close to a year. I told myself to remember to make an appointment. Quite likely, Liseth would be the one to make it.

"What do you want to eat?" I asked her.

"If they have good lobsters, I'll have one. Remember when we used to go to Sammy's on City Island and pig out on lobster and shrimp scampi? You remember those days?" She laughed when she said it.

"Me, you, Greta, and Victor. Those were fun days."

"Yeah, those were fun days. And then you had to go and spoil it by wanting to get married." Her voice and the expression on her face changed when she said it. "Why couldn't you just leave well enough alone, Delroy?"

It didn't stop you from fucking some doctor you thought was a big shot, having twins, and running off and getting married. That's what I'd like to have said to her, but I withheld the comment. Instead, I said, "Come on, Connie, that's a long time ago. Plus, we have moved on to other people."

"It's not that long ago," she said, and that expression returned to her face again. I had seen it before, and it always said she was not in a good mood. And right then, I started to ask myself why I was there.

"You said you have something to talk to me about," I said, changing the subject a little.

"We'll talk about it over dinner," she said with a smile that revealed something both devious and mischievous.

For dinner, she had a lobster, and I had a turkey sandwich with french fries. She had another glass of white wine, and I had a diet Pepsi. Since I was planning on going back to work, I figured I would keep my alcohol intake to a minimum. I wanted to ask her what she wanted to talk to me about, but I figured I would approach it from a different angle. So I said, "How are things between you and Kevin?"

"Same shit," she said without looking up from her lobster. She dipped a piece of lobster meat in the melted butter and offered it to me. She put the fork in my mouth, and I took the meat off and slowly chewed on it, savoring the succulent flavor. I must admit it was one of the better lobsters I've had in a long time. For $28, it ought to. I remarked on how good it was, and she offered me another piece, but I declined.

"So how are things between you and Kevin?" This time I was hoping to get an answer.

"Not any better," she said. "And I don't think it will get any better. Which brings me to the reason why I wanted to talk to you." She offered me another piece of the lobster. This time I took it, and I wished I'd ordered the same thing for dinner.

She took a mouthful of wine and held it for a while before swallowing it. She was searching for whatever she wanted to say. I studied her face as she wrestled with her thoughts. "If . . .," she stammered. "If . . . if only. If only we could change certain things." She finished the remainder of her wine and then looked around for the waiter. He was on the other side of the room but caught her signaling to him by holding up her empty glass.

"Are you sure you want another?" I asked her.

"I've only had two," she said. "I'll be all right."

"You were saying that if only you could change certain things—what would you change?"

"Marrying you," she said as the waiter replaced her empty glass with another. "It's one of the few regrets I have in life. Not only would you make a great husband and a father, but I know I would be much happier."

I must admit it satisfied me a great deal to hear Connie say those words, and if she had asked me, I would have readily agreed with her. After all, if I was a woman and was looking for a husband, I'd be looking for a man just like me. But hey, this was not the time to gloat. She was in enough pain as it was. "We all have regrets, Connie. Don't worry, I have regrets too."

"You?" she said, as if it was incredulous that I would say something like that.

"Of course I have regrets."

"Name one."

"Not living with you. Insisting that we get married. Those are my regrets."

There was an inscrutable look on her face when I said it. She reached over and put her hand on mine. She said, "Do you really mean that?"

"Of course I do. I'm practically living with Liseth now, aren't I?" I looked at my watch when I said it.

"You know something?"

"What?"

"The last time we were together and Liseth's name came up, you looked at your watch, and you did it just now. Why?"

"This time I have to go back to work."

"Do you have to?"

"Yes, I have to," I said and looked at my watch again.

"Have to, or want to?"

"What difference does it make? I have work to do."

"I miss you, Delroy. Do you know that?" Sadness engulfed her face when she said it. I had never seen Connie so sad before. "I'm so unhappy," she continued. I removed my hand from under hers, switching position. I looked into her eyes. They were wet, but no tears running. "Are you happy, Delroy? Really happy?"

I put my fingers through hers and said, "Yes, I'm happy. I'm very happy."

She took a sip of wine and tightened her fingers between mine. "Tell me about Liseth."

"Oh, come on, Connie. We're not here to talk about Liseth."

"I know, but just tell me. Is she a good person? I know she is smart. Ebony said she is. And she has to be to graduate from Columbia with straight As and got accepted to Yale Law School. Plus, I heard she blew them away on the LSAT. But is she a good and decent person, because God knows, Delroy, you deserve a good and decent person. You deserve the best. You know that." She wiped her eyes when she was finished.

"Thank you," I said. "Yes, she is a good and decent person."

"Are you in love with her, and she with you?"

"Yes, we are. Can we not talk about Liseth? Please."

"OK," she said, but somehow I was sure she wanted to stay on the subject.

"Can we talk about why you wanted to see me? You said you had something you wanted to talk to me about. What is it?"

"I'm so fuckin' lonely and unhappy," she said as she drank some more wine.

"Please don't order any more wine," I told her. "It's a long drive to Dobbs Ferry."

"I'll be all right."

"All the same, I think three is enough. Don't drink anymore. Please don't." But I knew she could handle the three, and maybe three more. Connie could drink any guy under the table and then drive home without incident.

"Maybe I'm not going straight home," she said. A slight smile crossed her face. I couldn't think of any other place other than Greta's that she would be spending the night. But even so, I didn't want her to show up at Greta's under the influence. So I repeated my objection to her having another drink, but she insisted again that she would be all right, and that I should not worry. She reminded me of the times when we would go out and get drunk and she would be the one who would drive us home. Nevertheless, she said she was definitely not going straight home, and she was not going to Greta's. Of course, I wanted to know if Kevin was out of town at some medical seminar or something. She said he wasn't, and that where he was had nothing to do with her decision to not go home that night, and that just as much as I didn't want to talk about Liseth, she didn't want to talk about Kevin. Without flinching or showing any sign of emotion one way or the other, she said, "Maybe I might just stay right here in this hotel for the night."

Not knowing what else to say, I looked at my watch. It was now ten minutes to seven. I know she didn't want to talk about it, but I had to ask. "Connie, are things really that bad between you and Kevin?"

"Delroy, I really, really don't want to talk about him. I really don't."

Somehow I didn't like where this was going, and just like at our meeting last Saturday, I started to wonder what the hell I was doing there. OK, so she was unhappy, and her life was miserable, and sure, I wanted to be a friend, but why couldn't I be of help long-distance? If I had just gotten up and left the worst that could happen was that she would think badly of me. And, what, I'd have a bad night sleep? Yeah right.

"You obviously have something on your mind that you want to get off," I said. "Connie, what is it?"

"Us," she said, looking me straight in the eyes.

Now, why was I not surprised. "What about us?" I said.

"You remember last week, when I told you I haven't had sex in close to seven months?"

I looked at her and said to myself, *I wondered when she would bring that up.*

She continued, "When a woman has everything she wants in the world except the one thing she wants the most, she loses her self-respect." She paused. "A woman should never want anything bad enough to lose her self-respect in pursuing it. When she does, she ceases to live."

I'd heard that line before. I'd heard it in a movie, but I couldn't recall what movie. Only that the movie had an ominous ending. Nevertheless, I said, "Are you that person, Connie? What is it you want so bad?"

"You and good sex," she said, still looking me in the eyes.

"There is more to life than good sex, Connie, believe me."

"How would you know? Look at the woman you're living with."

I ignored that.

She went on. "You know what I really miss?"

73

I thought she had just told me, but I asked anyway, "What?"

"I miss being talked to. It is so boring to make love in silence. I want a man to talk to me, to tell what's on his mind, to just say what he feels. Someone like you. Oh, I miss that. God, I miss that so much. I miss you, Delroy."

In my forty-something years, I have had my share of women, all bright and gorgeous. I once had a federal judge recuse herself from a case I was on because she was not professional enough to hear the case. All because she and I used to fuck. I even had an adversary remove herself from a case because we fucked a few times and she had to go and fall in love. Hey, they were good lays, but that was then, and this was strictly business. Considering the women I was accustomed to going out with, I should not have been; but I must admit I was flattered by Connie's overall behavior. Yet at the same time embarrassed. There I was in the dining room of the Sheraton Hilton, being seduced by a woman most men would do just about anything to get in bed with. God, she looked so fucking good. I was tempted to throw everything out the window and just go the fuck for it.

Somehow, during the conversation, she had slipped off her right shoe, and her toes had found their way between my legs, and I could feel them gently rubbing up against my thigh. I wanted to tell her to stop, but I must admit it felt good. And it felt even better when she started to rub them against my erect penis.

She said, "I'm going to order another drink, but first, let me ask you something, and I hope you're not surprised."

Considering everything she had said all evening, what else could she say to surprise me?

"Suppose I told you that I rented a room right here in this hotel, would you be surprised?"

The only response I had to her question was, "Now, I want you to answer one question for me, and this is very important to me."

"What?"

"Did you rent a room at the Holiday Inn last Saturday night?"

"No, but I thought of it. I didn't because I thought it would be presumptions of me. Why?"

"Never mind," I said. I was getting very uncomfortable and uneasy, and wanted to leave. "Listen, Connie, I have to go. I really have to go."

She removed her foot from between my legs, and just as the waiter was putting her drink on the table, she said, "Do you have to?"

"I'm afraid I have to."

"No, you don't. You don't even want to."

"Don't tell me I don't have to, or that I don't want to," I said, slightly irritated, but knowing deep down she was right.

"Well, go if you must. I don't want to keep you any longer than you want to be here. Go if you must," she said.

"Please don't say it like that, Connie," I said. I was sure she could sense the ambivalence in me.

"Don't say it like what?"

"The way you said it."

"Listen, if you must go, go. Don't let me stop you."

I was still standing, and I was now certain she saw my indecisiveness. I said, "It's just that I have to go back to work."

"No, you don't. You already lied to Liseth about working on an emergency motion. So you must have expected this."

"Expected what? That you would rent a room and that I would go upstairs with you? No, I didn't expect that."

She held on to my hand. "Sit down, Delroy. You're making a scene. People are looking at you. They're looking at us."

I felt silly, so I sat down. "Connie," I said, "I'm not really sure—"

She cut me off. "Not sure about what? What you want to do? Well, you may not be sure about what you want to do, but I'm very certain of what I want. I want you to take me upstairs and fuck me. I'm not asking you to leave her, and I'm not telling you I'm going to leave Kevin, and I don't know where we may be going from here, and that's not important right now. What's important right now is that I get fucked by you right now."

I looked around to see if anybody was really looking at us. There were two women, maybe in their sixties, sitting at the next table; and unless they were stone deaf, I was sure they had heard every word we had said. Listen, I'm far from being a prude by any means, but I'm not one for making a spectacle of myself, so I got up again, and this time I started to leave.

"Are you really leaving?" she said.

"Yes, Connie. I must go."

"If you want to know, I'll be in room 1724, if you change your mind." I offered to pay the check, but she refused. "Good night, Delroy."

"Connie, I . . . I . . . please don't—"

"Good night, Delroy. Go home."

Chapter 5

————⚬◯♥◯⚬————

$\mathcal{M}$ aybe for Connie it's easy to just fuck me and walk away, go back to her husband and not feel guilty about anything, and then wait for the next time we see each other, if we do see each other again. Maybe she can turn her emotions on and off. Maybe she can even live under the same roof with someone she is not in love with, yearning for and losing sleep for someone who lives with another woman and is in love with her. Maybe for her that's OK and she can deal with it. Maybe this is all part of the modern woman, like some celebrities who only want a man to father their child and then go away, but that's not what I want. I want love and affection. I want to be emotionally involved. I want to have some woman throw her legs over my body in the middle of the night and sometimes ask me to move over to the other side of the bed, and yet is always there for me. I want a woman to love me despite my loud farts in the middle of the night, and I want a woman who, despite her smelly breath in the morning, I still wouldn't want to wake up without. Hey, I'm not asking for perfection, nor am I asking for guarantees. I just want fucking honesty. I don't want to make love to some woman and, despite the sex being good, feel guilty afterward.

If those were the dos and don'ts I wanted in a relationship, then why was I pushing the elevator button?

I got to as far as the lobby; then I stopped and was thinking about what she had said earlier: a woman who had everything she wanted in the world, except the one thing she wanted most, and that a woman should never want anything bad enough to lose her self-respect pursuing it.

Why that line got stuck in my mind I could never figure out. And why couldn't I remember the name of the damn movie? All I could remember was that the movie ended badly. Even when I knocked on the door of room 1724, the line from the movie was still floating in my mind, especially the part about when she loses her self-respect, she ceases to live.

Connie indeed had everything she wanted, but her problems were being bored and not being in love with her husband. I suppose some people might find it hard to understand. After all, her husband was young, talented, and handsome, and made an incredibly decent salary to support their lifestyle.

Kevin Minto was a brilliant surgeon, who had written several books and lectured extensively on heart surgery and cardiovascular disease. At thirty-six, he was a giant in his profession. He was a man who in many ways I admired because of his drive and his dedication to his profession, and for how he and his older brother became doctors.

His mother and his father had both worked at Kings County Hospital in Brooklyn, which was where they met. His mother worked in the laundry washing bed linens, and his father was in maintenance. When Kevin and his brother Calvin were children, their parents would take them to the hospital, and it was there they got their love for medicine. And it was there Kevin vowed that he would not be poor. After he and Calvin graduated from Howard University College of Medicine, Calvin went off to South Africa to work. Calvin envisioned the eventual demise of the white power structure and wanted to be part of the majority when the new government came. He never returned to the States, except to visit their parents on holidays. Kevin, meanwhile, opted for making as much money as he could, catering to the rich and famous in the United States.

His salary was well in the high six figures, and from what Connie told me, he had invested wisely. Their house was worth well over a million dollars. She drove a late-model Benz, and he a BMW. They also had a third vehicle, a Jeep or something. They send Nicole to an exclusive private school and vacation in Europe and the Caribbean every year. Since Connie got pregnant with the twins, she has not worked an hour's wage, and didn't have to. Kevin was an old-fashioned guy who didn't want his wife to work, so he took care of everything.

"The door is open," was the response to my second knock on the door. I turned the door handle and slowly opened it. Connie was lying in bed. She had nothing on. "For a moment, I thought I'd have to sleep here alone tonight," she said.

"I'm not sure why I'm here." I wasn't sure I convinced her.

"You're here because you want to be here."

Talk about silly responses, I said, "I actually came up to see if you really rented a room."

"Now, Delroy, you and I know you could have easily found that out from the front desk. You didn't have to come all the way up here just to find that out."

Not only was it a silly response, but I was sure I looked silly saying it. She said nothing as I sat down on the sofa; and for the first time, I was acting like a teenage boy who was about to get laid for the first time. And not even on my first time did I act like that. My first time was bold and direct: at fifteen, I told this seventeen-year-old girl that if she didn't have sex with me, she could forget about us going out. It worked. As I sat there looking at Connie on the bed, I thought about all those fantasies I had about making love to her in the shower, and looking over at Liseth and seeing her instead.

"Relax, Delroy. If I didn't know better, I'd think this was your first time," she said. "And we all know you can't remember your first time. Not because of your age but because there were so many." She got a laugh out of me.

"I really shouldn't be here, you know," I said, in a voice that convinced no one, not even myself.

She got up out of the bed and walked over to the minibar and poured a drink. A brandy. "Here, drink this," she said as she stood in front of me. I took the drink and took one sip of it and then put the glass on the dresser. As if one sip of the brandy was all I needed to gain courage, I stood up and faced her. The smell of Pears soap was fresh, as if she had just taken a shower; and if my memory served me right, she must have. I undid my tie, and she kissed me as I let it drop to the floor. Her tongue was probing the inside of my mouth like a worm inside a succulent fruit. I wanted her in the worst way, and she could sense it. "I'm glad you changed your mind," she said.

"I may regret this tomorrow," I said.

"Let's not think that far. Let tomorrow think for itself."

"We can't just forget that there are other people involved, Connie."

"Are you going to fuck me, or are you going to talk about other people?"

I did not know what to say, and even if I did, I was not sure what difference it would have made. No one was forcing me to be there. I was there because I wanted to be there. I may very well regret it the next day, but that night, I had every intention of being face-to-face again with that little birthmark on her vagina. It was one of the few times in my life that my clothes came off and I couldn't remember how or who took them off. All I could remember was that I was in bed with Connie, and she was telling me how much she still loved me, and that she always will. That she had never loved a man the way she loved me. That we should never let another three years pass before we make love again.

"Connie," I said, "I . . . we—"

But she cut me off. "Shhh, don't talk. Just hold me. Hold me for a while. Before we do anything, just hold me, baby. Hold me, Delroy. Feel me in your arms. Let me feel your arms around me. I so longed to be loved, to be loved by somebody sincere, somebody honest, who is kind, and who makes love to me with kindness and compassion. Someone who is all man but not afraid to show their feminine side. Someone like you. I don't need someone to just fuck me. I don't need someone to prove to themselves they can maintain a stiff dick all night. It doesn't hurt, but it is so mechanical. You know what I miss, Delroy?"

"What?" I said in a barely audible voice, and with my tongue getting reacquainted with her body. It was still soft and smooth, and my mind journeyed back to the twenty-two-year old girl who kept me waiting nine months before she let me make love to her.

"I miss how after we made love we would hold each other for what seemed like hours. I miss eating ice cream in bed after we made love. I miss you so much, Delroy. Oh God, I miss you."

For nine months, I pursued her like the weak-minded pursued guidance in a cult. And I wanted her worse than a Christian wanted salvation, or a drug addict needed another fix.

"For the past seven months, Delroy, all I've ever thought about is you. God, why was I so stupid? Why couldn't I see that my happiness lies with you? That I'd be miserable without you? I wish time could stand still and tonight could last forever. It's so unfair."

I knew the moment I saw her that day in the barbershop that I wanted her, and that my single days were on the verge of being over. Everything I did when I met Connie was out of character. It never took me more than a month before I'd consummated any relationship I was in. It had gotten to the point where I would start to think I was losing it. And trust me, it was not for lack of trying. But the more I tried, and the more she resisted, the more she became desirable, and the more I wanted her.

"Tonight I feel like a woman again. I feel like a born-again virgin. I feel the way you made me feel the very first time we made love."

For nine months, I wined and dined her. I'd acted the perfect gentleman, and I'd made love to her mind. The first night I got her in bed, I spent half the night telling her why she was worth waiting for that long, and the next half making love to her without penetrating her. I told her that anything that was worth having was worth waiting for. And that she was definitely worth having.

Although at the time she had a four-year-old daughter, she was in many ways young and naive. Waiting nine months to make love to her left a lasting impression on her. With Liseth, it was different: about three weeks after we met, she gave me a blowjob in my Jeep, and that was only because she was having her period. Otherwise, I could have fucked her in the Jeep right there in the parking lot at Jones Beach.

"Delroy, you make love like a bitch."

Those were Connie's exact words the first time I made love to her, and had I been a neophyte, I would not have recognized the compliment. But despite her denial, I held on to the suspicion, to this day, that she had experienced a lesbian relationship in the past. Not that it would have made any difference.

"You think they might have any pralines and cream? If not, we could order some cheesecake and champagne."

Now Connie was playing unfair, for if there was only one thing she knew, it was my weakness for ice cream after making love, and cheesecake and champagne. Those were my weak points. And to mention it when I was at my weakest was, in my opinion, hitting me when I was down. And I was down in every sense of the word. The birthmark was still next to her vagina, and her pubic hair was neatly trimmed, just like it was the very first time I came face-to-face with it.

"I feel so safe when I'm with you, Delroy. You're all I need. Three years is too long, and the past seven months of my life have ceased to exist."

Far be it for me to pretend I was not enjoying the night, and had it been a year or so earlier, it would not have made a difference. I was enjoying myself, and a year earlier, it would have made a tremendous difference. This was a year later, and she was married, and I was very much in love with Liseth. Like with a lot of things, the next day I may very well wish I could change what had happened on this day, but it was too late for regrets or to turn back the clock. I was there in bed with her, and in up to my neck. I may not be able to change the past, but I had control of the future.

"Connie," I said, lying next to her and looking up at the ceiling, "all this talk about ice cream and cheesecake and champagne—those were about a time that was great, and I can't deny that I don't miss them too . . ."

"But."

"But . . . but we have to admit we are involved with other people. I'm not going to lie to you, I did fantasize about us making love. Just this past Sunday, while I was taking a shower, I pictured us making love in the shower like we used to, but I don't know if this can happen again. I don't want to hurt Liseth. It's not fair to her."

"Is it fair for me to be unhappy? For me to be miserable?"

Suddenly I remembered the movie: *Laura*. It stars Dana Andrews, Gene Tierney, Clifton Webb, and Vincent Price. In the movie, Clifton Webb's character is a man who has everything, but is obsessed with Gene Tierney's character, Laura. But Laura is in love with Vincent Price's character and is planning to marry him, and this Webb's character cannot take, so he tries to kill her. And that's where Connie got that line. It's a movie she and I had watched more than once. It's Clifton Webb's character who says it before he tries to kill Laura with a shotgun, only to be stopped by Dana Andrews, who shoots him to death. As I said, the movie has an ominous ending.

"Connie, I know this is hard for you to understand, but sometimes we just can't go back. I'm not going to say I don't have feelings for you, but sometimes we just can't act on our feelings. I'm not going to say this is not great sex, and that I don't enjoy making love to you, but as much as I would like to, I don't think it would be wise for us to do this again."

She got up out of bed and went into the bathroom. "Listen," she said as she peed, "I'm not going to hide the fact that I don't love my husband, and I'm also not going to hide the fact that I don't want a divorce. I'll live with him and perform the wifely duties, including spreading my legs every once in a while to make him happy. But I won't enjoy it."

I sat up in bed and listened to what she was saying with keen interest. Most men might have been flattered, and in a way, I was; but I pitied her more. She was married to a man she was not in love with, and felt trapped with nowhere to go. No one should live a life, or stay in a relationship that makes them unhappy. All the money in the world is not worth it. I didn't like where the conversation was going, and I told her.

"Listen to me for a minute," she said. As if I had a choice. "This is what, July? In a few weeks or more, Liseth will be going off to Yale—"

"End of August," I interrupted.

"OK, August. And you will be by yourself, unless you already have someone on the side, in which case you would not have been faithful to her as you claimed."

"I have been."

"So you're saying."

"I'm not just saying it. I have been. I don't have to lie to you."

"I know. I'm not the one you have to lie to."

That was low, but I guess I deserved it.

"If I know you well enough, and I think I do, you're not going to go long without sex, and it's a long drive from New York to New Haven just to get some pussy. By the time you get back to Long Island, it will have worn off, and you'll be wanting some more."

"You have me all figured out, do you?"

"No, it's just that I know you more than anybody else, including Liseth. You're an addict. You can't go long without pussy. You use sex to cure all your ills, unless you've changed. And I doubt it. Here is what I'm suggesting: I'm still in love with you, and you have some feelings for me—you just admitted it. So why don't we see each other on a regular basis while she is away. You can still go up to New Haven whenever you want. I'm not asking you to leave her, and until that motherfucka drops dead or somebody does me a favor, I'll stay married to him. What's so wrong about that? We can both have our cake and still eat it."

Connie came out of the bathroom and stood at the foot of the bed. The room was dimly lit. All this time in the hotel room, we didn't turn the TV on. The light from the bathroom framed her body as she stood there, and I wanted to just look at her for as long as I could.

"Stand there for a moment," I said.

"Why?"

"I just want to look at you. I haven't seen you naked in three years."

"Would you believe I didn't gain any more weight with the twins than I did with Nicole? And I lost it much quicker this time than when I was younger." She started to tell me how some women her age, and even some who were younger, with three children didn't look as good as she did, and she would have gone on and on if I didn't stop her. This time it was me who told her to shhh. I gently pulled her onto the bed. I figured that I was already there; the damage was already done, and like a condemned man who can't be executed more than once even if he killed again, I made love to her over and over, and I enjoyed it.

We lay in bed, she with her head on my chest and me running my fingers through her hair; and we talked about many things but stayed away from the topic of our respective partners. We were sure we had said all there was to be said. The room was a little cold from the air conditioning, but even so, we were sweaty, and the smell of sex lingered in the air. I had a feeling that whoever came to clean the room the next day would most likely say, "Some fucking did went on here last night."

Even though we didn't talk about our partners anymore, I couldn't help thinking about Liseth, and about what Connie had said earlier. About Liseth going off to Yale in August. I must admit that for a moment, the whole idea was intriguing. What would be so bad about it anyway? With Connie, it would be sex without commitment. We would both know that we had someone else. At least we would be honest.

I had a handful of her hair in my hand and was slowly guiding her head toward my penis when her cell phone rang.

"Is that you or me?" she said.

"It must be you," I said. "If Liseth was going to call me, she would call the office, and if I didn't answer, she would assume I was in the library. So it must be yours."

"Hello," she said as I walked into the bathroom. "It's Greta," she shouted to me through the door. At first I wanted to just empty my bladder, but suddenly I felt a great urgency to empty my bowels instead, as if I hadn't gone for days. I sat on the toilet during most of the conversation. She walked in just as I was getting up. She was still talking to her sister and sat down to pee as the flush was completed. When she was finished, she unrolled some of the toilet paper, wiped herself, looked at it—for what, I couldn't imagine— threw it into the toilet bowl, flushed it, and then walked back into the room still, talking to Greta. There were lots of laughter and serious talking, and my name was mentioned several times. Kevin's not once. But I knew she had to be talking about him when she said, "That's his fuckin' problem."

When she got off the phone, I asked her, "You told Greta you were meeting me?" I already knew the answer. Connie and her sister were very close and rarely hid anything from each other. Plus, in all likelihood, that was where the children were. And on the other hand, she would have to say she was somewhere Kevin wouldn't call or visit.

I lost track of the time until I noticed that it was close to twelve o'clock. I had stayed at the office until twelve one night; and more than once, when I was a young associate, I worked all night doing research in preparation for a brief. The legal profession is not a nine-to-five job, and for those who want to cheat on their spouses, it can provide great cover. As if it was one for the road, Connie gave me a blowjob before we got dressed.

We dressed partly in silence, mostly because I was wondering why for the second time in less than one week Connie had asked for me to meet her at a hotel. Was this part of a master plan? Was she hoping to seduce me the first time, or was she feeling me out for tonight? Did I say or do something last Saturday night to make her want to meet me again? Just thinking about it was not going to give me the answer.

"Connie," I said. I had noticed she didn't put her underwear on when she got dressed. Either she didn't wear one, or she put it in her pocketbook. I have seen her done both before. "There is something I have to ask you."

"What, darling?" she said.

"Did you plan on us going to bed last Saturday night, or was it an exploration?" If there was one thing about Connie I knew that would not have changed, it was her propensity for being honest. Sometimes too honest.

As we headed toward the door, she brushed her hair back from off her face and said, "Both."

***

I settled into the backseat of the limo and kind of just hunkered down and went to sleep. I was more tired than I imagined. The limo driver was familiar with Bay Shore, so there was no need to give him instructions on how to get there. Connie had wanted to give me a ride home, but I reminded her that since her intention was for us to be discreet (not that I agreed to it), it would be inappropriate for me to be seen getting out of her car in front of my house, with Liseth just happening to be standing at the window waiting for me to get home, or worse, just coming or going to the 7-Eleven because she ran out of cigarettes. "Thanks, but no thanks," I told her.

I saw her into a cab in front of the hotel so that she could retrieve her car on Seventy-Ninth Street and Central Park West. We kissed and said good-bye; again, we made no promises, but unlike last Saturday night, there was no need to make any promises, verbal or otherwise. What we had just experienced was too good for us to believe it would end there. And indeed, it was good. So good that being pure ego-driven, I started to think it was worth the risk. After all, how many men can say they have two young gorgeous women who are great lovers and both madly in love with him? If I didn't have an ego before, I was rapidly getting one.

It was about one thirty when the limo pulled into my driveway. Only the TV was on in the bedroom. The light kept flickering with the movement of the picture on the screen. Other than the lamp that was on in the living room and the TV, the house was dark. Liseth was either watching TV or she had fallen asleep with it on, or she was on the phone with her mother. I'd called her from my office when I went to pick up my briefcase and laptop and called the limo service. She was on the phone with her mother then. And when those two get on the phone, it could be for hours. I have never seen a mother and a daughter behave like them before. Their relationship is like one between friends more than a mother-daughter one. Esmeralda is like that with her children, and in particular her daughters. She and Liseth talk about everything, including Liseth's relationship with me, although I can't say Esmeralda was receptive to it at first.

It was not easy winning Esmeralda over. The age thing was a big factor, and Liseth warned me about her mother. Even after I pierced Esmeralda's armor a little, it took a while before Liseth introduced me to the rest of the family. Liseth said her mother felt awkward introducing a man my age to the family as her daughter's boyfriend.

The first time I met Esmeralda—this was after Liseth told her how deeply she felt about me, and that I was not going anywhere— it was at her apartment. Esmeralda and I were both uncomfortable. We barely said anything past the introduction. Liseth and her sister, Esther, did most of the talking. Esther was impressed with who I was, but Esmeralda was not. According to Liseth, her mother thought that once she got to Yale and got to know other students, especially those in her age group, she would think differently.

After about our fourth meeting, and Esmeralda realized that I was not going anywhere, I dropped in one evening at her apartment with the pretense of wanting to see Liseth, knowing fully well that she wouldn't be there. After the salutations, and after we were satisfied each other that we were fine, I admitted why I was really there. I was unable to pull anything over on her, and she told me she knew. Regardless of how Esmeralda felt about me, there was one thing she never was, and that was impolite or rude in any way.

"Are you hungry?" she said, still in that accented English that she had retained even after all the years on the mainland. Liseth was convinced it was her lack of education and her love for Puerto Rico, mixed with her desire to stay in the old neighborhood that contributed to her fragmented English. Esmeralda was not only a flag-waving Puerto Rican, but she never stayed away too long from the island. A year would not pass.

I was not hungry, but having been exposed to her epicurean skills, and wanting badly to have a one-on-one with her, I was not about to turn down the chance of feasting on the best fried chicken and biscuits since the invention of oil and fire. I got the feeling that Esmeralda, like myself, was waiting for that moment. She seated me in the sunken living room, and she sat next to me on the twenty-something-year-old couch that looked as if it had hardly ever been sat upon, and we both had a glass of sherry while the biscuits were cooking. Liseth often told me that when they were kids, they were not allowed to play, or did much, sitting in the living room.

The room was immaculate. There was the couch and two side chairs, in the same pristine condition as the couch, and an old but expensive-looking desk that she told me she got from the Plaza. The desk was in a corner next to the window looking out on 118th Street. In the opposite corner of the room was a table covered with a lace tablecloth with photos of the family going all the way back to her grandmother. Despite the divorce, she still kept several photos of Carlos, her ex-husband. There were two from their younger days—their wedding photo and one with him holding Liseth (the only one in color) when she was a baby.

Liseth, according to Esmeralda, was her father's favorite, but somehow Liseth despised him for abandoning the family for another woman. Despite Carlos having a second wife and family, Esmeralda always talked about him with affection, and still referred to him as her husband.

The walls of the living room were painted eggshell white, and the drapes were soft cream. The hardwood floor was preserved and stained dark, with an expensive Persian rug on it. Esmeralda rarely used that room; she usually spent most of her time in her bedroom watching TV or reading. There was no TV in the living room. Her youngest son, Juan, was the only one living there with her—that is, when he was not in jail. Liseth's room remained intact.

Esmeralda was an elegant woman of modest height and weight: five feet two inches and a few ounces over one hundred pounds. She was a throwback to the days when people dressed for dinner. Despite her and Liseth being blondes and having no problem keeping their weight down, the similarities stopped there. Liseth looked more like her father (who was over six feet tall) and walked and talked like her father. They even had the same personalities—at least I was told, since I never met the man.

Esmeralda's apartment was on the fifth floor in one of those prewar buildings. Those apartments in the prewar buildings were usually quite large in comparison to their postwar counterparts. It had three bedrooms and a large dining area, enough to hold a dining room suite with six chairs. It was where I was first exposed to her epicurean delights, and subsequently two scrumptious dinners, and where we would have the fried chicken and biscuits.

"Delroy, come join me," Esmeralda said in that lovely accented English, and beckoned me over to the dining area. "Here, sit," she said, pointing to the head of the table, where I always sit.

"Thank you," I said as I took my seat. She poured some lemonade for both of us. Frankly, I'd have preferred some more sherry, but I deferred to her judgment.

After putting the chicken and biscuits on the table, she took the seat closest to me. "Go ahead, help yourself," she said as she laid her napkin on her lap. In many ways, Esmeralda reminded me of my mother. Except for the height (Mom was five feet ten), they were both slim, and both radiate class and were arbitrators of good taste, especially in the field of couture. The more I knew Liseth, the more I agree she must have gotten her father's personality. A slave to fashion she was not.

"Thanks for allowing me to barge in on you," I said as I put two pieces of chicken and two biscuits on my plate. "It's very kind of you to allow me to invade your home like this."

"Come now," she said. "Don't apologize. We both knew that this would happen sooner or later. What had me worried was, what took you so long?" She put two pieces of chicken and two biscuits on her plate too.

"I suppose you could say I was waiting for the right time." I sank my teeth into the succulent fried bird. A breast. From my estimate of the chicken on the platter in front of me, and from what I saw still sitting on the top of the stove, I'd say she must have fried at least two chickens. I was prepared to talk slow. After taking a bite of the biscuit and drinking some lemonade, I said, "Esmeralda, can I be frank with you?"

"I'd be offended if you weren't," she said. She said it so flawlessly I started to wonder if her accented English was a charade.

"You're opposed to our relationship, aren't you?"

I always pictured Esmeralda as a woman who was economic in her speech, but that evening proved me wrong. "Let me also be honest with you, Delroy—by the way, would you like some more sherry, or some white wine instead?"

I was glad she asked, because I was ready to ask for some if she didn't mention it. Since we were eating chicken, I chose white wine. She went into the kitchen and returned with a chilled bottle of wine and two glasses. I offered to uncork it.

"Let me put it this way," she continued. "It's not so much that I'm opposed to your and Liseth's relationship—at least not in the way you may think." I poured us some wine. "Thank you," she said.

"Then what are you opposed to?" I asked. I took a sip of the wine. It was good. I took another sip. Actually, it was more than a sip. I drank some and poured myself some more. "Let's forget the age thing for a while, because I know that's what you're hung up on. Let's look at me from a different perspective: I come from a good family. I went to a good school. I have never been arrested. Both my parents are lawyers, and so am I. As a matter of fact, I come from a long line of lawyers. Now tell me something, if I was a year or two older than her, would you have any objections?" I looked at her face for a reaction when I said that.

She didn't give away anything. "I must admit you're right. I'd have no objections if you were just a year or two older than Liseth."

"But?" I said with a mouthful of wine.

"But the problem is you're forty-five. You're almost my age, and she is only twenty-two. She is still a baby, my baby, and . . ."

She was getting emotional on me, and that was the last thing I wanted, so I interrupted her. "Esmeralda, let me ask you something. What is the real problem here? Are you afraid that because I'm twenty-three years older than Liseth that I'll take advantage of her? Have you ever stopped to consider that she may be the one who is taking advantage of me? Not that anybody is taking advantage of anybody, but have you ever stopped to think you might have it the other way around? Liseth is no fool, you know."

"Oh, I know she is no fool," she said between sips of wine and blowing her nose on a paper towel. "She has too much of her father in her to be a fool, but I can't help thinking that she will get hurt."

"If you really believe that, then I'm afraid you don't really know your own daughter. Trust me, she will be all right. I can't give you guarantees, but I'll tell you this much: if I think for a moment that it's not going to work between me and Liseth, you'll be the first to know, and I'll exit with as much grace and class to make you proud. But may I say one thing?"

"What?"

I could see a lot more comfort and easiness in her demeanor after my little speech.

"I want to say with all humility that I'm the lucky one in this relationship. I'm lucky to have her in my life." I poured myself another glass of wine and then some for her too. She thanked me again. I had some more chicken and two more biscuits. And she started to tell me how much Liseth loved me, and how she had never seen her behave like this about a man before. We were in a high state of conviviality when Juan walked in, said hello to us, took a two-liter bottle of Coke out of the fridge, put several pieces of chicken in a piece of aluminum foil, and then went back out. Juan was not a person for too much conversation. He struck me as rather shy, someone who kept people at bay; but that was all right with me. Something told me I was not missing anything. Needless to say, after that evening, Esmeralda and I became good friends; and I gradually, to the delight of Liseth, started to meet the rest of the family.

It was not unusual for me to take a late-night shower, especially on a summer night. Tonight I took a quick one, put on a clean underwear, and then got in bed next to Liseth. The sheets were fresh and clean; they were the light-blue sets she had bought recently, and as usual, she washed them before putting them on. I love the smell of clean sheets.

I could see the outline of her body under the sheets, and something told me she had nothing on underneath. As I propped up my pillow, I looked under, and I was right: she had nothing on. I quietly searched for the remote control. I found it and hoped for two things: to not wake her, and if I did, that she was not in the mood for sex, because I was certainly too tired for any kind of activity. Though I was sure if she wanted to and I said no, she would have understood.

There was some movie on, with two girls making love. I was sure it came on after she fell asleep. Liseth is not big on watching these types of movies. I surfed the channels. The last thing I wanted at that time of the morning was to watch two girls making love. It was only going to put me in a mood that I was trying to avoid.

I settled on a Laurence Olivier movie on American Movie Classics. The movie was maybe halfway along, but it was one of my all-time favorites: *Rebecca*. I could catch the last ten minutes and I'd still recognized it. As I nodded off a little, Liseth said, "Did you get the motion done?"

"Yes," I said without elaboration.

"I hope you win this motion. I'd be pissed if you stood me up for a losing motion," she said as she snuggled up to me.

"When you become a lawyer, you'll realize that you'll win some and you'll lose some," I said.

"You can lose the others. Just don't lose this fuckin' one. I suffered for it tonight. I love you, baby," she said.

"I love you too."

She kissed me on my chest and said, "Good night."

I bade her good night and continued watching the movie until I fell asleep. I didn't know what time it was.

***

There is always a first in everything: the next morning, Liseth got up before me at ten thirty, and I was too tired to go running. Liseth may not be blessed with her mother's epicurean advantages, but our relationship will not suffer because of her cooking, even if we have to live on scrambled eggs and toasted bagels. If she flunked out of law school, she can also do well as a salad chef.

Eggs are not something I eat often—maybe two or three times a month—but when I do, I'd usually have a three-egg omelet or three scrambled with sliced lox. Actually, that's my favorite. I showed Liseth how to do it once, and she, being a quick learner, got it down pat. I'd usually take a slice or two of lox, chop it up, add it to three beaten eggs, along with some scallions, and then pour it into the frying pan. Scramble and serve. Not only was Liseth a quick learner, but she got to love it too.

We had brunch in bed; it was close to noon, so we just ate, watched TV, and then went back to sleep. It was almost three o'clock when we woke up. It was too late to go to the beach, and since we had to look at a gift for her aunt's wedding at Fortunoff at Roosevelt Field, we just stayed in bed a little longer and watched some more TV. And I tried not to think about the night before.

Chapter 6

I n law school, I had a friend who was older than me. Robert McKendrick was forty and was married to Pamela, a girl that he grew up with, who was two years younger than him and a lawyer. They had a five-year-old son. Everybody called Robert BobbyMac. BobbyMac had no intention of going to law school, until he was injured on a construction site and was laid up for about a year. BobbyMac recovered from his injuries and was on disability for another year. It was then that Pamela, who had been practicing law for thirteen years, encouraged him to go to law school. Before law school, BobbyMac was doing very well running his own construction company.

BobbyMac was the old man of our group. And a very wise one. We were all in our twenties. All of us had gone on from undergrad straight into law school, or from undergrad to study overseas, which I did, and then to law school. And we brought with us some of our reckless behaviors. We drank, got high, and fucked everything that wore a bra. BobbyMac was not averse to joining us, and as an Irishman, his affinity for drinking was legendary. But he would stay away from the drugs and women. He was faithful to Pamela without apologies.

One Friday night, BobbyMac and our regular group were at this bar in the Village. As usual, we drank without discretion, felt the effect of it, and behaved badly. I remember the night as if it was yesterday. I even remember the bar, although it is no longer there. The bar was Mulcahy's on West Fourth Street. That night, the bar was crowded with the usual Friday-night crowd: students from NYU Law School, New York Law School, Brooklyn Law School, and from Fordham. It was the week before Thanksgiving.

Among some of the people in the bar that evening was a close friend of mine, who was one of the most brilliant young men of our generation but who at the time was the biggest cokehead, and who today is one of the most influential people in the federal government, and who, for that reason, I'll call Nameless.

Back then, everyone, except BobbyMac and a few other people, did a few lines. I would occasionally do a line now and then, but I never developed a taste for it. But Nameless not only just did a few lines, he needed cocaine to function. According to him, he needed it to study, to stay awake, and, most of all, to fuck. I must admit that fucking while high on cocaine is an experience—like making love to two women at the same time—that every sane man should try at least once, although I wouldn't recommend getting hooked on the former. The latter I would definitely not seek any cure for. Anyway, one of our modes of operation was to see how many different girls we could fuck each semester, and from which different law schools. Columbia girls were no longer at the top of the list. We went there. They were no longer a novelty. Since we had had girls from NYU Law, New York Law, Brooklyn Law, and even St. John's and Rutgers, there was only Fordham left. That night, we set out to capture a Fordham girl.

I remember telling this to BobbyMac, and remember him saying that had he been single, he'd have given us a run for our money.

"You think Pamela would know if you slept with someone?" I remember asking him.

"Yes, she would."

"How would she?"

"Because I would tell her," he said. Now bear in mind I was about twenty-two or twenty-three, just starting my second year of law school and having the greatest time of my life, and some weird old guy is telling me he would tell his wife he fucked some girl. This was not only weird but abnormal. *What's wrong with this guy?* I asked myself. "Why would you tell her?" I asked him. Bear in mind again that we were stone drunk. "Because I love her," he said.

"And?" I said without missing a beat, between sips of rum and a beer chaser.

"Because I wouldn't lie to her," he said.

"What do you mean you wouldn't lie to her? It's easy. Everybody does it."

"I'm not everybody. I don't lie, and most of all, not to my wife."

I looked at him; drunk as we both were, I could tell he was serious. To ask him if Pamela would tell him the truth if she slept with someone would be in poor taste.

A week after we came back from the holiday break, I was in the cafeteria with Nameless, and we started to talk about my conversation with BobbyMac. Of course, Nameless believed him. "You really believe he would tell his wife he cheated on her?" I asked him.

"Shit, yes," said Nameless.

"Why? Two people meet in a bar, they have a little too much to drink, and one thing leads to another, and they may never see each other again, why bring it up by telling your wife?"

"I agree with you one hundred percent, but that's what makes us different from white folks."

"What are you talking about?" I said even though I sort of knew where he was going. You'd have to know Nameless to understand him. He was not only very bright, he was also very Afrocentric.

"You have to understand the nature of the white man," he said. "They can lie about history looking you dead in the eye. They'll even change history to suit their own end. That they don't have a problem with. But with their wives, they can't lie. When it comes to history, they are revisionists, but they will leave home and go all the way across the world on a business trip, fuck some bitch they know they will never see again, and what happens? Three months later, their wives are taking their suit to the cleaners, after having found something as simple as a matchbook from a strip joint. OK, so he went to a strip joint, but does that mean he fucked some bitch, even though he did? And here is the shit that kills me: she says to him, 'Don't insult my intelligence. Look me in the eyes and tell me you didn't cheat on me.' And what does the motherfucka do? Confess. Now ain't that a bitch? And here's the part that some people will never understand: the same son of a bitch, with his luck, becomes president. Then he gets on TV, look the American people in the eyes, lie to them, and then lead them into a war on the premise of that lie."

There might have been some truth to what Nameless was saying, but knowing him, all he needed was someone to agree with him, and you'd have to have a heart attack or fake one to end the argument, so I said, "Well, there is one of two ways to avoid that."

"And they are?"

"Either you don't get married, or—"

"Or—don't tell me, if you get married, be faithful, right?"

"Right."

"Let me tell you something, Delroy. One thing has nothing to do with the other. And don't get me wrong, I'm not condoning infidelity in any way, but at the same time, I'm not saying I wouldn't cheat on my wife if I was married."

"So what are you saying?"

"What I'm saying is that if I was married, I'm not admitting to anything under any circumstances."

"Even if there were evidence?"

"Let me put it another way: if I was married, and my wife walked in on me fucking some bitch and she took pictures—now you must remember that me and the girl are stark naked in my wife's bed and she has pictures to prove it—I'm still denying it. Fuck that shit, it ain't me."

"Even with the pictures?"

"I don't give a shit if Eyewitness News is there, it ain't me. And let me tell you something else, Delroy, my good friend—or rather, let me remind you of something: we are studying to be lawyers, and if we are hoping to be any good at it, we can't take this kind of attitude into the real world."

"What kind of attitude are you talking about?"

"Let me tell you a story a professor told me in undergrad—"

"What was that?" I sensed one of his legendary stories coming as I picked at my salad.

"One day—this was about my last year in college, and for a long time, I was trying to evade any and all math classes . . . oh, did I tell you I was terrible at math? Well, I was. In any case, one day I walked into the office of the head of the political science department. I told him how bad I was at math and asked him if there was anything he could do. I had taken one of his classes before. Right now, I don't remember the class, but I know I was outstanding in his class, and he remembered me, and that I had a four point average. I was afraid I wouldn't graduate unless I took the silly math classes."

"So what happened?"

"He told me to take statistics and not to worry about the rest, because in the real world of politics, two and two don't always add up to four. Delroy, my friend, politics and the law are the same fuckin' thing: everything is not always what it seems. And one other thing: lawyers make the best fuckin' politicians."

"I'm afraid to ask, but what if he had insisted that you take the math classes?"

He looked at me as if to say, *What a silly question*, and said, "Let's just say I didn't have to worry about it, but if I had to, I can assure you it would not have spoiled my GPA."

I believed him, and needless to say, of everything that I'd learned in law school, that was the best advice I'd ever had. It stuck with me forever. Admit nothing, no matter the evidence. And when necessary, attack the facts. Fortunately, I didn't have to lie to Liseth. She never asked. And had she asked, of course, I was not going to admit that the night before, I was not at work but instead in some hotel room with an old girlfriend. What am I, crazy? Now if she caught me in the act . . . well, let's just say I'll cross that bridge if I ever come to it.

All the way to the mall, and throughout dinner at the California café, I was not my usual self. I'm usually a very gregarious and loquacious guy, but that evening, I was quite and pensive. Liseth assumed it was work related, and I was not about to contradict her.

Much as I tried during dinner, I could not get Connie out of my mind. I never thought cheating on my girlfriend would cause that much anguish. Was that the way married men felt? I knew then what BobbyMac meant when he said he couldn't cheat on Pamela. But I kept hearing Nameless saying, *Fuck it, it's just a little sex. It's no big deal, unless you make it one.* But BobbyMac kept coming back with, *It's more than sex. It's character.* I had one of them on each shoulder. I could have rationalized my actions by making an argument, to myself or to whomever, that I was not married, which was true, but Liseth and I lived together, and although I had been in serious relationships before, this was the first time I'd ever lived with anyone—and that meant a lot, not only to me but to Liseth.

Our evening ended in the sort of way that had it been a first date, it might have been our last. When we got home, I gave Liseth the excuse that I had to review a file and spent most of the night in my study. I must have fallen asleep on the leather sofa. I had a legal pad with some notes scribbled on it. It was all silly jottings, but I knew Liseth was not going to read it unless I asked her to.

Liseth knocked before she entered and asked if I was all right, and if I wanted some tea. It was after eleven, so I said yes; and she went off to the kitchen to make it. She returned shortly afterward and told me she was making a pot and asked me if I wanted company. I said yes, even though I would have liked to have said *No, just leave me alone and let me think*, but that would not have been fair to her. She was too caring and honest to be treated that way, but I wanted some time alone, because the lie was too deep;

and somehow I was thinking that Connie would go away and my life would return to normal.

When she returned with the pot of tea, we sat down and talked for a while, and she wanted to know what sort of case had me so tense and pensive. I had many cases I was working on, so it was not a problem finding one. "You're working too hard, sweetheart," she said. "Don't you realize it? You should let some of the associates handle more of the work."

"You may be right," I said.

"I know I'm right. Promise me that when I'm at Yale you'll take care of yourself, OK?"

"What do you mean? I always take care of myself."

"I know that, and that's not what I mean. I mean you shouldn't spend twelve and fourteen hours at the office every day. You should try to enjoy yourself. Go out, meet people, have fun." That obviously didn't mean Connie. There I go thinking of Connie again.

Liseth moved closer to me, and I put my arm around her and pulled her close to me and kissed her on her left cheek and told her not to worry, that I'd be all right. "You shouldn't worry so much." I kissed her again and squeezed her. "I'll be fine."

"But I have to worry." She put her arms around my waist. "I want you to father my children and see them grow up. I intend to get at least thirty more years out of you."

"Only thirty?"

"I said at least."

"My grandfather is still active at ninety-one."

"I intend to grow old with you."

"I'll get on your nerves."

"I'll get used to it by then."

"Thank you."

"I love you," she said and kissed me, and asked if I was coming to bed as she got up to leave.

"You go on up," I said. "I'll be up soon."

"Don't take too long."

"I won't."

I sat there for a while and thought about the possibility of fucking up what we have. I thought of just letting the time pass, putting some distance, really just letting time pass between me and Connie, so that she would have time to think and she would realize that the whole idea of us having this torrid affair was wrong, and that maybe if she called me again, all I'd have to do was ignore her calls and she would eventually get the message. On the other hand, I was thinking *Why don't I just tell her we can't ever see each other again?* But I did that the last time we were together, and I left convinced that she didn't take me seriously. Then it occurred to me that the one person I may be able to talk to, who could convince her to give it up was her sister, Greta. Not only were she and Greta close, but Connie also had a great deal of respect for Greta; and in any case, Greta already knew that we were at the Hilton Hotel the night before.

The words of BobbyMac were ringing in my ears: that one must tell a second lie to cover up the first, and then a third to cover up the second, and so on, and so on; and then you either break down at some point and tell the truth, or you become so good at lying that it wouldn't matter anymore. Nameless would have said that truth and lies are subjective. They are not absolute. Maybe that's why he had been making more than $2 million a year before he went into government, and why BobbyMac was defending the rights of homeless people in New York City.

***

Twice each month, on a Saturday, there were two things I'd always do (if I was not away on business), I would get my haircut and visit my parents. Liseth would drop me off at the barbershop and then drive up to my parents in Pelham Manor, or she'd wait for me—that is, if Victor took me right away, which would be rare since the barbershop was always crowded on Saturdays, especially during the hours I usually showed up, which was generally somewhere between one and two, or later. Afterward, she would either pick me up or I'd go up to my parents' on my own, depending on how I felt, or if Liseth and my mother were out shopping, which they have done on many occasions.

Frankly, I'd much rather walk sometimes. Not only was it a relatively short walk—seven or eight blocks from the top of Boston Road up to Pelhamdale Road in Pelham Manor—but it reminded me of the walks I used to take with my parents when I was younger up and down Boston Road. Even though we had a car, my parents would walk to wherever they were going, whenever they could; and even now, with my dad at sixty-six and my mom at sixty-three, along with their daily laps in the pool, they still did as much walking as they could. Maybe that's why they looked so great.

Dad was six feet tall and a solid two hundred and twenty-five pounds. He was a handsome man, without any prejudice on my part, with not as much gray hair on top (as most men his age would have) but with extremely gray temples, and a neatly trimmed mustache that, when he was dressed in his pinstriped double-breasted suits, gave him a distinguished look befitting his profession or that of a diplomat. My mother was equally elegant and was as beautiful as Lena Horne, though not as fair skinned as Lena. The one thing about my mother was that she never, and for all she would eat, could ever weigh more than a hundred and fifty pounds. She had long hair, which showed more signs of gray all over than my father's, and she has a penchant for wearing hats. She had all kinds of hats and berets, and she loved scarves and sweaters. My mother and my father were made for each other, and after forty-five years of marriage, they were just as in love with each other as when they first met. I'd like to have at least two kids with Liseth and hoped that we can be just as happy and in love with each other as my parents were.

I was happy with the relationship that my mom and Liseth had. Unlike Liseth's mom, my mother had no reservations about our relationship, despite the age difference. Being that I was her only child, my mother was happy if I was happy, and she saw Liseth as the daughter she always wanted. Mom liked Connie too but thought Connie was not ambitious, and may have been a gold digger, which was not true. Mom realized she was wrong about Connie when I told her Connie turned down my marriage proposal. Interestingly enough, when she met Liseth, she was overjoyed, if for no other reason than at the prospect of finally having grandkids, and the fact that Liseth, a graduate of her alma mater, was Yale-bound.

"There is no need to ask if Victor is busy," Liseth said as she pulled up the car into the shopping plaza. All the parking places were taken, and cars were illegally parked all over the place, including on the sidewalk in front of the barbershop. Victor has always discouraged us from parking illegally. But it was not so much the patrons of the barbershop who were the main offenders as the customers of the Jamaican market separated from the barbershop by a Jamaican restaurant.

The Jamaican market, owned by some Chinese Jamaicans, was also part fish shop. Saturdays the place was filled to overflow capacity. The first time I went in there to buy a Red Stripe beer, it took me close to twenty minutes to pay for the one item. The next time, I just walked up to the head of one of the four cash registers, put the exact amount down, amid stares and reprimands about breaching Jamaican ethics, and just walked out. (One thing about those Jamaicans was their predilection for being polite, waiting their turn in a line to be served. British tradition dies hard.) But despite their passion for orderly standing in a line, they were the main offenders when it came to parking illegally all over the parking lot. A Jamaican friend once told me that it was those expensive cars they drove that they wanted everyone to see them getting out of. And there seems to be some truth to it, because you can only find more BMWs, Lexuses, and Mercedes Benzes on a car dealer's lot.

"Call me if you want me to pick you up," Liseth said as she kissed me before I got out of the car.

"See you later," I said. I watched her as she headed out of the plaza and turned north on Boston Road.

The barbershop was standing room only. All the usual faces were in the joint, and Victor was on the phone as he cut a customer's hair. I walked past his chair, the third from the front, and headed straight to the toilet in the back past the giant-screen TV and the soda machine. A bunch of children and a few adults were gathered around the TV, watching the Yankees' game. Victor's little office, adjacent to the toilet, was open; and Greta, who was also her husband's bookkeeper, was sitting at his desk working on the computer. I stuck my head in and said hello, and that I needed to talk to her.

"I need to talk to you too," she said in a way that indicated certain seriousness.

"Oh," I said, surprised. "What about?" I stood in the office doorway and was about to ask her again what she wanted to talk to me about, feeling like a child before his parent, guilty of something but unable to figure out how the parent found out.

"Why don't you go use the bathroom first," she said.

Greta and I had enjoyed an amicable relationship over the years. I regard her as a friend, and I could, without any doubt, say the feeling was mutual—not only because of my past relationship with Connie, but also because of my friendship with her husband. She and I had talked about many things that run the gamut, so the fact that she *needed* to talk to me should not have surprised me. And yet somehow I felt this was not one of our usual tête-à-têtes.

I tried to make it as brief as possible in the toilet, and my carelessness left a wet spot on the front of my khaki pants, which forced me to sit down immediately when I entered the office. "What's up, G?" I said as I positioned myself at an angle on the chair at the side of the desk where she would not be able to see the wet spot, although I was sure she saw it when I entered the office.

Not only did Greta and Connie look alike, but also, despite Greta being two years older, they could pass for twins. At five feet seven inches, Greta was an inch taller. Being married to the same man for all these years and resigning herself to the duties of mother and wife made the ten-pound advantage evident. Unlike Connie, Greta wore her brown hair short; but the one thing they had in common was that they always smelled the same—having always had a penchant for Givenchy's Amarige Eau de Toilette.

"Close the door," she said.

I really felt as though I was being busted by one of my parents for doing something wrong. "This sound serious," I said, trying to read her face.

She got to the point. "What the hell is going on between you and Connie?" she said in a slightly raised voice. Before I could say anything, she said, "What you and Connie are doing is dangerous, not to mention stupid. Connie I could understand, because she's a person who is very passionate when she's in love, and God knows she's in love with you. But it's you I don't understand."

I was totally speechless, and confused. I thought, from everything Connie had told me, Greta was cool with her seeing me. She even called Connie when we were at the hotel two nights before, and Greta, according to Connie, said hello. "I don't get you," I said.

"Well, let me put it this way: you're a very intelligent man. As a matter of fact, I always say you're one of the few men that I know who think with your head and not with your dick, but I guess I was wrong."

"You think that's what I'm doing?"

"Maybe not intentionally, but it's still the same. Don't get me wrong, Delroy. We—that is, the family—all wish you were the one she married, but she didn't, and that we all thought was a terrible mistake on her part, and we told her so."

"Thank you," I said. It felt good to hear it even though it was not the first time I was hearing it.

"Greta," I said, my voice breaking with emotion, "I did not mean for this to happen. I really didn't. You must believe—"

She cut me off. "I know you didn't, and I know you still have feelings for her, and I know you still love her in a lot of ways."

"I do," I said, unable to hide my emotions but trying to not let it get the better of me.

"Well, if you do love her and care for her, you're going to have to break it off with her. You must end it for everybody's sake, yours and hers in particular."

"Why?" I asked her, and the minute that word came out of my mouth, I wished I could take it back. I wanted to apologize for saying it, but that would only make me look sillier.

Greta paused, as if searching for the right response—a response that I could only think would not show her contempt for my stupid reply. Her next question was measured, and the pedagogue in her surfaced. I felt like one of the young kids in her Bronx public school classroom. "That's the kind of question I'd expect from anyone but you," she said. If she was trying not to show contempt for my stupid question, she was doing a poor job of it. I felt like a child, and I just sat there in my seat. I said nothing more as she lectured and berated Connie and me for what was in her opinion our reckless and selfish behavior.

We were, in her opinion, behaving like teenagers, sneaking behind our parents' backs, fucking at every opportunity, although we have met twice and gone to bed once, as reluctant as I was, thinking that eventually when they did find out, they would just say, "What the hell, they're just kids in love."

But we were not kids. We were adults with responsibilities to others, and she reminded me that Connie had young children and a teenage daughter and had more at stake in this irrational triangle we called love.

Greta warned me that unless I was willing to leave Liseth, which she didn't think I was willing to do, and do the right thing in marrying Connie, I should break it off, and that both of us should move on with our lives. She assured me that Kevin didn't know what was going on. That it was too soon, but that if we continued, he eventually would, and when he did, she knew him well enough to know that he was not going to be civil about it. She told me that Kevin was not her most favorite person, and at times not the most likable guy, but that he deserved better. That despite his ways, he treated the kids and Connie's kid well. That he was a good father, and he never hit her or abused her in any way. The only thing Kevin was guilty of was being old-fashioned: he didn't want his wife to work.

Something went off in my head. I was not sure I heard her right. "Did you just say that her husband never hit or abused her in any way?" I asked her, uncrossing my legs and sitting up straight in the chair when I said it.

"Did she tell you he hit her?" she said with a sense of disbelief across her face.

"Hit her, abused and raped her," I said. "She even told me you knew about it. As a matter of fact, you're the only one she said she told this to."

"Delroy, I can assure you this is the first time I'm hearing this." Disbelief turned to anger; her complexion changed, her face turning red. I wanted to believe Greta, because I knew she had no reason to lie to me. After all, she admitted that Kevin was not her most favorite person, and that at times he was not the most likable person. So she had no motive, and Connie could have, but what could it be?

And so my only reaction was to ask her. "Greta, are you sure?"

"Of course I'm sure. If he had done all those things to her, she would not stay with him, that much I know about my sister."

"But she told me how he forced himself on her, and that when he drinks, he not only forces her to have sex, but he sometimes gets violent."

"Delroy, this is why you're going to have to end this between you and Connie, because look what she's doing: she's making her husband out to be a wife beater and a rapist. It's not true, Delroy. It's not true. Believe me, it's not true."

I put my hand on my head. "I can't believe what I'm hearing."

"Kevin, I must admit," said Greta, "sometimes drinks one too many, but he never gets violent. Never."

In frustration, I said, "I don't know what to believe. I really don't."

"Did she tell you she hasn't have sex with him for months? Did she tell you that?"

"Yes, she did," I said, voice subdued, and although I should be feeling some relief that something was fundamentally wrong within the marriage for her to not have sex with her husband for months, I couldn't help feeling like a sucker.

"At least she told the truth about something," said Greta. "That and the fact that she loves you very much, and that she does not love Kevin. I know she wouldn't lie about these things, but the others, I don't know what to say. I really don't."

"Greta, how can you be sure Connie is telling the truth about anything? How can you be sure she really loves me and not her husband?" I don't know why I asked that question, and I don't know what good it would do to know that, or what difference it would make; but for some unexplained reason, I had to ask.

The phone rang. There was a knock on the door, and she looked at her watch, all at once, as she was about to say something. She picked up the phone first, said hello, and then asked who was at the door. It was Connie on the phone and Victor at the door. Victor walked in as Greta was starting her conversation with Connie. He was there to tell me that my turn was coming up.

"I'll be right there," I said.

"There's two before you," he said and then went back out the door. I was more interested in what Greta had to say to Connie.

"Connie, Delroy is here with me, and I have heard some very interesting things that I didn't know was going on in your life," she said, and before Connie could answer, she asked her if Kevin was home, and Greta's next response indicated that he was not. "OK, so you can answer my question, then. Where . . . no, you answer my question first before you talk to him. Where—no, you're not going to talk to him till you answer my question. Are you . . . are you. Connie? Connie, are you going to answer my question first? Then you're not going to talk to him, then. No, you'll not talk, then."

"Let me talk to her Greta," I said.

"No, let her answer my question first. She should answer my question first. You can't let her get away with this."

"Greta, I assure you she will not get away with anything." She handed me the phone. "Hello," I said.

"Hi, baby," Connie responded in a soft, seductive voice. "I miss you."

"Connie, you lied to me."

"What did Greta tell you?"

"That Kevin never hit you or ever raped you in any way, that he loves you and cares for you and the children, and that he's a good husband. Is this true, Connie?"

"She doesn't know the truth about everything," she said.

"What is the truth, Connie?"

"That some things you just can't tell your family. Some things are just too embarrassing to tell even your closest family. You wouldn't understand, Delroy."

"But you told me you told Greta, so one way or another, you lied to me. Why, Connie? Why?"

"Can we talk about this some other time?"

"I'm not sure we have anything to talk about."

"Don't do this to me, Delroy. Please don't do this to me."

"Connie, you lied to me. You lied to your sister, and God knows who else you lied to. What I don't understand is, why? For what? Just to fuck me? Is that what this is all about? Because if that's what this was all about, you didn't have to lie, Connie. You know you didn't have to lie, and you know something, I believed you."

"This is not the time to talk about this, Delroy." She was getting defiant, and before I could say another word, she said, "Let me talk to Greta."

I gave the phone to Greta.

The first thing out of Greta's mouth was, "Where the fuck do you get off talking about people like that? How dare you say those things about Kevin? You don't do that to people, Connie. If you want the marriage to end, seek a divorce. There is no court that would not give custody of children that young to their mother. But if you keep running around, every chance you get, with another man, you'll wind up the loser, and you know that. Connie, you're my sister, and I love you, care for you, and want the best for you, but you're going to wind up hurting yourself. You know the family will stand behind you no matter what, but don't do it the way you're doing it. It's not fair to Kevin and to Delroy." She paused, and then said, "OK. OK. OK. OK." Then she said to me, "She wants to talk you again." She handed me the phone.

I took the phone and held it to my ear and said nothing, afraid of what I might say. And as if she could smell me, Connie said, "Listen, you and I have to talk."

I still didn't say anything, but she was reading me well. "Please don't jump to any conclusions."

I finally said, "What choice do I have?"

"You could give me a chance to explain."

"OK, so explain," I said with an air of irritability.

"Not now," she said. "He's expected back any minute."

"When?"

"Let me call you," she said.

"When?"

"Soon."

"OK. Bye." We hung up. Greta was just as confused as I was, and I was sure equally disappointed. There was a knock on the door again, and Greta told the person to come in. A young man stuck his head in and told me that Victor was ready for me. I told him I'd be right there. Greta told me that Connie was coming over to her house the next day and that she would have a serious talk with her about everything. She told me to say hello to Liseth, and that I should be careful, that I could wind up losing both women. I thanked her for the advice, even though Connie was not mine to lose. Then I went off to get my haircut.

It was one of the rare occasions when Victor and I didn't talk about much. He asked me if I was going to be all right, and I told him I would be. Then he told me that he was sure I'd handle it in the right way. I said I would. When he was finished, I told him I'd see him in two weeks. And left without talking to anybody else.

Chapter 7

I flagged a gypsy cab that was going south on Boston Road. Another had come up just as the lights changed on my side of the street, but I didn't see it. The southbound driver made a U-turn and stopped in front of me, almost causing the other driver to rear-end him. Tires screamed and horns blared, and I was sure unkind words were said as onlookers stared. I hopped into the back of the Lincoln Town Car. The driver was a West African immigrant. He tried to make small talk, but I was not in the mood; and after several attempts, he gave up. The fare was $8, double the usual four since we were going over the city line. I gave him ten.

The sound of laughter greeted me as I walked up the pathway to my parents' house. The lawn was neatly manicured, and the hedges trimmed. The automatic sprinklers were on, and the labor of the Mexicans who came once a week to take care of the gardening was evident.

The sun bounced off the pair of white Jaguars parked in front of the three-car garage. The residue of water around the cars was evidence that it wasn't long since they'd been washed. Mom and Dad, like me, always wash their cars every Saturday.

The laughter grew louder as I approached the front door. It was Mom and Liseth laughing, which meant only one thing: Dad was telling one of his legendary funny stories. Mom's laughter almost drowned out Liseth's. You could always pick Mom out of a crowd by her laugh. She had a good-humored, healthy laugh that reached a crescendo and trailed off with a giggling that continued sometimes even after the joke was long over. Mom loved a good joke and loved to laugh. There were two things Mom said people should never stop doing: reading and laughing. Reading exercises the mind, and laughter makes the heart stronger. Both she practiced with undiminished loyalty.

Beatrice greeted me as I entered the house. It was always a joy to see her. She had been living with us since I was fifteen and was like a second mother to me. Mom and Dad met her on one of their many trips to Jamaica. I was ten at the time. They befriended her and sponsored her and her two children, who were both older than me. Her son, Kenneth, went on to graduate with a PhD in mathematics and went back to Jamaica to teach. I admired him for that. If many more Jamaicans did that, the country would be better off. Her daughter, Elizabeth, married a Baptist minister and was a housewife living in New Jersey, with three children, two boys and a girl. Elizabeth and her husband, who lived in a huge house and who changed their Mercedes Benz every year, would bring the children to visit Beatrice quiet often. Beatrice, a humble woman, couldn't stand Elizabeth's husband, with his jerry curled hair and diamond-adorned fingers. And it would embarrass her when they would show up in their matching full-length fur coats and flaunt their wealth. My only hope was that when her husband finally gets busted for misused church funds, he would have enough sense to hire me. Kenneth, on the other hand, couldn't have a mother who could be more proud of him than Beatrice was. He and I remained friends, and whenever I visited Jamaica, I would always make it a point to see him.

"Hello, Aunt Bea," I said as Beatrice and I hugged. I always call her Aunt Bea, and although I had many aunts on both sides, I was honored to call her my aunt.

In her thick Jamaican accent, she said, "Hi, bay-be Roy." That was her pet name for me, and she was the only one who ever called me that, and the only one I allowed to. Why she ever called me that I never knew; it just stuck, and I never told her not to, even though my parents knew I never cared for it.

"Did you cook one of your favorite Jamaican dishes, just for me?"

"Me make some curry chicken, some rice and peas fe tomorrow, and some corn bread. Me hope Liseth leave some fe you. Boy, that gal sure can eat." A modest woman at five feet eight and of large build, she always covered her mouth when she laughs.

"Sounds good, Aunt Bea. Where is Mom and Dad?"

"Dem in the living room," she said. "So wen you gone?"

I anticipated her full question and answered her the best way I knew how. "Aunt Bea, you'll be the first to know. That much you can trust me on."

"First, second, or last, me no care as long as you do it. You naw get any younger, and we a get olda before you."

"Maybe I should have a talk with Liseth."

"Maybe you should do more dan talk." We both burst out laughing and headed straight for the kitchen, and for the curry chicken.

Aunt Bea set a place for me at the table in the breakfast nook and then went off to get me some food. Liseth walked in. "Hi, baby," she said and ran her fingers through my hair. "Looks good," she cooed.

"What are Mom and Dad doing?"

"Your dad was telling me the funniest joke. It was so funny, you wouldn't believe."

"I know. I could hear the laughter as I came up the pathway."

"Are you OK?" She sat down at the table and flipped her hair off her face.

"Sure. Why?"

"Nothing. Just wondering."

"I'm fine."

"OK. Your mom and I were just talking about a friend she went to school with, and who is now teaching at Yale. She wants me to drop in on her when I get there. I think that's wonderful, don't you?"

"That's fantastic. What does she teach?"

"Constitution law and, I think, ethics. Are you sure you're OK?"

"Why do you keep asking me that?"

"You seem distracted, that's all."

"Liseth, I'm fine. Honest."

Aunt Bea brought the food and some of her homemade ginger beer. The only other person I knew who could cook Jamaican food, which could even come close to Aunt Bea's, was my old girlfriend's mother, Ma Saunders.

Liseth sat across from me, and as much as I was accustomed to her beauty, she was still a distraction. I knew that I was an attractive man, and that I looked younger than forty-five, and that by the time I was in college, I'd had more women of all ages, while some guys were still virgins; but I couldn't help feeling lucky that Liseth had fallen in love with me. "Did I ever tell you why I love you?" she said.

With a piece of chicken in my mouth, I said, "Tell me again."

"Because you are the most compassionate, warm, gentle, generous, self-centered, confident, arrogant, cocky son of a bitch I have ever had the good fortune to meet."

"Be careful now, my mom might be coming in."

"Oh, she knows how I feel about you."

Aunt Bea let out a slight cackle and raised her hand to her mouth. I wished she wouldn't because the few times she didn't, it revealed such a wonderful smile that justified why her three brothers were so protective of her when she was a young girl in Kingston, Jamaica.

"You and my mom talked about me?"

"Among other things."

"Like what?"

"Girl talk. What do you think we sit around talking about?"

"So it's like that, huh?"

"Hey, it's like that." She took piece of the chicken from my plate with her fingers and put it in her mouth.

Aunt Bea saw it from the kitchen and said, "You leave the mon food alone." She brought out a plate with some chicken on it, to replace the piece Liseth had taken, as if what she had given before wasn't enough. "Me no know gal whey you put all that food." This time, with the spoon and a plate in each hand, she was unable to cover her mouth; and that smile that must have kept her three brothers busy fighting off the neighborhood boys was there for all of us to see.

Liseth took piece of chicken off the plate and thanked Aunt Bea. "We love you, Aunt Bea," she said.

"You love me, where is me grand child? We waitin'."

"Talk about pressure, my God."

"Me a seventy-two, Enid sixty-three—that's pressure."

I knew that Mom would love nothing better than to be a grandmother by her sixty-fourth birthday, and I must be honest, I too would love nothing better than for Liseth to tell me she was pregnant, but I was not going to get her pregnant just to satisfy other people's desire, if she is not ready.

Curry chicken, hot and spicy, with rice and peas and corn bread on the side, washed down with homemade ginger beer. What a combination. For all those non-Jamaicans who have never drunk homemade ginger beer, you have been greatly deprived. To live is to have drunk homemade ginger beer. It's not for the faint of heart. It's nonalcoholic, but it's as potent as Kentucky moonshine, and it's a million years removed from that shit sold in stores called ginger beer.

Legend has it that it's made the same way they make regular beer, that it's left to be fermented for several days, some say over a week, before it's ready for consumption. It's usually stored in a jar or a long-necked rum bottle, and when it's first opened, it pops like a champagne cork. As I said, it's nonalcoholic, but it's potent.

I had a glass of ginger beer with my dinner and another after dinner. My parents, Liseth, and Aunt Bea were all in the living room. I joined them with my after-dinner drink. I love spending time with my parents. They were the type of people that anybody would just love to be around. They were so kind and wonderful. I often wondered if there was a person in the world luckier than I was to be blessed with such wonderful and caring parents.

My mother, Enid Dorothy Brown, the youngest of Edward Lester and Frances Imogene Brown's four daughters, married my father, Lloyd Francis Bradshaw, son of Delroy Lloyd and Elsie Bradshaw, when she was eighteen and he was twenty-one. She had just finished high school and was on her way to Columbia College when she learned she was pregnant. She was the first in her family to get pregnant before finishing law school, let alone starting college. Her parents were not pleased, but Dad, who was a Rhodes scholar, not that it impressed her family because they were from a long line of academicians anyway, was from a well-respected family who had all gone on to law school; so although they would have preferred for her to have a baby much later, they readily accepted Dad, and Mom took a year off before she started her studies. Mom often tells Liseth that story, but Liseth, coming from a different background and the first in her family to go on to a four-year college, is not about to displease her mother by not going to law school first. We all understood.

If there was ever a man I admire and want to be just like, it was my dad. There was nothing about my father that I didn't like. There was not one thing I can ever think of, or any moment in my life I can remember when he has ever disappointed me. I can't remember him not ever being there for me when I needed him. As far as I can remember, I always wanted to be like him. The way he walks. The way he talks. The kind of cars he prefer and, most of all, the way he dresses. My father is the most impeccably dressed man I have ever known. He is the epitome of sartorial taste, and he has a penchant for British clothes, cars, and mannerism. Each year in January, my father would go to London to shop for his shirts and shoes, and have several suits made on Savile Row. I remember when I was a boy, I would watch my father lay out those finely tailored suits on the bed as he meticulously chose his shirts and ties. "A well-dressed man should never buy his suits off the rack," he would say.

Except for having my suits made on Savile Row, I have emulated Dad in every respect. Although I would, on occasion, buy some materials in London, I would have my suits made in the Bronx by a just-as-excellent Jamaican tailor who charges far, far less than the Savile Row tailors.

Like me, my father's father was his role model. My grandfather, whom I was named after, had seen action in World War I, and he too had come to admire the British and their mannerisms; and he encouraged my father and his brothers and his sister to study in England. And my father didn't have to talk me into it. Right after I finished my undergrad at Columbia, I wasn't a Rhodes scholar; instead, I went off to Oxford for a year. It was during my father's study in England that he became enamored with the British mannerism, and except for the accent, he's as British as they come. To my father, the British are the most civilized, industrialized nation around. He doesn't forgive them for being part of the slave trade and populating the majority of the world, including America, with people of African heritage; but they didn't, unlike the Americans, have domestic slaves, even when they had slaves in the colonies. Some may argue that they are just as racist as their American cousins, and that may be true, but the United Kingdom, as a country, is less polarized, racially, than the United States. And what impressed my father the most is the fact that the British does not find it necessary to arm themselves against their citizen. I have been there prior to, and subsequent to, studying at Oxford; and I must say, I couldn't have felt safer in an industrialized country. After all, how many young black men have we heard of in the UK being shot twenty-two times, in his doorway, holding his wallet?

As distinguishably furnished as my parents' home was, with its fine Old English furniture, imported rugs, and chandeliers, there were no other pieces of furniture in that old six-bedroom, four-bathroom house that they had bought from the family of one of the original Robber barons that Dad loved more than his old-brass studded leather chair. The chair was old, and the leather was cracked in several places, but that was Dad's favorite chair. Believe me, the damn chair had seen better days, or as they would say in Britain, "It has passed its sell-by date." But Dad loved that old chair more than any other piece of furniture in the house. Mom and I, on many occasions, had threatened to throw it out and buy him a new one; but neither one of us was brave enough.

"Good evening, sir," I greeted my father. I did not always greet my father in such a formal manner, and at times, he and I can be like any two guys in a bar.

"Hello, son," he replied.

"How are you, sir?"

"Very good."

"It seems I was a little late in catching you holding the floor. I could hear the effect as I approached the house."

"You missed a good one."

"I'm sure it was," I said as I took a seat on the couch and was hoping he wouldn't repeat the joke. Not that I didn't like his jokes, or that I didn't find him funny; but some of his jokes can be a little bland.

A Saturday night at my parents' consists of dinner and after-dinner drinks. They were not big drinkers, but they enjoy a glass of wine or two with dinner, and a brandy afterward. Then they would relaxed in the living room—Dad, of course, in his favorite chair, and Mom on the couch. They would watch some TV, and then read a book, and then go to bed by twelve.

Dad's favorite show on Saturday nights was Kavanagh QC, a British legal drama on PBS. If he was not home, Mom or Aunt Bea would tape it for him. I must admit I'd grown to love the show too, and watched it not only when I was at my parents' but also at my house. Liseth thought the show was unrealistic, because that air of acrimony between lawyers, as was customary in their American counterpart, was absent.

After the show, we would talk about things going on in our lives. That Saturday night, of course, I left Connie out of it.

Since my last, visit I'd taken on a new client. I was suing a stock brokerage firm on behalf of Michael DeLuca, son of the late

Dominick DeLuca, who has headed, for twenty-five years, the Galante crime family, one of the five families that run New York City. Michael was not accused of being the head of the Galante family; that was bestowed upon the notorious and flamboyant Frank Carbono, who was in federal prison doing life without the possibility of parole.

Michael DeLuca operated a number of supermarkets in and around New York City and, along with his brother and sister, was a champion of the poor and downtrodden. Among some of the things they did was run several soup kitchens in the South Bronx. It's alleged that all the illegal money they made from gambling, drugs, prostitution, and extortion was what afforded them the opportunity to be as generous as they are. The question is, *why?* It's interesting to know that despite all the accusations, and all the alleged criminal connections, except for a $75,000 fine and nine months in a federal prison for tax evasion, Michael DeLuca was never arrested for a crime in his fifty-seven years. Some criminal.

Regardless, that's not my problem, or rather, my concern. All I know was that he wanted to sue someone, and a colleague recommended me. He never complained about my fee, and his check cleared the bank.

Dad, like everybody else, was entitled to his opinion: that Michael was well connected to the Galante crime family. Among some of the proof that were being bandied about was Michael's thirty-year-plus marriage to the late Alphonse "Al" Galante's only daughter, which was attended by the Who's Who of organized crime. Al Galante—along with Lucky Luciano, Meyer Lansky, and Joe Bananno—was a founding member of the committee that organized crime in New York in the 1930s.

I was not in the morality business. I am a lawyer, and in my profession, I'd taken an oath to defend the rights of my clients. And my clients are those who, for whatever reasons, think the government or another citizen has aggrieves them. They are people who are seeking a certain redress from the courts, and they come to me to protect their interest. I am also an American, and Michael DeLuca is an American. I don't have to like him, and I liked very few of my clients. Although I'd never represent a child molester, or a rapist, I love the law, and it's my job. It's what I do. And I'm good at it.

Dad had a problem with me representing alleged gangsters, and I can understand that. And the word here is alleged, and you know what? Who cared if they were? Some of Dad's best clients were major corporations, and oh yes, a few insider traders, and as much as my father, I was sure, wouldn't represent a child molester, I'd never question his right to defend one. Every person accused of a crime is entitled to not only a fair trial under our constitution but also to a lawyer of their choice.

"You know, son, I have heard of ironies, but this is the mother of all ironies." Dad took his feet off the ottoman and straightened up in his chair as he said it. He stood up and headed toward the kitchen, and Mom and I looked at each other.

"I take it he's not happy with my latest client?"

"I wouldn't worry about how your father feels," Mom said. There was a big smile on her face when she said it. "He knows as well as anyone of us that all lawyers have a right to defend whomever they please."

"What is he worried about?"

"That you might just win the case." She, Liseth, and Aunt Bea all laughed.

"I am glad for the vote of confidence, but it's not like the man is charged with a crime or anything. He's not on trial."

"We know, but it's sort of funny that a man like him would decide to sue someone for stealing his money. That's the irony your father is talking about." Dad came back from the kitchen with a tray, with a pot of tea and enough cups for all of us. "Would you like some tea?"

"I'm not sure Aunt Bea would approve of me not finishing her delicious ginger beer."

"Go on, have some tea. Me make nuff ginger beer, fe last two weeks," Aunt Bea chimed in.

"Thanks, Aunt Bea."

Dad remained standing as Mom poured his tea, put some sugar in it, and handed it to him. "Sit down, Lloyd," she said.

"What are you worried about, Dad?"

"I am not worried about anything," he said as he stirred his tea.

"OK, what are you concerned about?" I studied his face for a hint of some sort of answer, but if there were any, he wasn't betraying it.

"I am neither worried nor concerned. I am just opposed to you representing those kinds of people."

"Why?" Before he could answer I continued, "A bunch of guys—in this case, four—decided to go into the stock brokerage business. They applied to the SEC for a license and were approved. Once the Securities Commission approved them, they agreed to abide by certain rules. Just like your client years ago agreed to abide by the rules, and then violated those rules when he engaged in insider trading. These guys violated those rules when my client entrusted them with his money, and what did they do? They inflated the performance of certain stocks for their own aggrandizement, and when the stocks did not live up to expectations, they used their clients' money to bail themselves out. My clients are not the only ones who are suing them."

"You kept saying 'clients'—who else are you representing in this case?"

"His brother and sister."

"So you are representing Michael and his brother and sister too?" Dad said as he slowly sipped his tea.

"Yes."

"What I'm really worried about—"

"So you're really worried about me," I interrupted him with an air of satisfaction.

"Of course, I am worried about you. You are my only child."

"OK, so tell me, what are you really worried about? That I'll go into court and prove that my clients were really swindled out of their money?"

"Not that I don't think you're a brilliant attorney, because I think you're one of the best around, but I also don't want to deflate your ego either. But proving those brokers swindled the money will be the easiest part. Getting your clients' money back, if it's not already left the country, will be another subject."

"That's why we're getting a judge to freeze everything we can find."

"Good luck. Boy, times really have changed. Imagine how lucky a horse must have felt." Everybody burst out laughing.

"They only put horses' heads in people's beds in the movies Mr. Bradshaw," Liseth said.

"But seriously, Delroy, I am worried because I remember what happened to that lawyer who represented that mobster from the Bronx. He was sanctioned and lost his license to practice."

"That was a different situation, Dad. His client was charged with murder, and under the RICO statute. He'd also made himself a spokesman for his client and was all over the place claiming that his client was an honorable man. I am not a spokesman for my clients. All I'm trying to do is get their money back. I'm not going to their houses for dinner, nor will I be going to any clubs they own. Any contact between them and me will be in my office, and all payments will be by checks. This is totally a business relationship."

"Just don't get too involved with these people, Delroy. Please don't."

"Will you stop worrying?"

"All right, boys, can we talk about something else?" Mom cut us off. "Enough of this love fest."

"I'm glad I'm going to be a tax attorney, like Ebony," Liseth chimed in. "Litigation is too complex. Plus, I won't have to go to court, at least not as often."

"Trust me, girl, it won't be much better being a tax attorney either. You will have your share of malefactors too," said Mom.

With a wide grin on his face, Dad said, "Didn't Michael DeLuca do some time in prison for tax evasion?"

Mom rescued me by asking Liseth about Ebony. "How is Ebony these days?"

"She is fine," Liseth answered.

"If I'm not mistaken, on top of the sentence, he was fined close to a hundred grand, wasn't he?" Dad persisted.

"Lloyd!" said Mom with a look on her face that said it all, and that was enough out of him.

Mom continued the conversation with Liseth. "I haven't seen her for years. The last time I—oh God, I can't even remember."

"I'm still her protégé. She thinks that taxes is the best area of practice," said Liseth.

"They all have their good sides and bad sides," said Mom.

I loved those little sparring sessions my Dad and I would have from time to time. They were great bantering, that I wouldn't exchange for anything. At times, Dad made me feel like a younger brother. We would go shopping, out to dinner, to the movies. We'd catch a ball game, and we would both root for the Knicks, until I switched to the Lakers and he would call me a traitor, and I would tell him that the Knicks don't know how to be winners, and he would say that loyalty is sticking with your team even when they are losing, and I'd say that they would never be winners, and he'd say that I'd come running back, and I'd say, "Yeah right." But we would stay loyal to the Yankees. Go Yanks.

***

Despite the closeness and the great friendship between my father and me, I always felt awkward in discussing certain things with him. My father was so proper and disciplined, and always projected that air of loyalty to family and friends, that I would feel a sense of betrayal, to him, in telling him that I'd cheated on Liseth.

I've always felt that this was the sort of thing you discuss with your best friend over a glass of beer, and my father was indeed my best friend, but discussing infidelity with him was not something I would think appropriate. I could just hear him when I told him that I'm torn between two women: "Young man, the most important thing in a man's life is the love of a good woman, and the best way to preserve that love is to be loyal and faithful. If you lose that, you lose everything." And I'd just sit there with my head down, with nothing to say, because I have let my father down. And he'd continue by giving me a speech about divided loyalty.

Dad thought that marriage was a sacred bond, that when made should not be broken, unless the relationship is broken down and the parties are ready to go their separate ways. Dad was sort of like BobbyMac. Respect the vows of matrimony, or move on.

I remember, when Liseth moved in with me, he said to the both of us, "You kids may not be legally married, but you have just made a commitment to each other. Do not take it lightly." I took his words seriously, and had on many occasions told him how happy I was, and that I hoped one day to make it official. Dad was happy for me. I couldn't imagine me telling him that I was cheating on Liseth, nor could I imagine me baring my soul to him, telling him that I didn't want to lose Liseth but Connie just happened to be back in the picture. No, I couldn't imagine it, and I wouldn't want to talk to him about it, because I wouldn't want to see the look of disappointment on his face. I just couldn't.

I certainly would rather not have to discuss what was going on between me and Connie with my mother either, because I was determined to put an end to it before it got out of hand, but I knew that if I had decided to talk to her about it, she might not agree, nor would she approve; but she would have understood. After my disagreement with Dad on my representation of Michael DeLuca, and after we watched *Kavanagh*, and then talked about more pleasant things—like Liseth and me going to England before she started school—they all went up to bed and left me and Liseth downstairs.

We decided to watch cable, but right after the movie started, she said she was tired, and she went up to bed. How anyone can be too tired to watch a Bogart retrospective, especially *Casablanca*, is hard to accept.

Bogart was giving Ingrid Bergman his speech about why she should get on the plane and leave Casablanca with her husband when a voice softly echoed from behind me.

"A timeless classic, you'd have to agree." Mom was standing behind me, and from the look on her face, I could tell she had been there awhile. I reached for the remote, turned the sound down, and asked her if the TV was too loud. "No, I was on my way to make some hot chocolate when they shut down the joint." Mom was referring to the part in the movie when the German general ordered the Italian colonel, Louie, to shut Rick's Cafe` down.

"You have been standing there awhile?" I said as I shifted on the couch so I could see her as I talked.

"Would you like some hot chocolate?"

"I'd love some."

As Mom headed toward the kitchen, she, Humphrey Bogart, and I said, "Louie, this is the start of a beautiful friendship." I followed her into the kitchen and got my old mug from out of the cupboard. I have had that mug since I was ten or twelve. I got it when we went to Disney World. It had Mickey Mouse on one side and Daffy Duck on the other. It was, at my age, too big for me, although I would always finish my hot chocolate and say, "See, Mickey and Daffy, I have drunk all of it." I had neither grown too big nor had I outgrown that mug; and I remember that when Liseth moved in with me, she brought her cereal bowl that she had since she was a little girl. I told her about my Mickey Mouse mug, but that I'd never take it from my parents' house because keeping it there, along with my room remaining the way it was, made me feel that I had never moved out.

"Would you believe that Ronald Reagan was one of the actors they wanted to play Rick Blaine before they gave the part to Bogart?" Mom poured some milk in a pan and put it on the stove.

"We can only hope that had he gotten the part, he would have been a big star, and America would have been spared the embarrassment of having him as president." I sat on the kitchen counter like I did when I was a child.

"True, but I just couldn't see him saying 'Play it again, Sam.' But then, as we know, stranger things have happened."

We both laughed and said in unison, "I know."

Mom poured the hot milk into the mugs and stirred them as she did. As the color of the milk turned light brown, and then became creamy, I was reminded of when I was a child and used to sit up on the kitchen counter as Mom made me hot chocolate, particularly in the winters, when there was snow on the windows. We were living in neighboring Mount Vernon back then. Mom would tell me stories about when she was growing up with her three sisters in St. Albans, Queens. Mom was seven years younger than her sister Edna, and was born at a time when her parents thought they were through with having children. Being the youngest of four girls, Mom was doted on by everyone.

I held my mug with both hands and sipped my hot chocolate, and the memories came gushing back. I knew what was coming next. Mom reached for the English tea cookies and put the opened container next to me. I never could take just one of those cookies. I put two in my mouth and sipped my hot chocolate. I could feel my mother's eyes bearing down on me. And I knew a question was coming.

"You want to talk about it?" she said.

I looked at her, and she was looking at me over her mug. I said nothing.

"We are alone," she continued.

"You could always read me, couldn't you?" I took another cookie.

"You're my only child. I know you." She went back over to the fridge and got the milk. It was going to be a long night. It was times like this that I wished I had a brother. "I also know that whatever it is, it's something you can't talk to your father about. So it has to do with sex, and not just sex, in the common vernacular, but it has to do with you, sex, and another woman. I think I can safely say Liseth doesn't know anything about it yet, because if she did, she would have said it to me. And I think that whoever the woman is, she is somebody from the past, which brings me to one person. Did I leave anything out?" She poured some more milk in the pan and turned the stove back on, but this time keeping the flames low.

God, she is fuckin' good, I said to myself. No wonder she was such a great trial lawyer. Soft, subtle, unimposing questions that let the witness spill their guts. How could I lie to her, even if she was not my mother?

"No, you haven't left anything out."

I finished the last of my drink and pushed the mug over to her. She turned on the faucet and rinsed the mug out, and then she heaped two spoons of chocolate in it and looked at me, and I indicated for her to put another. She put the same amount in her mug, and poured the hot milk in them. As she stirred the milk into the mugs, I could tell there was something on her mind. I had seen that look on her face before, and I could tell she wasn't pleased when she had that look. "Is it who I think it is?" She handed me my mug. Her eyes fixed on mine, and I felt as though she was looking inside of me. I averted my eyes and blew on the content of my mug and told her the truth.

"How long has this been going on?" She was still looking deep inside of me.

I told her the whole story, and without adding the full details, I even told her about Connie's night with me at the hotel. Mom was visibly displeased, and it had me wondering if this would have hurt her more that it would my father.

"First, I'd like—"

I interrupted her and excused myself to go into the living room. I looked around and came back into the kitchen. "I'm sorry, Mom. I thought I heard somebody in the living room."

She continued. "There are a few things I'd like ask you."

"OK."

"First, are you in love with Liseth? And second, what are your feelings towards Connie?" She untied the sash on her robe and retied it a little looser; then she sat back down. Her eyes penetrated me, and although it was just me and her in the kitchen, I couldn't help but feel there was somebody else listening.

"Mom, there is one thing I'd like you to know, and that is I would never lie to you under any condition."

"If I'm not sure of anything else, it's the one thing I know for sure about you."

"I also want you to know that I'm deeply and helplessly in love with Liseth, and I wouldn't want it any other way."

"And Connie?" she said, with her right elbow on the arm of her chair and her palm supporting her cheek, like a judge weighing the evidence.

"I'm not in love with Connie, Mom. This you must believe. It might be difficult for some people to understand, but just because I'm not in love with her, doesn't mean I don't love her. You understand that, don't you?"

"If you mean do I understand the difference, yes, I do. But I know Connie well, and as much as she is a rational person, she has the proclivity to behave irrationally. After all, she did say she didn't want to leave her husband, and that you and her should carry on while Liseth is at Yale"

"I told her it's not possible."

"I am not sure I like what I'm hearing, but here is what I think you should do." Mom removed her elbow from the arm of the chair, and sat back. She closed her eyes for a moment as if to think, and then she said, "Delroy, I'm very disappointed in you. I know you love women, and that as far back as I can remember, you always have some girl or another calling here or dropping in to see you, but that was then. You know, you were the last person I ever thought would live with anyone, let alone get married. But how can you expect to marry Liseth if you want to still behave like a playboy?"

"Come on, Ma, that's not fair." I got down off of the kitchen counter and sat on one of the chairs in front of her.

"Don't talk to me about fair. I'll tell you what's fair." Her voice went up a notch. It was not loud enough, but I told her she might wake up the rest of the house. "You want to know what's fair—or rather, what's not fair? What's not fair is what it would do to Liseth if she found out. That's what's not fair. Let me tell you something else: I love that girl like a daughter, and I think you are darn lucky to have her." Mom paused, and took a sip of her hot chocolate, which by then was cold. She got up and walked over to the fridge and took out a bottle of white wine that was already opened. She took a glass from the cupboard and poured some wine in it. Then she took her seat back at the table in front of me. She put the glass of wine on the table and the bottle beside it. I looked up at the clock on the kitchen wall. It was almost three in the morning. Liseth was not a light sleeper, so I wasn't worried, and since Mom had a habit of going into the study to read when she couldn't sleep, I wasn't worried about Dad. Aunt Bea was not really a heavy sleeper, but when she locks her door at night, what goes on in the rest of the house was none of her business.

"I am going to tell you something I have never told anybody, not even my sisters. For close to thirty years, I have kept this to myself."

Oh great, I said to myself. *We're keeping family secrets.* My perfect mother had an affair, when she was younger, that was shy she was behaving like that. I sat there, and I couldn't believe what I was about to hear—that my mother had cheated on my father and he didn't know it. Boy, was I glad he didn't know, because Dad hated divided loyalty with a passion. I suppose in a sense, I wasn't surprised, because Mom is such a liberal, who was active in the movement of the sixties, while Dad is more of a checkbook liberal.

"For nearly thirty years, I've never told anyone what I'm about to tell you," Mom said as she drank some of the wine.

My father was my mother's first boyfriend. Dad met her when she was fifteen and he was eighteen, at a yearly attorneys' picnic both their families were attending. Mom had never kissed a boy before she met my father, so I could understand that maybe when she was in college or law school, she wanted to try something different, and so she cheated on Dad. *That's OK, Mom, I understand. There's nothing to be ashamed of, but it's good to know you were human too.*

"When you were about eight and we were living in Mount Vernon, your father was a young associate and used to work very late—you know how it is? The business hasn't changed over the years. Sometimes he would work until midnight." Mom paused and poured some more wine in her glass. The glass was not even half empty. She filled the glass but didn't drink any.

It could not have been easy for Mom to be telling me what she was about to tell me. The only thing I could say—to myself, that is—was, *So it was not while you were in college or law school. It was while Dad was a young associate. In any case, this happened when you were young. You were twenty-six and just out of law school and was home by yourself, and lonely, and this happened once, and you kept it from your sisters and from Dad. That's OK, Mom. We all have our moments of weakness. Go on.*

"Your father was having an affair with a girl he worked with. She was an attorney, and they were working together, and it just happened."

My father! I screamed inside. I looked up at my mother, and I could tell she knew exactly what was going on inside of me.

"Oh yes," she said. "Your father, who believes that one should not have divided loyalty. Your father, who believes that marriage is sacred, and that the family comes first. But you know what, my son, I don't want you to think differently of your father because of this. This only means that he is human, and in a way, you're both alike. But I'm glad you did this before you're married to Liseth, and that she doesn't know about it."

I was sitting there, and I couldn't explain why, but knowing that my father cheated on my mother was more of a letdown than had it been my mother. Both were decent, wonderful people who had always been there for me, but my father cheated on my mother? Why? How could he? What about trust? What about honor? What about loyalty and respect?

I walked back into the living room, because I swore I heard somebody moving in there. The first person who came to mind was Liseth. It could have been her. She could have come down the stairs and hid in one of the closets and left the door open enough to hear us in the kitchen, and then when I entered the living room to investigate, all she had to do was close the door; and unless I looked in the closet, I wouldn't know she was there. The thought crossed my mind, but I resisted it.

"Let me ask you something, Mom," I said as I reclaimed my seat at the table. "How did you find out, and what did you do after you found out?"

Mom ran her fingers through her hair, let out a yawn, and smiled. It was an uneasy smile. "You know, now I can look back on this and laugh about it. But believe me, it was not funny back then." She yawned again and rubbed her moist eyes. It was not tears, just the moistness that gathered in her eyes when she yawned. "I didn't know for sure," she continued, "but I had a feeling something was going on."

"But you weren't sure?"

"I didn't know anything. All I had was a feeling." Her yawns became frequent, and the contagion was spreading.

"So what did you do?" I put a hand over my mouth and stifled a yawn.

"Having supportive parents was very important . . ."

"But I thought you said nobody knew?"

"That's right, but my parents always told me that I was welcome home at any time, so I just packed my things and waited until he came home and told him that I was leaving him." She was running her fingers over the rim of the filled glass of wine. "You should have seen the look on his face. Up until that moment, your father and I had never had an argument or a fight or a disagreement that would threaten our marriage. In he walked that night, and I'm sitting in the living room. It was the summer, and you were playing, oblivious to what was happening. I just told him that I was moving back to my parents'."

I was struggling to keep my eyes open. I wanted to hear the whole story. "And what did he say when you told him that?"

"I think he was too shocked to say anything other than *why*."

"That's all he said?"

"The poor man was in a state of shock, not to mention having to face my father, who would have killed him for hurting his little girl. In any case, I told him my reason for leaving was so that he could be happy." Mom smiled again. This time I sensed there was some satisfaction behind that smile.

I smiled too, and then asked her, "What did Dad say when you told him your reason for leaving?"

"'I don't understand, Niddie. What did I do?'" She did an impression of Dad that was not too far off. "Then he went on to explain how he didn't understand what I was trying to say, and how happy he was being married to me. So I just came right out and asked him, if I made him so happy, why was he sleeping with another woman?"

"But you were bluffing. You didn't know anything."

"Until that moment, I knew nothing, but he told me everything, right there and then. Who she was. Her name and how long it was going on."

"What if he had denied the whole thing?"

"You know the funniest thing about the whole situation? I would have believed him, but your dad was such a poor liar."

"So did he end the affair with this woman?"

"Yes, he did. And he made me a promise, and I am sure he kept it."

"Can I ask you something?" Both of us were fighting hard to keep our eyes open. We were yawning in unison.

"What?" she said.

"What if he had called your bluff, and not only denied the whole thing but let you walk out the door?"

"I suppose I wouldn't be sitting here with you, and he wouldn't be upstairs in bed where he belongs. But I was young and headstrong, and not to mention impulsive."

Chapter 8

I was no different from most children who idolize their parents. And the fact that I was an only child made me see them as even much larger than life. There were quite a few of my parents' friends who have had some messy divorces. We even had a few on both sides in our family. But my parents, who had never taken separate vacations, were the closest I have ever seen any couple could be. Even after all those years of marriage, they still tell each other "I love you." And my dad, ever the romantic, still sent his Niddie roses without there being a special occasion. They had the kind of relationship I'd always envied, and notwithstanding my father's transgression, to the best of my knowledge, they had lived up to my expectations. I had every reason to believe that was the one time my father ever cheated on my mother, because from everything he and I talked about, it had to be.

I can remember once, when my father and I were in London. Mom was representing a young Jamaican, who was in the country illegally and was caught in a spot check in Harlem with three other Jamaicans who were here legally. They had four kilos of cocaine and three loaded guns in the car that belonged to Mom's client.

Dad's clients were crooks of a different breed. They were more the corporate types. But in any case, he had given Mom as much moral support as possible. The trial went on for three weeks, and Mom was unable to get away, so Dad and I, on the spur of the moment, decided to go to London for a weekend. Actually, from Thursday until Tuesday. I was in my twenties at the time. I had already finished law school, so I must have been about twenty-eight. Anyway, we were in London, and we were doing the town like two bachelors. We shopped. Did the theater and hung out in a few pubs.

That Saturday night, we were in a pub in Mayfair when in walked this girl in the shortest, and tightest skirt that was ever made. (Those who may not know, the miniskirt were a British creation.) The girl was a brunette, with a body that had to be made in a lab by a mad scientist, who, for some unexplained reason, wanted to wreak havoc on the male species. She must have been at least twenty, not a day older than twenty-one.

I took one look at her and said to my father, "Just for the hell of it, I'd love to wake up next to her."

And I remember him saying, "My son, do as much and as many as you can, because when you find the right one, like I did, you'll have to put all of this behind you."

I remember asking him that night how one knows when one finds the right girl, and if he had any regrets marrying Mom. His answers were clear, and unequivocal. "You know you find the right girl when after meeting her everything else becomes unimportant. As far as regrets, I have a few. There are things I wished I'd done differently, but as far as marrying your mother, I have no regrets."

Dad never told me about his regrets, and I can only assume he was talking about his affair with the young lawyer; but at the time, I took them to mean regrets in general terms.

Anybody who knew my mother as a young girl would never have believed she would grow up to be such an outspoken liberal, left-wing, storm-the-palace, burn-the-flag, antiestablishment person, considering the kind of family she came from, and that she grew up at a time when women, particularly black women, were not as vocal as their white counterparts. Mom believed in and supported every left-wing cause that ever existed. Had my mother been a child of the sixties, I could see her not only marching in Washington, like she did in that great civil rights march of 1963, but she would have been there with Stokely Carmichael, H. Rap Brown, Angela Davis, Huey Newton, and the rest of the gang. I could see her as a member of the Black Panther party. I could also see her burning her bra, using drugs, and engaging in free love. Dad, on the other hand, as much as he believed in the revolution—I couldn't see him throwing an egg at a passing car, although he'd defend your rights to throw the egg, and he might even buy as many eggs as you'd need.

In all my life, the thought of either of my parents being unfaithful never crossed my mind. But if I'd sat down with anyone, and for some reason was asked which of my parents I think were more likely to have sex outside the marriage, I would have said my mother.

***

Liseth was asleep when I went upstairs. It was after four. It had been a long time since I'd stayed up that late with my mother. Our late-night sessions had always been more pleasant.

I got undressed down to my shorts and got into bed, and just lay there for a while, with my hands under my head, looking up at the ceiling.

I wasn't sure what time I fell asleep. All I knew was that whatever time passed before I fell asleep was spent thinking about what I'd say to Connie when I saw her. It's times like this that one develops the worst thoughts. I started to think of calling her husband's job. I didn't know his number, but that wouldn't be hard to find. I thought of anonymously telling him that his wife was having an affair with an old boyfriend, and that she didn't love him but was still in love with her old boyfriend. I gave it a great deal of thought, and it seemed logical; and yet at the same time, the irrationality of it could not be denied.

One of the things my mother told me the night before was that if I didn't put an end to what was going on between me and Connie, it would only get worse. "Complacency will only feed into irrationality," she said. I thought about what she said, and it didn't take me long to realize that not only was what she said true, but that I definitely had to put an end to it.

The smell of coffee stirred me from my slumber. It was a little after ten, and Liseth was sitting up in bed with a mug of coffee. She had on a white T-shirt and a pair of my boxer shorts and was looking so beautiful with her hair pinned up and without a trace of makeup on. I just wanted to have her for breakfast.

"Good morning," she said as she sipped her coffee, and as much as I never touched the stuff, the aroma was one that I always enjoyed.

"Good morning"—I yawned—"darling."

"What time did you come up last night?"

"Oh, I don't know. About four, or close to."

"What did you and your mom stay up talking about?"

How the fuck did she know I was up with my mother? Did she come downstairs last night and hear the conversation? Without giving away anything, I asked her, "How did you know I was up with my mother last night?"

"She told me at breakfast. She said she didn't think you'd be able to make it, because you were both up late."

Relieved, I said, "Yeah, we hang out. It was like old times."

Inquisitively, she said, "So what did you guys talk about?"

"Mother-son stuff. You know."

"No. I don't know." She changed her position, from sitting with her legs straight out and her back on the headboard to a cross-legged position in the middle of the bed, facing me. "Don't forget I'm not a son."

"If you were a son, I'd break my wrist."

Comments like that usually get a laugh out of her, but she didn't laugh. Instead she said, "You and your mother stayed up till close to four in the morning and all you talked about was 'mother-son stuff.'"

"I'll tell you one thing, babe, and the rest you'll have to get from my mother. Most of the discussion was about you." I put my hand on her leg and ran it up her shorts, to the crotch of her thong, and was about to negotiate my fingers in her bushy path when she said, "You must be hungry. Would you like some breakfast?" And she got out of bed.

"As a matter of fact, I am." My erection was protruding through my boxer shorts. But both of us knew it would be unwise to encourage what was brewing at ten in the morning at my parents' house.

I finished my breakfast: juice, tea, and two of the pancakes that the rest of the family had for their breakfast. I flipped through the *Sunday New York Times*, but I couldn't get into it. Liseth was reading the sports page, but somehow I had the feeling she wasn't into it either. She seemed to be preoccupied with something. I still couldn't shake the nagging feeling that she had heard our conversation the night before. Well, I was not going to ask her, because that would tell her something she didn't know, and if she already knew, it would be for her to bring it up; and if she didn't want to bring it up, well, I suppose she had her reasons. Then again, maybe she was waiting until we got home. OK, so it's like that, huh. When we get home, the Spanish tigress would be unleashed.

When Liseth and I first started going out, she told me, that very first night we met, to be honest about my intentions, and that she didn't want anybody to fuck with her head. She told me she was aware of my reputation with women, and that she didn't want to be anybody's plaything. If I were looking for some sort of trophy, she wouldn't be the one. I assured her that was not my intention. She also gave me clear warning that the first time she had the slightest hint that I had cheated on her, she would be out of there as fast as she could.

Liseth had never forgiven her father for cheating on her mother, and for eventually leaving her for another woman. She could never understand, as much as she loved her mother, why after having her heart broken by her father, her mother could still love that man, after all these years, and with her father having another family.

I was not sure what hurt more: her father cheating on her mother or the fact that he married another woman who was carrying his child. It took a lot of reasoning, but if all her father had done was cheat on her mother, admit his intransigence, ask forgiveness, and ask to come back home, she would, she said, have forgiven him. It would have meant that his family was important to him. I once asked her if she would have forgiven her father had he fathered a child outside the marriage but decided to stay with her mother. It would have been hard to deal with, because her sister would have been a constant reminder that he disrespected her mother, "but it would have shown that he loved us enough, and that we were important enough for him to stay." In a way, she sounds a little like my mother. Mom said a man as young, rich, and handsome as my father was is going to have all sorts of women throwing themselves at him.

I took some comfort in the fact that we are not married. We have no children, and if she were listening last night, she would have heard me telling my mother that I had never cheated on her before, and that I loved her and didn't want to lose her. She would also have heard me telling my mother that I would break it off with Connie. She would also have realized that Mom was mad enough to almost slap me, for the first time in my life, for doing that to her. Then I thought if she didn't hear anything last night, then I had nothing to worry about. I went back to sleep and woke up sometime after two.

"Well, look who finally decided to get out of bed," Dad said as I entered the kitchen and headed toward the fridge. He was coming in from the yard. I took the orange juice container out of the fridge, and had he not stood there, I would have put it to my head. At my house, and at Liseth's constant rebuke, I would put the container to my head. I took a glass from the cupboard.

"Where is everybody?" I asked.

"Your mother, Liseth, and Beatrice went up to White Plains," Dad replied and then went upstairs.

I looked out of the kitchen window. From there, straight ahead, I could see the swimming pool; and a little off to my left, I could see the driveway. I drank my OJ, and picked up the phone. I punched in Victor's home number and was hoping he would be the one to answer. I kept my eyes on the driveway. Joe answered on the third ring.

"Joe, Delroy."

"Yo, wha'sup?" Victor was not from Jamaica, but he was like most West Indians. To a certain degree, they sounded alike. "Mon all right?" he continued.

"I'm fine. You?"

"Me a chill. We never get to talk 'esterday."

"I know. But I'm sure you know the whole story."

"Ya, mon. But whey you goon do?"

My eyes were fixed on the driveway. "Listen, Victor," I said between sips of OJ, "right now everybody but Liseth and Connie's husband know what's going on." I didn't tell him I suspected that Liseth might have overheard my mother and me talking last night. "I am hoping to end this shit before either of them find out."

"Me agree. So wha' you gonna do?"

"I need to talk to her, because she seemed to be not overly concerned about her marriage, but I care about Liseth, and I don't want to ruin what we have. She is going off to law school in a couple of weeks, and Connie has this weird thought in her head that she and I will be fucking while Liseth's away. I have got news for her: it's not gonna happen."

I was twisting the telephone cord as I spoke. Everything was all tangled in a mess, but I never took my eyes off the driveway.

"Wha' you wan' me to do?" he coughed. "'Cause me know, Connie."

"Why, all of a sudden, why after having twins and married to a successful doctor, is she still carrying this blazing torch for me? Why, Victor? Can you tell me?"

"The girl never stopped lovin' you, and she was not crazy in love with Kevin. With the pregnancy and marriage, she decided to give it a go, but—"

"But what? What went wrong?"

"Him fuckin' some doctor"—he coughed again—"and she—"

"What's that you said?" I wasn't sure what I heard.

"Him was havin' a affair with a doctor, and she found out—"

"Hold on a minute. Greta told me that he was a devoted and good husband. That he loved Connie and that he gave her everything she wanted."

"True, but, mon to mon, between me and you, the boy fuck everything him see, mon. Greta no know dat, and Connie won't make a big deal out of it, 'cause she never really love him." He coughed for a third time.

"Are you OK?"

"Me OK," he said as he coughed for a fourth time. The previous coughs were single coughs. This time there was an outburst.

"Are you sure you're OK?" I was getting concerned.

"Ya, mon. Me a smoke a spliff, and the weed good," he said amid another coughing outburst.

"Yeah, that will do it." I smiled. "You were saying that Kevin cheated on her a lot and that she knows? You were also saying that Connie don't want to make a big deal out of it? Why?"

"Listen, she no love him, but she figa, wha' the fuck. Why should she give up the life he can offer? So she let him do wha' him want."

If Victor could have seen my face, I was sure he'd have asked why I was looking so pleased with what he had just said. But I couldn't deny that I was finding some comfort in her misfortune.

"That don't sound like the Connie I knew."

"Really?" He sort of laughed when he said it. Then before I could say anything else, he said, "You just said dat she wan' fuck you while you girlfriend is away, and at the same time live with Kevin. Wha' dat tell you?"

For a moment, it had me thinking. My mind raced in more than one direction. Victor broke into my thoughts. "Dat should tell you dat Connie changed over the years."

The white Jaguar slowly turned into the driveway and rolled to a stop beside Dad's. Liseth got out first and walked around to the trunk. Aunt Bea got out next. Mom joined Liseth at the back of the car and helped her with some packages out of the trunk. They were both carrying Nordstrom, Saks Fifth Avenue, and Victoria's Secret shopping bags. I knew which belonged to whom. Chances were that Liseth bought herself another pair of jeans and some thongs and bras at Victoria's Secret, but Mom was not so immune from succumbing to the intimate apparels of Victoria's Secret. In Liseth she had found her equal, even if their taste in clothes were different. Knowing Aunt Bea, she had just gone along for the company. There was some light banter as they approached the house.

"Listen, Victor, Liseth and my mother just drove up, so we'll have to talk about this some other time."

"Yo, me friend. You keep you head on, OK."

"We'll talk some more."

I hung up as they entered the house. Their mood was jovial. Liseth spoke first. "Hi, babe"—she kissed me on the cheek—"what time did you wake up?"

"About two o'clock. You didn't tell me you were going shopping."

"I didn't know I was going shopping. Your mom wanted company, and I couldn't resist going into Victoria's Secret."

"That would be asking too much," I said, and was well pleased in saying it. It was one of the times I would not have minded if she had spent every penny I had to my name. She was in a good mood, and that told me that she could not have heard what was said last night.

"I treated her to some things," Mom broke in. "I hope you don't mind."

"If we are not married yet and you're spoiling her like this, I can only imagine what you'll do to her when we are."

Mom looked at me, half surprised. I'd never mentioned marriage in Liseth's presence before. I'd spoken to my parents about marrying her, and I did tell Liseth I'd like to marry her someday, but I have never mentioned marriage in the presence of either of my parents.

"If that's a proposal, I have heard worse," Mom said.

"If this is a proposal, he should be on his knees," said Liseth.

"If him a propose, it's about time," said Aunt Bea.

"If this was a proposal, I'd need a ring," I said.

"And you'd need to ask my mother. She'd want to know she was asked. You know how she is."

Aunt Bea poured herself some ginger beer. Liseth excused herself and went upstairs. Mom took her shoes off and sat down at the breakfast table. She pulled out the chair in front of her and put her feet up on it. When I was a child, I'd always massaged her feet when she did that. I lifted her feet off the chair, sat down, and put her feet in my lap. I took the pair of size 7's in my hands and gently massaged them. "You guys did a lot of walking?" I asked her.

"That's not what you really want to ask me, is it?" Mom replied.

"What's the point of me ever opening my mouth when you always know what I am going to say before I say it?"

"When a woman has a child as young as I did, and are as close to him as I am to you, they tend to know what they are thinking. And no, she didn't ask me anything about last night, which means you'll have to handle this in the most expeditious way. The next time you come over, I want to hear that you have taken care of it, because if she asks me, you know I'll have to tell her."

I nodded my head and continued massaging her feet. It had been a while since I'd given her a foot massage. Next to me sitting on the kitchen counter and drinking hot chocolate, massaging my mother's feet was the only other intimate moment when we talked about whatever was on our minds.

"Delroy," she said. Her voice was calm but stern, "Not that she had to tell me, but that girl loves you very much."

"I know. And I love her too."

"I know that."

"But?"

"There are no buts. It's just that I want you to remember that you're forty-five years of age. You're not getting any younger. Ahh, that feels good," she said, referring to the massage, and then removed her feet. "Delroy, it's time you settle down. I need grandkids. Connie now has three children. Maybe she doesn't want any more."

She would have gone on and on if I didn't stop her. "OK, Mom. I get the message."

"I'm not sending you any messages." She got up, and I remained seated. I could hear Liseth coming down the stairs.

"OK, Mom. I'll handle it."

"I'm sure you will."

Liseth entered the kitchen with the Victoria's Secret bag and a few things she'd left there. "Are you ready?" she said.

I looked at my watch. "Let me get dressed." I went upstairs while she went out to the car.

Mom and Liseth were standing next to my car, talking, when I approached the back door. Mom was doing most of the talking. Liseth nodded her head several times. There was a somber look on Liseth's face as I exited the house, and paranoia overcame me. They embraced as I got closer. "I definitely will," Liseth said as they released each other and Liseth got behind the wheel.

Mom and I embraced. "Don't forget what I told you," she said.

"I won't, Mom. I love you."

"I love you too, son." She kissed me. "See you soon."

"Bye, Mom. Say good-bye to Dad and Aunt Bea for me."

She told Liseth to drive safely and headed back up the house.

***

From my parents' house, we headed down the Hutchinson River Parkway up to the Whitestone Bridge toll booth. The sun had gone down, but the heat had lingered on. The humidity was high, and the air felt stale. There was a funky smell coming off the river that penetrated the car even with the windows up. The river between the Hutch (as all New Yorkers referred to the Hutchinson River Parkway) and the Bronx was an environmental disaster. The water was green and had a permanent oil slick and added to the waste that was constantly thrown in it. In the summer, you could smell the stench from any direction. Traffic was light heading toward the Whitestone Bridge but was bumper-to-bumper headed toward City Island.

Except for the pulsating sound of the music coming out of KISS-FM, there was nothing said between us. The silence hung in the air like the residuals of the joint she'd just smoked. I looked over at her, and she looked over at me. I loved the way her eyes looked when she smoked ganja. There was a come-hither look in them. I could also tell she was thinking, and I wondered what she was thinking about. Her behavior had been inconsistent all morning. From being loving and affectionate to slightly chill. Maybe she was expecting her period. I knew how she was when her period was due. On the first day, she can be a little irritable, especially if she was planning on having sex.

Traffic was also moving freely at the tollbooths, except for the couple that were cash lanes. As we approached the E-ZPass lane, I broke the silence. Turning down the radio a little, I said, "Before you got into the car, I heard you told Mom that you 'definitely will'—what was that all about?"

Liseth looked at me again with those eyes—only this time there were no come-hither look in them. This time it was the opposite.

"I figure you were telling her that you would definitely see whoever that professor is she wants you to see when you get to Yale."

She looked at me. A smile crossed her face, but I could tell it was not real. She turned up the volume on the radio. "Maybe," she said.

"You are acting strange all of a sudden. What's wrong with you?"

"Why would you say I'm acting strange? Why would you think something is wrong with me?"

"I can't put my finger on it, but there is something strange about the way you're behaving." I turned the radio down again.

"I don't understand why you would think that." Her voice was calm, but I sensed an edge to it.

"Why I'd think what? That—"

"I'm talking," she said. There was a definite edge to her voice.

I said nothing, but I had to wonder what was bothering her.

She continued talking. "Is there any reason, in your mind, why I should be acting strange? Because if there is, maybe you can tell me. Or maybe there is, and I just don't know it. If you know, maybe you might care to share it with me." Her conversation became a convoluted babble, and when she was finished, silence ensued. For a few seconds, maybe five, nothing was said. Then she said, "You can finish what you were saying."

Rancor may be too harsh a word, but there was nothing else to compare what I heard in her voice to. Choosing prudence over possible confrontation, I said nothing. Instead I put my seat in a reclined position and closed my eyes. She turned the radio up again.

Like all couples, Liseth and I have had our share of disagreements and arguments. Some were silly. Some were on principle. Like me refusing to go to her aunt's upcoming wedding, unless I was invited. Liseth's argument was that she and I were living together, and her aunt knew it, so if she was invited, then naturally, I was invited too. I differed with her. As a matter of principle, I told her, I would not go unless her aunt sent an invitation to the both of us.

Liseth's aunt, Olga Lynette Flores-Mercer-Smith-Rogers, soon to be Kazinsky—and we all hoped this one would last longer than her three previous marriages combined—was one of her mother's two sisters. Olga was the younger. There was an older sister and a brother, who was also older. Olga was a social climber, and an amateur snob. She was also an enigma. She had only met me once, and outside of us saying hello to each other, we had never talked; but she had never liked me. It could not have been because I was older than Liseth, and it certainly was not because I came from a wealthy family, or that I was doing well on my own, because Olga's last two husbands were both older and wealthy men who left her richer than when they met her. Very little was known of her first husband. There was only one other reason I could think of why Olga would not be supportive of Liseth's relationship with me: I was black.

Despite Olga's three childless marriages, she loved Liseth as though she was her own daughter, and would not think of getting married without Liseth being there. And Liseth would not think of going to the wedding without me. And I would not go without being invited. But I was sure she'd deny it.

Liseth thought I was overreacting.

"About what?" I asked. Liseth thought that our relationship was still young, and that given time, her aunt would come to accept us like her mother did. She also thought that deep down in her aunt's heart, she realized that there was no way Liseth was going to attend the wedding without me.

"That's all well and good," I told her, "but part of being invited is an act of recognition."

"What is my aunt going to do?" Liseth said, incredulously. "Ask you to leave if I show up with you? She wouldn't, 'cause she knows I would leave."

To insist that her aunt invite me was, in Liseth's opinion, tacky and in bad taste. Inviting me to the wedding must be a decision Olga made on her own, Liseth concluded. To show up at her aunt's wedding uninvited, I told her, was more tacky and in worse taste. "I'm not going," I told her.

Whether it was Esmeralda or Liseth who talked Olga into inviting me, or it was Olga's decision, I may never know, but the fact that the invitation came last weekend had averted a possible crisis. It would have been interesting to see how this would have played out.

Comparing the wedding standoff to my affair with Connie would be like comparing the Iranian seizure of the US Embassy with the Cuban missile crisis. Both were volatile, but only one could lead to disaster for both. My affair with Connie was my Cuban missile crisis. Like the missile crisis, if handled wrong, it could have been the end of things as we knew it. I'm not going to deny that I would miss her. This is where the religious person would invoke the name of God to make his point in how much he would miss her. Since I am not a religious man, nor do I accept the theory that there is a god, I can only say "You get my point." I'm was also not going to say life would be the same without her, or that I wouldn't get over her. Of course I would, but like life after a nuclear war, it would be a long and painful recovery.

I was convinced—as a matter of fact, I could feel it in the pit of my stomach that Liseth knew something. But if she did, she was stepping out of character. Liseth is a blunt, straightforward, decisive person. But then again, when the heart is pierced, the rational becomes the irrational. The decisive becomes indecisive. Love has a way of making cowards of us all.

I wanted to look in her face, to see her eyes, to see if she was crying. The eyes are the true barometers of our feelings. Our eyes say things about us that nothing else can. To use the cliché, the eyes are the windows to our soul.

I couldn't see her eyes, because she had put on her sunglasses; and since the sun was not out, I could only conclude she was crying.

"Are you OK, baby?" I asked, sheepishly.

She didn't answer, but when I asked her again, she retorted, "Can I concentrate on driving?"

I was right. She knew. She was downstairs last night. *OK, Delroy, when we get home, the shit will not only hit the fan, it will be all over the wall. So you better get ready to endure the stench.* Oh yeah, I was ready.

At Exit 38, traffic was slowing down on the LIE. Everybody was trying to get on the shoulder to get on the service road. "Shit," she said. "That's just what I fuckin' need."

I sat up from my reclined position as she carefully guided the car onto the shoulder. The snarled traffic didn't last too long, but there was a guy next to us in one of those new Mercedes Benzes, a 450SL something. It looked as though it had just been driven off the showroom floor. The guy—black, maybe about thirty—looked so relaxed he couldn't have cared less if the traffic never moved. He had his finger up his nostril, digging as though he was trying to find his next car payment. He just sat there digging away and tapping on the steering wheel with the fingers of his other hand. I, in the meantime, was feeling like a jerk. I felt guilty and terribly remorseful, and felt like confessing; but despite my feelings,

I heeded the words of Nameless—to not admit anything, even when faced with overwhelming evidence.

Except for the short tie-up at Exit 38, the Sunday evening traffic was light. I returned to my reclined position, and despite the annoyance of the hip-hop station she had on, which I was sure was deliberate, I tried to block her and everything else out. Whatever awaited me at home, I was prepared for it.

I didn't have to look up to tell that the Meadow Brook Parkway was empty. The weight of Liseth's foot on the accelerator was evident. I was never worried about how fast she drives, and even if I was, it was certainly not the time to raise my concern. If I were keeping records of how quick she'd made it home from the toll bridge, save for the slight delay at Exit 38, I'd say she had broken her own record.

Charles and Mildred were just passing by my house when we pulled up. They said hello to us, but Liseth barely answered. She just took her bags and went into the house, leaving me there with them.

"What's wrong with her?" said Mildred. And before I could answer, she said, "Don't tell me, she found out?"

"I'm not sure, but something is certainly bothering her," I said. "And whatever it is, it's serious. But so far, she hasn't said anything."

I told Mildred and Charles about the conversation I had with my mother the night before. Of course I left out the part of my father cheating on my mother. I told them my fears—that Liseth might have been downstairs and overheard us, and of Liseth's inconsistent behavior all day. Mildred said that had to be it. That she too would have acted the same way.

"Right now she is hurting," said Mildred, "and she is torn. I know her well enough. The fact that you admitted it to your mother, and that she heard you telling your mother that this was the first time you cheated on her dulled the pain a little, but the *who* is the big problem. Don't forget you had proposed to this woman before."

"So you think she did hear us last night?"

Mildred looked at me, as if to say, *You're a lawyer and you can't figure that one out.* "Of course she heard you. What's the worst thing you guys ever argued about?"

I scratched my head. "I don't know."

"How about the disagreement about going to that wedding of her racist aunt? She told me she would not go if you were not invited."

"She really said that?"

"Delroy, let me tell you something: that girl loves you very much, and not only that, but she has a great deal of respect for you. She really wants to go to that wedding because she loves her aunt very much, but she is not going to have her aunt disrespect you like that. She really hopes she won't have to make the choice. But if she has to, she is going to side with you and not go to that wedding."

"But she never told me that."

"Do you think I tell Charles everything?"

Charles looked at her. His face was sort of bland. I couldn't read it. "Are you keeping secrets from me?" he said.

"We can't tell you everything, but don't assume the things we don't tell you are stuff that would damage the relationship. They are just girl stuff."

"It's good to know that," Charles said.

"Delroy, you mean a lot to Liseth. And the fact that she came home with you after hearing what she heard says a lot. You're convinced she heard you and your mother talking last night, aren't you?"

"I suppose. Yeah, I am."

"So then, you gotta ask yourself this: why is she up there crying her eyes out? Because, trust me, she is not up there packing."

I looked up at the bedroom. It and the rest of the upstairs were in darkness. Not even the TV was on. Downstairs was also without light. It was close to eight in the evening, and the advantage of daylight savings time made the evening longer. But for Liseth to not have any lights on at that time of the evening was unusual. And to not have the TV on was even more unusual. Liseth is a person who can have the TV on while she reads a book.

Charles agreed with his wife. Liseth was up there in the bedroom, crying in the dark.

"Delroy," he said, "I'm one of your best friends. Mildred and I love you and Liseth very much." He paused. "I have to say I'm glad she found out, but on the other hand, I'm—and I'm sure Millie feels the same way—"

"About what?" I asked him.

"That we were put in a position. Well, let's just say that . . . what I'm trying to say is we know that you didn't swear us to secrecy, although I'm sure it was implied. But I hope she will understand it was not our place to tell her. I hope she'll understand that."

"Listen," said Mildred, "if I were in her place, I'd be a little pissed that a person who claimed to be my friend didn't tell me something like this, but on the other hand, being in my position, I don't think it was my place to tell. Can you understand that?"

"I do."

"I hope she'll understand."

"I hope so too," said Charles.

"You guys are great friends. Don't worry, I'll handle it," I assured them.

"I feel relived, because I just couldn't carry around that burden much longer. Delroy," Mildred continued, putting her arms around me and squeezing me, "don't forget that Liseth has never had to deal with this before. And one other thing: Don't go up there as a lawyer. Go up there as a man. Talk less. Listen more. Be contrite. Be sensitive. But most of all, be sincere, and be honest. We love you. Good luck."

That certainly did move me. It left me with both moist eyes and weak knees, but I felt honored to have friends like them.

I turned the doorknob and entered the house. Even when I lived alone, the house was never that dark when I came home. It felt like I was entering a strange house, like I didn't know where to turn. I put some lights on, Liseth's bag from Victoria's Secret, and the overnight bag that had the clothes she brought from my parents' house were sitting in the middle of the foyer.

I went into the kitchen and got a beer from the fridge. There were three left in the six-pack I'd put in before we left the day before. I'd say Liseth had taken more than a drink upstairs with her. With any luck, she would drink herself to sleep and I wouldn't have to deal with things tonight. I sipped my beer and lingered downstairs as long as I could. I went into the living room and sat on the couch. I sat there for a while before I turned the TV on. Nothing seemed to interest me. I jumped from channel to channel, still not finding anything. Comedy Central had a female performer on whose whole act was about men who cheated on their wives. The girl was fucking funny, but it was the last thing I wanted to hear.

There were footsteps upstairs. Then I heard the toilet flushed. Then footsteps again. This time she was coming downstairs. A figure moved from the foyer toward the kitchen. The light from the fridge illuminated the kitchen. Something was thrown into the sink as the light disappeared, and the figure moved back toward the foyer. The footsteps were heading upstairs, then across the floor. Then silence. Several minutes passed. Maybe five. Six maybe. Then footsteps again. Silence. Then footsteps. Then silence.

I went back into the kitchen. I turned the lights on and went to the fridge to get another beer, but there wasn't any left. OK, so she took the last two. So maybe I didn't need it. Maybe I'd pour myself a brandy. I went over to the cupboard to get a glass. There was cap from a bottle of beer in the sink. I started to pour the brandy, but I stopped, and wondered if I really needed it. I didn't, but I poured it anyway. I went back into the living room, sat back on the couch, sipped my brandy, and watched whatever was on TV, which didn't hold my interest.

About fifteen minutes passed. There was no movement upstairs. Good, she was asleep. I finished my brandy, and left my glass on the coffee table, and went upstairs. I entered the bedroom, and save for the open curtains and the glow of the moon, there was no light in the house. Liseth's still figure lay in bed. She was lying on her back. I couldn't see her eyes or tell if she was sleeping, but I felt her eyes watching me as I moved about the room.

The French doors were open, and the breeze off the ocean made the evening feel good for sleeping. On nights like this, I would sometimes lie out on the balcony outside my bedroom with a couple of cold beers, staring up at the sky and listening to the waves lapping up on the beach. Before I knew it, I'd fallen asleep, and when I woke up, dawn was breaking.

I went into the bathroom, closed the door, and felt for the switch and turned the lights on. I emptied my bladder and looked at my face in the mirror. And then I went back into the bedroom. The lights shone into the bedroom, but not enough to light up the whole room; nor could it light up the area where the bed was—just enough to identify who was on the bed, if one was familiar with who it was. Before I could get outside the bathroom, Liseth said, "Could you turn the lights off?" The tone of her voice, although normal, was contemptuous.

As calmly as I could, I said, "I want to change my clothes. I need the lights on."

"But I don't need them on," she said. There was force in her voice.

"What's wrong, baby?"

"There has to be something wrong because I don't want the lights on? Why is it something always has to be wrong because I don't want the fuckin' lights on?"

"OK, OK, OK, OK. Jesus Christ, I'll go in the other room."

"How fuckin' convenient."

"What are you talkin' about?"

"Delroy, could you do me a favor and just leave me the fuck alone? Could you just do that? Please." Her voice was breaking with emotion. She was angry, and I could tell she was on the verge of crying.

I was tempted to ask her why she was behaving the way she did. But who was I kidding? I knew why she was behaving that way. The last thing I wanted was to patronize her. Neither of us was stupid. She knew that I knew why she was behaving that way. And I knew that she knew. The best thing for the both of us, if we were holding out any hope of salvaging what was left of the relationship, was to face the truth.

"Liseth, can I ask you something?"

She didn't answer, and whatever her answer would be, I was going to ask the question anyway.

"Were you downstairs last night when my mother and I were talking?"

"Finally. So now we know what the fuckin' problem is. Now we can stop asking me every fuckin' second what's the fuckin' problem, and I can stop goin' around lookin' like I'm fuckin' crazy."

Sometimes in life we want to get at the truth, but when we get at the truth, we are not always happy with the results. I wished I could see her face. I wished we didn't have to talk in the dark; but the look on her face when I admitted my affair with Connie was a look I was sure was better left in the dark.

"Liseth, I . . . I . . . I'm sorry. I didn't mean to hurt you in any way. I—"

"You're fuckin' sorry! You go out and fuck some bitch. You lied to me—not once, but twice in one week—and all you can say is 'I'm sorry.' And then you come home and fuck me as if nothing happened. And then you say 'I'm sorry.' Here I'm thinking you were under work pressure. That you're working too hard. And all along you were fuckin' lying to me, and all you can fuckin' say is 'I'm sorry.'"

"Liseth, let me—"

"No. Don't you say a fuckin' thing. I don't want to hear anything you have to say, OK. Nothing you have to say right now is important, or would interest me. Nothing."

I was sitting in one of the chairs at the opposite end of the bedroom. The bedroom was huge. Twenty-two by twenty-six. I'd knocked out the wall of a smaller bedroom and made it into one huge bedroom. I'd knocked out another wall and expanded the bathroom, and the closet, with a sliding door between them, and a dressing area. I'd replaced the regular windows facing the ocean with huge ones, so I'd have a better view of the ocean. From where

I sat, I could see Liseth now sitting up in bed, and as much as I would have loved to have some lights on, the dark gave me some kind of cover. Some protection. I felt safe. Just in case she decided to throw one of those beer bottles.

"What the fuck is wrong with you, men? Can't you keep your fuckin' dicks where they belong? First, it was my father. Then it was your father. And now you. Is it a weakness with men that they have to prove something? What the fuck are you trying to prove anyhow?" She lit a cigarette, and for a split second, I saw her face. Her face was wet. Drenched. I couldn't tell if it was from crying or from sweat, or both. She pulled on the cigarette, and the fire on the end was all I could see.

"You know the irony of the whole situation? Most men cheat with a younger woman. But you, you have to do everything different, don't you? At forty-five, and with a twenty-two-year-old girlfriend, you have to cheat with a thirty-something-old woman with three fuckin' kids." She pulled on the cigarette again. And the lit end burned brighter. "What's the matter, Delroy, don't I satisfy you anymore? You're not getting your dick suck good enough? Don't you enjoy fucking me anymore? If she were younger than me, I'd think I was getting too old for you, and maybe I could understand that, but I don't know. I really don't know." Another pull on her cigarette, and then: "I really don't fuckin' know. I wish I did. I really wish I did. You know, if I'd wanted this kind of aggravation, I'd have gotten involved with a guy my age, not some man twice my age, who I expected better from. But I guess you're all the same."

I just sat there, and I really didn't know what to say. I just listened and let her get it all off her chest, and hoped she didn't throw anything. Maybe I deserved something being thrown at me. Maybe being in the dark was saving me from being hit with one of the bottles. Maybe she wanted the lights off, because she couldn't resist throwing something at me if she was looking at me. Had she thrown something, I might not have moved. I'd say Thank you.

She took the last drag on her cigarette and crushed the butt in the ashtray. She was not one to smoke in the bedroom. She usually goes out on the balcony or in the kitchen. But that night, I suppose she didn't really care how I felt. She lit another one right after she put out the last one. Again the flame from the lighter revealed her face. It was not as wet this time, but she looked haggard, and she was definitely crying.

That was the first time I had done anything to make Liseth cry. The only other times I'd see her cry was when she talked about her brother and his drug addiction. She pulled on the cigarette, and the lit end glowed in the dark. That too was unusual, for her to smoke two cigarettes back to back.

She moved across the bed, and I followed her hand with the cigarette as she brought it to rest on the ashtray. She stood up and came toward me. There was something in her right hand. I shifted in my chair, and she sensed it. "Don't worry," she said, "I'm not gonna throw it at you, even though I should."

My eyes followed her into the bathroom, and watched her as she closed the door behind her. The toilet flushed; then the shower ran. I got up and turned the lights on, undressed, and put on my robe. Four empty Red Stripe beer bottles were on the night table next to the ashtray with the burning cigarette, and a blunt. The bathroom door swung open, and she walked out with a towel wrapped around her head, and nothing on.

"I don't want to see your fuckin' face," she said as she turned the lights off, picked up her cigarette, and went back into the bathroom. I wanted to use the bathroom, but I had a feeling she had locked the door, so I went downstairs to use the other one. I poured myself another brandy while I was at it. I might as well; the night was going to be long.

She spent some time in the shower, and when she came out, I decided I'd have my say. "Listen, Liseth, I have to say something. You have to know what happened. You have the wrong impression."

She went on the attack again. "What the fuck you gonna tell me, that her marriage is falling apart and she ran to you for comfort, and you had to fuck her and get your dick suck, just to prove you could still do her?"

Why the fuck am I even trying? Fuck you. I am not married to you. I don't owe you any fucking explanation. I can fuck whomever I damn well please. If you don't like it, you can leave.

I could have told her all those things, but that was only if I didn't care. That was only if I was looking for a way to end the relationship. Which I didn't want. So I let her go on.

"Is this a revenge thing because she turned down your proposal and married him? Is this an ego thing, Delroy? OK, so you got your revenge. So you satisfied your ego. Now what?"

I shot back, "It's not like that." Even though in a way it was.

"Well, if it was not like that, then we have a b-i-g problem. If this was not about revenge, or an ego thing, then where does it put you and me?"

She was standing in the middle of the room, and the bathroom lights were on. The rays from the bathroom lights and the moon brightened up the room—not enough to read, but enough to see each other clearly. The towel was still around her head, and one around her body. She dropped the body towel and stepped away from it.

"Be careful how you answer it, Delroy"—she unscrewed the cap of the lotion bottle and squeezed some into her hand—"because it can't be struck from the record."

I laughed. A slight laugh.

"You think this whole thing is fuckin' funny?" The expression on her face didn't encourage anything to laugh about. She applied some lotion to her body.

Why is it when a man is having a fight with his woman he always wants to have sex with her more than at any other time? Much as I knew she would not have accepted, I offered my help with the lotion. The look on her face said it all.

"No, I don't think it's funny." I was getting irritated. "It's just that in this whole argument, you chose a courtroom metaphor to make your point."

"And you think it was funny? Yeah, this is a joke to you, right?"

She unwrapped her hair and toweled the ends. Her body movement accelerated my heart rate, and I wanted to throw her onto the bed and make love to her.

"Liseth, you have to listen to me for a moment. Even if you disagree with me, you have to let me talk." She started to say something, but I cut her off. "Goddamn it, Liseth, will you listen for a moment." Typical woman; they never shut up. And it's even worse when they know they are right. Yap, yap, yap. I wanted to stuff something in her mouth. She demurred. "I am not trying to justify or defend my actions. There is nothing to defend or justify. I'm sorry you found out the way you found out, and no, I was not going to tell you. I was going to handle it my way. I was not going to sleep with her again, but I was going to see her again and put an end to it."

I told her about my conversation with Greta and Victor. She went back into the bathroom. Out of impulse, I walked in behind her.

"I'm not deaf, Delroy. I can hear you from out there."

She returned, wearing one of my boxer shorts and a tank top. At thirty pounds sterling, from Harvie & Hudson on Jermyn Street in London, it was good to know I was not the only one enjoying custom-made monogrammed boxer shorts.

"In a way, I'm glad you heard me last night, because that way, you can choose to believe what you heard. I was not saying just what I wanted you to hear, as anything I might tell you can be misinterpreted. What you heard, Liseth, was the truth. I don't know if you can understand, despite what happened, that I love you with all my heart, and that I don't want to lose you. I hope you realize it's not a contradiction. You studied philosophy. You understand human nature."

She was sitting on the edge of the bed. "Fuck philosophy." She leapt to her feet. "This is not the time for reasoning. This is about my heart. About my feelings. This is about my head." She went downstairs and came back with a bottle of wine and a glass.

"That's not going to help the situation," I said, raising my brandy to my head.

"No, but yours will?" Sarcasm abounded.

The phone rang. I was closer. I answered it. "I can't talk right now," I said and hung up. "That was Mildred," I told her.

"So now you feel you have to tell me who's calling." She poured some wine in the glass. "Tell me, Delroy, did you tell them that you fucked your old girlfriend?"

I ignored both questions.

"I told you, Delroy, not to fuck with my head. I begged you not to. I begged you." She started to cry. In the middle of drinking the wine, she was crying. "I begged you not to. Delroy, why are you doing this to me?" The tears were flowing down her cheeks as she put the bottle to her head. I moved closer to her and put my arms around her. At first she resisted, but I held her, and she stopped resisting. I took the bottle from her and put it on the center table. "Why are you doing this to me, Delroy? Why? Don't you know I love you?"

With tears in my eyes, I held her flaccid body closer. "Yes, I do," I replied softly. "I love you with all my heart."

"Then why? Why, Delroy?"

What could I have said? What could I say to ease the pain? Saying I was sorry was so inadequate and, I was afraid, without meaning. But, how could I repair the damage? Now I truly understood what Bobbymac meant. I'd already told Liseth two lies, and had she not overheard me and my mother, it's fair to say I would have told her a third. And where would it have ended?

We both sat on the edge of the bed. I held her like she was a big baby. I thought the crying would never stop. Then she pulled herself away from me and sat next to me. She wasn't crying anymore, but her face was all wet, and so was her upper body. "I have never been hurt so much in my life." Like a child, she wiped her nose with the back of her hand. "The worst part is that for some reason, I wasn't expecting this from you of all people. And what is making this even tougher is that I'm still in love with you."

She wiped her face with the towel she had around her head. Blew her nose in it and took a deep breath. "There are two things I want you do: Don't make me any promises, because a promise is a comfort to a fool, and I'm not a fool. After this, Delroy, what you do is more important than what you say. The next thing you will have to do is go see this woman, and whatever you do, put an end to it. I am not making you any promises either, but if you have any hope of us continuing, you'll have to end it between you and her, and then we'll see about us."

"But, Liseth, believe me, with Connie, there is nothing to end. There is only us. You and me."

"The next time you see her, tell her that. Don't tell me." She wiped her face again and reached for the bottle on the center table and drank from it. "In two weeks, I'll be going off to school, and I don't want to start school with this on my mind. I want to put this behind me. As a matter of fact, after tonight, I don't want to talk about it." She drank some more of the wine from the bottle. As an act of contrition, I remained silent.

"I'm serious, Delroy. Before I leave for school, I want you to put a complete end to what's going on between you and her. As I said, what you do is more important than what you say. So I will assume that if you drive up to New Haven with me, you will have made me a promise. But that will not mean that everything will be all right between us. It will only mean it's a start. Right now, Delroy, I'm going to get drunk, and you should get some sleep."

"What will getting drunk do, Liseth?" I asked, without an alternative.

"Other than getting drunk? I don't know. But it's how I feel. And it's what I'm going to do. I'm going to finish the rest of this wine, smoke a joint, and if I feel like it, I'll open another bottle of wine. I don't have a job to go to tomorrow. You do, so you should get some sleep." She got up, took the rest of the wine and her pocketbook, and went downstairs. I fell asleep after midnight and woke up at six thirty the next morning, with Liseth next to me, smelling of wine and ganja, and with nothing on. I had my boxers on.

Chapter 9

—⚬❤⚬—

$\mathcal{C}$onnie and I planned on meeting in this little Italian cafe on McDougall Street, in the Village. I was meeting her with certain ambiguities. On the one hand, I had to talk to her and make it clear that she should go on with her life, with or without her husband, but certainly without me. On the other hand, I was meeting her because I couldn't just walk away and leave things unsettled. It would be like running away. I'd feel like I was hiding. I had to face her. I had to look her in the eyes and tell her it was over. Hard as she might take it, I had to tell her it was the best thing for everybody. It certainly would be the best thing for me. In time, I was sure, she'd understand. And in time, I was sure, she'd get over it.

The cafe was an old familiar place that Connie and I used to frequent. It was a small restaurant with no more than eight tables that seats four, covered with crisp white linen tablecloth, with vases that had fresh roses daily. There were no more than two waiters at any given time, who were not only waiting on tables but waiting for their big acting break. The restaurant sold liquor but had no bar where you could sit at the counter. It had only an area with a small counter that had behind it glass shelves supported by steel brackets to the wall. On it were liquors of all description. On one side of the

161

little bar was a jukebox, and on the other side a double curtain that led to the kitchen, which you had to pass to get to the bathroom.

You'd part the curtains and then immediately make a turn to your left and go up four flights of stairs, then make another right, and the bathroom, which was unisex, was straight in front of you.

The place was owned by the same husband and wife for the past fifteen years, and was known for its seafood specials and great pasta dishes. For Connie and me, it was our own private little hideaway. We had never gone there with anybody else. We had been there so often the owners, Giuseppe and Marlo, had become good friends of ours and had taken my check, even though they didn't take credit cards. The restaurant is Mannetti's Cafe.

After Connie, I had never been back to Mannetti's, and as I thought about it, I wondered, without an answer, why I never took Liseth there, even though I'd always thought of Mannetti's as a date restaurant. It was such an intimate place that no one would ever think of going there by themselves.

After our breakup, Connie hadn't been back to Mannetti's either. She said she couldn't go there with anyone else. "It's our special cafe," she said. "And the memories are too personal."

So when I told her where to meet me, it was no surprise when she expressed her delight. But she wanted to know why that restaurant of all places. I told her it held a special place for me. But the real reason was to meet somewhere that didn't have rooms upstairs.

We were to meet at six thirty. It was a Wednesday. A week and a half after Liseth found out about us. Connie was late getting to Mannetti's. It gave me a chance to think, and I was willing to wait however long it would take for her to get there, because it would probably be the last time I would ever see her.

Before I took my seat at the window table, I went into the kitchen to surprise Giuseppe. Marlo was behind the bar. She was surprised to see me, and we embraced each other. I asked her not to alert her husband of my presence. Giuseppe, as usual, was cooking one of his specials for a customer. I snuck up behind and tapped him on the shoulder. The look on his face was that of a father seeing his son for the first time after a long separation, and since he and Marlo had only girls, one of whom works in the restaurant and the other an actress, he had oftentimes made me feel like a son.

"Holy Mother of Mary," said Giuseppe in his fragmented English. His heavy Italian accent was ever present. "Howaoyudo?" And being true to his Italian roots, he hugged me and kissed me on both cheeks.

"I am fine, Giuseppe." The old man, at close to seventy, still had some strength in his grip. "I am just busy."

"For two years? Getoutahere." There was disbelief in his voice. "Is Connie here?"

"She'll be here soon."

"Good. I'lla make you something special." The aroma of pasta sauce and the fresh herbs and vegetable made you aware of being in not just any kitchen but Mannetti's kitchen.

"Marlo," he shouted, leaning his head toward the front, "Delroy is here." He never could pronounce my name correctly, but I'd always liked the way he said it.

"Go, have some vino. Let me know when Connie come. Imakeayou something special. Justletameknow when she come." And he went back to doing what he was doing.

Since the last time I'd seen him, he hadn't changed. Except for his hair getting a little whiter, his short, squat frame was still plump, and his smile welcomed. Marlo, who was two years younger than her husband, was taller by at least four inches. At five feet nine inches, she always looked up to Giuseppe. And they were the kind of couple who always finished each other's sentences, and after thirty years, they were still doing it. Giuseppe insisted I have some vino, but I ordered a beer instead and took my seat at the window table.

One of the two waiters was a tall young white guy in his early twenties. The other was a girl, who couldn't be much older than Liseth. He poured the beer into a tall chilled glass and started to tell me what the day's special was. I told him I was waiting for someone, and that Giuseppe would be making me something special. He told me to let him know when my guest arrived. He was a polite young man and spoke with a Southern accent. Chances were he wasn't working there the week before, and come the following Wednesday, he might be on his way to Hollywood, and I would someday have to wait in a long line to pay eight-fifty to see him blaze across the screen.

The clock on the wall behind the cash register said seven twenty-five. My watch concurred, and I was on my second beer. It was cold. I'd much rather have a Red Stripe beer, but Heineken was not a bad substitute.

From my window seat, I could see up to Washington Square Park. Mannetti's was below the park, behind New York University. Greenwich Village was always a busy place. People were always on the street twenty-four hours. There were the people who lived in the Village, going to and from work. There were the hustlers, the wannabe hustlers, the tourists, and the just-plain curious. But whatever they were, they were in Greenwich Village.

The restaurant was getting busier, and I was finishing my second beer. An hour had passed, and my waiter had hoped I would have ordered something to eat. If he was worried about Connie not joining me, and that I wouldn't be ordering dinner, and him not getting a decent tip, he shouldn't. If Connie didn't show up in the next twenty minutes, I was prepared to make an excuse to Giuseppe and Marlo and give the waiter a twenty-dollar tip. And if she showed up, which I was sure she would, we would stay awhile, and I'd tip him handsomely.

It was precisely ten minutes to eight when Connie came into view, emerging from the park talking on her cell phone. Some guy approached her, and the reputation of the area had me assuming he was trying to sell her something illegal. She was wearing a white cotton dress and had sunglasses on. Whoever Connie was talking to was not a long-lost friend with welcome reacquaintance, or a person who was endearing to her heart. Whoever it was, was on the receiving end of her ire. And how fortunate; they could have been standing in front of her.

She had to pass by the window to enter the restaurant, and she waved to me and mouthed the word *hi* as she passed. I said nothing and watched her as she paused in front of the restaurant and continued arguing with the person on the other end. The conversation went on for maybe over a minute before she entered the restaurant.

As she took the seat across from me, I could see her black bikini through her cotton dress. The arguing with Kevin continued. I had no proof it was him, but any doubt I may have had was erased when she said, "So what if I'm meeting him?"

Being struck by lightning would have been a more welcome feeling than what I felt. My first reaction was to ask her what the fuck she was doing But my legal training prevailed. And although I was sure she was talking about me, there was no evidence she was talking to her husband. That is, until she folded her phone and said, "I swear to God sometimes, I could kill that nigga."

She apologized for using the word but explained how angry he had made her lately, and that she just couldn't take it anymore. Before I could say anything, she asked how I was doing. And before I could answer, she asked if I had been waiting long, and a series of questions came at me before I could say anything.

Giuseppe came over and greeted her. She returned the greetings and asked us if we would like some salmon for dinner. It was delivered today, he said. She wanted lobster, but he insisted we should try the salmon. I acquiesced, but she insisted on the lobster. Giuseppe went back into the kitchen, and she turned down my offer for a drink. She had iced tea instead, which was encouraging. At least she would listen to me with a clear head. And all throughout, she kept her sunglasses on.

"Listen, Connie," I said, "I'll just get to the point, because there is no other way."

"And what might that be?" she said as the waiter set her iced tea down. She asked for some extra lemon.

"Come on, don't act as if you don't know why we are here."

"Why are we here, Delroy?" The waiter brought a saucer with three slices of lemon, plus the one that was on the rim of the glass. "What happened, he couldn't find a whole lemon?"

165

I ignored the sarcasm and went straight to the point. "Why did you lie to me about your relationship with your husband? Why did you tell me all the things you told me knowing they weren't true?"

"What did I lie to you about?"

"Everything. That Kevin raped you and that he hit you. I think you lied to me about both. Your husband is apparently sleeping with other women, so why would he rape you? It doesn't make sense."

"That's a good argument for a jury, but we're not before a jury, and rape is not about sex as you very well know."

"I know. I know."

"Listen, I can't prove to you or anyone that he raped me, unless I have someone examine my pussy right after he raped me—and even then, who's to say we didn't have consensual sex? After all, we're still married. But—" She pulled off her sunglasses and revealed a swollen left eye. The eye was partly closed, with black and pink rings around it; and tears slowly fell from the right one. And any doubts I had were removed with the sunglasses, and I felt like shit as she said, "I am certainly not making this up. Or unless you think this was self-inflicted."

It had been over six hours since I'd eaten. I had a grilled chicken salad for lunch, but I could taste it in my mouth. I wanted to throw up, but I didn't. I was just revolted and felt sick by what I saw. I couldn't find the words to express the anger that was brewing inside me. All I could think of was, what sort of man would do this to a woman? How could a man who had sworn to preserve life do this to a woman, to the mother of his children.

The tears trickled from her right eye only. I supposed the left eye was too damaged to shed a tear. I had a feeling she was not crying because she was hurt or in pain. I had a feeling she was crying to free herself from something, but I didn't know what. She calmly replaced the sunglasses, and said, "This is not the first time he hit me. I told you that before. Now you believe me?"

"I . . . uh, I . . . I don't know what to say."

"Of course you don't know what to say. You thought I was lying to you. You thought I was making it up just to fuck you.

What kind of person you think I am?" Behind her anger, there was disappointment in me. She pulled down the right shoulder of her dress and revealed a bruise on her shoulder running down her back. "Don't say how sorry you are."

"But I am."

"I know you are, but just the same, don't say it. I don't want your sympathy." There was something cold about the way she said it.

"What can I do to help, Connie?" I looked around for the waiter. He was at another table. I waved him over.

"Your dinners should be ready by now. Let me check with the kitchen," he said.

"That's all right. Bring me another beer. Please."

"OK, but I'll check with the kitchen anyway."

"Thank you."

He went to get my beer.

"What can I do, Connie?"

"Just always be there for me." Tears rolled down from under her sunglasses and down her cheeks, and she just let it roll down uninterrupted. The tears fell in the glass of iced tea as she held it to her mouth.

"Connie, you must get outta there. I know a very good divorce lawyer, and from what Victor told me, there is no judge who wouldn't give you temporary custody of the twins and remove him from the house. I just don't understand why you didn't tell anybody about his abuses."

She finally wiped her face. I was glad she did. She had started to look pitiful. The waiter brought my beer and our dinner, and I suddenly lost my appetite. And I almost forgot what I wanted to talk to her about.

"What is it you wanted to talk to me about?" she said. She asked the waiter to bring her some more iced tea.

I had planned on being as blunt as I could be. I was not going to spare her feelings, but I didn't expect her to show up with the shit beaten out of her. It didn't matter that her husband may have been irritated by having me thrown in his face. It didn't matter that her actions may have been stupid, to say the least. I couldn't go through with what I'd planned. Despite how I felt, I must admit it would take an unusual man to not literally want to kill his wife for telling him she was fucking her ex-boyfriend, even if he was also fucking other women. I can't think of any man, despite his own infidelities, who wouldn't be tempted to. I really felt sorry for her, but how could she disrespect her husband like that?

It's a rare occasion when I lose my appetite for salmon, to the point of not even wanting to taste it, but after what she'd just told me, there was no way I could have enjoyed that meal.

"What were you thinking of, Connie? Why would you want to tell him about us?" I pushed my plate away and poured the rest of the beer in the glass. She had nibbled on her lobster a little, but showed no more interest in it than I did in mine.

"I am sorry," she said, and the sudden transparency of the extremely dark sunglasses revealed eyes, however damaged one of them might be, that indicated she was sincere. "I didn't mean to tell him—at least not like that—but we were arguing, and he got me real angry, and I couldn't hold it back."

"What do you mean not 'like that'? Connie, I don't know what's your reason for telling your husband about what happened between us. It was just one night. A night that shouldn't have happened, but it happened, and we can't take it back. But we can do something about it. Which is the reason why I'm here."

"Which is?"

"Liseth found out about us—and no, I didn't tell her."

"So how did she find out?"

"She overheard me and my mother talking, but that's irrelevant. Connie, you're a good person, with a lot of love to give. I wish it could have been different, but our time has passed. You're still in love with me, and you obviously don't love your husband. Him I can't speak for, but—and I don't mean to be indelicate—I am not in love with you, Connie. I am in love with Liseth, and someday I'd like to marry her. I hope it's not too late for us. Connie, you're still young. Divorce him and move on with your life."

At first, it looked as though she was playing with the food on her plate, but she was digging the fork into it with too much force to be playful. It was as though she was trying to make it suffer. Maybe she was thinking of Kevin.

"Maybe I should have something stronger," she said.

"I don't think you need that right now. Plus, we won't be here too long." I look up at the clock on the wall. It was twenty minutes to ten. Almost two hours. I didn't think we were there that long. "I'm meeting Liseth at Ebony's," I said.

Giuseppe came over and asked us if everything was all right. "You no touch-a the food. What-a the matter?" he said, not too pleased.

"We are all right, Giuseppe," I said. "We're OK."

He looked at us, unconvinced, but didn't press the issue and headed back to the kitchen. Connie called the waiter over and asked him to remove her plate. Then she ordered a rum and coke, with a slice of lemon. He asked if something was wrong. I told him we were all right, and that he could take my plate too.

"When did you start drinking rum and coke?"

"This has been my companion many a night. I found it helpful when I wanted to sleep. At home, I usually put more rum than coke, but don't worry, I'll only have one, and I'm quite sure their rum is not as strong as the ones Victor gets from the island, so I'll be OK."

"Connie, why are you putting up with all these physical abuses? It's obvious you didn't lie to me about the abuses and the rest, but why did you tell me you told Greta?"

The waiter brought her drink and asked me if I would like another beer. I said no, but as he was leaving, I looked at my glass and asked him to bring another.

Connie squeezed the lemon into her drink and stirred it with the little stick that was in the glass, and took a sip of it. "Just as I thought. Certainly not 120 proof, but it will do."

As I looked at her, I thought of how much she had changed, and how different our lives had become in so short a time. She had twin sons, got married, gave up her career, and was extremely miserable. She was having the shit beaten out of her, and periodically raped by the one person she should trust the most. And if all that wasn't enough, she was becoming a lush.

While I was still single but was living with a woman who was half my age and on her way to Yale Law School, and who made me extremely happy. This was a woman who wanted to have my children, and who would round out my life by marrying me—that is, if I didn't fuck it up.

Yes, indeed, our lives had taken different turns—one of those turns that were irreversible. At least I didn't want to reverse mine. It's interesting how life's events can take on these weird and sometimes-interesting twists. For a long time after Connie and I broke up, I had held out hope that we'd get back together. I waited for her even though I was dating other women. I waited for her because I never stopped loving her. I loved my bachelor life and everything that came with it—the freedom to come and go as I pleased—but I would have given it up for Connie. I knew I'd taken a vow to remain a bachelor, but that was because I didn't have her in my life.

The events in our lives don't usually happen the way we want them. Or when we want them. A year earlier, it would have made a big difference. A year earlier, and even with three kids, I would have given the idea of Connie and me getting back together more than 90 percent chance. But it was too late. I cared for her and loved her, but I was not in love with her anymore. I was in love with someone else, who has never given me any reason to disrespect her; yet I did, and I felt terrible, and I had to work hard to regain her trust and respect.

I watched her as she finished her rum and coke. She scooped up one of the ice cubes with her fingers and put it in her mouth. She sucked on it for a while; then I could hear it crunched between her teeth. "I should have another one," she said, referring to the drink, "but I won't."

Do you know how much fuckin' difference a year makes? Do you realize that a year ago I'd have pushed you as hard as I could to get a divorce? Yes, I would.

"What are you thinking about?" She interrupted my thoughts and didn't answer my earlier question. She scooped the other ice cube out of the glass.

"Nothing, really." Of course, I am not going to tell you what I am really thinking about.

"Are you thinking about what it would have been like if Liseth wasn't in your life?"

You'd never know. And you never will. "I think we should be going, Connie. It's getting late, and I told you I'm meeting Liseth at Ebony's house."

"You know how long I haven't seen Ebony?"

I am quite sure you're going to tell me, but I have to go. "Listen, Connie, I want you to think seriously about getting in touch with this lawyer." I wrote his name and extension on one of my business cards. "He's one of the top lawyers in our divorce department. Call him."

She put the card in her bag. "Fuck it," she said. "I'll have another drink." She ordered another, and I asked for the check. The drink and the check came together.

I apologized to the waiter for us not eating the food. He said it was OK. He understood. I gave him the check and two one hundred-dollar bills and told him to keep the change. With a tip of more than $50, his expression of gratitude was intense.

I went back to the kitchen to say good-bye to Giuseppe and told him about our lack of appetites. He asked me not to stay away so long again. I told him I wouldn't. He said he'd very much like to meet Liseth. Marlo said she had a feeling that I'd finally found a wife. I told her she was right. We all wished each other well, and the waiter said he was going on an audition the next day, and that he felt good about getting the part. We all wished him good luck.

"I think Giuseppe is watering down his rum," said Connie when I came back from the kitchen to find her standing by the door, talking on her cell phone. I didn't hear any of the conversation and had no idea who she was talking to, but she ended the conversation in a better mood than the one she came in with.

I walked her to the garage over on 13th Street. At first I resisted, but she insisted, and I accepted a ride from her to Ebony's house. I had her drop me off on Saint Nicholas Avenue and 148th Street. I didn't have to lie this time to Liseth.

Liseth had wanted to say good-bye to Ebony and Dalton before she went off to school. After all, she was Ebony's protégé. She credited Ebony a great deal in her decision to go to law school, although she had toyed with the idea. Teaching was her first love. She'd wanted to teach political science. Being in court, possible every day, was not something she'd wanted to do, but when Ebony told her that tax attorneys sometimes never go to court, and that they make an enormous amount of money, she was sold. After meeting me, her path was irreversible.

I rang the doorbell and was let in by Dalton. "Hi," was all we had time to say to each other. He had just come off a twelve-hour shift at the hospital; the last four were in surgery, saving a little boy who shot himself with his father's gun. Ebony and Liseth were in the living room. Ebony was on the love seat, and Liseth was curled up on the sofa. They were watching TV.

"Hi, Ebony," I said.

She returned the greeting, and they both laughed at something on the TV; and I walked over to the sofa, and Liseth pulled up her feet to make room for me.

"What are you guys watching?"

Their next laugh brought my attention to a *Sanford and Son* rerun. A "Good night" echoed from the kitchen, and Ebony returned it with a "Good night, sweetheart," and Liseth with a "Good night, Dalton," and I bid him the same.

"How are you, baby?" I said to Liseth.

"I'm OK," she said without elaboration, but more laughter followed. "That guy Redd Foxx was funny as a motherfucka," she added. She got up and stretched as the show ended and said she'd be right back, and headed upstairs.

"So I heard you met Connie tonight?" was the first thing out of Ebony's mouth when we were alone.

I looked in the direction of the stairs. "She dropped me off on the corner," I said.

"Why'd you think she went to use the upstairs bathroom? So you and I could talk." Ebony straightened herself up in the love seat. "She told me everything."

It didn't surprise me. Ebony was the closest friend Liseth had outside her family, and with Ebony and me the same age, she had taken on a surrogate mother role.

"Remember when you first met her, right there in the kitchen?" I didn't answer. "What did I tell you? We won't go over it word for word, but I told you she was not a pushover, and she isn't, but right now, she is hurting, big-time."

I thought the best thing for me would be to listen to her. If there was anybody I could learn anything from that would help me, it would be Ebony.

"You know, one of the reasons why she fell in love with you was you are older, and wiser, and she felt that you just might be ready to settle down. Isn't that ironic? She felt that guys her age didn't know what they wanted and were more inclined to cheat on her. With you, she figured you have had them all, so now you'd be ready to be tamed, and she'd be the one. And you know what? I agreed with her. I also told her, when she came to me this time, that this was more of a get-even tryst than for the pleasure of it."

I remained silent, but my eyes were fixed on the stairs. I knew that unlike the events at my parents' house, there was no way Liseth could hear us talking, but I kept looking at the stairs.

"Delroy," Ebony continued, "you and I have been friends since college. I know you as well as anybody will ever know you. I know what you like, and I pretty much think I know how you think." She shifted slightly in her seat. "Liseth is more than a friend to me. What she wants more than anything is stability. If you were her age, she wouldn't have gotten involved with you. I wouldn't have encouraged it either. Only because I knew you when you were her age." Ebony shifted again. She was like that when she was uncomfortable about something. "Because I know you that well, I think I can safely say I not only know you wouldn't lie to me, but also when you are lying to me."

If you shift one more time, I swear I'll wring your neck. And shift she did. "Listen, Ebony"—*so I won't wring your neck*—"this is not my proudest moment, and everything you said is true. I took no pleasure in what happened between me and Connie. Not even in the fact her marriage is falling apart, because you wouldn't want to see her tonight. She looked like a battered breadfruit. Her husband is beating the"—I paused—"shit out of her. But, Ebony, I spoke to her frankly and honestly, and I think she understood. There's nothing between us, and I encouraged her to get a divorce. I gave her the number of a good guy in the firm. It's up to her, Ebony. I'm going on with my life. My life is with Liseth. I love her."

"I know that, Delroy. I know that. And she knows that too, but she's young, and a little confused."

"What did she tell you?"

"If you're asking me if it's over, the answer is no. But, you have a lot of work to do." The shifting had stopped, thank goodness. "Delroy, that girl loves you. I know that for a fact. She loves you like I loved you when we were younger. But I knew from the start that I'd have a lot to put up with, and had Dalton not come along, I might have put up with it. But that was then."

She got up and walked over to me. She took me by the hand and pulled me up from the sofa. With my hand in hers, she led me to the kitchen. Slipping her arm around my waist, she said, "Delroy, this is a good girl. Her future is paved. She is guaranteed a job at my firm. We will be bringing her back every summer, and when she graduates, we'll take her on full-time. Not many young girls her age can say they have a future that secure." She opened the fridge and took out some orange juice. "You want something?" I took a Red Stripe beer.

"Delroy, don't deny me the pleasure of getting drunk at your wedding. I have waited a long time for it. Did you know that you're the only one of our class that's not married?"

"Or divorced."

We laughed, put our arms around each other, and walked back into the living room. Liseth was waiting for us.

"How many beers you had tonight?" she said.

"This is my fourth."

She looked at me funny. "We should be going. It's getting late."

"Yeah, we should be going. Thanks for the talk, Ebony."

"You're welcome."

Ebony walked us to the door. We embraced and said good night.

Chapter 10

*T*he fall term at Yale Law School began at 8:30 a.m. on Tuesday, September 7, 1999. Liseth and I drove up the Saturday evening in her Jeep and stayed at a hotel until the Tuesday when she went to orientation and moved into her room. I was glad we could spend that weekend together. We got a chance to check out some of the local places, had dinner at a nice little restaurant, and cleared the air on certain things.

I left New Haven that evening feeling a little better about our relationship than for the past two weeks. I was not worried about losing Liseth, but even after a weekend of making love and admitting to myself that I'd come close to losing the greatest woman in the world, I knew I still had some work to do. The hardest thing for me was to say good-bye. I missed her before I'd even left New Haven, but I knew that she would be home on October 22, when she went on her fall recess.

I got off the train in New Rochelle and took a taxi to my parents' house, where I'd left my car, and where I would spend the night. Dad was not home when I got there, and Aunt B was visiting her daughter, which was unusual but long overdue. I had a snack with my mother, talked about Liseth and the future, and I let it drop for the first time that I would ask Liseth to marry me when she came home for her fall recess. Mom was delighted that I made the decision, which, until I told her, I didn't even know I had wanted to do. But as I talked about it, I realized it was time for me to settle down. Maybe it was what Ebony said to me, that I was the only one in our class who was not married. It also made me realize that I was in my midforties, and if I let this girl get away, I may never get married and end up being an aging playboy trying to recapture something that was long gone. All my cousins were parents. I was the last holdout. I looked at Mom and realized it was time.

Liseth promised she'd call me before I fall asleep, and sometime before midnight, she kept her promise. We talked for more than half an hour. She told me about her room and her roommate, and about meeting some students from New York, orientation, and just that overall felling of being at Yale and being away from her family and loved ones. She had just gotten off the phone with her mother before she called. They talked for nearly an hour. Her mother was crying, she said. She missed her but was happy that she had a daughter at Yale Law School. Her mother and her sister, Esther, had wanted to go up to New Haven with us, but Liseth told them she wanted to spend some time with me. She never told them, of course, what had happened between us. Her sister understood the need for us to spend that weekend together. Her mother was a little reluctant, but eventually understood. It was not every day she had a daughter going off to Yale. She, however, spent Friday and most of Saturday with her mother, before meeting me at my parents'.

"Delroy, I am glad we got to spend time together," she said. "It was really important to me."

"I am glad too," I said. A surge of emotion overcame me as I said it. And I sensed the same in her voice as she continued.

"I miss you very much, Delroy." She paused. "It's not even a day yet, and I miss you already."

"Are you crying?"

"No." She was lying. "I just want to say"—sniffles—"that I really miss you"—double sniffles—"and that I love you very much."

"I love you too, darling. Now you should get some sleep. You have early classes tomorrow, and I have work."

"I know. Good night, baby."

"Good night. I'll call you this weekend."

I had breakfast with my parents the next morning. Aunt B spent the night with her daughter. Dad congratulated me on my decision to propose to Liseth. The look on his face would have rivaled a Cheshire cat's. I told him I hadn't proposed, only planned to, and that Liseth didn't even know, nor did I even buy a ring. I told him that until I mentioned it to Mom the night before, the thought hadn't crossed my mind.

Dad and I rode into the city together. I dropped him off at Grand Central Station, and he took the train down to his office on Lower Broadway. Mom had to be in federal court in White Plains, so she left after us. I was happy about how my parents felt about my decision to get married. I hadn't even told Liseth yet, and my mother was already planning the wedding.

I worked that evening until eight. For the rest of the week, I went in early and stayed late. I immersed myself in my work. Just what Liseth asked me not to do, but I missed her, and I had to find something to keep me busy.

My first weekend without Liseth, after less than a year of living together, and I was feeling like an old married man who had just lost his wife of many years. Even though I was a good cook and knew how to run a washer and dryer, I felt helpless. As if Liseth knew how to cook, or was one who was inclined to use the washer and dryer, unless she ran out of clean underwear. Lucky for me I was not looking for domestication in a woman. But I missed her.

Friday I got home at about nine, had some leftover chicken, watched TV, finished the bottle of wine that was in the fridge, and had no idea what time I fell asleep; but I woke up before nine the next day. I went running by myself, because Charles and Mildred went earlier. Then I took a shower, had something to eat, caught up on some work, and just hung out in the living room until Jasper came by to do the lawn and the car. I wasn't in the mood to talk to anyone, so I just let him do his work. I stayed out of his way.

Saturday night I ordered chicken broccoli from the Chinese restaurant up the street. I opened another bottle of wine and put on a Miles Davis CD. After the food and the wine, I fell asleep in the living room. Sunday was a repeat of Saturday. The only difference was that Liseth called. We talked for close to an hour.

***

The following weekend, I wanted to go up to see her, but she asked if I would rather come up the other weekend instead. She was overwhelmed with her workload that first week, and just wouldn't be good company. She would love to see me, she said, but the first week was so hectic. I understood. It was over twenty years ago, but I remembered my first week at law school.

The week that I was supposed to go up to see her, I couldn't make it. I had taken on a new client and had to get familiar with an enormous amount of facts on short notice. I spent the weekend at the office with four associates and an army of paralegals going through dozens of boxes. She was not disappointed, even though she had asked me not to work too hard. She too had lots of studying to do.

It was only about seventy-six miles from Midtown Manhattan to New Haven. Without traffic, I could do it in ninety minutes. Add thirty more minutes if I was coming from home. We both promised to make time for each other the following weekend.

That week I had depositions scheduled Monday and Tuesday, and court appearance for Thursday and Friday. Wednesday, there was a meeting with the executive committee. I was in my office going over some fact sheet before the meeting when I got a call from Brian Taylor, the attorney I recommended to Connie. He called to thank me for the referral, but that he would assign it to Gloria Lemke, who would meet with Connie later that week. He just wanted me to know. I told him it was fine, and that I was confident Gloria would do a good job.

That weekend I told Liseth everything that happened since she'd been away, and she told me about school and how tough it was. I, however, stayed off the subject of Connie, and I didn't mention marriage. The first year at law school is always the hardest. With core classes to take and law review, we didn't have much time for each other, so I drove up late Saturday and came back Sunday evening.

It was good to see her. And after a week of all those depositions, court appearances, meetings, and her classes and long hours in the library, making love was certainly what we both needed. It rejuvenated me for the week ahead. And no Connie. I didn't want more pussy by the time I got to Long Island, and I didn't have someone on the side.

Gloria Lemke was a rock-solid woman—about thirty-four, about five six, with short black hair, and had a preference for tailored man trousers, French cuff man's shirt, and loafers. The buzz around the office was that she was one of the best matrimonial attorneys in the firm and was on the partner track.

She was an extremely pretty woman, although she looked less feminine than she would have had she wore a dress and put on some makeup. And that rock-solid body of hers, which had to be a result of hours spent in the gym, made her looked even less feminine. But her sexual preference was her business. What was important was that she hated men enough to tear Connie's husband apart.

Gloria dropped by my office at about 2:30 p.m. I was not a divorce lawyer, but she wanted to talk to me, and I didn't mind.

"Hello, Delroy," she said, extending a hand that was soft and more feminine than her appearance. She had on a blue suit, light blue shirt with white collar and cuffs secured by multicolored silk knots, and her hair was cut in military style. Despite us both being lawyers, we had one other thing in common: our love for fine clothes. And I was sure that like me, she had a personal tailor. That suit was definitely not off the rack.

"Good to meet you," I said, offering her a seat on the opposite side of my desk.

"Thanks for taking the time to see me," she replied.

"How may I help you?"

"I am representing a woman named Constance Darby-Minto in a divorce proceeding, and I was just wondering if you might tell me something about her?"

I hadn't heard anybody call Connie Constance in such a long time I'd almost forgotten that was her name, and to the best of my knowledge, she never used the name *Minto*.

"What do you want to know?"

Connie had told Gloria that we were friends, and she wanted to know how well I knew Connie. I told her the truth, without going into the latest details, except I told her that Kevin hit her because she mentioned my name. Gloria's stay was short. She wrote some things on a legal pad and then left. She would be filing a divorce petition sometime the next week, as soon as she drafted the complaint and had Connie sign it.

"If there is anything I can do, please let me know," I said.

She thanked me, we shook hands, and she left. I was relieved to know Connie was going forward with the divorce. At least now she'd be able to get on with her life. I would try to stay informed and find out how it was going, but I wouldn't call her.

Connie didn't tell Kevin about the divorce until it was filed. Gloria told her not to. Serving him would not be a problem. He could either be served at his home or at his job. He wouldn't be hard to find.

I could have easily found out through the litigation department if the summons and complaint were filed, since they would use a litigation clerk to do the filing; but as much as I would love to know, I didn't want to ask questions. And it would be a breach of ethics for me to pry. Matrimonial cases are confidential, and the information is privy only to the parties involved, or to the attorney of record. I was neither. But I didn't have to pry into it. That Saturday, at the barbershop, Victor told me that the summons and complaint were filed, and that Connie was seeking divorce on the grounds of adultery, cruelty, and mental anguish. Her attorney was asking for a protective order against her husband and for him to stay away from the matrimonial home, and for temporary child support, and for him to pay all the bills until the divorce was final.

Gloria moved expeditiously, but not fast enough. Kevin had hired a well-known divorce attorney who was known to play rough too. In one well-known case, he tore into a wife on the stand so hard she broke down crying, left the stand, and wouldn't return. She settled the case for less than what her husband was offering. A fraction of what she had wanted in the first place.

Kevin's lawyer had filed his summons and complaint before Connie and served her before she could serve him, and so they had the upper hand. Kevin didn't list adultery as one of his grounds for divorce, for which I was glad. He listed irreconcilable differences and Connie's refusal to have sex with him for the past eight months. Kevin also moved out of the house and agreed to pay all the bills until the divorce was final. It seemed Connie was getting what she wanted, and without a fight from him. It worried her, but Gloria told her to accept it; if there were any tricks she was prepared.

Liseth was getting ready to come home for her fall recess. Our plans were for me to take the train up and drive back with her. She'd be home from the twenty-second to the thirty-first of October. Classes resumed on November 1, 1999. I was looking forward to our time together.

On Saturday, October 16, 1999, I was trying to make room for some new suits I'd picked up from my tailor. At the rate I was going, I might have to expand the damn closet. I was excited about Liseth's homecoming. The phone rang, and I dashed across the bed to get it. "Hello, darling," I said. But it was Greta.

I knew right away something was wrong. Greta never called me at my house before. The first thing that came to mind was Connie was hurt. She was crying, and it took a while for her to calm down enough to get a word out.

"Greta, what's wrong?" I sat on the edge of the bed. "Greta, what's wrong?"

The crying sounded like a wailing. The kind you'd hear at a wake. I asked her if Connie was all right.

"No," she said. Then, fighting to overcome her hysteria, she said, "Delroy, Connie . . . oh God, what has she done? Delroy, can you come?"

"Greta, I can't understand what you're saying. Is Connie all right?"

"She . . . she . . . she killed her husband."

What the fuck was she saying? Was I hearing her right? "She what?"

"Connie killed Kevin." The words staggered out of her mouth, and the only thing I could hear on the other end was uncontrollable crying.

"Greta . . . Greta . . . Greta, can you hear me?" She didn't answer. "Greta!" I shouted as loud as I could.

"I didn't know who else to call."

"That's all right. Calm down and tell me what happened. First, when did this happen?"

What Greta knew was patchy. She'd gotten the news from her father, who was called by an old friend on the Dobbs Ferry Police Department. All she knew was that Connie was beaten up pretty badly by Kevin and, as a result, was in the hospital—which one Greta was not sure, but whichever it was, she was in police custody at the hospital until she was released, at which time she would be taken to jail. Nicole was also in the hospital. It seemed she witnessed the killing and was traumatized by the event and had to be hospitalized as well. Greta didn't know if Nicole was in the same hospital. It all happened earlier that evening. She started to cry again.

"Greta, you gonna have to calm down. I can't understand you."

"I'm so sorry to get you involved, but I didn't know who else to call." The crying stopped, a little. Only for a second. "Delroy, she is my only sister." And off she went again. Crying. I swear if she was in front of me, I'd have slapped her face. "What will happen to her?"

Dobbs Ferry was a village on the banks of the Hudson River, about forty miles north of New York City. Very little happened there. Mexican day laborers getting drunk on Saturday nights and driving reckless was a major epidemic. Every now and then, a person might go into the local A&P and leave without paying for something. Other than that, the soporific village was not used to having one of its residents killed by their spouse. So when something of that nature happened the person was taken to the local jail; and then to the village court, where they would be arraigned; and then to the Westchester Correctional Facilities at Valhalla, from there they'd be taken to court in White Plains, where bail would be set.

I told Greta that since Connie was in police custody at the hospital, there was nothing that could be done until the hospital released her and she was taken to jail, and then to court. It was quite likely, I told her, that since the firm was representing her in her divorce, we would be representing her in any criminal charges. If her injuries were severe enough to keep her in the hospital too long, we could move to have her arraigned at the hospital and have bail set. I was confident, given her and Nicole's condition and the twins, that bail would be set. I reminded her, though, that Kevin was a prominent doctor who was murdered by his wife, so the family should be prepared for the DA to be nasty.

The facts would not be known for days—at least until Connie was questioned, and it would only be her version. They would also want to talk to Nicole, but depending on how traumatized she was, that might have to wait. How and why it happened was known only by three people, and one of them was in the county morgue, the other would obviously tell her version, and the other was a possibly permanently damaged young girl two months shy of her fourteenth birthday. I told Greta to call me as soon as she knew more. I left her my cell phone number.

I called Gloria. It was after eleven. She wasn't home. The voice on the answering machine wasn't hers. It was another woman's. I left a message. I didn't go into details. I just asked her to call me back. I left my cell phone number too. I called Ebony and told her. I asked her not to tell Liseth if she talked to her. I would tell Liseth. I told her I would wait until she came home. That was a good idea, she said.

Gloria called me back right after I hung up. She called in and picked up her message, she said, and was calling me from a bar. It was hard to hear her over the noise. I asked her if she was on her cell phone, and could she step outside and talk to me.

Once she was outside, we didn't have to shout to hear each other. Either Gloria was the coldest bitch there was, or she was expecting it. "So now she won't have to worry about the divorce," she said.

"Yeah, but how about murder," I said.

"She won't be convicted."

Maybe Gloria was right, but it was the way she said it. As if Kevin's life was nothing. Gloria was also a litigator, and had only switched to matrimonial four or five years ago. She had tried cases and understood the criminal justice system. As Connie's attorney, she said she'd go see her and represent her at the bail hearing. She would, of course, talk to Brian first. I told her I'd talk to him before her. I called him as soon as I hung up with her and explained the situation to him. He was the supervising partner. It would need his OK.

I called Greta back. She sounded better. I told her Gloria would be at the bail hearing. Then I called Ebony again and told her the firm would represent Connie at the bail hearing. She too was glad. Then I called my mother and told her. She didn't take the news too well. She was worried about what this might do to the children, even if Connie beat the charge.

It was the most restless night I'd ever had. Sleep was elusive—at least until six the next morning. I slept until past noon and must have left or knocked the phone off the hook. The pounding on the back door, coupled by loud shouts, woke me.

I stumbled out of bed and ambled out onto the balcony, shielding my eyes from the midday sun. The shadowy figure below was not identifiable, but the voice was. "Hey, Delroy," said Charles, "I've been trying to call you for the past three hours. You OK?"

I mumbled something I was sure he didn't hear. I think I told him to hold on, or something to that effect. In any case, I went downstairs and let him in. He repeated the query: was I OK?

"What time is it?" I grunted, rubbing the sleep out of my eyes.

Without looking at his watch, he said, "One o'clock. Did you know your phone was off the hook all morning?"

I felt as though I had a hangover. My head was splitting. I put the kettle on and put a tea bag in the mug. Charles was looking in the fridge for something. I asked him to hand me the orange juice. I took three Advils and guzzled some juice to wash them down, wiped my mouth with the back of my hand, and left the container on the kitchen counter.

"We haven't been seeing much of you since Liseth left." Charles and Mildred had gotten addicted to Aunt B's ginger beer. Each time I'd go up to my parents, with them in mind, I'd bring some back with me. He poured some in a glass with ice. "We hardly run together anymore. What's happening?"

I excused myself and went into the bathroom, took a leak, returned, and poured the boiling water for my tea. "Besides the fact that I have been busy, nothing's happened, except Connie killed her husband last night."

I went out front to get the Sunday papers. I heard him ask as I opened the door, "Who killed whom?"

"Connie killed her husband," I said as I returned with the paper and took it out of the blue plastic bag and laid it out on the counter.

"That's what I thought you said. How did it happen?"

"He beat the shit out of her, she plunged the kitchen knife in his chest, he's in the morgue, she's in the hospital, and her daughter, who witnessed it, is hospitalized for shock."

"That's terrible news. I'm sorry to hear. Where are the twins?"

I didn't know, but I assumed they were with her mother, since it was likely Greta would be doing a lot of running around. Charles had never met Connie, but he showed genuine concern for her and her children, and as much as he didn't condone Kevin's actions, he was sorry that his life should end like that.

One of two things will happen if you continue kicking a dog: it will either run away or bite your ass. I suppose it would have been easier for Connie to run away; she'd had to endure so much by herself. I was quite sure that as much as she didn't want to go back to her parents with three kids, they would have welcomed her. But maybe she thought she had nowhere to go. That is, maybe she thought no matter where she went, she couldn't hide. Maybe she thought as close as she was to her family, she was alone. Maybe she thought there was no one to turn to, and that like everybody else, I failed her. That must have been the worst part. For her to run to the man she loved and trusted. Her true love, and what did I tell her? "Get a divorce, and get on with your life." That must have pushed her over the edge.

Not many people can recognize their problem and solve it themselves. Some of us need somebody to talk to. Somebody to confide in. To share our innermost secrets with. To bare our soul to. Connie was close to her sister; but she couldn't, for whatever reason, confide in her. For some reason, she kept the abuses she suffered from Greta. She stayed up in Dobbs Ferry and endured the humiliation and the indignity of being a battered wife. She must have sworn Nicole to secrecy or something, because they both kept the secret until she told me. She thought she could come to me, and that I'd be there for her, but I let her down.

"I don't think it would be in the papers yet," Charles said. I was looking through the metro and the Westchester sections. "I'm sure it will be on the news at six."

"I just feel I could have done something, and I didn't." I folded up the paper and shoved it aside.

"What do you think you could have done?"

"I don't know, but I had a feeling she came to me for help and I turned her away."

"But you didn't know at the time she was crying for help, did you?"

"No."

"So you can't hold yourself responsible for what has happened. Listen, she was in an abusive marriage for God knows how long. Maybe this was the only way she could get out of it, unfortunately. But, Delroy, you can't blame yourself."

"I just felt like I could have done something."

"Only if she had wanted you to, and I'm afraid you would have gotten hurt."

"Maybe you're right."

"I'm right. Are you going running?"

"I don't think so."

"Don't skip too many days now. Are you finished with this?" He held up the orange juice container. I told him I was. He returned it to the fridge and put his glass in the dishwasher. "Listen, my friend, you tried to help her the best way you could. You advised her to get a divorce. You did what a true friend would have done. There was nothing else you could do. Come over later and have dinner with us." I didn't commit myself, but I probably would. I told him I'd call him.

I went back up to bed. Not necessarily to sleep, just to get back in bed with the Sunday papers. It had been a long time since I did that. Even if I'd wanted to sleep, I couldn't. The phone kept ringing every fifteen minutes. My mother. Greta. Ebony. Mildred. Greta again. Someone who dialed the wrong number, and just about anybody who had nothing to do on a Sunday afternoon.

I called Ebony back and asked her if we could have lunch sometime before Liseth came home. We only had a few days. Tuesday was good, she said. Wednesday would be better, I said. We agreed.

Chapter 11

~oOvOo~

I had six to seven hours of sleep. I was up and out of bed the minute the alarm went off at five thirty. I was feeling better than I did the morning before. Lately I'd been slacking off on my running, but no damage was done. My weight remained the same. I'd hate for Liseth to come home after seven weeks and see me looking like the Pillsbury Doughboy.

There is one thing about America in general, and New York in particular: people are news vultures. Stories about prominent people are usually beaten to death. Kevin was a prominent heart surgeon, and he was killed by his wife. And what made it even bigger news, whether we wanted to admit it or not, was that he was a brilliant black doctor, with advanced degrees from Harvard, Cambridge, and Havana. He had worked in the United Kingdom, Cuba, Germany, and France, and had assisted his brother on occasions in South Africa. His expertise was sought after, on many occasions, by the governor, the president, and many hospitals. Not to mention his reverence in the black community. And he was killed by his white wife, who was a registered nurse, with only an associate's degree from a community college. This was big news. For the black community, white folks had finally got their O. J. Simpson.

And news it was, indeed. And Connie was being maligned. Kevin was the boy who came from humble beginnings. Whose parents had worked at Kings County Hospital, in maintenance; saved their money; and sent their two sons to medical school. Kevin was the kid from the housing projects, whom every kid in every project aspired to be like. He was the kid who grew up and took his parents out of the projects to a comfortable home in Hackensack, New Jersey. If there were bubble gum cards for doctors, he could have been included. Connie was the daughter of retired Irish American parents. Father, NYPD for thirty-five years, then a security consultant for corporations. Her mother, New York City public school teacher for twenty-five years, then five in the suburbs, until ill health forced her to retire.

Boy, they sure did dig into their backgrounds real fast. But they made Connie look bad. Connie was the spoiled little white girl from a middle-class family, who had killed the black Horatio Alger. She had killed the "American dream" of all black kids in America. The late Arthur Ashe once lamented on why, he being a great tennis player, should he carry the weight of all black Americans on his shoulders. That was too much burden they were putting on Kevin's shoulders.

But the press, as usual, was contaminating the jury pool. In less than forty-eight hours, the case was being tried in the public, and Connie was being condemned. The public was told that Kevin had filed for divorce and had moved out of the house. That he was giving her everything she wanted, but it wasn't enough. One or two reporters raised the question as to why she was in the hospital, but most were not interested in her condition. It was then I knew it was Dobbs Ferry General Hospital. But the few who were interested in her condition didn't bother to find out that her husband had beat the shit out of her. For all they knew, she could have sustained those injuries while Kevin was fighting her off. No, she was a cold-bloodied killer. This would be a slam dunk for any prosecutor. But that was what they said about the O. J. Simpson case.

It was on the 6:00 a.m. news. At noon, for those who had missed it, it would be on again. And in case you missed that, "Live at Five," would repeat it. And then the "News at Ten," and at eleven. And the next couple of weeks, the talk shows would have nothing else to talk about. I was afraid to buy a newspaper. The public was getting one side of the story. This was not the Connie I know. OK, Gloria, get out there and tell your client's side of the story.

I took a half-hour run, showered, shaved, had breakfast, and was ready to go by eight when the phone rang. It was Liseth. "Good morning, darling." There was nothing new in her calling me early in the morning. She had called earlier on one or two occasions just to say waking up without me was taking some getting used to. But there was reservation in her voice, but she managed to sound upbeat.

"You caught me on my way out, but I'll always have time for you. How is school?"

"School is great. As a matter of fact, I am a little late for class."

I sensed this was more than a call to tell me how much waking up without me had taken a toll on her well-being. "What's up, babe?"

"Did you see the news?"

My jacket was over the chair, and my briefcase and laptop case were by the door. I was hoping to catch the 8:26 out of Bay Shore, but I sensed I might not make it. Without equivocation, I told her I did, and what I knew. "I was just going out the door. I want to catch the 8:26. Call me on the cell phone."

Ten seconds later: "Is there anything you can do?"

I looked at the clock: it was 8:05. I should get to the station in fifteen minutes. "I'm not sure, but one of our lawyers will be in court this morning. We will see what happens, and then we will take it from there. The first thing we will do is try to get her out on bail. Then we will see what kind of case we have."

She sighed and wondered about Connie's children and asked if things were that bad between her and her husband. I told her about the children but said as little as possible about her marital woes.

"Are you going to get involved, personally?"

That was a fair question to ask. "I'll be involved one way or another, but I don't think I'll be making an appearance in court."

"That's what I thought. There is no telling which direction this case may go, and I'd hate to see you dragged in for the wrong reason. You know representing her could create a conflict. You know that, don't you?"

I am not sure what kind of response you're expecting, but I'll tell you this much: "We have dozens of litigators who are capable of doing a great job. And who knows, she might even go with different lawyers for the trial. Right now, we are only involved because we were retained for the divorce, which has now become moot."

"In any case, I hope for the best for her. Listen, I have to go. You take care of yourself. I love you."

"I love you too." I made it to the station with nine minutes to spare.

One of Gloria's strategies was to have Connie arraigned that Monday, no matter what. She wanted the judge to see how beaten up she was. And I heard she was beaten up pretty bad. Gloria had gone to visit her in the hospital. She had also taken a video camera and shot her in the hospital. She also asked her doctor to release her that Monday. Gloria was thinking fast. I could picture her having Connie wheeled into court in a chair. I was quite sure if she could, she would have had her wear the hospital gown opened down the back in the court. The best the prosecutor could do would be to ask for a high bail. There was no way they could oppose bail, and no judge would even listen to it. Great move, Gloria.

I had twelve messages in my inbox. Two from Ebony. Three from Greta. My mom called once, Gloria once, and the rest were of no importance. I called my mother first. She wanted to know what was happening. Ebony wanted pretty much the same information. There wasn't much to tell either of them. Greta, I figured, was too emotional, so I would pass up on calling her.

Gloria was at the hospital when I reached her. Over some strong opposition, she convinced the doctors to release Connie. She would be taken to the Dobbs Ferry village court for arraignment.

Gloria was hoping to see the judge before noon, but it didn't seem likely. Connie was not released from the hospital until about eleven thirty, and she was to be taken to the police lockup before going before the judge. The best she could hope for was some time in the afternoon. I told her to call me back.

Gloria called back a little after three. The judge in Dobbs Ferry remanded Connie to the Westchester County Correctional Facility at Valhalla pending a hearing at the county court in White Plains the following Monday, when she would apply for bail.

"She will die in that place, Delroy." If I didn't know better, I'd swear I heard a tinge of emotion in Gloria's voice. "There is no way we can let her stay in there for a whole week. That place is a hellhole. She will be put in with the worst of Westchester's criminal elements."

The one thing a lawyer should never do is get emotional involved with their client. I could only hope, given Gloria's position on men and Connie's vulnerable condition, that she wasn't getting emotionally attached. I tried to assure Gloria that we would do all we could.

"She doesn't have to. Tomorrow we will go to the county court and file a petition for a bail hearing. Hopefully, we can have her out by the end of the day. She won't have to spend more than tonight in Valhalla. Where are you now?"

"I am still at the courthouse in Dobbs Ferry, with her parents. They are willing to put up the bail money."

"Let me talk to Bill."

Gloria put Connie's father on. It had been a long time since I'd seen Bill or his wife, Carol. I didn't know how they felt about Kevin, but I knew when Connie and I were going out, I was always welcome in their home. I had a great deal of respect for them, and I was sure the feeling was mutual.

"It's been a long time, Bill," I said. "Too bad it has to be under these circumstances."

It was not one of Bill's proudest moments. The tough ex-cop was fighting back the tears. Poor man. Had to see his baby girl go through this. "I tell you, Delroy, I wish I'd die before I'd see this day. I'll do anything to get her out of this."

It must have been hard for him to express his emotion in front of Gloria, but his daughter had killed the father of his grandchildren, and she was about to spend the night in a place that for years he had put people in. It couldn't have been easy for him.

"I know you'll do anything for her, Bill. And we will do everything we can. Don't worry about it. Gloria is a good lawyer."

"She has been nothin' but good to us."

"We'll do everything we can to get her out tomorrow. You know, the bail could be high. We'll push for a low bail, but you have been around, so you know the bail could be high. The district attorney will push for it."

"I know. You do what you have to do. I'll have her out of there in an hour after they set bail."

"I'm sure they'll grant us bail. I just hope it's something reasonable."

"I'll call a few people and get certain things in motion. Cash or bond bail, I'll be ready. You just do what you have to do."

"How is Nicole? Is she with Greta?"

Bill's voice cracked a little, and he blew his nose. I asked him if he was all right. "I'm all right. I'm all right. I have been through some tough times, but this . . . this, I don't know what to compare it to." He sighed. "That's why you have to do all you can so I can bring my baby home. Nicole is not doing good. She hasn't talked since this whole . . . this whole unfortunate incident. This thing is too traumatic for the little girl. She is just not talking. You have to do something, Delroy."

I told him we would be there first thing the next morning. He thanked me, and I asked him to put Gloria back on. I explained to her what must be done the next day. That no time should be wasted. She said she'd be the first one in court the next day. I knew she would be. I thanked her and told her how much it meant to me. She told me she knew.

***

I left the office sometime after eight that night, but not before Liseth called me. I updated her on what was going on. She asked how Connie was doing, and about her children. I told her what I knew. "I can't wait for you to come home, baby."

"I'll be home this weekend."

"I know, but I still can't wait. I've got a surprise for you."

"That's interesting."

"What is?"

"You having a surprise for me."

"Why?"

"Because I have one for you too."

"Really? Is it a good surprise or a bad surprise?" She knew me well enough not to tell me she had a surprise for me. I was only going to keep asking until I knew what it was.

"I can't say if it's good or bad. You'll have to determine that when I see you."

"Now you have me wondering."

"Isn't that the whole idea behind a surprise?"

"I guess so."

"That ought to hold you for a while."

"OK, I won't ask any more questions, but tell me one thing: will I get it when I pick you up or when I we get home?"

"You said you wouldn't ask any more questions. It's late. Why don't you go home. I have some studying to do. Maybe I'll call you before I go to sleep. I miss you."

"I miss you too."

***

I sat up in bed with a brandy and tuned in to the eleven-o-clock news. Sue Simmons, on NBC, led off the news: "The thirty-two-year-old Dobbs Ferry housewife and mother of three who killed her thirty-seven-year-old husband, a prominent heart surgeon, was released from the local hospital and was arraigned in the Dobbs Ferry village court this afternoon. Bail was denied, and she was remanded to appear at the county court in White

Plains next Monday, when she will be formally charged and bail will be set. Until then, her home will be the Westchester County Correctional Facility at Valhalla."

Throughout the reading of that segment, alternate photos of Kevin and Connie were put up behind Sue Simmons, and when she read the last sentence, she did it amid a backdrop of the palatial contemporary two-story house Connie and her husband shared in Dobbs Ferry.

I am sorry to disappoint you, Sue, but she'll be home with her children by tomorrow night.

I took a sip of the brandy and put an additional pillow, from Liseth's side, behind my head. There was a full moon that gently caressed the ocean as the waves slowly rolled up and pounded the shores. I took another sip and another of her pillow and hugged it like I would her. It smelled of her, even though they were clean linen on the bed. I squeezed the pillow and would argue with anyone who said it didn't squeeze back. I even had an erection.

I lay there with the poor pillow in my embrace, too helpless to resist, or enjoying the clinch. Either case, I was too tired to resist sleep. And I would have succeeded in becoming a victim of heavy eyelid syndrome had Liseth not called. It was brief. She just called to tell me she had just finished studying and was going to bed. *Great, you woke me just to tell me that. I have sued people for less than that.*

It took me another half hour to fall asleep again. In that brief respite, I had time to wonder about the surprise Liseth had for me. When a man had everything he could ever want, it was hard to figure out what else he could get that would surprise him. But whatever she had in store for me would be no match for the 2.5-karat diamond ring I was picking up later that week.

***

Gloria Samantha Lemke was a native New Yorker. Born and raised in Manhattan. She was a Lower East Side kid. Alphabet City. Went to public school. College: NYU. Law school: New

York Law School. She did several years in the Manhattan district attorney's office. She headed the sex crime and domestic violence unit. She was a tough prosecutor. She pushed for jail time in all her cases. She usually got her way. Most defendants would rather cop a plea than have her angry at them. She was batting a thousand. The few cases she lost, if you could call it a loss, were when the victims changed their minds. When this happened, she would threaten to prosecute them for making false statements. She thought they were being further victimized. Sometimes it worked.

Very little was known of Gloria's family. People who were close to her said she talked very rarely, if not at all, about her family. One could only speculate about the relationship between her and her father. But whatever it was, she hated men with a passion. Which was good for us and Connie. She walked into that courtroom in White Plains early that Tuesday morning and laid out her case before the judge. We had sent one of our crack litigators, who had tried several criminal cases, to assist her. But she asked him to let her handle the hearing. She had created a bond and developed a friendship with Connie that she thought would be better left that way. Gloria was emotionally involved.

Gloria was also up against one of Westchester County's best prosecutors, and was about to show him her balls were as big as his. The prosecutor—knowing he could not oppose bail for a woman who was never arrested before, who had roots in the community, with young twin sons and a daughter in the hospital, and whose father was an ex-cop—had decided to ask for a million dollars in bail. Gloria asked for Connie to be released on her own recognizance. The judge refused both, but set a bond of $50,000.

Connie did not have to be in court for the bail hearing, but her father and her sister were there. The whole ordeal had taken a toll on her mother, so she stayed home with the twins and Greta's children.

When a court sets bail, they set it under one of two conditions: cash bail or a bond in the equivalent. Cash bail has always been considered the harshest, because the person would have to come up with the cash before they can get out of jail. With a bond equivalent, all they would have to do is pledge a piece of property that's worth at least that much. Most people would go to a bondsman, give him 10 percent of the bond in cash, sign a confession of judgment on a piece of property they own, and the bondsman would do the rest. Bill didn't have to do that. With his experience of the system, he bypassed the bondsman and put up the deed to his house. He saved $5,000.00. But he wouldn't have to worry about losing his close-to-one-million-dollar house. His daughter was not a risk.

The judge set the bail and signed the bond, and the whole process was done before noon. They then had to go over to Valhalla, which was about ten or twelve miles away. Getting Connie out of Valhalla would take longer. Hopefully, they would not get there between two thirty and three thirty, when the guards were changing shifts.

Everybody except Frank Lambert, the attorney we sent to handle the case, went to Valhalla. Frank was satisfied that Gloria did an excellent job, and even suggested we kept her on the team when we went to trial.

It was 1:05 p.m. when they pulled up into the parking lot of the correctional facility. By the time they were processed and had submitted their request for Connie's release, it was 1:45 p.m. Then they had to wait. They were caught in the shift change, and Connie, who was in a separate wing of the facility and who also had to wait until a thorough statewide warrant check was performed to see if she was wanted anywhere, was not released until almost six that evening.

I told Gloria to call me the minute Connie was free. It was ten minutes after six when a tearful Connie called me from the parking lot. I could hardly hear her over the crying. I tried to calm her down, but the emotion was too much. And I could understand. I was pretty emotional too.

When the crying subsided, she thanked me and Gloria for all we had done, and was about to tell me how everything happened so fast, had I not stopped her.

"Right now, Connie, I just want you to go take care of Nicole. This is the most important thing right now."

I could hear her take a deep breath. Then she exhaled. Then another. Good, she was trying to control her emotions. I waited until she had taken another, and then she said, "Delroy, I'd do anything to change that moment."

"I know you would, Connie. I know you would. But unfortunately, we can't. But let's not talk about that right now. We can do that later. We have time. Go look after Nicole. She needs you."

"He ruined my daughter's life. Now mine." She started to cry again. "I have to go to the hospital. I have to go see my baby. I have to go."

"Call me anytime. Let me know how she's doing."

Bill took the phone from her. The rage in his voice came out at me but was not directed at me. It was as though he was standing in front of me. He was angry. And it became evident why Connie could not share the abuses she suffered with her family. Kevin would have been dead a long time ago. What irony: Connie saved Kevin's life, only to take it. It wasn't easy, but I was able to calm Bill down.

"What's going to happen to my little girl?" he asked. His voice cracked under the strain of the emotion. "How could this happen to my family? Why?"

The sound of horns and vehicles wheezing by suggested they were on the highway.

"Bill, I want you to listen to me very carefully." I had his attention. "Connie is not going to go to jail. That much I'll promise you." It was a promise, I was sure, I didn't know if I could keep. But what else could I tell him? His daughter was facing possibly up to twenty-five years in jail.

First thing we had to do was find out if we would be retained as the attorneys of record for the trial. Then we would see what the DA had. Then we would listen to what Connie had to say, and then we would formulate a strategy.

"Delroy, I want you to handle this case personally. I want you to do whatever you can legally to get my little girl out of this mess. I'm goin' to talk to some people I know and see what we can find out 'bout Kevin. I don't care what has to be done. My daughter's goin' to beat this." His voice raised, and I could hear the anger fighting against him trying to stay calm in Gloria's presence. Bill was not a man to show any emotion. He was a man who prided himself on remaining calm under any circumstances. He once told me that as a cop, he was not supposed to show any sign of emotion. "It's sign of weakness," he said. But this was his daughter's freedom on the line. It was personal.

I was happy that he had enough confidence in me to want me to handle the case, which meant the firm would represent Connie. The part that worried me was that he wanted me to handle it personally. I made sure to prefaced my answer with the word *we*.

"We will do everything we can, Bill. Don't worry about it. You take care of your daughter and granddaughter. Leave the lawyering to us."

I spoke to Gloria and thanked her for the great job she did. She thanked me for the opportunity. Then we said good night.

***

Wednesday would be a busy day for me. I had a meeting with a client to discuss an offer of a settlement. We were suing a developer for breach of contract. We were asking for $25 million in compensation. Fifteen million was for what my client would have made had the developer kept his part of the agreement. Ten million was for punitive damages. My client, who was a small businessman, was an electrical contractor. He was contracted by a real estate developer to do the wiring of two apartment complexes the developer was putting up in Manhattan. And two more he had set to break ground on. The apartment would be co-ops. And the starting prices were $800,000 for a studio to $2.5 million for a three-bedroom. In a handshake agreement in front of witnesses, the developer agreed to give my client the contract to do all the electrical work on the two buildings and was promised the option on the other two, if the zoning permit was approved.

The developer was familiar with my client's work since my client had worked for a competing developer and was lauded for his professionalism and his ability to finish a job on time.

After several telephone discussions between my client and the developer, they both agreed to a formal contract. One was drafted, by another attorney, and sent to the developer for his final approval. The developer sat on the contract for over a month, and at the last minute, without even as much as calling my client, gave the job to another contractor. We sued on the grounds that we had an implied contract based upon the handshake in front of witnesses and the subsequent phone calls, which my client made, in the presence of witnesses, on a speaker phone. Their last telephone conversation ended with him telling my client, "Messenger over the contract, and I'll sign it and we can start moving."

Five weeks passed without a word, and the next thing my client knew, somebody else was doing the work, and he was being told they didn't have a deal. Oh yeah. We would let a jury decide. We filed an injunction to stop all work. And with him unable to go forward, he was losing money. That's when he decided to seek a settlement. He offered five mil. We told him to go fuck himself. Then he came back with seven point five, and we told him that if he enjoyed the first fuck, the second one should be heaven. And anytime he was tired of stretching his dick, he could give us a call.

We didn't tell him in those exact words, but he got the gist of it, and $15 million, including attorney's fees, was put on the table. He and his lawyer were due in my office at ten thirty. It shouldn't take more than twenty minutes if they brought a good faith attitude and cashier's check. I was meeting Ebony for lunch at one, and my father at three thirty. My best friend and I were going to look at diamond rings.

The money would be paid out over two years. The first installment of $3.75 million in cashier's check was handed over, with the rest to follow at the end of the first six months, and every six months subsequently. If the agreement was breached, we would reinstate the lawsuit for the remainder. Our fee was $3 million.

***

It had been so long since Ebony and I had lunch I couldn't even remember when. The Rockefeller Center Cafe was a place we often loved to eat. She was seated at her table when I got there. It's hard to get a table at lunchtime in the Rockefeller Center Cafe without a reservation. She saw me from across the room and waved. She signaled to the waiter as I sat down, and he brought me a white wine. Thanks, I told Ebony as I sat down.

"It's been a long time, but I remember," she said.

"I'd be worried if you forgot." I laid my napkin across my lap. If there was one thing I was proud of in my life, it's my propensity to pick beautiful women. Ebony and I are a year apart, but I was beginning to wonder if I'd made a mistake in not marrying her when I was younger. But then I had to be honest: she and I would have been divorced by now, and I was sure I'd have lost a friend. It was better the way it worked out.

"What's the latest on Connie?" She looked over the menu as she spoke.

"She made bail last night."

"How does it look?"

"I haven't sat down and talked to her yet. She has to go to court Monday."

"I'm sitting here, and I know it is true, but somehow it seems like a nightmare. It just doesn't seem real." The waiter took our order. I was having seafood salad on a bed of lettuce. Ebony was having the grilled chicken. "I just can't," she continued, "see Connie killing anyone. Especially her husband."

"Anybody can commit murder, if they are pushed too far."

"I don't know, Delroy, there must be more to it than we know right now."

"I don't want to make it sound simple, but he beat her one time too many, and she put a stop to it. It's self-defense. When Nicole gets better, she will be our prime witness."

The waiter brought our lunches, and we ordered another drink. Ebony finished the remainder of her drink and put a piece of cucumber in her mouth. I took a mouthful of the seafood. It was good.

"He just didn't look like the type that beats women," Ebony said between bites of chicken. "He seemed like such a nice and gentle person."

"You met him?"

"Once or twice. Actually"—she paused—"now that I think about it, I met him twice. Once, when Connie was pregnant, Dalton and I ran into them with Nicole in Bloomingdale's."

"Did Nicole remember you?" I was quite sure Nicole did, but I asked anyway.

"Of course she did. As often as she and Connie used to be over the house with you, of course she did. That day in Bloomingdale's, Connie introduced me to Kevin, and I introduced Dalton to him; and since he and Dalton had something in common, they did most of the talking. I found him to be a charming and likable person. There was, at least from what I saw, nothing phony about him. As a matter of fact, we had lunch that day. Dalton and I found him to be a highly intelligent man."

"He was. Where did you meet them again?"

"I never met then again—not together, that is. I met him one evening when I was visiting a friend at Beth Israel Hospital. I remembered him and everything about our first meeting, except for his name. He had a great memory. He remembered my name and Dalton's. He was not only intelligent, but he was a very good-looking man as well."

"He fooled you too, didn't he?"

"Why, because I'm saying he's intelligent and good-looking? But it's true, he's intelligent and good-looking."

"Was." I found myself suppressing a sick sense of delight in a man's death, however tragic, and even if he was a notorious wife beater.

"Was," she corrected her tense. "All I'm saying is that to me, he didn't look like the kind of man who'd beat his woman. That's all I'm saying."

"What do you think, the wife beaters all have a sign hanging off them?"

"Of course not." And as if to rile me, she said under her breath, "He was good looking."

"I heard that," I said. We both laughed. "You know, you'd think I asked you to lunch to discuss Kevin's lack of virtue."

"I'd hope not, because I'd hate to spoil a good afternoon talking about something beyond our control." She leaned over and, with her napkin, wiped something off my nose. "Dressing," she said.

"That you."

"So what's up?" she said as she chewed on a piece of her chicken. "I must say that despite our sparring session, there's something that pleases you. What is it?"

"Maybe I'm just happy." I drank the last of my wine.

"Yeah, but happy about what?"

"You remember when Liseth and I were at your house the last time and you said that I was the only one of our class that was not married?"

"No. Don't tell me. You have decided to get married!" She looked both surprised and happy.

"Still can't hide anything from you after all these years, can I?"

"Oh my God, Delroy. You have decided to marry her. Does she know?"

"No. I've only told my parents, and now you."

"Holy shit, I can't believe this. I gotta call Dalton. He'll be so happy to hear."

"Tell him later. I gotta talk to you first."

"Did you buy the ring yet?"

"No, I'm meeting my father later today. He's taking me to a jeweler friend of his on Forty-Seventh."

"What size?"

"At least 2 karats."

"She gonna die. I just know it." People in the restaurant started to look at us. But I didn't care. "I just knew it. I told Liseth that you might do something like this. I told her—"

I interrupted her. "What did you tell her, and when?"

"She and I were talking, and she was wondering—not enough to change her mind about how she felt about you, but she was wondering—where you'll go from what had happened. And I told her that after what happened, you might just pop the question."

"So I don't suppose she'll be surprised when I propose this weekend?"

"Unless you told her you're going to—are you kidding? Of course not. She'll be surprised."

"I hope so."

"Anything over 2 karats will leave a woman too numb to be surprised. But, trust me, on this one, she'll be surprised. Oh my God, I'm so happy for both of you. Are you having a big wedding?"

"You know my mother. She'll take over the whole thing and do it the way she wants. But we'll wait till next summer to get married."

"What was the first thing your mother asked you when you told her? I bet she wanted to know if Liseth is pregnant? Did she?"

"As a matter of fact, she didn't. As a matter of fact, I am sure, between me, her mother, and my mother, I'd be the last to know if she was pregnant. But Mom was just as excited as you when I told her."

"Oh yeah, she would be. Yes, she would be. I could just see her face. Now if you had told her Liseth was pregnant, you might have had to sedate her. I know how much she wants a grandchild."

"Tell me about it."

It took a while, but Ebony finally calmed down. We finished our lunch. We shared a piece of cheesecake and journeyed down memory lane. She told me that she thought the time was right for me to get married. That getting married at my age, and that stage in my life, would make for a happy marriage. That had she and I gotten married when we were younger, it would have lasted maybe a year, and our friendship maybe less. As much as Connie loved me, Ebony was convinced that even if she had said yes to my proposal, it would not have worked. But with Liseth, she was sure it would work.

Liseth, she said, had always had certain goals. To go to college, then graduate school, get married before she reached twenty-five, have at least two kids before she reached thirty, and live in a big house with a pool in the suburbs. But she didn't want to marry anyone in her age group. She was concerned that they would somehow think there were still mountains to climb. That they had not sown enough wild oats. Five years into the marriage and they'd think, *Oh my God, I am not thirty yet, and there are things I haven't done*; and by the time they reached forty, younger women would look more attractive. Older men were more established and were inclined to be better fathers. She would always look younger and would always be appreciated by an older man. *OK, since I fit into all the categories, except for the pool, does that mean I will have to sell the house? Please don't ask me to sell the house. I love that house. I don't have a pool, but I have the ocean in my backyard.*

Chapter 12

•┅━◦⊙♥⊙◦━┅•

One sure way of knowing what your spouse will look like when they get old is to meet their parents. A man should meet his girlfriend's mother, and a woman her boyfriend's father. This way, you'd know if you want to wake up next to that person thirty years from the time you marry them.`

The receptionist called me directly to tell me my father had arrived. I told her he could come in. He knew the way. Dad was immaculately dressed, as usual. He had on a light-blue lightweight suit. A dark-blue striped shirt with English spread collar and French cuffs. The blue tie with the red and pink dots and the crisp white linen handkerchief in the jacket pocket complemented the ensemble. Only my dad could make a double-breasted suit looked better than I could.

I was not by any means condoning my father's past indiscretion, but I could see why women would find him sexy. Even my mother admitted he was a lady killer when he was younger. At close to seventy, he still turned the heads of younger women. And when this tall, lean, impeccably dressed man walked through my office, all the women, even after he left, couldn't stop talking about him. Dad was the classic symbol of that cliché, "Age is nothing but a number." I knew what I'd look like when I grew old.

"I'll be ready in twenty minutes," I said as Dad sank into the sofa. He looked around, and Mom's influence was everywhere in the office.

When I first made partner and was wondering how to decorate my office, she was the one who brought her friend, a renowned decorator, to my office one week and decided on everything. The drapes. The valance. The rug. The desk. The pair of Louis XIV chairs. The sofa, and even the plants. She and her friend did an excellent job. My office, with its Old English look, was a showpiece. It had been featured in many magazines and had been used as the office of a power attorney in a major movie.

Dad told me not to rush. "We have time," he said.

I looked at my watch. It was close to five. We were meeting a friend of his, who was a diamond merchant and who could get me the ring at below market price. I would save a lot of money.

Dad's friend was an old Arab. One of the few successful diamond dealers in a business dominated by Jews. Omari Maadi had been in the diamond business for over thirty years. Dad had known him for more than ten years. They met through a mutual friend who defended Omari when his landlord wanted to evict him. The building was taken over by a new owner who spent a lot of money to improve the building and then wanted to raise the rent. Omari, who at the time had seven years left on a ten-year lease, refused to pay the increase, and so the new owners took action and lost in court. The new owners, of course, said it was not true.

It was the third time I'd met Omari, a short, thin man, in his mid-seventies, of dark complexion. He was, maybe, I think, from one of the Gulf states—Omar or Kuwait, I was not sure—but he still spoke, after more than forty years in the United States, with that thick Arab accent that made him sound as though he'd just come over. He was a very polite man, who loved to tell stories about great adventures of Arabian warriors. And when Dad told him I was buying an engagement ring, he couldn't help telling me a story about a great Arab warrior who at age forty-two married a young girl of sixteen, who went on to bear him five sons. The young girl, he said, was also the warrior's fifth and favorite wife, because she gave him five sons while his other wives, between then, gave him four girls. Of course, I asked him if the story was true; and of course, he left the ambiguity hanging in the air.

The ring was a 2.5-karat round diamond, surrounded by twenty-three sapphires—one representing each year for how old Liseth would be on her next birthday. The setting was white gold and platinum, twisted together. I designed it myself, and Omari would have it ready by that Friday. I insisted, and he promised.

The cost of the ring was too vulgar to talk about, but if I should stupidly break off the engagement, Liseth would be left with enough asset that, if invested wisely, would have her set for life. Omari jokingly asked me if I was going to have a bodyguard follow her around at Yale. I told him I wouldn't; but of course, I was having it insured for every penny it was worth. One thing he, the Arab warrior, and I had in common: we all thought that a man should spoil his woman.

***

I intended to make a short day of Friday. The ring would be ready by noon. For what Omari was charging me, I should have had it that same day. Connie and her father would be at the office at one. The interview should take an hour. Ninety minutes at the most. We mainly wanted to hear her side of the story. I didn't have to be there. Brian would do the interview, and Gloria would sit in as support. They were capable of handling things without me. But even if all I had to do was observe, I had to be there.

Although I had no doubt of his craftsmanship, the thing that impressed me most about Omari was his punctuality. At eleven forty-five, he called to tell me the ring was ready. "Would you like for me to send messenger over with package?" he asked. "They bonded."

I told him it was OK. I could be there in ten minutes. Plus, I couldn't wait to see it; and although the messenger was bonded and the insurance company would pay if the messenger went south, I didn't have the luxury of time on my side.

Omari's showroom was on Forty-Seventh Street, between Fifth and Sixth Avenues. It was a small showroom, with his workroom in the back. To get in the front door, I had to be buzzed in and out. The same to get into the workroom. Part of the security, including the armed guard inside the showroom, was closed-circuit cameras. Omari had never been robbed, but he was aware of the risk that came with the business he was in, and having known people who were robbed, and one who lost his life, the cost of being cautious was cheap.

Maybe Omari was right. I might have to hire a bodyguard to follow Liseth around Yale. The ring was more beautiful than I'd imagined. It was gorgeous. If I was in doubt of Liseth's love, the ring would do one of two things: make her fall madly in love with me or scare her off. The fact that she was head over heels in love with me was no guarantee she wouldn't take one look at such an ostentatious ring and said the whole thing was too much for her. Maybe the idea of walking around with that much money on one finger, although I was not about to tell her how much it cost, would be too burdensome. But this was the first and only time I intended to get married, and I was willing to spoil her like rotten bananas.

***

One of the advantages a black woman has over a white woman is that she can just get the shit beaten out of her. She can have her face used as a punching bag, and with enough makeup, save for the swelling and missing tooth, she can throw on a pair of sunglasses, and you wouldn't know she had her face pushed in earlier. White women are different. All you have to do is try to get away from them, and they'll have red marks all over their body. All Connie would have had to do was call the police, and with her neck or hands red from the struggle, Kevin's ass would have been in jail faster than he would be able to explain what happened.

When Connie walked into my office, no amount of makeup or the sunglasses could hide the fact that she had had the shit beaten out of her. She was not one to go heavy on the makeup, but that day, she laid it on with a trowel. But after a week, all the makeup in the world still couldn't hide the silver-dollar-sized bruise on her right cheek and the stitches under her left eye that the sunglasses could not fully hide. And thank goodness she didn't attempt to put any lipstick on. It would have only made her half-healed and crusty lips look worse. She tried to smile when she saw me, brave woman; and the smile revealed a missing upper tooth. I was glad Gloria had enough sense to take pictures of her in the hospital, because the key to winning this case would be to convince a jury that she acted in self-defense.

The sight of her made me angry. It was obvious the bastard beat her mercilessly. For a moment, the amount of trouble she was in was unimportant; I was just glad the son of a bitch was dead. What kind of depraved animal was this man? How could he just finish saving a life and then beat the living daylights out of his wife, the mother of his children? The agony Connie must have lived through, knowing she couldn't tell anyone in her family because Bill would have surely killed this mad animal.

Brian and Gloria were not there yet. It gave me a chance to put professionalism aside. I had to take her in my arms and comforted her. I couldn't have done any less. This was my friend. A woman I was at one time in love with. A woman I had wanted to be my wife. A woman I still had feelings for.

"Oh, Delroy," she said, "I'm so scared. I'm so afraid." She was shaking and started to cry. I calmed her and sat down beside her on the sofa and poured her some water.

"Look at what this man did to my little girl," Bill said, pacing my office. "How could I not see this coming? I'm supposed to be able to be a good judge of human character. I'm a cop, for crying out loud. How could I not detect this?" He kept pacing back and forth in my office.

"Sometimes we fail to see the obvious, Bill. Don't blame yourself." I was trying to calm him down. I offered him a drink. He declined but sat down on one of the chairs.

"I really am scared, Delroy. I really am," Connie said as she leaned her head on my shoulder.

"I know you're scared, baby, but you'll be all right. Don't worry about anything. We'll take care of everything." For a moment, I'd almost forgotten where I was. I just wanted to never let her go and comforted her as much as I could. The knock on the door and her father's assurance that it was self-defense reminded me of my surroundings.

"You did what you had to, Connie. You had no choice," her father said.

"Your father is right, Connie," I said as I released her and stood up to let Brian and Gloria in.

I introduced Brian to Bill. Gloria said hello, shook his hand, and I took my position behind my desk. Brian sat in one of the chairs. Gloria sat next to Bill, who sat next to his daughter. Connie shook her head as she slowly drank some more water. Silence engulfed the room. Then Brian spoke first. "Are we using a stenographer, or would you rather I recorded her statement?" He was directing the question to me.

"Use a tape. We can have it transcribed later," I told him.

Brian put the tape recorder on the center table. He looked at me as if for my consent to start the proceedings. I nodded my head.

"Are you OK, Mrs. Minto?" Brian used her married name. She answered affirmatively, and he continued. "Mrs. Minto, there are a few questions I'll have to ask you." He paused before he continued. "I know this is painful for you, both physically and emotionally, but you understand it's necessary." He paused again. "I'm sorry to have to put you through this again." He told her again that it was necessary, and then looked at me and her father.

Bill put his arm around her and told her it was OK. She looked at me, and I gave her a slight nod. She drank some more water, dabbed her eyes without removing her glasses, and then said, "It's OK, ask me anything."

"Thank you," Brain said. "I want you to tell me exactly what happened that night." He pushed the tape recorder closer to her and pressed the Play button. He stated his name and named everyone in the room. The date and time. Then in a low voice, she started to talk.

***

Connie was not expecting her husband that night. She had wanted to spend the evening with her children. As much as the separation was the right thing to do, and it was best for everybody, she was finding it hard living alone with her children. She was explaining to Nicole how different things would be. And what the change would mean. She was not sure how long they'd be able to live in that huge house. As much as she would hate to move, she had accepted the reality that she would have to. The expense was enormous, and even if she went back to work, which eventually she would have to, any salary she'd make would not be enough to pay the mortgage, living expenses, and Nicole's tuition after the divorce became final. Gloria had told her she'd definitely get a settlement, but any settlement would usually include selling the house, although it would not be unusual for a judge to let her keep the house and order her husband to pay the mortgage. It had been known to happen.

Connie was taking the breakup a little harder than she imagined. Not so much for losing Kevin but for being a failure at marriage for a second time in her young life. Surprisingly, Nicole at her age, saw it as a necessity whose time was long overdue. To Connie's joy, it was the first real mother-daughter chat they'd ever had. For Nicole, it was a mature, adult conversation.

Nicole told her mother not to cry over spilled milk, and to move on with her life, and that she should consider going back to school for a bachelor's degree. It was a surprisingly frank discussion with an almost-fourteen-year-old, but it was honest and true. And it moved Connie.

Connie and Nicole were in the living room, laughing like two teenagers at a sleepover. The telephone interrupted their moment of levity, and Nicole dashed to the kitchen, still laughing, to answer it. It was Kevin. Her mood changed, but she was polite. She said hello, and then called her mother to the phone.

Kevin wanted to come over to see the twins. It was early in the evening, a little after five; but Connie thought he should have given her prior notice before he came over. She told him he should give her at least twenty-four hours' notice. That the next day, Saturday, would be more convenient.

"For whom?" he asked.

"For everybody," she said.

That's when he said, "Why do I have to have permission or give prior notice to come to my own home?"

And she told him it was no longer his home.

***

"And what happened after that?" Brian asked her.

"He got angry and asked me if my lover would need permission to come over, and I told him that it was absurd."

"And why would he accuse you of having a lover? Do you have one?" Brian was also taking notes.

"No."

"But why would he think that?"

She looked at me, and I shook my head as if to give her my consent to answer the question. I had told Brian about Connie's past relationship with me, but not about our recent tryst.

"He seemed to think that Delroy and I are lovers."

There was no reaction from anybody when she said it. Not even her father, and least of all Gloria. I could see it in her face. I could very much tell what was going on in that lesbian mind of hers. I couldn't have been more right about what she was thinking. It was as though I was inside her mind.

You men, she was saying. *You're all dogs. You all think with your dicks. The idea of being faithful and being a man is a contradiction.*

Yeah, right, and you lesbians are paragons of monogamy, I shot back.

Then as if to confirm my belief, she looked over at Liseth's picture on the console behind my desk. Then she looked back at me and blamed me for the mess Connie was in. *It's your fuckin' fault, you fuckin' pig.*

I sat there and calmly took her mental abuse. Then I after I'd had enough, I shot back, *You know what your problem is? You haven't been fucked by a real man. You penis-envy, bitch.*

We both looked at each other, and I managed a slight smile. *Yeah, bitch, you know why I'm smiling.*

She remained stoic.

Brian broke up our mental jostling. "Were there any truth to his suspicion? That is, was he right about you and Delroy?"

Brian didn't look at me when he asked the question. Neither did Connie when she answered him.

"No," she said.

Brian was a complex and brilliant man, who could be very passionate but aloof at times. As co-chair of the litigation department, his work had brought him in contact with distraught wives faced with losing lifestyles they'd become accustomed to. And as a litigator, he had seen grown men brought to their knees when faced with a long stay in prison. But despite caring deeply for the people he represented, he tried to keep his emotions in check. He knew Connie was in deep pain. He knew what she was going through. He'd represented wives who had killed their husbands before, and he'd had to ask them some very tough and personal questions. This was when Brian would seem aloof and uncaring. But anybody who knew him intimately would know he was one of the most passionate and caring people who ever existed.

Unlike Gloria, Brian Taylor and I had a lot in common. He was the product of the legal establishment. His parents were both lawyers. He was literally conceived and delivered in a law firm. His mother and father, who were married to other people at the time, were working at the same law firm. Work threw them together, and among other things, they shared long nights, takeout food, and Brian's father's office desk. Nine months later, but three weeks shy of her due date, Brian's mother, who by then was working at another firm, had her water break in the middle of a conference;

and her client, who happened to be a doctor, delivered one of the toughest cross-examiners I have ever seen in action.

Brian was named after his grandfather, an old-time liberal, who was a union leader, and Brian's hero. The old man died when Brian was a young man, but he lived long enough to teach him that the essence of a man was for him to work in every way to further the cause of his fellow man. He also taught him that nothing one achieves in life is achieved on their own. Someone, somewhere, known or unknown, has helped them in achieving their goal. And for that, they owe a debt to their fellow man. Brian and his father lived the old man's philosophy.

Liberalism was not just a thought for Brian and his father. It was a way of life. They practiced what they preached. They would not only donate money to all causes that benefitted liberal ideals and minorities, but they would donate their time building affordable housing for the poor and a vast amount of time representing those who couldn't afford quality representation. He didn't bring in as much business as the average partners, but his pro bono work made the firm look good.

I once asked him why he was so passionate about his causes, and he simple said, "Delroy, us whites will never understand how lucky we are to belong to a privileged class. And the fact that I'm white and living in America makes me doubled lucky."

I suppose it's a white thing, and I'd never understand. But Brian and his wife, who was born into great wealth and privilege, were, if there was such a term, "subway liberals." Despite all their wealth and his wife having gone to private schools, they were sending their two teenage children to public schools.

Brian had few failures in life, in and out of court; but the one thing he had failed miserably at, at forty-three was maintaining his weight. He was a member of one of the top health clubs in the city, not that he ever had time to go, and was constantly on a diet, but that didn't stop him from wanting to lose at least forty or fifty pounds off his five-feet-seven-inch frame. He was not a slave to fashion, but he loved to look good in his clothes.

Brian shifted his huge bulk in the chair, and then leaned forward and poured himself some water and asked Connie if she'd like some. She passed on it. Bill looked a little uneasy. Gloria still had that cold look on her face that somehow only she and I knew why. Connie wasn't that comfortable either. I tried to remain unmoved by everything, but I was sure Gloria could tell that deep down I was hurting for Connie. I couldn't help it. Despite who Kevin was, she had killed a man. A life was taken, and even if she walked on this, she would have to live with it for the rest of her life. And someday she would have to explain it to her sons, and it wouldn't be easy.

"Are you sure you don't want some more water?" he said. We could take a break if you'd like."

"It's OK," Connie replied. And her father gently rubbed her back.

"You sure you want to go on, baby?" her father asked.

"I'm sure, Dad. We might as well get it over with."

"Mrs. Minto, before I ask you about what happened last Friday night, I'd like to just ask one more question about the relationship between you and Delroy. If you would like for him to leave the room, I'll understand."

She looked at me and then at her father. "Only if he wants to." Then she looked in my direction again, and the dark glasses became transparent. Her eyes revealed her pain. Then for some reason, she asked her father if it was all right.

"The truth is what we are her to get at," he responded.

"Delroy!" Brian said.

"I'm OK. You can go on." I wanted to be there because I wanted to hear everything.

"OK, then, I'd like you to tell me," Brian said, "have you and Delroy been having an affair? Bear in mind, this is something the prosecutor will want to know. And when they ask you, they'll make it look ugly. They will want the jury to, to put it mildly, hate you."

"No, we were not having an affair, but we slept together once. And only once," she said it without emotion. She looked over at me when she said it.

"How and when did this happen?"

"Kevin and I had been having problems for a long time. I had been putting up with his infidelities for a long time. I should have said something about it sooner, but I didn't. Later, I found out the reason why I didn't was because I didn't love him. When I started saying something about it, he became abusive, especially when he was drunk. Then he started accusing me of still being in love with Delroy." She paused and asked for some water. Gloria filled her glass. She drank half of it. There was a look of anger on her father's face, and I was sure it was not because she was still in love with me. It was because he didn't know of the abuses.

"Go on," Brian said.

"I must admit I never stopped loving Delroy, but I had not seen him since I got married. I wanted to, but I had two young sons, and I wanted to give my marriage a chance. I was divorced once, and I didn't want to fail again. Then the abuses continued, and I stopped having sex with him. I just didn't feel anything for him. I only called Delroy because I knew I could rely on him. I knew he'd always be my friend. I couldn't talk to anybody else about what I was feeling, and I knew he wouldn't be judgmental."

She looked over at me again, and I didn't have to say or do anything for her to know that she was right. She drank some more water. And then she went on.

"I must admit that when I went to see Delroy, I also wanted more than a friend to talk to. I also wanted us to make love. I hadn't had sex for a long time, and I wanted to make love to someone I loved. But I didn't realize how much he'd changed. He was in love with someone else." With her glasses still on, she wiped her eyes. "I tried to seduce him, but he resisted. He gave me comfort, but we didn't have sex."

Gloria looked at me. She and I were in our own element. She and I were telepathically communicating, and she was shocked.

Yes, bitch, there is some honor in some of us men, I said, well pleased.

Brian asked her how many times we saw each other before we slept together, and she told him about the incident at the Hilton. Connie had told Gloria a lot of things in the short time they knew each other, but Gloria was hearing some of this for the first time, and she was not pleased.

Brian tried to remain indifferent to what he was hearing. He was more concerned that this kind of information could be damaging in the prosecutor's hand.

"So what happened last Friday night?" he asked.

***

Kevin had come over. He rang the doorbell, and Connie had refused to answer it. Then he started to pound on the door. She heard keys shuffling in the lock, but she had changed the locks right after he moved out. He threatened to break the windows if she didn't let him in. He promised to leave if he'd only get to see the twins, and that he'd call next time. She let him in.

He went upstairs to the twins' room. He was up there for about ten minutes, and then he came down angry about some silly scratch on Francis's face that was self-inflicted. He started to accuse Connie of not only sleeping with every man in Dobbs Ferry, including the poor sixteen-year-old-boy who flirted with her at the supermarket, but also of being an unfit mother. That was when she told him he was being ridiculous, and asked him to leave, or she would call the police.

He refused to leave, and she picked up the phone, and from the corner of her eye, she could see him swinging at her. The blow landed on the right side of her head, knocking the phone out of her hand. For the first time in her life, she was not afraid of anybody. She faced him and was ready to defend herself. A stupid move on her part. She was no match for him. He outweighed her. And outmatched her.

He hit her again in the middle of the kitchen. The full force of his fist landed flush on her mouth. He hit her so hard a tooth fell out, and she struck her head against the kitchen counter as she went down. She struggled to pull herself up, holding on to the counter for support. She barely made it to her feet before he hit her again. The blow landed her against the counter again, but she didn't go down this time. Her face was bloodied. Blood was coming out of her mouth from the missing tooth, and a gash opened under her right eye, but before he could raise his hand again, she grabbed one of the knives from the seven-piece Ginsu set, and with one thrust, plunged the carver deep into his chest.

Kevin grabbed his chest with the knife sticking out of it and spun around, facing Nicole, who had come downstairs after hearing the fight. Kevin staggered toward Nicole, and gasping for breath, he fell forward in her arms, and they both tumbled to the ground. Him on top of her.

I was sure Connie's father, an old pro, had heard what we were all hearing. He would not have been a good detective if he had not insisted on her telling him first. I was sure when his friend on the Dobbs Ferry police department called him he must have told him to tell her not to talk to anybody until he arrived. And that was exactly what happened. A cop will always be a cop. The fact that he had long been retired would not have obviated his need to act like one. He would not have changed her version of what happened. That is, he was not going to tell her, "Here is what you should tell them." But I was sure he would have told her, "Here is what you shouldn't tell them."

The fact that her father was fighting back tears was not because he was shocked at hearing the story for the first time, but because it was his little girl who was telling it. Bill wiped his eyes with his handkerchief and then squeezed Connie's shoulder. She removed her sunglasses for the first time and revealed bloodshot, tired eyes, and the gash under her right eye was longer than I'd imagined. Her eyes were swollen, not from being hit in them but from all the crying and lack of sleep. The swollen eyes, the lack of makeup, and her crusty lips made her look older than her age.

Gloria was stoic but obviously moved by Connie's story. I could tell she was. She might be able to keep her emotions in check, but she didn't fool me for a minute. She was falling apart inside. And I was sure she had a crush on Connie. The first time she was alone, by herself, she would break down and cry.

I was sure Brian was thinking what I was thinking: self-defense. There was no case there. But would the DA see it that way?

The meeting lasted a little over ninety minutes. I walked Connie and her father to the elevator. Bill asked me if I'd be in court on Monday. I told him I didn't have to, but that Brian and Gloria would be there. He was familiar with the court system, so I didn't have to tell him that all the DA would do on Monday was present his evidence and convince the judge that there was enough evidence to go to trial. We would, of course, say otherwise. The judge would then send the case to a grand jury, who would look at the evidence and then decide.

In any case, I'd be spending the greater part, if not all, of the next week with Liseth. I also didn't think it was the right time to tell Connie I was going to propose to Liseth.

***

"Holy shit, it's a quarter after two," I said as I walked back to my office. One of the secretaries sitting across from my office said, "The day is young."

I shot back, "For you it is." And then I closed the door. I stood behind my desk and looked out the window, and I knew I'd never make it to New Haven in time, even if I'd leave then. Who knew what train I'd catch and when I would get there.

I rang Liseth's cell phone and got her on the first ring. I started to apologize for not leaving the office yet. She told me she had called my office earlier to tell me she was coming in with a group of girls that were planning on spending their fall break in the city, and that my secretary told her I was in a very important meeting and shouldn't be disturbed.

"She told me if it was very important, she'd interrupt you, and I told her it was all right, I'd call you back. I called your mother and told her that I'd be stopping by with some friends from school. They'll be taking the train into the city."

"Where are you now?"

"I am actually not far from your parents' house."

"We're in Rye," a female voice echoed in the background.

"We're in Rye," Liseth said.

"Tell you what," I said, "you and your friends go by the house, relax a little, have something to eat. Mom won't be there. Aunt B should. I'll try to get out of here as quick as I can. I'll see you later."

"How was the meeting with Connie?"

"I'll talk to you about it later. I love you."

"I love you too."

I called my mother at her office. She was in a meeting but took my call. There was never a time in my life when my mother was ever too busy to talk to me. No matter what the circumstances, even if she had to talk to me for only a couple of seconds, she always had time for me. I would always love her for that. Dad was the same. If I could be half the parent to any child or children I might have, I'd be fortunate. I told Mom that Liseth would be stopping by the house with some friends from school, even though she already knew. Then I called Aunt B and told her to expect them. She too already knew. Then afterward I called Ebony and told her how pretty the ring was.

"Are you nervous?" Ebony asked.

"About what?"

"You know. Proposing. Are you?"

"No. Should I be?"

"Some people would be, especially after being a bachelor for so long."

"I suppose so, but I'm not."

"Good. I can't wait to see the ring."

"You'll see it this weekend."

"You'll be a great husband, and someday a terrific father."

"Thank you."

"Oh, I almost forgot. Liseth called me, but I didn't give anything away. And I think she has a surprise for you too."

"Yes, she told me that, but wouldn't tell me what."

"And I won't tell you either. Tell her to bring her friends by the house before they go back to school. I wish I could be there to see the look on her face when you give her the ring. Talk to you later."

***

I was getting ready to leave when there was a knock on my office door. "Come in," I said. It was Brian. "Come in, Brian." I beckoned him. He sat on the sofa and put his feet on top of the *New York Times* that was on the center table. "What do you think?" I said, referring to Connie's case, of course.

"It's a clear-cut self-defense. In my opinion."

"I agree with you." I put some files in my briefcase as I spoke to him. Then I removed them. They were about four files. He looked at me, sort of strangely.

"Are you OK?" he said, still looking at me with that puzzled look on his face.

"Yeah, I'm OK. Why?"

"Nothing in particular, except." And he stopped. And I could tell there was something bothering him. But I had to be careful. This was a brilliant lawyer I was dealing with. I was not about to say anything that might be a leading question.

"Except what?" That's neutral enough.

"Well, let me put it this way: what was going on between you and Gloria?"

"What are you talking about?" The very fact that he asked the question was enough to tell me he read what was going on between us.

"The two of you were scratching at each other's face all throughout the meeting. The scars are showing. What was that all about?"

And we thought we were being discreet.

"Hey, I'm a good litigator," he said, clasping his hands behind his head and stretching and yawning, "because I can read people's body language, and you and Gloria were at each other's throat."

"It's nothing. As a matter of fact, I hope it's something. This way, she'll be occupied with someone else."

"What are you talking about?"

"I'll tell you someday, but not today." To tell him that I hoped Gloria and Connie would become lovers, so she would stay away from me and Liseth would be tacky, to say the least. But what difference would it have made to me?

He looked at me with probing eyes. And I felt the need to drop the subject. And whether he sensed it or not, he said, "I just want you to know one thing: she is a very good lawyer."

I told him I knew and left it at that.

"What's with the file shuffling?"

"I need you to do me a favor for next week," I said.

"OK."

"As you know, Liseth is coming home today from Yale, and she'll be home for the next week."

"I know, and you want to spend some time with her. That's OK. You want me to cover a case for you? That's OK too."

"Well, you're right about everything."

"But don't tell me there is more?" An inquisitive expression crossed his face.

"Well, there is." I walked over to the door and turned the lock. He didn't say anything. I walked back over to my briefcase and took out the box with the ring and showed him the content. His eyes popped out of his head like some twelve-year-old seeing some pussy for the first time. I answered the question that he was too stunned to ask. "Yes, it's what you think it is. And I'm popping the question this weekend."

He walked over to my minibar, took out the bottle of brandy, and poured some into two glasses. "This calls for a drink, wouldn't you say?"

"If you're buying," I said. And we knocked glasses.

"Can't do the bachelor thing anymore, eh? Well, it's about fuckin' time, you old cradle robber. Good luck. You know Elizabeth and I are very happy for the both of you? When is the wedding?"

"Sometime next summer. I'll let Liseth handle that."

"Now I'll have to go get a stupid tux." We both laughed.

"Do me a favor," I said.

"Another one?"

"Keep this in your house, until I make the announcement. Will you?"

"You got it."

Chapter 13

◦•——◦❧♥❧◦——•◦

I must have looked at the ring more than a dozen times before I got to my parents' house, and that was all before I left my office. Each time, the thought of spending over $50,000 on a ring made me feel lucky to be getting married to a girl like Liseth. No other girl in the world would be worth that kind of extravagance. She might have been getting a very expensive ring, but I was getting something priceless: her love and affection.

I took a car service to my parents' house. To avoid the Friday evening traffic, I asked the driver to go through Harlem. We went through Central Park, before it was closed for the weekend, and up Seventh Avenue. At Yankee Stadium, we caught the FDR Drive to the Cross County Parkway, and made it to my parents' house before four thirty.

Neither Mom nor Dad was home. Liseth's jeep was in the driveway, and I could see Aunt B moving around the kitchen as I got closer. A delivery van drove up the driveway as I pulled on the screen door to the kitchen. It was from the liquor store up in New Rochelle. The young man, a young Hispanic, asked me if this was the Bradshaw residence. I told him it was and signed for the delivery. He asked where to put the boxes. Aunt B came out and told him to bring them into the kitchen. A case of champagne.

Half a case of white wine, half a case of red, and four bottles of brandies. Not unusual for my parents. They always keep a stocked bar.

In the kitchen, turkey was being thawed out on the counter. Had to be at least eighteen or twenty pounds. There were also several bags of groceries waiting to be put away. And then there was the cheesecake. My favorite. Now with all that air of festivities, I didn't have to think too hard about the reason for all that liquor, turkey, and groceries. My parents were killing the fatted calf for my engagement announcement.

But this was Friday. When was this celebration supposed to take place? I was making my announcement tonight, I said to myself. Then it dawned on me: I'd make the announcement tonight, and my parents would invite Liseth's family over on Saturday. Made sense. On the counter were also some fried fish and chicken that Aunt B had prepared earlier. I nibbled on a piece of fish and asked Aunt B how she was; and just to see if she would tell me, I asked her why the air of festivity. But she just grinned from ear to ear. She couldn't contain herself. I had to ask her if she'd given Liseth any hint. She assured me she didn't. I thanked her.

Liseth and her friends were in the living room. She was standing at the window talking on the phone with her mother. She was looking out the window. Her friends were on the sofa watching TV. She turned around as I entered the room. She looked thinner, or was it because I hadn't seen her for so long? Her hair was definitely longer. And she was looking just as radiant and sexy as the first night I met her at Ebony's house. Except for the torn jeans she had on that night, there she was, standing in my mother's living room. In the room that I grew up in, in faded blue jeans and a white T-shirt. And just like the first night I met her and I knew right then I wanted her to be my woman. As I walked over to the window, I knew I wanted, without a doubt, to marry her.

"I'm talking to my mom," she said. She waved her hand for me to come closer to her. She put her left arm around my waist. And I put my right arm around her neck. We stood like that: she squeezing my midsection and me rubbing her shoulder, until she finished talking to her mother. She told Esmeralda that we would stop by on our way home.

"Hi, baby," she said when she hung up the phone. "God, I miss you."

"I miss you too," I said. And we kissed—a long passionate kiss, with her friends looking but trying not to make it obvious.

Trying not to make a spectacle of ourselves, we unclenched, and Liseth introduced me to her friends.

"Toni, Carla, Claire, this is Delroy." Our arms were still around each other. Toni was closest to us. She was drinking beer. She stepped forward and introduced herself. She was a light-skinned black girl, and I could tell, from the texture of her hair that one of her parents was white. Probably her mother. She was thin with curves, and had adequate chest to go with it. And despite having supermodel written all over her, I found out later that she loved drinking beer from the bottle, smoking weed, shooting pool, and had a proclivity for telling dirty jokes.

"So you're Delroy," she said, extending her hand. "I've heard so much about you." Her hand was as soft as her appearance. And her smile was just as soft and engaging. She was the kind of girl any man would love, but underneath that engaging smile and behind those supermodel looks and soft hands was an extremely smart girl who had breezed through UCLA in three years, gotten an MBA from Wharton, and was in her second year at Yale Law School, and she wasn't even twenty-five. What the hell did this girl do in her spare time? I know, drink beer from the bottle, smoke weed, shoot pool, and tell dirty jokes.

"I'm pleased to meet you," I said.

Then Liseth introduced me to Carla—a plump, bookish blond Puerto Rican who, I would later learn, could read a book and watch TV at the same time, and digest the information enough to regurgitate them if asked. She had an encyclopedic mind and a photographic memory, and though she was pretty underneath that baby fat, at twenty-three, she was still a virgin. She struck me as a future bureaucrat. Some government department was just waiting for her to get out of law school for her to head it up.

Claire was different from the others. She was—well, let me put it this way: Claire thought she was "all that." And I had to be honest, from a man's point of view, she was. She was not only extremely beautiful, and sexy, but she was street-smart, and from Detroit with a troubled past. Toni was from Los Angeles, and Carla was from Puerto Rico. She was a real Puerto Rican, not a Nueva Rican like Liseth. She grew up and was educated on the island. And although she had relatives living in New York and had visited there on more than one occasion, she had never lived there.

Claire had gone to college to avoid going to jail, and excelled. With an arrogance and cockiness about her, she felt that if some of the lawyers who she'd encountered during her stint as a juvenile delinquent could get through law school, she could do it sleepwalking. She was accepted to Yale. The only school she'd applied to.

Claire jumped up from the sofa and greeted me with a friendly embrace. "At last I finally get to meet you," she said. Then she walked around me, as if to inspect me, and then said, "You were right, Liseth. He's fine. I can see why you missed him so much. I would too. He looks younger than his age, and mad cool."

Two things I found out about Claire on our first meeting: she was not subtle, and she knew how to make a man blush. They all laughed out loud, except for Carla. She just smiled. Then Claire started with a barrage of questions. What kind of law did I practice? What did I like most? Was it exciting trying a case before a jury? Did my firm have an entertainment practice? What was it like growing up in a family of lawyers? And at what age did I know I wanted to be a lawyer? And she just went on and on and on. Then she apologized for going on like that, but I understood. She was a young white girl who had never been out of Detroit until she went to Yale. She was also the first in her family who had ever finished high school, let alone college. She was fascinated by New York and everything about it.

The three girls were supposed to meet up with some other girls and guys from school and do New York. They were supposed to stay at a hotel on the West Side and then meet up back with Liseth the next Saturday and drive back up to New Haven. For what I had planned for Liseth, their plans would be altered.

"You said you had a surprise for me," I said. "Where is it? You know, once you told me, I'm never gonna stop thinking about it until I get it."

"I know. You're a kid when it comes to that, but you'll have to wait." She took me by the hand and led me into the kitchen. She took a piece of chicken from the platter. I took a beer from the fridge and asked her if she wanted one. She said no, but asked me to get her a soda.

"Aren't you gonna ask me what my surprise for you is?" I said as we sat in the kitchen.

"No. Because if I insist, you'd only insist on knowing what I have for you. So we both can wait. When are your parents coming home?"

"What time did Mom and Dad said they'd be home?" I asked Aunt B.

"You ma should be here anytime soon. You fathda 'bout six. Six thirty." Aunt B busied herself about the kitchen as she talked.

"Aunt B looks as if she's preparing for a party this weekend. Are your parents having people over?"

"Not that I know of."

"They sure look like they're expecting people."

"You know Mom and Dad—they know a lot of important people. Could be an important client."

Toni came into the kitchen, and Mom's car came up the driveway. Toni asked if she could have another beer. I pointed her to the fridge. She twisted the cap off the bottle and whispered something in Liseth's ear. Liseth told her my mom had just driven up. And I knew she was asking about them smoking some weed.

Mom walked into the kitchen and didn't even put her things down before she and Liseth were hugging each other and telling each other how much they missed each other. They were actually crying. They were like mother and daughter. This went on long enough to draw the attention of Claire and Carla. I was in the kitchen with six women, and two were in a tight embrace crying, and Aunt B was looking on, on the verge of letting loose. I knew Mom loved Liseth and thought a great deal about her, but it never accrued to me she'd miss her that much. The three girls were standing there looking puzzled, wondering why my mother was so excited to see my girlfriend.

"I miss you," Mom said. "How are you? How was school?"

"She looks like she lost weight," Aunt B said.

Mom pulled herself away long enough to look for herself. "Maybe about five pounds," she said.

"Lots of studying. Not eating right. Missing the people I love. It's hard work, you know."

"I know, but this is what you were born to do."

Claire, who was standing closest to me, remarked in a low voice, "You sure this is not your sister?" I laughed.

"This weekend alone will put that five pounds back on," Aunt B said, and Liseth smiled.

"Enid, I'd like you to meet some friends I met at school." And she introduced her friends to Mom.

"This is a beautiful house you have here, Mrs. Bradshaw," Toni said. "Great architecture. I'd say this was built somewhere in the twenties, or thirties. Some Wall Street robber baron built it, I'm sure."

"It was built earlier. And was built by one of those." Mom didn't elaborate. "Are you into architecture?"

"In a way. I just love older houses. I'd love to someday, when I get married, buy an old house and renovate it. They have more character."

Mom agreed with her. Then she was introduced to the others. As usual, Carla said very little. Claire asked a million questions about Mom's years as an attorney, and Toni asked if she could see the rest of the house. Mom asked them what time they were being picked up, and if they'd like to stay for supper. Nobody was picking them up. Liseth was supposed to drive them into the city, where they would meet up with the rest of the group. Mom asked them to stay awhile, and that Liseth and I would take them into the city. They agreed.

It was close to seven when Dad got home. He'd called to tell Mom he'd be a little late. My parents were like that—no matter how slight it might be, even if it was five or ten minutes, they'd call to say they'd be late. Dad also spoke to Liseth when he called. He also told Mom to go ahead and have supper without him, since she had company. He'd have drinks with us when he got home.

Fridays, when we didn't eat out, were always the same at home. Supper was always light. Usually salads. Aunt B, in addition to the fried fish and chicken, had made some seafood and pasta salad. We had that with some white wine and Italian bread. Dad got home before we were finished. He nibbled a little and joined us for drinks.

Another one of Dad's Friday traditions was to bring my mother flowers. That Friday, along with his customary two dozen roses, were a dozen roses for Liseth and a new hat for Aunt B. For church.

"Who are the other gifts for?" I asked him.

"Certainly not for you," he said.

"Just asking. Just asking. Considering that I'm your only son, not to mention your only child, I just thought you'd buy me something. You know, to show your love."

He walked over to Liseth with the bouquet in one hand and arms open. "Come here," he said. "Give the old man a big hug."

"Hey, leave my woman alone."

"You can hug mine. I won't mind."

"You think I won't." And I hugged Mom. "I'll even kiss her too," I said.

The moment of levity and family closeness impressed Liseth's friends.

"My father is only behaving like this because you're all here," I said to the girls. "Normally, we would be throwing things at each other, and the police would be banging on the door."

"I don't believe that for a minute," Claire said. "You guys look too happy. Now in my family, that'd be a different story. My father, that was when he was sober enough, would—"

Carla cut her off. "All right, Claire, we have heard that story before. I'm sure Delroy and his family are not interested." Claire clammed up and gave her a dirty look.

Liseth put the roses on the side table, and then she and Dad sat down. Mom sat on the other side of her, and Claire sat in Dad's favorite chair. He was in too good a mood to notice or mind. Carla sat in one of the side chairs. I snuck a peek in one of Dad's shopping bags. A Barney's bag. Which meant ties. There was another bag with a gift already wrapped. It was about twenty by fifteen. I wondered what it could have been. For the size, it could have been anything, but it was sort of heavy. So it wasn't clothes. A card was in the bag. Liseth's name was on the envelope.

Aunt B had joined us in the living room. All of us sat around talking. For some strange reason, in all our jubilation, Liseth, although it was obvious she was having a great time, wasn't drinking any alcohol. Since she came home, she hadn't touched a thing. No beer. No wine. Nada. Usually, she'd put away at least four bottles of beer already. She wasn't drinking, but she sure was eating enough to make up for it. If she'd been eating like that, how could she explain the obvious weight loss? The rest of the girls were also making up for her abstinence. Even introverted Carla had more than one glass of wine. The second she nursed. If I was certain Liseth wasn't having a good time, I'd ask her why she wasn't drinking. But I let it go.

The phone rang, and Aunt B answered it. "It's for you," she said to me. It was Liseth's mom.

"Hi, Delroy," Esmeralda said. "Is it official?"

"Not yet," I said.

"When?"

"Soon."

"Can't talk, eh?"

"Right."

"Is she in front of you?"

"Sort of, but we'll call you."

"You guys are stopping by tonight before you go home, aren't you? If you're not, let me know."

"We will. I promise."

"Did your mother tell you she's having us for dinner on Sunday?"

"That's great. I'll talk to you later."

"Who was that?" Liseth asked when I got off the phone.

"A friend," I answered, unconvincingly but without inviting any question.

When I told my parents that I was planning on proposing to Liseth, Mom told me to ask her mother for permission. Mom said it would be the right thing to do. And that it would show respect for her mother. Mom said she was sure Esmeralda would not be adverse to us getting married, but that the proper thing to do was to seek her permission. She'd feel snubbed if I didn't ask her, Mom said, and that if she was in Esmeralda's position, she feel that way. So I stopped by the next evening after I told my parents and formally asked Esmeralda for her daughter's hand in marriage. And she said yes without hesitation.

It was after nine o'clock, and I didn't want to keep Liseth's mother waiting all night. I asked Dad to come into the kitchen with me. This was a man thing. I needed a man's advice.

"What do you think, Dad?" I was nervous. "Should I just go back in there and pop the question, without a speech?"

"Well, you certainly have to go back in there, for one thing," he said. "And on the other hand, you already have the ring, so you can't change your mind."

I wasn't thinking of changing my mind, but, "What if she says no in front of all her friends?"

"She won't say no."

"How do you know that?"

"Because she loves you. And why would you think she would say no, anyway?"

Mom and I had agreed we wouldn't tell Dad about my Liseth-Connie problem. To tell him would mean we might have to discuss his past indiscretion. And that would be the last thing we would want to discuss.

"I know she loves me, but you know women. This is her first time away from home, meeting new friends, and experiencing new things—maybe she's not ready to get married. She's only twenty-three and just started law school."

"I can't believe it. You're scared, are you?"

"Damn right I am. Weren't you?"

"It was so long ago, I don't remember."

I peeked into the living room. "Look at her sitting there having a good time with Mom, Aunt B, and her friends. It's not like she's drunk, so I could catch her under the influence. Come to think of it, why isn't she drinking like everybody else? Did you know she haven't had a drink since she got home? Why?"

"Maybe she's pregnant. How the hell would I know? Delroy, go in there and propose to that woman now."

I took the ring out of my pocket and looked at it. I showed it to Dad, and he held it under the light. Claire walked in, and it was too late for us to hide the ring. The sight of it almost blinded her. I'd only known her for less than six hours, but I was sure it was the first time in her life she'd ever been speechless. She just stood there and looked at it, with utter amazement. There was no need to tell her what it was.

"Claire," I said, pulling her by the arm, "I need your cooperation on this."

She put her right hand over her heart and asked, "Can I just touch it? Please," she whispered.

I put the box in her hand, and she put her hand over her mouth, and I hoped it was to keep from screaming. But she said nothing, except—in a low voice, almost a whisper—"It's beautiful."

I gently took the box from her hand and asked her to go back out and act as if nothing had happened. Mom came in as Claire was going out and wanted to know what was keeping us in there. With Claire back in the living room, Dad told her, "Your son is getting cold feet."

"So now it's my son, huh!" she said.

"When he regains his courage, he'll be mine again," he said.

"All right, Dad," I said as I took a beer from the fridge.

"You might need something stronger," he said and poured me a brandy.

"I'm going to go in there and propose to the most beautiful woman in the world, next to you," I said and kissed Mom on the cheek.

"That's my boy," Dad said. An old-time slap on the back followed as he went into the living room.

"Delroy," Mom said as I headed out the door, "let me talk to you for a minute."

I leaned against the kitchen counter. "What's the matter?"

She came over to me. "You're ambivalent, aren't you?"

"Not really."

"But—"

Before I could finish answering, she said, "But you're worried she might say no. You're worried that after what happened between you and Connie, she might not have gotten over it enough to say yes to your proposal? That's what you're worried about, isn't it?"

"Well, sort of. You know what happened the last time I asked someone to marry me?"

"I think we're dealing with two different situations. Not to mention two different people. I wouldn't compare—"

Liseth interrupted the rest of her sentence, but I knew she was going to tell me not to compare the two situations or people. And I should have, but—

"What are you doing in here so long?" Liseth asked. Curiosity all over her face.

"We were just coming out," I said.

"Come here," she said and held on to the back of my pant waist. I turned around and faced her. Mom went out and left us alone. "Are you keeping secrets from me?" She said it playfully, but it kind of caught me off guard.

She sensed the defensive tone in my answer. "What makes you think I am keeping secrets from you?"

"I'm just kidding. Relax." She put her arms around my neck and pulled me close to her. She kissed me, and I kissed her back.

"Do you still love me?"

"What a silly question. Of course, I still love you. I've always loved you, and always will. I'm madly in love with you." She kissed me again. "I'm crazy about, don't you know that?"

"I love you too, with all my heart, and I never meant to hurt you. I want you to know that. You mean so much to me. You know, don't you?"

"And you mean a lot to me too." She wiped the lipstick from my mouth.

"Liseth, I just want you to know that I'm very sorry, and I—"

She cupped her hand over my mouth and told me not to say any more. "Let's not talk anymore about the past. Let's leave it where it belongs. In the past. Just know one thing: that I love you very much."

She had just given me the answer I wanted, and the courage I needed. "How come you haven't drunk even a beer since you got home?"

She laughed and said, "I'll tell you about it later."

"And when am I going to get that surprise you have for me?"

"I'll tell you about that later too. How about the surprise you have for me?"

"Let's go outside, and I'll give it to you."

"In the living room? In front of all those people?" She put her hand down the front of my pants and got a handful of my erect dick. It swelled even bigger. She nibbled on my ear and whispered, "I miss feeling this in the back of my throat." She squeezed it as she bit my ear.

"That's not the sort of surprise I had in mind."

"Oh!" she said.

"I suggest we go out into the living room before they think we're fucking in here."

"Maybe you should walk behind me when we go out. If you know what I mean." We laughed and kissed again.

Everybody was waiting for us to return to the living room, as if they were waiting for a curtain to go up on a play. We entered arm in arm. I asked Liseth to sit down. She took a seat between my parents. Toni said something, like she thought we forgot them and about how late it was. I was sure she said it in jest, but Claire told her to shut up and asked her if what she had to do was more important than hanging out with my parents. Toni was getting an

236

attitude. Not because Liseth and I stayed in the kitchen too long, or because they were there that late, but from Claire talking to her the way she did. Mom told them they were welcome to stay the night if they wanted to. Carla apologized for their behavior and told Mom that she was having a great time. Mom thanked her and said her offer still stood.

Breaking into their conversation, I said, "There is something I'd like to say."

Dad knocked his ring on his glass, and everyone was silent. "I think my son has something he'd like to say."

"Thank you, Dad."

"You're welcome. But you'll make it brief, won't you?"

"I'll ignore that for now."

"Let the boy talk," Aunt B said.

"Thanks, Aunt B." I looked at Dad, as if to ask him if I may continue. He raised his glass in assent.

"First, I'd like to say to my mother and father, two of the greatest people I'm positive I'll ever know. If I were without parents and was looking for a mother and a father, you would be the ones I'd choose. No one can ask for better parents. You have loved me, respected me, nurtured me, spoiled me, and, when it was necessary, disciplined me. Though some people, I'm sure, would question your concept of discipline. I suppose some people could also interpret your idea of love was to not have another child, so that you wouldn't have to share your love for me. If that was your intention, I can only say, what an extreme way of showing your love for me. In many ways, I wish I had a brother or sister, and I'm sure you both wish you had a daughter, which explains the reason you guys are so crazy about Liseth. And who wouldn't be? Just look at her."

My parents both put an arm around Liseth, and she looked on with subdued delight.

"Mom, Dad, I can't imagine life without you. I can't imagine being far from you. You have taught me everything I know. Dad, you have taught me how to dress. How to deal with adversaries. How to handle and face the real world. And most of all, how to be me. You taught me independence and individuality. Thanks, Dad."

Dad was about to stand up—no doubt to take a bow, but Mom told him to sit down. We all laughed.

"Mom, you have taught me sensitivity. You taught me how to handle my emotions. Mom, you and I were so close, and we still are. When I was younger, someone once remarked that studies showed that any boy, particularly an only child, that is that close to his mother ran the risk of being effeminate. I wonder what studies they were following?"

Everyone laughed.

"Some of you would be amazed, or even turn blue, if you knew some of the things my mom and I talked about."

Mom cleared her throat loudly.

"We won't get into that now. I'll save it for my book."

"He was a quiet boy, until he went to school in England for a year. Then he came home with the proclivity to make long speeches. It's all your fault, Lloyd," Mom said, looking at Dad. "You were the one who insisted on sending him to Oxford." Dad stood up and took a bow. The room roared with laughter.

"Sit down, Dad. This is my parade. But seriously, folks, unlike most guys, my mother taught me everything I know about girls. She taught me how to appreciate them. How to love them. How to please them."

"Wow," Claire said.

"Not the way you're thinking, Claire."

Claire put her hands over her face and bowed her head, resting it on her knees.

"But you were close. Just kidding," I said to the sound of more laughter. "But . . . but I just want to say one last thing: my mother taught me the most important thing of all, and that is what it takes to be a real man. Thank you, Mom. Thank you, Dad. I would also like to say a special thank-you to a wonderful lady. One who has played a great role in helping this family in every way. A lady who came into our home and treated me like her own, and who have made Liseth feel at home when she is here. Thank you, Aunt B. We love you."

Mom and Dad joined in expressing their sentiments for Aunt B. And we all raised our drinks and shouted, "To Aunt B."

"I'm sure you're all wondering why I'm standing here heaping deserved praises on my parents and Aunt B. Well, there is a reason for it. This won't take long." I looked over at Liseth, and we smiled at each other. "This is really about me and Liseth," I said.

Liseth straightened up in her seat and smiled at me again. We looked at each other, and I continued speaking without taking my eyes off her.

"Liseth," I said. Our eyes locked, and our gazes intensified. "I would like to say that since I've met you, you've brought me and this family nothing but joy."

She mouthed the words *thank you* and blew me a kiss.

"I'm glad you and my parents love each other. Which brings me to the reason for standing here while you're all sitting, and I'm a nervous wreck."

At that point, I was sure everybody had figured out what was coming next. If they didn't, the fact that I was by now on one knee in front of Liseth was a dead giveaway.

"Liseth, my love, my joy, my friend and soul mate, I'm not good at making speeches."

"No," Dad echoed.

OK, so I've known to give a speech or two."

"Or three, or four," he said, laughing.

"And most of the time, I managed to get through them uninterrupted."

"OK, OK," he said, putting his index finger to his lips.

"Thank you. As I was saying," I continued, "Liseth, I have taken the liberty of asking your mother's permission, like most gentlemen would, for your hand in marriage, and she has given us her blessings, and now I'm on one knee in front of you asking you, will you marry me?"

The box with the ring was already in my hand, and when I opened it, the whole room gasped.

"Oh my God," Toni said.

Carla said something in Spanish I didn't understand, but I could tell she was excited. Which was the first time all evening she'd shown any sort of emotion, or demonstrated any inkling that she could have fun.

"Thank you, Jesus," Aunt B said. She sounded surprised, even though she knew I'd be popping the question. Mom and Dad and Claire—of all people, if you could believe it—were silent. Dad got up and went into the kitchen.

I removed the ring from the box and started to put it on Liseth's finger before she could say yes. It slid on easily and fit as if the jeweler had taken her finger size. She kept saying yes over and over again. She was on her knees with me, and we were kissing. And she was crying, and her tears were in my mouth. And then she stood up, and I remained on my knees. And everybody was looking at the ring. Dad returned to the room with a bottle of champagne and glasses for all of us. The expression on his face understated his excitement. "I think you can get off your knees now, Delroy."

"So this was the surprise you had for me?" Liseth said. And before I could answer her, she said, "It's worth the wait."

Dad popped the bottle of champagne and poured a drink for everyone, including Liseth. Then he knocked his ring against the bottle and asked everyone for their attention. He asked us to pick up our glasses. We all did, including Liseth. Then he started to talk. He started by telling us how proud he and Mom were of me. And how he'd like to set the record straight—that Mom didn't deserve all the praises for teaching me everything I knew about girls. She may have taught me some things, but not everything. He said he taught me how to recognize, like all good fathers did, a good woman when I saw one. And that he was happy and overjoyed that his teachings had born fruit in my recognition of Liseth.

Dad was beaming with pride when he talked about me and Liseth, and how he'd waited for the day when I'd get married, and that even if it was at my age, he couldn't wait to be a grandfather. "Let's drink to the happy couple," he said and raised his glass. We all raised our glasses, including Liseth. And we all drank our champagne, except Liseth.

240

"Is everything all right?" Mom asked Liseth.

"Oh yes," Liseth answered with emphasized enthusiasm that erased any doubt. "Oh yes, indeed."

"You're glowing like—what's that word Aunt B would use?"

"Fireflies in a jar," Aunt B chimed in.

"Thank you, Aunt B. So if you're glowing like fireflies in a jar, why aren't you drinking your champagne?"

Liseth looked over at me, and her eyes sparkled brighter than the diamonds on her finger. She put her glass down and came closer to me. "I have something I'd like to say. I won't give a long speech like Delroy, or any speech for that matter. I just want to say—"

"Oh my God, you're pregnant," Mom interrupted with unbridled glee.

Tears cascading down her cheeks, and visibly shaking, she said, "Yes, I am." She didn't just say it. It busted out of her mouth and rolled off her tongue, like a projectile coming at us. I got the feeling she couldn't wait to tell the world. I had a feeling she'd kept this to herself ever since she'd found out, and telling us was a heavy load unburdened.

"So that was why you were throwing up every morning?" said Toni. "And you said it was because you weren't getting enough sleep and not eating well."

"Shit, I knew she was knocked up all along. That crap about not enough sleep and not eating well didn't fool me," Claire said, smiling and refilling her glass.

"And I'm sure you're talking from experience," said Toni. Her sarcasm was evident. It erased the smile from the childless Claire's face. But she didn't respond, except to say, "Double congrats to the both of you."

Toni and Carla joined in congratulating us. You could feel the sincerity in Toni's voice. In Carla, you could tell she was being polite.

The look on Mom's face could have only been matched by an unemployed mother of four on the verge of being evicted, only to be told that her last $2 invested in the lotto had just made her $20 million richer. Mom couldn't have been happier if she'd gained an acquittal for the entire Black Panther Party against the federal government. Dad was equally ecstatic. Aunt B was giving Jesus all the credit.

After my parents pulled themselves together and they remembered I was in the room, the first thing out of Dad's mouth were names for his grandson. Mom didn't care about the sex. She was just happy over becoming a grandmother. Her main concern was what Liseth planned on doing about school, and what her mother's reaction would be when she got the news about the pregnancy.

"I suppose now is the time to tell you," Mom said to Liseth, "that your mother and sister and brothers are coming to dinner Sunday. I took the liberty of inviting them, so both our families could sit down and celebrate your engagement."

"Thank you," she said, hugging Mom and kissing her on the cheek.

"You're welcome, but I have to say—and I'm saying this as a mother, and one who has been in the same position as you, except I was younger and had just finished high school. As you know, Esmeralda always wanted the best for you, and you know she was not always crazy about your relationship with Delroy. You know, the age difference."

"I know," Liseth responded, fidgeting with the ring on her finger.

"You know, it never bothered me, but then I'm the mother of a son. A son who is a good son. The best there is. A first-class litigator, and who I'm sure will make an outstanding husband and superb father. But I'm not the mother of a daughter, so I can't tell you how I would react. But I remember how my parents reacted when I got pregnant the first year I finished high school. You're older than I was, and you and Delroy were practically living together, but mothers being what we are, your mother will want to know if you're going to finish law school."

Liseth must have felt like she was being scolded. She had that look on her face as if she was caught red-handed doing something she shouldn't have. But Mom wasn't really scolding her. She was just pointing out the facts. Esmeralda would be concerned about her finishing law school. And as much as I was overjoyed at being a father, I had to take her mother's concerns into consideration.

"You have to believe me when I say I never planned on having a baby until after I finished law school. I didn't even know Delroy had marriage in mind."

"Liseth, let me admit something to you, and this may sound selfish of me, but I have to be honest. Lloyd and I are not getting any younger. Delroy is forty-five."

Liseth friends looked at me with disbelief, which told me she never told them my real age. Claire, in particular, looked at me, and I could read that mind of hers. And I responded, *Yes, bitch, I'm forty-five, and I look this good.* Her eyes also told me that at another place and another time, she would have been among my conquests.

Toni's mind was hard to read, but I thought age would not have been a factor in a relationship. Carla, on the other hand, was not pleased to hear that I was forty-five to Liseth's twenty-three. I was sure Liseth didn't tell her I was thirty-something. She might have told her I was forty. So what was five more years?

Mom continued. "Being selfish, I can't wait to be a grandmother, so it wouldn't have bothered me if you had gotten pregnant earlier. It was a decision for you and Delroy to make. It's your mother I'm worried about."

"I have always wanted a family. At least two children." Liseth looked at me, well pleased with herself. The look told me she was concerned over how her mother would react to the news, but it also told me she was an adult; and as much as she loved her mother, she would make her own decision. "I would not have minded if this had happened after school, but it's here, and as much as I wanted to make my mother happy, my happiness comes first." She came over and sat beside me. We put our arms around each other, and looked at each other. "I haven't been to the doctors yet, but based on when I last had my period, I'd say the baby is due about May or early July. I'll finish next semester, have the baby in the summer, and go back to school in the fall. I'm not going to disappoint my mother. I'm going to be a lawyer. A working one. First, I have to decide when I'm getting married. Delroy and I will talk about it this weekend."

Dad brought another bottle of champagne from the kitchen and filled the glasses all around. I didn't mind getting drunk. Liseth would be driving. Mom asked Liseth what kind of wedding she had in mind.

"I'm not sure, but it will be either before I go back to school next semester or during spring break. I could even wait till after I have the baby. Delroy is not going anywhere."

"Tonight, tomorrow, whenever you're ready. It's up to you on this one," I said as I sipped my champagne.

"Thanks, baby," she said.

"I just want this to be exactly the way you want it. I know Mom will want to play a great part in this. After all, she has waited so long for this, but, baby, this is yours. You call it the way you see fit. I'm sure Mom will understand and help you in any way."

"Oh, of course. That goes without saying," Mom chimed in.

"Your mother and I agree on more things than you'd imagine. As for my mother, as long as I finish school, there won't be a problem. As I was saying, I'll spend the summer with the baby and then go back to school. I'll miss him or her, but—"

"Him," Dad interrupted.

"Or her, but I'll—"

"Well," I interrupted, "you could transfer to Columbia. That way, you wouldn't have to be away from him or her." I emphasized the *her*, looking at Dad.

"That's a good idea," Mom said.

"Or we could rent a house with a full-time nanny up in New Haven so you can finish at Yale." The girls looked at me with disbelief at that remark.

"That's way too extravagant," Liseth said. "Columbia sounds more practical, but right now, I can't make any decision."

Chapter 14

•——••❧♥❧••——•

We must have put away five or six bottles of champagne. Champagne never gets me drunk. Anything else would. Beer certainly, but never champagne. But I was feeling a buzz from it. Thank goodness Liseth was driving. Between Dad, Claire, and myself, I'd say we drank four or four and a half bottles. Mom and Toni had a few glasses. Aunt B had one glass when we toasted, and Carla had maybe one and a half. After asking for Mom's permission and being told by her and Aunt B that no harm would come to the fetus, Liseth drank a glass of champagne.

I was feeling a buzz, but I was steady on my feet. A lot less than I could say for Claire, although she tried to control her gait every time she would go to the bathroom. She might have been a tough streetwise girl from Detroit who had stood her own with many boys in the hood, but that night, old Dom Perignon was too much for her. She didn't fall over or bump into the furniture, but I sure was glad she wasn't operating a motor vehicle that night. Old Dom not only got to her head, but he also loosened her tongue.

Claire talked about and asked about everything. From her troubled past to her law degree from Yale. She had high expectations for her future. And why not? She already had a degree, with honors, in the art of bullshitting. All she needed was a law degree from Yale, and if she played by the rules, there was no telling how far she'd go.

Mom called a car service to take the girls to their hotel. They all thanked Mom for a wonderful evening. Toni hugged me and kissed me on the cheek and told me she was happy to have met me. Claire did the same, except she kissed me on the lips. I wasn't surprised. Carla shook my hand.

"Why do I have this feeling that Carla doesn't approve of our relationship? Not that I give a fuck," I said to Liseth as we pulled out of my parents' driveway. I was trying not to hide my displeasure in what I thought was rudeness on her friend's part.

"She has a problem with our age difference." Liseth blew her horn to signal her departure as she sped up the street.

"No fuckin' kidding."

Liseth laughed.

"What's so funny?"

She laughed again. "She's just a kid."

"What do you mean she is just a kid? She's your age."

"Yeah, but in comparison to me, she's a kid."

"In what way?"

"She's a virgin."

"As in never been fucked?"

"As in never been fucked."

"You're telling me a guy has never scored on her? You're kidding."

"Not only never scored on her, forget about first base. Girlfriend has never even heard of baseball, if you know what I mean."

"Maybe the guys she met don't know how to play baseball. Where the fuck was she raised, in a monastery on a hill on an island?"

Liseth laughed again. "No, but she's a nice person, once you get to know her."

"No wonder she looked at you funny when you said you might even wait till after the baby was born before we get married."

"There is one girl who'll be a virgin on her wedding night."

"She and Claire," I said, with my tongue firmly planted in my cheek.

"Not even you, in your wildest days, been with as many women as Claire's been with men. And another thing, that's one person you'll never meet again, if I can help it." She didn't look at me when she said it, and good sense prevented me from asking why.

I was tired and could still feel the buzz of the champagne in my head. I leaned back and closed my eyes. A call from her mother invaded the silence. The conversation was brief. She told her we were on our way, and then she hung up and I drifted off to sleep again.

Rita Mendoza's voice entered the jeep like a mad herd of buffalo entering a baby's nursery. She was loud, abrasive, and had the manners of a pig at slop time. But what Rita lacked in good grace, manners, and human relations, she made up for in beauty and a body that if seen by Hugh Heffner of *Playboy* magazine, would never be the same again. But despite being blessed with great beauty, a body that could make her famous, at five feet eight inches, with brown hair and a year younger than Liseth, she was the most worthless person I'd ever met in my life.

Besides consistently being worthless, Rita had never been consistent at anything. She never finished high school (she dropped out at age thirteen or fourteen), she didn't know who her father was, she had a less-than-civil relationship with her mother, and she had minimal contact with the three kids she had from three different men. But somehow, and for some strange reason, Liseth loved her like a sister. Rita loved Liseth too, but in my opinion, only because she was generous.

"Hola, Liseth. Que tal?" Rita's sandpaper voice, which was damaged from smoking two packs of cigarette a day and too much weed, jolted me from my sleep. I opened my eyes and was greeted by a combination of the most gorgeous pair of green eyes and the stench of the worst tobacco breath I'd ever encountered. She was on my side of the jeep, and her head was in the vehicle. "Whasup, nigga? You still lookin' pretty."

I hated when she addressed me that way. And I could never get used to it, but there was no use complaining.

"I'm OK," I grunted.

Liseth returned the greeting in Spanish as she unbuckled her seat belt. They said a few more words in Spanish and laughed, and then Liseth walked around the vehicle, and they locked arms around each other.

"Congratulations, girlfriend. Bitch, you in Yale. You go girl." She gave Liseth a high five. "Bitch, I knew you got it in you. Got a rich nigga. Roof on the beach, and now Yale. Shit, bitch, you too much." Then she burst out laughing again, and they hugged each other again.

Liseth thanked her and asked her how she was doing, and about the kids. She said they were all right. Then she saw the ring on Liseth's finger; and before she could ask, Liseth told her, and they both started screaming.

"Get the fuck outta 'ere," Rita said. "L'me see that chunka ice." Liseth held her finger up to her face, and Rita took hold of her hand. "That's a lotta fuckin' money. How much?"

"He won't say," Liseth said, looking at me, as I stood there on the sidewalk watching them going crazy.

"I have something else to tell you, but I have to see my mother first. You gonna be around when I come down?"

The look on Rita's face said it. She knew Liseth was pregnant, but despite who she was, she had certain loyalty and respect for Liseth that would prevent her from saying anything to anyone without Liseth's permission. But Liseth owed it to her mother to tell her first.

"Shit, yes, I'll be 'round. I wanna hear more shit." Then she touched Liseth's belly, laughed, and said, "Bitch it's 'bout time."

"Let me tell my mom first, OK."

"Word. Your Mom gonna have a major fit, but don't sweat it, girlfriend. You be a'right." Then she looked at me. "This nig—I mean Delroy—will take good care of you. He loves you big-time."

I could have sworn to God, if there was one, that the bitch didn't know my name.

I couldn't help but laugh, and I thanked her. They hugged each other again, and Liseth and I went into the building.

Esmeralda was waiting up for us when we entered the apartment. Liseth still had her keys. We apologized for being so late. It was close to one in the morning. But it was Friday, and Esmeralda had been off from work since the day before and was not expected back at work until the next Tuesday. Then she'd be off again from Thursday until the following Tuesday. She was also watching us and Rita from the window.

"Was she asking you for money?" Esmeralda asked. She was visibly upset at the thought of us giving Rita money, but we didn't. And even if we did, we wouldn't have told her. Which, come to think of it, with all the excitement, Rita must have forgotten to ask Liseth for money.

"Ah, come on, Mommy. I don't give Rita money every time I see her. And even if I do, I don't give her more than ten bucks."

Liseth was not telling her mother the truth. She would always give Rita money, and it was always more than $10. The last time it was $50.

"You know how I feel about that girl." Esmeralda rolled her eyes when she said it. "That girl is no good."

Liseth disagreed with her mother, but this was not the time to be disagreeable.

I doubted Rita would have been the topic much longer, but her brother saved the day.

"So I hear you're getting married?" Juan said. They threw their arms around each other and kissed each other on the lips and on the cheeks. Showing their affection for each other was nothing new. They genuinely loved each other. But for the first time, I saw Juan cry; and in a way, it surprised me. Not that junkies don't cry. It was just that one could never tell when they were ever sincere about anything. Crying was the least of them. Esmeralda looked on with pride as her son and daughter professed their love for each other.

"Are you happy, Liseth?" Juan asked as he wiped the tears from his eyes.

"Oh yes, I'm happy. Mucho, mucho happy."

"Are you really, really happy?" He was unable to hold back the tears, and the infectious bliss was too much for Esmeralda to avoid. She too was crying.

Liseth sat down with her brother on her mother's prized sofa and assured him of how happy she was. Juan had no doubt his sister was happy, but like all older brothers, and without a father around, he had to protect his sister. He walked over to me and extended his hand and congratulated me and wished us both good luck.

Liseth showed them the ring, and all Juan could say was, "Damn, girl, you realize how much that shit cost?"

"Don't ask me, Juan, because I don't know. And please don't ask Delroy, because that would be rude."

"I won't, but am sayin' that shit, girl, even though you're from the hood, you be careful flashin' that rock."

Her mother looked at the ring and beamed with delight. She remarked how beautiful it was and said Juan was right—she should be careful. For the first time, I felt as though I might have done more harm than good buying her that ring. If all everybody was going to talk about was the ring and its perceived value, pretty soon word would get around, and trust me, in Spanish Harlem, it would. The next thing you knew, some junkie would want to take the finger with the ring. Maybe I should buy her a cheaper ring to wear when she visited her mother.

"Mommy, there is something I'd like to talk to you about." That was a hint for me to go get a beer from the kitchen. The nap on the ride over, the excitement with Rita, and then the emotional duet with Liseth and her brother had diluted the buzz from the champagne. Going into the kitchen would also give Liseth and her mother some room.

I had a can of soda instead of a beer. I drank it from the can as I flipped through a magazine that was on the counter. Juan came in, and we engaged in a bit of small talk about Liseth. How he loved her. And how he was happy that she was getting married. He said he was sure I'd make her happy. And wished us luck again.

The clock on the microwave oven said a minute after two. I found an interesting article in the magazine and was halfway through it when Liseth and her mother walked into the kitchen. The look on her mother's face was not one of a displeased person. They had their arms around each other, and the mood was jovial. As they came closer, a smile came across Liseth's face, and her mother managed a smile too. It made me relaxed.

Liseth kissed me and stuck her head into the fridge. "I thought you said you had fried chicken in here?" she said.

Juan had eaten several pieces of chicken while he and I were having our small talk.

"There were at least four or five pieces in there," her mother said.

"Well, there are only two pieces now." She took the plate out, asked if I wanted a piece. I said no, and she took the plate with her and went into her room.

Esmeralda filled the kettle with water and lit the stove. She took a mug from the cupboard and asked me if I wanted some tea. I said yes, and she took out another mug. She put the tea bags in the mugs and took a lemon from the fridge. She cut the lemon in wedges and placed one next to my mug. She squeezed a wedge in her mug, and I followed suit. Then she heaped two spoonfuls of sugar in her mug and the same in mine. And then she poured the water. Finally, she said something. "Promise me one thing." We stirred our tea, and I jiggled the bag in my mug. "Promised me you'll let Liseth finish law school. I don't care if she never works as an attorney. God knows it won't be for the money, but I want to see that piece of paper from Yale."

I felt relieved. I thought she was going to tell me how displeased she was and give me that talk that grown-ups have and only grown-ups understand.

"I promise you I will," I told her, and a smile engulfed her face, and I had no doubt it was genuine.

We sipped our tea in silence, and I watched her face as she leaned against the kitchen counter. The number on the microwave clock changed to 2:45 a.m. Esmeralda was visibly tired. She hadn't slept since she got up at six the morning before. She was like me, an early riser. But she was still looking radiant. And I wondered what it would take to make her ever not look good. I tried to picture Liseth at her age. I'd be in my sixties by then. Retired. And hopefully two more kids.

Esmeralda yawned in two short successions. The night was getting to her. It was getting to me too. Except for the nap on the ride over, I'd been up since six too.

"Thanks for being so kind and understanding," I said between yawns. "It means a lot to me."

"I've learned a lot in a short time when I look at some of the girls in this neighborhood, especially Rita. She is a year younger than Liseth. When I look at many of them, I can't complain. Liseth promised me she'd finish school. And I know she'll keep her promise, but I wanted you to promise me too."

"She'll finish school, that much you can count on."

"Sometimes, Delroy, in life, we have to accept the situation that falls on us. That's one of the things I've learned. My daughter taught me that. She's a good girl, and I'm proud of her."

"You have every reason to."

Liseth came out of her room with some things she wanted to take home with her. She had on a jean jacket over her T-shirt. "What are you two talking about?"

"You," I said.

"I would hope so. Are you ready?"

"Yep. Are you taking those home?" I pointed to the bags on the floor.

"Yeah."

"I'll take them down."

"Thanks, baby. Let me talk to my mother for a while, OK?"

I walked over to Esmeralda and gave her a hug. I thanked her for everything and told her I loved her. She thanked me too and said she loved me. I told Liseth I'd get the elevator.

She stayed and talked to her mother for maybe five or ten minutes. As I waited for the elevator, some girl and her boyfriend came out of the apartment across from the elevator cursing at each other. She promised him she'd kill his ass the next time he cheated on her. He said he wasn't, that he couldn't talk to a girl without her accusing him of fucking her. She said she knew him, that if he talked to a girl he was not related to, he'd either fucked her or was trying to fuck her. He kept denying it, and she kept calling him a liar and telling him that she'd kill him. And she sounded like she meant it.

I could have walked down to the lobby and back before the elevator came, but in a way, I was enjoying the sideshow. And I had a feeling the guy was glad for my company, because although he was obviously bigger and looked older than her, something told me that the little Spanish spitfire scared the shit out of him.

Liseth and the elevator came at the same time. She and the couple exchanged greetings. On the way down, Liseth asked about the girl's two children, and she congratulated Liseth on getting into Yale. She had known the girl, Rosa, since they were teenagers. The guy, Armando, she hadn't known as long, but long enough to know that the scar on the left side of his handsome face was put there by Rosa, after she caught him in her bed with another girl. The girl ended up looking worse, and Rosa spent four months on Rikers Island awaiting trial. She was acquitted of the charges because the girl refused to testify against her.

"I told you how Armando got that weird scar down the side of face, didn't I?" Liseth said as we put the bags in the back of the jeep.

"That was the girl you told me about who almost killed the girl she caught her boyfriend with?" I knew full well why she brought it up.

"Yes, that's her. And that's not her boyfriend, that's her husband. If that was me, I'd have killed the bitch and cut his fuckin' balls off. In my house?" Her voice wasn't raised, but she didn't have to.

"Are you trying to tell me something?"

"I hope so."

"I thought we were putting certain things behind us?"

"I am. I just hope you will."

That remark was really uncalled for. But I suppose I deserved it. She started the jeep and drove up to the corner of Lexington

Avenue and pulled up on the other side in front of the bodega, got out, and went across the street into the store. She emerged with Rita, and they talked for a while. They laughed a little. Rita patted her belly. They laughed some more, and then they came across the street. Liseth got into the jeep, went into her purse, and took out some money. She only had twenties. She asked me for a ten. I gave it to her, and she gave Rita fifty. Rita ground her cigarette and thanked the both of us. I told her she was welcome.

"I bet you wanna boy," Rita said, smiling. The tobacco stench on her breath was even stronger.

"I hope it's a boy," I said, trying not to show any sign of discord between me and Liseth.

"I'm sure you'll get a boy, but whatever it is, good luck to the two of you." She took another cigarette from the pack and lit up. "Hey, bitch, come see me before you go, OK."

"Yeah, I will," Liseth said as she started the jeep.

"Maybe you'll invite me out to that fancy house for Christmas?"

"You take care of yourself, Rita."

"Love you, girl."

"Love you too." She put the jeep in gear and slowly moved away from the curb.

I waited until we were through the toll bridge and over the Triborough Bridge before I said something.

"Why did you have to bring that up back there? Liseth, I love you very much, and I apologize deeply for what happened. It was stupid on my part." I reached out and touched her hand, not knowing how she would react. But she didn't pull away. I put my hand up to her face, and she rubbed her face against the back of my hand. "Darling, I promise you it will never happen again. Never, but it's important that you not only forgive me, but that you trust me. We're getting married, and we're having a baby. You're getting a law degree, and we're starting a new life. I need you."

My hand was still next to her face. She rubbed her face harder against my hand, and I could feel her breath on the back of my hand. It was warm, but I could tell the hurt was deep. "Are you OK?"

"I'm OK. I'm sorry about that outburst back there."

"It's all right. And it was not really an outburst—plus, I deserved it."

"It's just that when I saw Rosa and Armando arguing, it just triggered something. She almost killed that girl, you know."

"You told me."

"And that was in her house. Her house. And nobody would blame her if she did."

I wanted to tell her I'd never do that in our home, but what would I be saying? That I'd cheat on her again, but not in our home? That was what it would sound like.

"She wouldn't be convicted. It would be a crime of passion," I said.

"Delroy, I love you. And I do forgive you, and I will trust you, because you're a good man and I'm going to marry you and have your baby. And I promise you, I'll never bring it up again." She kissed the back of my hand, and at sixty miles an hour, she tilted her head over to kiss me. She did, and the jeep swerved.

"Keep your eyes on the road," I said. We laughed, and I put my hand between her legs. She reciprocated, and my dick got hard. We looked at each other. She stuck her tongue out at me, and I squeezed her leg.

By the time we unloaded the bags from the jeep, got into the house, undressed, and got into bed. It was almost 4:00 a.m. We wanted to make love, but we were too tired. We talked for a while. She asked about Connie's case. I started to tell her, but by the time I got to the bail hearing, she was snoring.

There were three things I had never done before: bought an engagement ring for $50,000, got a girl pregnant, and made love to a pregnant woman. Two I was sure of. Buy the ring, although I would have bought Connie a ring of similar value. And I had never made love to a pregnant woman before. At least not to my knowledge. Getting a girl pregnant was questionable. In my last year at Columbia, a month before I graduated, a girl I went out with a few times skipped her last few classes and graduation. The word around was that she was pregnant and had an abortion.

Three years later, when I again was getting ready to graduate law school, I ran into her in the city. She was with two other girls. She introduced me to her friends, and I pulled her aside and asked her about the rumor. She denied it and said she didn't want to talk about it. And for good reason—she had an impressive wedding ring on her finger. Since she denied it, and I had no way of proving otherwise, I'd have to say there were three things I'd never done before.

I got up the next day a little after eleven. Liseth was out of it. And I could understand. She hadn't slept in her bed for close to two months. As usual, I could have fucked her, and she wouldn't have known it. The temperature was a little crisp, but not cold. A blanket was necessary. Even so, we both slept in our underwear. As she lay there in her black thong, I tried to imagine what she'd look like at six or seven months pregnant. She would start to lose her shape and those thongs wouldn't look good on her anymore. She'd be fat. Maybe her feet would swell. Maybe she'd gain sixty pounds, who knew; but I would still find her sexy and desirable.

I pulled the blanket over her and kissed her on the forehead. I slipped into a pair of khaki pants and put on a sweatshirt with my firm's name on the chest. I went downstairs and took a quick inventory of the cabinets and the fridge. There was not much food in the house. There were a few crackers in a box. A can of tuna, a few slices of bread, half a carton of orange juice, and an unopened box of pasta. Pasta was one thing we were never out of. There weren't even any eggs in the house. I jotted down a few things. Eggs, bread, OJ, bagel, cream cheese, fruits, and, oh yes, half-and-half. Liseth wouldn't drink her coffee without half-and-half. Not that I expected her to wake up, but I left a note on my pillow. Just in case she did. The note said I went to the supermarket, that I'd be right back.

I ran into Mildred in the supermarket parking lot. We were both getting out of our vehicles, and we both walked in together. She asked if Liseth was home, and I couldn't help telling her of our engagement and pregnancy, but I swore her to secrecy first.

"You have to promise me you'll act surprised," I said to her. "It's important that you do."

"I promise I will. I won't even tell Charles." I wasn't expecting her to go that far, but if she wouldn't tell even her husband, then I supposed she'd act surprised when they came over that evening and we told them the double news.

I picked up some smoked salmon while I was at the supermarket. I hadn't had salmon and eggs since Liseth went away. Come to think of it, I couldn't remember cooking anything since she left. I made a batch of salmon and eggs with sliced tomatoes on the side, toasted bagels with cream cheese, poured some OJ, and cut up some cantaloupe. I made her coffee, of course, and put everything on a tray with a vase with a rose in it and took it up to her. As expected, she was still asleep at almost 1:30 p.m.

I set the tray at the foot of the bed and thought of waving the mug of coffee, or the salmon and eggs under her nose, hoping the smell would wake her up, but decided on something else. I figured, why not wake her in a way she enjoyed. I pulled the blanket off her. She was lying on her side. One of her legs was bent, with her knee up to her chest. Working from behind, I moved the sliver of material to one side and ran my tongue between her cheeks, gently holding them apart as I inserted my tongue in her warm pussy. As I licked away, I could tell she was feeling me as she thrust her ass in my face so that I could get more of her wet vagina. It was good to taste something familiar.

I turned her on her back, and with her thong still on, I continued giving her oral pleasure, bringing her to a climax.

"Oh God, I needed that," she said. "You have no idea how much I miss you and miss waking up in my own house, in my own bed, especially like this. It's worth not going back to Yale."

"You're trying to get me killed." I moved up in bed next to her. And we snuggled.

"Most men would die to die this way. Ah, that smells good." She let out a yawn and stretched. "Is that salmon and eggs? Now I know I'm really home. Thank you, baby. I love you." She kissed me and pulled the tray closer to her and dug into the salmon and eggs. "I guess both plates are for me, because you ate already."

"I didn't say you were trying to kill me. I said you're trying to get me killed." She was wolfing down the salmon and eggs like a hungry baby attacking his mother's breast. "You know, Esmeralda would kill the both of us if you drop out of school."

"Don't let her scare you. Besides, who said anything about dropping out? Can I have some of your eggs?" She reached for the mug of coffee. "Baby, this is cold."

"I'll get you some more."

"Just stick it in the microwave."

She bit into the bagel and shoved some of my eggs onto her plate.

I made myself a fresh mug of tea while I was downstairs. She was halfway through the half of my eggs when I got back upstairs.

"My goodness, you were hungry. Would you like the rest?"

"You sure you don't mind? I feel like I haven't eaten since I left home."

"Like you said, I ate already."

"Thanks, baby. I need to build up my strength. I'm going to fuck your brains out when I'm done."

To hear her say it put a smile on my face would be an understatement. I asked her if I could at least have my bagel.

"You can have half," she said, and we both laughed.

"Seriously, Liseth, you're not thinking of postponing school or anything, are you?"

With her mouth full, and between chewing, she said, "No, silly. I was just joking. If anything, I'd transfer to Columbia."

"A better school," I quipped.

"Yeah, you'd like that, wouldn't you?"

"I'm not the only one who would."

"I know. Is there anybody in your family that didn't go to Columbia?"

"Hey, don't forget you're a Columbia girl too, and you're marrying into a Columbia family. You know, there is always a first for everything." I ate my half of the bagel and sipped my tea.

"This is much better," she said, sipping her coffee.

"If you dropped out of Yale, it would not only be the first time I'd make love to a pregnant woman, but it'd be the first time I'd make love to a pregnant Yale law school dropout."

"Wait till I gain forty or fifty pounds and you can't get on top of me."

"If you continue eating at this rate, it won't be long."

"They say most pregnant women are either constantly horny or hungry. I hope in my case, it will be the sex. I don't mind fucking every day, but I certainly don't want to look like a fuckin' cow."

"If you stay away from certain foods, you'll be all right. You just have to—"

The phone rang. "I'll get it." It was Ebony.

"Am I interrupting anything?" she said.

I breathed hard into the phone. "Yes, you are."

"And you stopped to answer the phone? You must be losing it."

"OK, don't get personal now." We both laughed.

"Where is the future Mrs. Bradshaw?"

"Right here, just finished eating two plates of salmon and eggs. That's five eggs, plus one and a half bagel with cream cheese. Not to mention about four ounces of salmon."

"Sounds like she's pregnant."

If there was one person in the world Liseth would tell before her mother, it would be Ebony. But what I heard sounded like a question, not a comment. I put my hand over the receiver and asked Liseth if she had told Ebony. She said no, and I handed her the phone.

"What's up, girl?" Liseth said, putting a piece of cantaloupe in her mouth. Chewing on the cantaloupe, she said, "I'm OK." Then, "It's good to be home. I missed this place."

I was hungry, so I went downstairs and made myself a bagel, lox, and cream cheese sandwich. I doubted Liseth would be that hungry, but I ate half of it before going back upstairs.

"About six weeks," were the first thing I heard as I reentered the bedroom. She was telling Ebony how many weeks pregnant she thought she was. I remembered her telling my mom and us that the baby was due in late May or early June. So it had to have happened when I took her up to New Haven. It had to be then. I didn't have a condom, and getting pregnant was the last thing on our minds. And why should it. We had had sex without a condom before, several times, and beat the odds.

"I thought it was the stress of our fight and starting law school," she said to Ebony. "I've never missed my period before."

Ebony must have asked her how she knew she was pregnant. She said, "Well, I don't know why I did it, but I bought a pregnancy test kit and tried it four times, and it was positive each time. I thought the first one was a mistake, but four times? No way." Then she laughed. She expressed her happiness and how she thought her mother was going to kill her, and how surprised she was that her mother took it so well. Then she told Ebony about the ring.

"Girl, I can hardly lift my left hand. The motherfucka is so heavy. My mother and, especially, my brother thinks it's dangerous walking in Harlem with it on." More laughter followed.

"You'll see it tomorrow. We're going up to his parents' for dinner. My mother and my sister and brothers are invited." She laughed some more, and then she got serious. She did a lot of listening and said a lot of "Yeses," and, "I knows." Then she wiped her eyes. Then she said, "I know she didn't mean anything to him. Of course I know he loves me. He's my life. I'm going to give him at least two more kids. Hire some live-in old woman to help raise them while I go out to work."

I was beaming with pride, but most of all, with great love and affection for my woman. Then she said good-bye and handed me the phone.

"Hey, what's up?"

"I thought you'd never do it, but better late than never," Ebony said, unable to contain her laughter.

"I was waiting for you to match me up with the right girl."

"I told you I would, didn't I?"

"Yeah right," I said. "All you did was throw a party. I found her myself."

"I think that girl was in love with you before she met you in person."

"I think you're right."

"And you know, if I didn't talk good about you, she wouldn't want to know you."

"I think you're right again."

"You will stop by tomorrow, won't you?"

"I promise."

"I love you."

"I love you too."

"Bye, pops."

"Watch it." We both laughed.

"You know what I'd like to do the rest of the day?" Liseth said, taking the phone off the hook. I took the breakfast tray off the bed and put it on the floor. Neither one of us had touched our orange juice. "I'd like to spend the day in bed with my man. I'd like to just have one of those quite days without the phone ringing every fifteen minutes. No TV. No radio. No distraction. No—"

"Sex," I said.

"There are limits. And I wouldn't go that far. There are two things I wanna do today, and they are two things I haven't done in a long time. I'd like to make love to my man, and then have some pralines and ice cream." She snuggled up to me and started to kiss me. "And please don't tell me there is no ice cream in the house."

"Oh my God. I knew I forgot something," I said to myself. There was no fucking ice cream in the house—the one thing I should have remembered when I went to the store. And even if I wanted to, it was too late to go out and get some. My dick was in her mouth. Ah, fuck the ice cream. I'd worry about it later.

I came faster than at any other time. It was understandable. I hadn't had sex in close to four weeks. Another first.

"You really missed me, didn't you?" she said after spitting in the mug and drinking some of her orange juice.

I was a little flaccid, but I was beginning to feel a rise again as she started to lick the head of my dick and then ran her tongue down the shaft.

"That's what happens when you go away from your man for that long."

"Columbia is starting to look good all of a sudden."

I had a full erection by then, and it was in the back of her throat. I could literally feel it brushing on her palate. And she wasn't even choking. And no, in case you're wondering, I had a more than adequate size. But that was what made my woman, at twenty-three, good at what she did.

My hands were full of clumps of her hair, and her tongue was teasing the tip of my dick. The most sensitive part. Then she started to slowly take it in and out of her mouth. And each time I felt like I was about to come, she'd squeeze the base of my dick; and not only would the feeling go away, but I was becoming bilingual.

Liseth and I had had great sex, in places too numerous to mention, and in positions unimaginable. Our frequencies were marathon at times. I couldn't think of any that was better than the other, but that Saturday was a day that would be remembered from then on as *the* Saturday. From then on, when we talked about good sex, we would say, "the Saturday."

Chapter 15

—————◦❦◦—————

Heavy pounding on the front and rear doors and the ringing of the doorbells jolted me from a deep sleep. The pounding on the front door shook the house. A woman's voice was calling my name. It sounded as though the neighborhood was being evacuated or something. But Liseth didn't even stir an inch.

"Who the fuck," I said, jumping up without putting anything on and looking out the window. The house was in total darkness. The motion light lit up the driveway. Mildred was standing at the door looking up and yelling at me. I totally forgot I'd told her and Charles to come over. I put my robe on and went downstairs. I opened the back door to let her and Charles in.

"You had your phone off since two thirty," said Mildred. "We have been trying to call you for the past five hours."

"Actually, we have been sleeping since four or five. What time is it, anyway?" I asked.

Charles told me the time. It was almost eight.

"Millie insisted that we come over tonight, even though I told her to wait until tomorrow," he said, looking embarrassed, thinking that perhaps he had invaded our privacy.

"It's all right," I said.

"Millie insisted she had to see Liseth tonight. I kept asking her if it couldn't wait till tomorrow, but she said it couldn't. I figured you guys wanted to spend some time together and we'd come by tomorrow."

"We're going up to my parents' tomorrow for dinner, so I asked Millie to come over tonight. By the way, do you guys have any ice cream? I forgot to buy some today."

Charles looked at me kind of strange. "Millie cooked some lobster for dinner. She bought about six and saved some for you."

All that fucking and sleeping had made me hungry. Mildred said she'd go get the food and bring the ice cream back with her. It was rum and raisin, she said. I told her it was OK. We looked at each other and laughed. Then she and Charles left to get the food.

"What time is it?" Liseth said as I woke her.

It wasn't exactly eight-thirty, but I just told her it was after eight.

"I'm so fuckin' tired," she said. "Can I go back to sleep?"

"No. Mildred and Charles are coming by. And they are bringing food."

"And I'm hungry too." She sat up in the bed and stretched. A loud yawn followed. She looked ravishing with her hair all over her face, and God knows, if she had asked me to make love to her again, I would have. "God, Delroy, I'm so tired. I don't know why. What did you do to me? You know I can make love all day and night and sleep twenty-five hours and wake up still feeling like I'm ready to fuck, but right now I feel like I have been drugged or something. I must be getting old." She held her arms out and said, "Come here."

I was sitting at the foot of the bed. I shuffled over to her, and she put her arms around me.

"Are you nervous or scared?" She kissed me.

"About what?" I pushed her hair back from her face.

"About being a father? About getting married?"

"Honestly?"

"Yeah, honestly."

"No. I'm neither nervous nor scared. I really hope, though, it's a boy. Only because if we never have another child, I'd like to have a son to do things with."

"Don't worry. Unlike you, this won't be an only child. After I graduate, I want to get pregnant right away."

"Talk about pressure on a guy."

"But look at all the fun we'll have in between."

"Wanna have a quickie?"

The doorbell rang. The door opened, and Mildred's voice came upstairs. Liseth went into the bathroom and asked me to tell Mildred she'd be down in a minute. I still had my robe on. I shouted from the top of the stairs that we were on our way down. I pulled on a pair of shorts and the sweatshirt I had on earlier.

Charles and Mildred were in the kitchen. He was drinking a beer. They'd brought two six-packs of Red Stripe, the food, and of course, the ice cream. I twisted the cap off one of the beers and raised the edge of the foil. The aroma of curried lobster came up at me. In the other container was plain rice, and in another steamed broccoli.

I went to the foot of the stairs and was about to shout for Liseth to come downstairs when she appeared at the top. She had on a white terry shorts set. The top was sleeveless, with a hood. She stood at the top of the stairs before she started down. Her hair was much longer than I'd thought. It came down past her shoulders. I'd seen it longer, but I'd always asked her not to cut her hair. And I was glad she didn't. I loved long hair on her. Something to grab on to when she was between my legs. I waited at the foot of the stairs until she came down. We kissed. The ends of her hair were wet.

"I took a quick shower," she said. "I needed to wake up. Now I'm hungry enough to eat the farm."

I told her about the curried lobster, rice, and broccoli. We walked into the kitchen with our arms around each other. She and Mildred embraced, and remained in a clinch for what seemed like five minutes.

"You look different," Mildred said.

"Must be the weight," Liseth said. She waved her left hand in Mildred's face, supporting it at the elbow with her right hand. Leaning to her left, she said, "All the weight is on this side."

It would not have taken much for Mildred to catch on, even if I hadn't told her. Charles, sitting at the counter, saw the huge ring on her finger and let out a sigh. Then: "Holy shit. Can I see that?" And he walked over to Liseth. "I have only seen ring like this in the movies or in store windows." He held her hand and brought it up to his face.

"For a moment there, I thought you were going to whip out one of those little things that jewelers put on their eye to inspect diamonds," Mildred said. "The way you looked at it."

"It is awesome," Charles said, releasing Liseth's hand. He twisted the cap off a bottle of beer and handed it to Liseth. She refused. He didn't say anything. Neither did Mildred even though she knew why. He handed the beer to me and took another for himself.

Liseth and I sat down to eat. Before she started, she said, "I'm so hungry, but I've to tell you something before I eat." Then she put an arm around Mildred's waist. "I'm pregnant," she said.

Mildred burst into tears, and Liseth put her arms around her. Charles walked around the counter, shook my hand, and congratulated me. I thanked him while Mildred was still crying.

"I'm so happy for you," she said to Liseth. "I really, really am." She took a napkin off the kitchen counter and dabbed at her eyes. Then she started to cry again. Liseth's eyes were moist too.

I was sure Mildred was genuinely, unconditionally happy for us, but it never occurred to me that when I told her earlier, I might have been insensitive. Knowing how much and how badly she wanted to get pregnant. And on top of it, asking her not to tell her husband. I wanted to apologize, but that might only make things awkward, so I let it drop.

Mildred asked how many weeks and put her hand on Liseth's belly. Even though there was nothing to see yet, Liseth pulled her shorts down a little so she could see it. They were now laughing like two teenagers. I dug into my meal and drank some beer.

Charles, between swigs of his beer, calmly said, "You know, I'm happy for you and everything, but right now, I don't know if I should love you or hate you."

Before I could say anything, he said, "You know the kind of pressure you have just put on me?"

He said it in way a friend would say it to a friend, but I felt a little embarrassed.

"Don't listen to him, Delroy. That's not true," Mildred said.

The only thing I could say was, "I'm sorry."

"Well, you know how much you want a baby," Charles said.

"Yes, but don't put it like that. You make it sound as if the minute we get home, I'm going to rip your clothes off and ask you to do it." We all laughed. "OK. OK. So I want a baby badly."

"We know," we all said in unison.

"I'm going to be forty soon. I don't have time. You're, what, twenty-two?"

"Twenty-three," Liseth corrected her.

"OK, twenty-three. Big fuckin' deal. But you're a woman. You can understand how I feel, can't you?"

Liseth put her arms around her friend and, nodding her head, acknowledged her plight. "You know who you sound like just now?" she said, "Delroy's mother, and how badly she wanted to be a grandmother."

"And she's approaching seventy, and me in my mid-forties. Charles, my boy, you don't know pressure." I drained the last of my beer and twisted the cap on another. "When the pressure is from a third party, it's even harder than if it's internal." We all laughed.

Liseth finished her food, and just when I thought she'd never asked, she said, "Since I can't drink or smoke—at least I don't want to—where is my ice cream? If there is no ice cream in this house, and I've seen how well stocked the fridge is"—she smiled at me—"you're one dead mother—"

"Watch your mouth."

"I'm talking 'bout *Shaft*," Charles and Mildred chimed in. Then the three of us started singing the *Shaft* chorus. "Da dap, da dap, da dap, daa." All four of us ended up laughing like a bunch of kids at a sleepover.

"Would I not have ice cream in the house knowing you were comin' home?" I winked at Mildred. I took the ice cream out of the fridge and showed her.

"When did you start eatin' rum and raisin?" She looked at Mildred. "Did you bring this over with the food?"

Mildred looked on sheepishly and shrugged her shoulders. "I had nothing to do with it."

"Yeah right. I suppose it will have to do. He knows if I don't have my ice cream what he won't get?"

"You would go that far, baby?"

"You were worried enough to ask Mildred to bring it, weren't you?"

Mildred took a beer for the first time. She twisted the cap, took a long swig, and said, "Hey, Liseth, this one is better than your flavor. It's got rum in it. And it's half a gallon."

"Is it OK?"

"Is what OK?" Mildred asked.

"The ice cream with rum in it?"

"Girl, drink a beer. It's not going to kill you or do the baby any harm."

Liseth took a sip of my beer, and I took it away from her. "That's all right, baby. You can have the whole half gallon of ice cream. I won't mind."

It was past midnight when we said good night to Charles and Mildred. Charles and I had finished the beers and moved to the den and had two snifters of brandy, while Liseth and Mildred went upstairs to girl talk. I didn't mind getting drunk. I was home. Charles wasn't too steady on his feet either, but he didn't have far to go, and the next day was Sunday anyway.

Liseth was standing in the middle of the kitchen eating the ice cream straight from the container when I walked back from the front door. She dug the spoon in the container and raised it to her mouth. Ice cream was already on her nose and chin. More got on her nose. She repeated the process two more times, with the same result.

"Hey, go easy on that," I said. She stuck a spoonful of ice cream in my mouth as I came over to her. Ice cream got on my nose too. "You're sloppy, you know that?"

"I'm also eating for two."

"No, you're not. At least not yet."

"Listen, life begins at conception, so I'm eating for two."

She dug into the ice cream again and had the first two spoons, then gave me the third. I had her up against the kitchen counter, my arms were around her, and she was feeding me every third spoon, and there was ice cream all over our faces. I lifted her and put her on the counter; her legs were around my waist and her breasts in my face. She asked me to take her top off. She had no bra on. These were the breasts that would be filled with milk in the next nine months. That my son would be sucking on daily. How lucky could a kid get?

She put some ice cream on her breast, smearing it all over. A little started to run down her stomach, but I stopped it with my tongue before it traveled to her navel. She put some on the other breast, and I caught it before it could get on her stomach. But when she put some more on the other breast, this time I was not quick enough to catch it before it ran down her stomach, passed her navel, and settled at the edge of her shorts. I was trying to get the ice cream before it got down into her shorts, but she was laughing and putting more on her breast as the watery, sticky substance seeped into her shorts and onto her pubic hair.

I pulled her shorts down. She had no underwear on. I pulled the shorts far enough to get my mouth on the ice cream on her pubic hair. This was another first for me—eating ice cream off her pubic hair. She complained about how cold the counter was on her ass, but nothing about the ice cream. I got her leg out of her shorts and got better access to her crotch. Her ass was making squishing sound as she slid on the counter. I cupped both her cheeks with my hands and held her bottom firmly, balancing them on my elbows. I raised her bottom up to meet my face. I inserted my tongue and found the spot, and I could feel her body responding, and she held on to the back of my head. She said a few words in Spanish—God, I loved when she did that—and then she moaned and gripped my head tighter, and then her body relaxed. Then she pushed me away.

That weekend was full of firsts. I rolled over in the bed, and Liseth was not there. I looked up at the VCR clock. It read ten thirty. She was not in the bathroom either. Ah, she must have gone downstairs to drink some water or sneak a cigarette. It was OK if she smoked. She was in the early stage of her pregnancy. I was sure she would eventually quit.

I went into the bathroom, emptied my bladder, and got back in bed and waited for her. I lay there playing with myself. Fifteen minutes passed, and a fist full of dick, and she still hadn't come back upstairs. I wondered what was keeping her and went to investigate.

As I hit the first step on my way down, I heard a voice ring out, "Get your ass back in bed till I tell you when."

The command startled me, and I raced back into the bedroom without comment, but I was on the steps long enough to smell something cooking from the kitchen, but I couldn't identify it.

Ten minutes later, she entered the bedroom with a tray. On it were two plates with stacks of pancakes, a bowl of fresh strawberries, and freshly squeezed carrot juice. There was a jar of maple syrup and a mug of Earl Grey tea, and her coffee, of course.

Not only did Liseth get up before me, but she made breakfast for us. If this was what impending motherhood was doing to her, I supposed I'd just have to keep her pregnant.

"Where did you learn how to make pancakes?" I drank some of the carrot juice first. I didn't even know she knew how to use the juice extractor. "Don't tell me you learned this at Yale. Did you?"

"Go ahead taste them."

"What is this, an experience?" I poured some of the syrup on the pancakes and cut into them with my fork and bravely put a piece in my mouth.

"Well?" she said, looking at me, not touching her own.

I slowly chewed and swallowed. Then I took another piece, and I must admit, it tasted good. I continued eating without comment, and was halfway through it, when she said, "They taste good, eh? They're obviously good, or you wouldn't be eating the way you're eating."

"Great deduction, Mrs. Holmes, but you could be overlooking one factor." I put another piece in my mouth.

"What is that?"

"Maybe I just want to get married." Not only did they taste good, but I was hungry. I finished the pancakes and put a strawberry in my mouth. She punched me in my upper arm. "Ouch. That hurts." It didn't, but I acted as if it did.

"Serves you right. These are good pancakes even if you won't say so."

"Did you make them from scratch—breaking some eggs, pouring milk, and measuring flour and everything?"

"Aunt Jemima did all that. I just opened the box."

"You're a genius, you know that? You're a genius. By the way, where did you get pancake mix?"

"You are not the only one who can get up early in the morning and sneak out to the store."

"What happened, I can't trust you now? Do I have to tie you down when I go to sleep?" We both laughed.

She finished her pancakes and started on the strawberries. I told her the pancakes were very good. She said she knew but thanked me for saying so.

Liseth and I were standing in the middle of the bathroom, naked. We were getting ready to take a shower. We wanted to leave early. First we'd stop by Ebony's. Then we'd pick up her mother and her sister. And maybe Juan. Then we'd go up to my parents'. We wanted to get to my parents' early so both our parents could spend some time together. It had been a while since our parents got together.

Liseth turned the shower on and was gauging the hot and cold water when the doorbell rang. The bell rang with an air of authority. Two long rings. The kind of rings that would make a member of the criminal element head for the back door. But then there would have been someone out there waiting for him. Usually, when one's doorbell rang with such authority, it was followed by a heavy knock on the door. Instead, the bell rang again. A softer ring.

"Who could that be?" Liseth said.

"I'll go see." I put my robe on and headed downstairs without bothering to look out the window. The frosted glass in the side panels of the door revealed a figure standing in the afternoon sun. It was a man's figure. He reached out to ring the bell again as I opened the door. It was Jasper. Since Liseth had left for school, I hadn't seen much of him, although he would come by every week to cut the lawn and do the gardening. I would usually leave his money in a mutually-agreed-upon place. I'd leave a check in the shed.

"Good afternoon, Delroy." His greetings were friendly, and we shook hands. "Did I catch you at a bad time?"

"We were just about to take a shower. We're going up to my parents' for dinner." He apologized and said he had stopped by because he saw Liseth's Jeep. There was something bothering him, I could tell. Besides the fact that he looked deprived of sleep, I could tell by the look on his face that something was bothering him. He was there for other reasons than seeing Liseth's Jeep in the driveway. But I had known Jasper enough not to pry.

"How is Liseth?" he asked. He also looked nervous.

"She's fine." I led him into the kitchen. "Can I get you anything?" As a lawyer, I'm trained to read body language. His lips weren't moving, but his body was saying enough. He was there for a reason. And whatever it was, he would come to me because I was the only one who could help him. If it was something that needed a lawyer, he had come to the right person. Finally, the son of a bitch would ask me for help.

"All right, spit it out, you bastard," I said to myself, with some satisfaction. I figured the proud son of a bitch would break down and tell me everything about his past, including whatever or whoever he was hiding or running from. I decided I'd throw him off his game by acting imperceptive. "I proposed to Liseth Friday," I said.

"Congratulations," he said. His handshake was not comporting with his complements. Where his handshake was amiable at the door, it was now stiff and clammy.

"She's pregnant too," I continued. "Isn't that wonderful?"

I was expecting something more than a feeble "That's wonderful." It was too disingenuous for me to not say something.

"What's wrong, Jasper?"

Liseth came to the top of the stairs and shouted, "What's keeping you? Will you come get ready?"

I walked to the foot of the stairs and told her it was Jasper.

"Great. Tell him I'll be right down."

There was an urgent look on Jasper's face. "Listen, I have to talk to you about something before she comes down." His voice betrayed him, but it didn't tell me much. Only that he was willing to reveal more than he normally would.

"Sure. Are you sure I can't get you anything?"

"I'm sure. Listen," he went on, "I need a favor. I can't go into details." There was a certain absoluteness when he said it.

He said he wouldn't go into details, but I had to ask, "Are you in trouble?"

"No, I'm not."

If there was one thing about Jasper I had come to know, it was his honesty. I didn't think he was lying. By omission, yes, but not deliberately.

"Delroy, you and I have known each other for a long time. We are not young men. But we are far from being old. And let's just say at this stage, our lives are different, and leave it at that. Maybe I'll have a beer, if it's all right."

I didn't have any more. Charles and I had finished the two six-packs the night before. And I hardly thought Jasper would want anything stronger. He was not a heavy drinker. And for him to ask for anything stronger would only lead me to assume he was in serious trouble.

"I'm sorry, but I'm out of beers. Would you like—"

He interrupted me before I could ask him if he would like some tea. "That's OK. Listen, as I was saying, I need a favor, and you're the only one I could ask. This is not easy for me." He paused and took a deep breath. "There are certain things I'd rather not go into, but I'll say this much: I have a daughter about Liseth's age. She's my only daughter, and she's in trouble"—another pause—"and I need to borrow $2,000."

That was certainly not what I was expecting, but it confirmed Charles's suspicion that he had a daughter somewhere. He did say she was his only daughter, but he didn't say she was his only child. So I couldn't help thinking that he had a family—a wife and children somewhere. And what about this daughter? Who was she? What kind of trouble was she in? Drugs was the first thing that came to mind.

"Listen, Jasper, man to man, you don't have to tell me more than you think I should know. You might not understand that I would, but I do understand. Say no more." I went into the den and wrote him a check. I handed it to him and didn't ask him about repayment. I wasn't worried about getting my money back. I had no reason to.

"Thank you very much. You'll never know how much this means to me." He folded the check and put it in his wallet. "I'll pay you back every month for the next four months. I'll put it in writing if you want."

I would have settled for his word on a handshake, but I was not about to dissuade him from putting it in writing. I told him it was up to him.

Liseth came downstairs as Jasper handed me his signed self-composed note that said he owed me $2,000, and that he'd pay me $500 a month for the next four months.

"What are you men up to?" Liseth said as she embraced Jasper. "Shouldn't you be getting ready?" she said to me.

"Jasper, I have to go take a shower. I'll talk to you later." He thanked me again.

"Baby, did you know the phone was off the hook all night and all morning?" Liseth said to me as I headed upstairs. "Our parents must have been going crazy trying to reach us. I'd better give my mom a call."

"I think you should wear something else," Liseth said as she came into the bedroom to get her pocketbook. She was dressed beautifully; she had on a new dress, in a way. I'd bought it for her some time ago, but she was wearing it for the first time. It was a cute black minidress that she and I saw in a store in the Village one night. This might be the first and last time she would wear it. Five or ten more pounds, and she wouldn't be able to fit in it. The accessories were also another kind of first—a single-strand pearl necklace and matching earrings. She'd had them too for some time. Her hair was pinned up, and she looked more beautiful than I'd ever seen her before.

"Did Jasper leave?"

"Yes." She looked herself over in the mirror. "You don't have to wear a suit, but that don't mean you have to wear jeans either. Lately you've been jumping into jeans every chance you get. And please don't wear those sneakers."

She said it disapprovingly. When we first met, she said I never wore anything casual, but now I was wearing jeans too often. What the fuck got into her? I was going to wear the jeans, but certainly not the sneakers. I changed into dress pants, put on a button-down shirt, and pulled a sweater over it. For footwear, I wore my English slippers with the crest. I asked her if my new attire was OK. She didn't answer, but she didn't have to. I didn't mind her telling me what not to wear; it was just that she seemed upset about something.

Both our parents had been trying to reach us all morning, and my mom sent a car to pick up her mother and sister. Her brother wouldn't be coming, but I doubted that was what upset her. It wasn't.

"What were you and Jasper talking about?" she asked as she backed the Range Rover out of the garage. She hit the button on the remote for the garage door.

"What did he tell you?" I asked cautiously.

"Nothing, but he was not a good liar." She checked her makeup in the mirror and ran her little finger over her bottom lip.

"What made you think he was lying?"

"I just know he was."

"Why would Jasper not telling the truth bother you? Assuming he wasn't."

"Because I care about him, and I know something is wrong, and he's not telling me."

"We can't say for—" Some woman cut us off on Montauk Highway, causing Liseth to slam on the brakes. At fifty miles an hour, and without our seat belts, we would have both been kissing the windshield.

"You fuckin' bitch. You goddamn—did you see what that bitch did?" Liseth shouted at the woman in the blue Cadillac that turned down a side street. "I swear, if I lose this baby, I'll go after that bitch and kill that motherfucka."

"How you gonna find her?"

"Don't worry, I'll find her, and I'll make her wish she'd never driven a car." Liseth pulled over the jeep and held her belly. I asked her if she was all right.

"You want me to drive?"

"No, I'll drive." She took a deep breath. "I need a fuckin' cigarette." She dug around in her pocketbook but didn't find any. "I need just a drag. Just one drag." She let out a sigh. "Some people shouldn't be allowed to drive a car. I can understand now the meaning of road rage." Another sigh followed, and she then said she'd be all right. "You were about to say something when that idiot almost killed us—what was it?" She put the jeep back in drive.

I was about to tell her that we couldn't be sure Jasper was lying, but I didn't. Instead, I said, "Did you know that Jasper has a daughter 'bout your age?" She looked at me very surprised. The jeep swerved a little. I reached out to hold the steering.

"I'll be OK," she said. "He told you that? So that's what it was. We all figured he was hiding something, but I had no idea it was this. Did he actually tell you that?"

"Yes. And not only that, but she is in trouble, and he asked me to lend him some money."

"What kind of trouble?"

"He didn't say, but it was enough for him to want $2,000."

"Did you—"

"Yes, I did."

"Thanks," she said and put her hand on mine. You'd think they were related the way she behaved. "You know, I think he has a family somewhere. He's such a sweet and lonely man."

"I agree with you on both."

"Did he say what his daughter's name is?"

"No, he didn't, and I didn't ask."

Jasper's visit was certainly unexpected, not to mention his problem. Mom sending a car to pick up Liseth's mom and her sister was within character, but we felt a little embarrassed. We'd promised Esmeralda we'd pick her, Esther and Juan up and take them to my parents'. So with no need to go down to 118th Street, we decided not to go to Ebony's house.

Liseth got Ebony on the phone and explained the situation to her and told her that since it was likely we'd be taking Esmeralda and Esther home, we would stop by later. Ebony told her she understood, and that since Liseth had a week off, if we couldn't make it that night, we could get together one day in the week.

Chapter 16

Both sets of my grandparents and just about half my family had met Liseth, and they all thought she was the most wonderful person. Although my grandparents didn't make a big deal of her age, I can't say they didn't wish she was older. Well, except for my mother's mother. Grandma thought at my age, the only way Mom was going to be a grandmother was for me to be involved with a much younger woman. Grandma loved Liseth from the outset. After the rest of the family got to know Liseth, they were easily won over. This was a day that both sets of my grandparents had wanted to see more than anything: my decision to get married and my impending fatherhood. They wouldn't have missed this for all the world, but Dad's father was not feeling well, so he and Grandma stayed home. Mom's parents were there, and the look on my grandmother's face when I entered the living room was enough. Before anybody could say anything to me, Grandma hijacked me.

"Come here, boy," she said, beckoning me and patting the sofa, indicating that I sit next to her. "I thought all us old folks would die before you got married and became a father. But I guess it's never too late."

Any attempt to describe the look on my grandmother's face would serve her no justice. My grandmother loved all her grandchildren, but I don't think I'd be overstating it if I said I was her favorite, although I was sure she wouldn't admit it. But very few people who knew us would disagree with me.

I snuggled up to Grandma, and we slid our arms around each other's waist. We kissed, and she picked something out of my hair. "Where is that pretty young mother-to-be?"

Liseth was in the kitchen with Aunt B and both our mothers. Esther and Ray, her son's father, were in the living room. So were her older brother, Pablo, and his wife, Rosalie. Dad and his father-in-law were in Dad's study, and Pablo's three children and Esther's son were in my old playroom in the basement.

Grandma whispered in my ear, "You made a great choice, my boy. I'm proud of you. You know that, don't you?"

"I know, Grandma. And I love you." Tears were in my eyes.

She wiped the tears under my eyes and kissed me again on the lips. "I love you too, even though you let me wait this long. Being an aging playboy was starting to not look good on you anymore." She made me laugh, and I put my head on her shoulder like a little twelve-year-old boy. And she patted me on the head.

Liseth entered the living room, and Rosalie was the first person to greet her. Rosalie was a shy woman, whose beauty said more for her than she would ever say for herself. She was also a very modest and very unexciting twenty-seven-year-old who tried not to draw attention to herself. Although she wore decent clothes, clothes were never her passion. Nor, to her discredit, did she wear makeup. But she was a devoted mother and housewife whose husband was just as devoted to her children. Ray was the antithesis to Pablo. Rumor had it that he was constantly unfaithful to Esther. And for that reason, although Liseth was civil to him, she was not crazy about him. But Esther and Ray had been going together since they were sixteen. Ray was her first and only man, and she would never listen to anything anybody had to say against him. This was where Liseth parted company with her mother and her sister.

You could sit through a Ricky Martin concert with Rosalie, and you wouldn't get a peep out of her; but that afternoon, she let out a scream that would have had the whole neighborhood sticking their heads out their windows. Both our parents rushed out of the kitchen to investigate. Rosalie, too, was from Puerto Rico and spoke and understood English well but would rather speak Spanish. When she did speak English, she couldn't help pronouncing many of her words with an accent. Like when she said my name, for example. She'd say "Jelroy" instead of "Delroy," never being able to pronounce her *D*s. Just like she was unable to pronounce her *V*s. It would come out as *B*s instead.

Liseth and Rosalie hugged and carried on in Spanish. Then Esther stood up and joined them, and all three started to scream. And when they saw the ring, the scream grew louder. Pablo, Ray, and I were sitting with my grandmother; and we just watched our women in the middle of the living room going crazy. Dad and Granddad emerged from Dad's study. With everybody looking on, Liseth and company were oblivious to their audience. Spanish dominated their conversation, but you didn't have to understand the language to know that they were in a high state of ecstasy. They were in their own world. Women!

"I sure hope all the excitement hasn't taken a toll on your appetites?" Mom said. "Because dinner is ready, and we have a lot of food."

"You might have to force-feed Liseth, because I doubt she's in any mood to eat today. Would you?" Esmeralda said with obvious pride. Everybody roared with laughter as she walked over to hug her girls.

"I think this is a perfect time to drink to the happy couple," Dad said as he asked Aunt B to get a bottle of champagne from the kitchen.

Granddad walked over to Liseth and hugged her. "I won't tell you how happy I am about this lovely and beautiful young woman that is about to be a member of this family. But I'll tell you this much: the fact that she'll be a lawyer makes all the more difference." His speech was interrupted by intermittent applause, and he would wave his hand to quell it. "As much as this boy had done everything in his life right, choosing to marry Liseth was one thing he couldn't have topped." He looked at me when he said it.

"I heard that," I said.

"I meant for you to. Come here, boy." He opened his arms. A wide grin creased his face. "I'm proud of you, son. We all are proud of you."

I thanked him as we embraced. I was glad that Liseth's family was there. It wouldn't have been the same had they not come. At least for me. And I was sure for Liseth too. I just wished Juan was there, but with the hold drugs had on him, it would have been unpredictable. He would probably have sneaked off into the bathroom to shoot up. As much as Liseth and I wished he was there, we realized there was nothing we could have done. And although Liseth and I believed we could have kept him under control, if for nothing else than for the respect Juan had for Liseth, we both figured it was best after all.

It would have been nice if my whole family was there too, but my family was large and their schedules were diverse. For the wedding, if we opted for a large wedding, and which would be Liseth's decision, we would have had to get a very large place.

I had hoped that at some point I would get the chance to meet Liseth's father. Growing up the way I did, I just couldn't see going through life not being in contact with one's father. But even if I never met her father, looking at Pablo would have sufficed. Esmeralda's children were split down the line. Pablo and Liseth were direct chips off Carlos's genetic block. And Juan and Esther were identical to their mother in every way.

Pablo parted company with his father as far as devotion to family was concerned. But Pablo didn't hold it against his father. They remained close, and Pablo had a relationship with his father's children from his second marriage. As a matter of fact, Liseth was the only one who was estranged from her father and his second family. She couldn't even bring herself to say his name.

When she did talk about him, she referred to him as "my mother's ex-husband."

"Thanks for making my little sister so happy," Pablo said. "It means a lot to me, and the family."

"It means a lot to hear you say that," I told him.

"Congratulations," Ray said, shaking my hand.

Esther and Rosalie broke apart long enough to hug me, wished me the best, and told me how lucky Liseth was. I corrected them. I was the lucky one. Esther laughingly said I was right. And Liseth coming to my rescue said we were both lucky.

Dad popped the champagne and poured for everybody, including Liseth. Mom said it was all right for her to have some.

"I'm going to have more than one glass tonight," Liseth said, reaching for her glass.

"Since I'm the oldest one in the house and my grandson let me wait this long, I'm going to insist on giving the toast. I'm sure nobody will mind." Granddad stepped forward with his glass in his hand.

"As the saying goes, 'Age before beauty.'" Dad patted his father-in-law on the back and eased back.

"When I was your age, I was much better-looking that you are at your age, Lloyd," Granddad retorted.

We all laughed.

Granddad cleared his throat. "First, I want to say that my wife and I are immensely proud of this young man. He's a fine boy, and have lived up to all our expectation. We're both lucky and proud that all our grandchildren have made us proud. We'd also like to say how equally proud we are of having a fine young woman like Liseth, whose mother I'm sure is proud beyond words of her, as a member of our family." He reached out for Liseth's hand, and she took it. "Liseth, I speak for the entire family when I say we're honored to have you as a part of this family."

"Isn't that the same speech you gave before?" Dad said.

"It's shorter than any you've given," Granddad replied.

Liseth kissed the old man on his cheek and thanked him and told him how happy she was. Her mother joined in expressing her sentiment and thanked us for making her and her family feel welcome and at home. Granddad finished his toast and was about to drink his champagne when Pablo asked to say something.

As the person who had been standing in for their father, Pablo stepped forward. He was not an articulate man in any way. He had never finished high school. But he had a good head for business. Having started working since he was fifteen, sweeping the floor of the barbershop around the corner from his mother's apartment and rising to owner ten years later. But Pablo didn't have to be articulate to express his heartfelt love for his sister. "I'm not good at making fancy speeches—or any speech, for that matter—but when I do, I'm usually half drunk before I'd have the courage to say two words, but tonight is special. Tonight I don't need a drink to say how much I love my little sister and how proud I am to stand here and wish her and Delroy good luck and a long life." He raised his glass. "May your firstborn be a boy."

"To Delroy and Liseth," everybody shouted, and we all downed our champagne.

"Since my husband has a proclivity to make long speeches, something he has passed on to his son"—laughter ensued—"let me just say, because if I let my husband start talking, dinner will be cold by the time he's finished." Laughter again.

"That's not fair," Dad said.

"I know, but I can't let two men talk consecutively." She threw Dad a kiss. "I'm very happy to be standing here today, a wonderful day. The happiest day since I gave birth to this wonderful boy, who, I don't have to tell anyone, I love very much. But I'm going to tell you anyhow. There is no one I love more than I love my only child. And when I say today is the happiest day since I gave birth to him, I suppose the only thing that will surpass it is the birth of my grandchild, which I've waited so long for." She looked over at me, and I sort of lowered my head. "My son has always made me proud, but I was afraid he might have made a secret, irrevocable deal with the bachelors association, because I was giving up on being a grandmother. But nevertheless, here we are. My son is getting married, and I'm going to be a grandmother, and I've gained the daughter I'd always dreamed of." Tears welled up in my mother's eyes as she choked on her words. Dad went over to hug her. I joined him.

"You know me, Mom," I said, kissing her. "I always hold out for the best."

"For those who are non-lawyers, two things you should know about a lawyer: they rarely give short speeches, and they very seldom get emotional when they give one."

Dad wiped the tears from Mom's cheek as he spoke. "We all are overjoyed by our son and Liseth's engagement and the prospect of being grandparents."

Mom thanked Dad and finished her speech, even though I thought we were short-changed. The food was ready, and the aroma had already penetrated the rest of the house; and although I was sure the rest of our guests were too polite to say so, my stomach was starting to make noise.

***

If anyone has seen the movie *The Remains of the Day* with Anthony Hopkins, they will remember him preparing the table for the world leaders' dinner conference. After the table is set, he goes around the table with a ruler, measuring how far the silverware are from the edge. For him, the whole settings have to be just right. I was sure my mother didn't go to such length to get her table right, but she sure would have made Sir Anthony Hopkins's character proud.

Mom's table was magnificent and beautifully set. Everything was in the right place. Dinner plates. Salad plates. Soup bowls. Side plates. Water glasses. Wineglasses. Sherry glasses. Dinner forks. Salad forks. Soup spoons. Desert spoons. Dinner knives. Butter knives. Salad knives. Bone dishes. Crisp white linen napkins. Fresh flowers were in the center, and our places were designated with our names. Not one single detail was missed. And if there's anything I didn't mention, it's not because it wasn't there but because I wouldn't be good at setting a perfect table.

Dad, as usual, was at the head of the table. Liseth was next to him on his right, and between him and her mother. Mom would sit at Dad's left, my grandfather next to her, and Aunt B next to him. I was at the other end of the table, and my grandmother was to my right. Pablo would sit at my left, and his oldest son between him and Esther. Between Esther and Ray was their son. Rosalie was beside Liseth, and Rosalie's daughters were next to her.

Leave it to Aunt B to give God the credit for all the hard work she and my mother put into preparing the wonderful meal. But that was Aunt B. She meant well. And for all the years I'd known her, she had never once tried to talk me into believing what she believed in. Although on more than one occasion, when I'd told her of my triumphs, she would say she had prayed for me.

Aunt B had just finished blessing the table. She asked God to be merciful and kind to all of us, and especially merciful and kind to me, Liseth, and our unborn child. Maybe for once God was cooperative: the minute they all said "Amen," the phone rang. It was my other grandfather, and it was for me. He called to say how sorry he was for not being able to be there, and to wish me and Liseth the best.

The old man sounded good and strong, and said he'd wanted to be there, but that my grandmother and his doctor advised against it. We joked a little, and he promised me he'd be at our wedding even if it killed him.

I talked to my grandmother too, and she assured me that it was purely precautionary why granddad was not there. He had a bad cold, and for a man in his nineties who'd had fairly good health all his life, if it meant keeping him well so he could be at the wedding, I had to agree. Then Grandma asked to talk to Liseth. And after Liseth got off the phone, Dad talked to his parents. A few more family members called to give us their best wishes and their apologies for not being there.

We were all enjoying our meal and chatting away. Pablo and I were engaged in a conversation about the law and how he would like to expand his barbershop. He had four chairs in his shop and more clients than he could handle, but he wanted to expand to the empty store next to his. Pablo had great ideas. If he could get the adjoining store, he could have at least ten chairs. But he needed capital, and his credit ratings were poor. He wanted to know if I would be interested in investing in the barbershop. I said it was something I'd be willing to think about, but that I wouldn't be able give him the answer then.

"I'll give it maximum consideration," I told him. My response was sincere.

He thanked me just as the phone rang. Everybody around the table were engaged in different conversations and were enjoying their meal. Mom was closest to the phone but was not about to leave her position to answer it. The answering machine picked it up.

"Good evening, Mrs. Bradshaw." The woman's voice was demure. I recognized it immediately. "My name is Gloria. I'm . . . I'm one of the associates in Delroy's office. I apologize for interrupting your evening, but this is important. First, let me congratulate Delroy and Liseth on their engagement. Good luck, you guys, and—"

Mom interrupted the rest of the message. "Hold on a minute. He's right here," she said. "You can take it in the next room."

I told her I'd take it in Dad's study.

"I got it, Mom. Gloria, what's new? We were in the middle of dinner."

"Brian told me you were having an engagement party today." She apologized and congratulated me again. "When is the wedding?"

"Liseth will decide. I'm quite sure it will be before we have the baby." That just slipped out—not that I didn't want her to know.

"You guys are having a baby too? Double congratulations. This is fantastic. Brian didn't tell me anything about a baby."

"I didn't know until this weekend. And she didn't know that I would propose."

"Now that's what I call true love. Both of you having a pleasant surprise for each other." I was sure she was happy for me, but her excitement was uncontainable. We almost forgot why she called.

"Gloria, you said this was important. The rest of the family is waiting."

"I almost forgot. I'm sorry. The reason I called is to tell you that there are new developments in Connie's case."

"Good or bad?" I was sure it was good. She wouldn't have interrupted my dinner with bad news.

"Oh, this is good. Too good." A sense of pleasure came through the phone at me. "I'm at Connie's." A pause followed. I didn't comment, but somehow I had a feeling she wanted me to know. "She asked me to spend the weekend with her."

"What's the good news you have to tell me?"

She went straight to the point. "Well, it seemed our boy Kevin was married before, with a son—eighteen years old."

"There is nothing illegal about that, or bad for that matter. Is that the good news?"

"Are you OK?"

"Of course I'm OK." *You fucking bitch, you finally got to sleep with her, didn't you?* "But I hope you didn't call me away from my engagement dinner to tell me that Kevin was married with a teenage son. I don't see how that will help our case."

"It will help our case if he didn't get a divorce, which our boy didn't bother to do. And on top of this, he used to beat the shit out of her too."

As much as I was glad to hear what she had to say, and I was sure it would make a difference in how we handled our case, I was also sure it could have waited until I was at the office. But letting me know she was spending the weekend at Connie's house was something she couldn't have waited for me to hear.

I was sitting on the edge of Dad's desk. I moved around to the other side and sat in his chair. The case had just taken on a new twist. Kevin was not only a wife beater but a bigamist.

"What do you have to back this up?"

"Plenty." Her confidence was overwhelming. "Listen to this: when he was in college, he got some girl pregnant, and they were secretly married. Right after that, she dropped outta school and was not heard from again."

"Where's she from? And where is she now?"

"She's from Jamaica, and from a very wealthy family. She moved back there, had the baby, put everything behind her, and moved on with her life."

"How did you find her?"

"Our private investigator tracked her down, and, listen to this."

"I'm listening."

"She was willing to talk to him. She told him everything. How he beat her. And here is the good part: there is no divorce on record in the States or in Jamaica. Our man is getting a signed affidavit from her and is due back in the States on Monday. We also found another old girlfriend whose jaw he broke as a parting gift. This one is living in the States and is willing to testify in court."

The news I was hearing was no surprise. When you're an attorney, you learn that investigation will uncover just about anything. But when you're close to the case, it seems unreal. For Connie to have married a bigamist and a notorious wife beater was not easy for me to accept.

"May I speak to Connie? Where is she?"

"She is right here, Delroy," Gloria said. Her voice sounded conciliatory. "Connie was not feeling well, and she didn't want to be alone. There was no one to stay with her. She asked me if I could come over—"

And you didn't want to, but she dragged you kicking and screaming. Yeah right, you bitch. "I understand."

"Thanks. I'll see you Monday?"

"I'm not sure, but make sure Brian has a complete report from your investigator."

"I will."

I could literally smell the liquor on Connie's breath. She didn't sound drunk, but I could tell she was drinking. "Sincere best wishes to you and Liseth."

"What the hell is going on over there?" I retorted. "Are you out of your mind?"

"What are you talking about?"

"Don't act as if you don't know what I'm talking about. And you're drunk. Where are the twins?"

"They're at my parents'. And where were you when I needed you? You're never there when I need you the most, so don't go telling me who I can have at my house as guest. You're getting married and having a baby."

"So that's the problem? Me and Liseth getting married? And you jump in bed with a woman?"

"Do you know how ridiculous you sound?"

I was beginning to believe her when Dad's knock on the door interrupted us. I told him to come in.

"You're keeping your family waiting," Connie said. "Give my best wishes to Liseth. Good night."

"Is everything all right?" Dad asked just as she hung up on me.

"New development in Connie's case." I remained seated.

"Good, I hope." He sat across from me. "So why the less-than-excited look on your face? Listen, son," he said before I could answer, "you don't have to answer if you don't want to, but you and I have been honest with each other for too long to stop now." Then he went straight into it, without equivocating. "Is there more to you and Connie than you'd want to admit? If there is and you want to talk about it, man to man, it will remain in this room. On the other hand, if you'd rather not talk about it, the same goes."

"There is. At least there was." And then I went straight into the details. I told him everything.

"And you're sure it's over? Done? Behind you? Liseth have nothing to worry about?"

"Dad, look at me." We looked each other in the eyes. "I'm ready to get married. I'm making you and Mom grandparents. I love Liseth. I'm happy."

"I'm glad to hear that, because, son, let me tell you something"—the expression on his face changed—"it could take years to get over these mistakes." Then he told me for the first time of his indiscretion, and how it took him years to make it right with Mom.

There is never a right time for a parent to tell a child that he or she had cheated on the other. And had my father told me when I was younger that he had cheated on Mom, I was not sure how I would have handled it. As a matter of fact, I am quite sure I'd have felt let down. But when we had that talk in his study, the time and the situation was right. I could handle it.

Everybody was halfway through their dinner, or close to finishing it, when Dad and I returned to the dining room. Several conversations were going on. Liseth's eyes caught mine across the room. Her eyes betrayed the questions on her mind. Questions that deserved answers.

"I'm sorry, folks. Business. The office has a way of following you around." I took my seat. My dinner was cold, but I ate it anyhow.

"Is that the hotshot young lawyer you told me about?" Mom asked.

"Yeah, she's doing all the groundwork on Connie's case. She's a fearless litigator."

"She had good news, I take it?"

Since Liseth and I were engaged and expecting a baby, her family was not, in the true sense of the word, strangers anymore, so it was all right to discuss the case, to a certain extent, in their presence.

"Oh my God, what a terrible man," Esmeralda exclaimed.

"The fact that her husband was, or I should say is, married, and with a grown son, and had abused her doesn't mean Connie has a good case for self-defense." My grandmother was a soft-spoken woman, but she was an exceptional legal mind who commanded attention when she spoke. In her days, she had defended some complex cases. Cases that were headline grabbers, that looked to the layperson, impossible to win. But she always found a way to pull off the impossible. "No case ever looks the way it seems," Grandma continued. Liseth's family was spellbound by my grandmother's comment. Esmeralda, in particular, looked visibly confused.

"I don't know the law, but it seems to me this man was no good. Only an evil person would do that to a woman." Carlos may have been unfaithful to Esmeralda, but he had never hit her.

"You may be right," Mom said to Grandma. "But if she was your client, you'd love to have that kind of information on your side, wouldn't you?"

"You bet I would," Grandma replied. Turning to Esmeralda, she continued, "I'm sure this man was an evil, no-good so-and-so who deserved what he got." Grandma was from the age when a motherfucker was known as a so and so. "But if I was the district attorney, I'd fight to suppress any information that would taint him. And you can bet she will."

"She?" Liseth intoned.

"My dear girl, you have to learn something about the law: it's devoid of any emotion. There is no room for it. They'll have to assign this case to a woman. That way, she can be as mean as she wants to be without being accused of sexism."

"Do you think, Grandma?" Liseth asked again, "that this man, who was not only a bigamist but a man who beat women, and had even broken some girl's jaw because she wanted to leave him, can be portrayed to any jury in any way as decent or sympathetic?"

"My girl, as I said, I think this man had no redeeming qualities. I think he was all the things the investigator uncovered and worse, but without corroborating evidence, it will be hard to prove self-defense."

"I'm afraid Mom's right, Liseth," Mom said. "The only person who knew Connie was being abused during her marriage is her daughter, and right now she's too ill to talk."

"I think the first thing the defense will have to do is take their case to the public," Dad joined in.

"Lloyd is right," Grandma said. "Trying the case in the press first will be the defense's best move."

"Getting the public on her side would not be a bad idea," Dad replied. "I'd put her on every talk show I could find from here to Singapore. I'd have her talking about how often he beat her and how she was afraid to talk about it, and I'd paint a picture in the public's mind that there would be not one person on this planet who hasn't heard about the case by the time we go to trial, if we go to trial. By the time I'm finished, she'd be the most loved person in America. And he the most hated."

"I have to agree with Lloyd on this," Mom echoed. "It's a strategy that has more advantages than disadvantages."

"This has no reflection on you, honey"—Liseth looked over at me—"but the first time a man put his hand on me, I'd move to a shelter with my children if I have to. I'd never stay with a man who hits me. No matter how many children are involved."

"You wouldn't have to," Esmeralda inserted. "You'd always be welcomed home."

I sensed where this may be going. Liseth and I had never talked about domestic abuse before. I suppose we just took it for granted that we were intelligent enough to talk about our differences without resorting to anything physical. And although I knew Liseth was speaking hypothetically, I felt I had to allay any fears her family might have. "There are no perfect people. And only perfect people make perfect relationships, but, thanks to my parents as examples, I was raised to respect women enough to not resort to violence, no matter what. I love and respect Liseth with all my heart, and I'm sure, overtime, we'll have disagreements, but we'll find a way to settle those disagreements like civilized people."

"We'll disagree but won't be disagreeable, babe," Liseth said, puckering up her lips.

"Thanks, baby." I puckered back. "And I promise you one other thing: I'll let you win all arguments."

"How do you think I stayed married all these years?" my grandfather chimed in. A chorus of laughter followed.

I didn't know what was on Esmeralda's mind, but I could understand if she was concerned after hearing of Connie's plight. I could also understand if she felt I might have been obsessive of Liseth, considering our age difference. Most people seem to think that in a relationship where the man is much older than the woman, especially if he's a man of means, he'll be obsessed with her. People tend to think the worst about relationships like ours. She's young. He's older. He's got money. He must be keeping her. As if they couldn't be attracted to each other for other reasons.

In any case, I had to keep in mind that Esmeralda was not crazy about our relationship in the beginning.

The rest of the evening was not spent on Connie and whether she was justified in killing her no-good, bigamist husband. We finished the dinner that my mother and Aunt B spent loving hours preparing. We had fresh fruit and cheesecake for dessert and put away a fair amount of alcohol. In between, we found merry things to talk about. We even found time to reject some names for the baby. Liseth and I reserved the right to choose our own names. If we had to accommodate everybody's choices of names, he or she would have the longest name in history.

Some of the names were just too ridiculous to be even considered. Not that they were ridiculous names; they might be perfect for some people, but I was certainly not going to name any son of mine Jesus, no matter how well intended it may be. And I didn't care how important a role Esmeralda's aunt had played in her life when she was growing up in PR, I was not going to name my daughter Conchita. It could very well be that people would call her Connie for short. Which I was sure would not sit too well with Liseth. But worse, children, just to be mean—and we all know how mean they can be—might call her Chita. *Conchita?* Definitely, absolutely not.

The kid may very well grow up resenting us for one reason or another. Who knew. But for sticking him or her with some stupid name shouldn't be one of them. I must admit, some of the boy's names were not bad, including *Lloyd*—not that I was entertaining having another Lloyd in the family, but *Carlos* was absolutely, definitely, not a choice. Liseth wouldn't even go near it, not even in two lifetimes, although I was sure her mother said it in jest. Despite everybody's good intentions, nonetheless, I felt it was a man's right to name his firstborn.

Chapter 17

I was glad I didn't have to go to the office the next day. Liseth and I didn't get home until sometime after two o'clock that morning, even though we left my parents' house a little after ten o'clock. On our way home, I started to feel sick, and we pulled over, and I threw up every fucking thing in my stomach. Liseth kidded me about having morning sickness. Could have been. I have heard of men having morning sickness when their women were pregnant, although the phenomenon was rare. In my case, my sickness was more from overeating and the mixture of different alcohols. My father, grandfather, Pablo, Ray, and I had decided to have a slugfest with a couple bottles of brandies. Granddad, at his age and to my grandmother's disapproval, could still put away a fair amount of brandy. I would have hated to hang with his crowd when he was younger.

Luckily, Liseth pulled over the Range Rover before I started to throw up. Some of the vomit got on the side of the vehicle, but the interior was spared. There we were, close to midnight on the side of the road on the Long Island Expressway, with me bent over at the waist and barfing like a common drunk while every vehicle passing had their headlights trained on me. Some even put on their high beam as if to get a better look. And Liseth standing there beside me, with a towel we had in the Range Rover, wiping my face in between. And complaining how stinky a drunk's vomit smelled.

"I'm glad you did this before you got home," she said. "I'd hate having to clean this shit up."

The last time I threw up after drinking was with Connie. If I remember correctly, we both threw up, although not simultaneously. It was at her house. I made it to the bathroom. She threw up after me but didn't make it to the bathroom. The stench was unbearable, and one that only a person madly in love with you would endure. That was the only time I could remember throwing up after drinking, although I couldn't say the same about Connie. She could hold her liquor much better than I could or any of our friends, but every now and again, she'd throw up after a drinking bout. I often wondered if there was a method to it when she did throw up after a night of heavy drinking. Was it a way of cleansing her soul? Was it her way of avoiding a hangover? Because unlike me who'd wake up the next morning feeling as though I'd been in a barroom fight, or been hit by something that fell out of the sky, she'd wake up the next morning with fond memories of the night before. And possibly ready to start again. I'd wake up not only feeling as though I had the crap beaten out of me but promising I'd give up drinking, or that I'd drink less. Neither promises, to this day, I'd ever kept.

After I'd emptied everything from my stomach—at least that's how it felt—I apologized to Liseth; but she said it was all right. That there was nothing I could have done to prevent it. And that she'd be throwing up a few times before she went back to school. I washed my face with a bottle of water that was in the back of the vehicle and then dried off. I got back in the vehicle, and we drove to the next Mobile service station. I had a large container of tea and lay in the backseat while we parked there for a while.

I didn't remember finishing the tea, or falling asleep, but I must have because the next thing I remembered was Liseth waking me up in our driveway and telling me that my mother had called her and they both had a good laugh about me puking on the side of the road.

I didn't vomit on my clothes, but Liseth suggested they go in the hamper. She undressed me, and when I hit the bed, I felt as though I'd been hit on the head with a blunt instrument. The room was spinning, and the floor felt like it was raising to meet the ceiling; and although it was cold outside, I was sweating as though it was the middle of the summer in a room without air-conditioning, with all the windows shut tight. This went on for several minutes, at least as much as I could remember; and then I blacked out. And the next thing I knew, it was daylight, and Liseth was sitting on the side of the bed, asking me how I felt. I said I was fine, but I was not. It was the day after a fight the night before. This time I went the full distance with an angry Mike Tyson, who showed me no mercy. And I, for some inexplicable reason, refused to stay down each time he'd knock me down.

"Why don't you go take a shower," she said. "I'll bring you some orange juice, tea, and toast."

"And four Advils," I said.

"Four? You sure?"

"Yeah, four. Nothing less will get rid of this headache."

"OK."

I looked in the mirror. I was still as handsome as the day before. Not a mark on my face. Mike Tyson didn't hit as hard as everybody thinks. But I felt as though I'd been pulverized. I took a nice, long hot shower. I let the shower message pound my head. It helped, and Liseth was standing in the bathroom with the glass of orange juice and the four Advils when I opened the shower partition. I stood right there in the shower and took the Advils and drank all the orange juice.

"Thanks."

"The tea is in the bedroom." She handed me a towel. "I thought of making you some eggs, but I wasn't sure you'd want it."

"No. Tea, juice, and the toast are fine for now."

"I didn't think you drank that much last night. What did you men do in your father's study?"

"We put away two bottles of brandies. Your brother was fucked up. I don't know he managed to drive."

"He didn't. Esther did."

"For a guy who loved to talk, Ray was very quiet most of the night."

"That's one person I'd like to keep drunk all the time."

"I didn't think I was all that drunk. As a matter of fact, I think I could have driven home."

Liseth looked at me with a *Yeah, right* look. "Confidence is everything," she said as I finished my tea. "Would you like some more?"

"Yeah, thanks. Are you saying I couldn't have driven home last night?"

She laughed, kissed me on the cheek, and said, "Not with me you wouldn't. I love you too much to let you do that." She took the mug from me and headed out the room. I reminded her to bring the toast when she returned.

I was dressed by the time she came back upstairs. "I'm sorry I forgot the toast. They're plain. I didn't put anything on them."

"That's fine." She put the mug of tea and the plate with the toast on the night table. I sat on the edge of the bed. Two pillows behind my back. Two more behind my head. She sat in the chair. I took a bite of the toast, chewed, and swallowed. Then another bite of the toast. Then a sip of the tea.

"I suppose if I was alone, I'd have had to drive home."

"No, you wouldn't. Your mother wouldn't let you. Last night when you talked to Gloria, you talked to Connie also, didn't you?" She said it all in one sentence, without pausing, as if to not give me time to think. But whatever her reason, I was not about to lie to her.

"Yes, I did."

"I thought so."

"Was that why you looked at me like that when I came into the dining room?"

"Like what?"

She was looking at me with that look again. "Like you're looking at me now. Like, *Don't let me have to ask you, just tell me.*"

"OK, then, so tell me."

"Well, Gloria was calling me from Connie's house, and Connie was drinking. As a matter of fact, I think she was drunk."

"That doesn't explain the look on your face when you entered the room. You were upset about something."

"Did I ever tell you that Gloria was gay?"

"No, you didn't, but why should that upset you in any way?"

"I think she is taking advantage of Connie's condition."

Liseth started to laugh, as though she'd just heard the funniest joke.

"Why, is that funny?"

"I don't know, but I was just thinking . . . let me ask you something." She laughed again. "I'm sorry, but I'm finding it hard to keep a straight face. Is Connie gay?"

"No, she's not."

"You sure about that?"

"I'm very sure."

"So why the concern? Are you saying that . . . let me ask you another question: did Connie ever have a lesbian affair before? Because a lot of girls when they were younger had had these sort of experience, some mainly out of curiosity. But you know, there is a difference between gay and just having a lesbian affair. You know that, right?"

"Of course I know that, but I'm not sure."

"Not sure about what?"

"I don't know, but . . ." I rummaged in the bed, looking under the pillows for the TV remote.

"What are you looking for?" she said, handing me the remote from under the chair cushion.

"Thanks." I turned the TV on and flipped through the channels.

"What are you not sure about, that she might have had a lesbian affair? You seem a little uncomfortable about this subject. You're the one who brought this up, remember."

"Not really." I continued flipping the channels.

"Not really what? What the hell are you looking for on the TV?" She gave a slight smirk. "If you're not uncomfortable talking about it, why are you hesitant about your belief of her ever having a lesbian affair? Either she did, or she didn't. What's the big deal?"

"This is kind of sensitive, and something I'd rather not talk to you about."

Without missing a beat, she exclaimed, "Holy shit, don't tell me you and her had had a threesome." She started to laugh. "Shit, Delroy, that's nothing to be embarrassed about. Most men would die to be in bed with two women. And she's a very pretty and sexy woman with a good body. I can't believe I'm saying this about a woman who I should despise. Don't tell me you've never fantasized about being in bed with two women?" She looked at me as though she already knew the answer.

"That's not it." I was glad she found it funny. "And of course, I've done that, but not with her, and I'm not going to go into details."

"And I wouldn't want you to. But if that's not the case, what is so sensitive that you don't want to talk about it?"

"Well, you know, other than saying this person was great fun to be with, or that she was smart, or she was dizzy, I've never really discussed my sexual relationship with any woman I've been with, but—" I really felt embarrassed, and she sensed it.

"I can't think of anything you could've done with her, sexually, that would make you embarrassed. Whatever happens, consensual, between and a man and a woman is nothing to be ashamed of."

What the fuck, I might as well tell her. "Well, the first time I made love to her, she told me I made love like a girl—something no woman had ever told me. At first, I was sort of embarrassed, but she told me it was a compliment."

"It is."

"How would you know?"

"Women know what women like. And it doesn't mean she had been with another woman. It's just a woman thing. Now maybe Connie had been with a woman before, but that doesn't make her a lesbian. Hold it a minute." She paused. "Is that what you're sensitive about, she saying you make love like a woman?"

I didn't answer. I just rocked my head side to side, looking sheepish.

"Well . . ." She walked over to the bed and sat on the edge, facing me. I slid over a little. She put her arms around my waist and her head on my chest. I ran my fingers through her hair. "You do make love like a girl. You're the most sensitive and passionate man I've made love to. And I've only been with two men before I met you, and they were not really men. They were boys. Both in age and maturity. But you were not only a man, you were a sensitive man who was not ashamed to show emotion while making love. Something rare in a man. You didn't just rush in and try to prove how long you can stay. You took your time and touched me in places that only a woman would know where to touch."

"So how come you never tell me?"

"I don't know. I suppose I figured that you being twice my age, it might be . . . I just think it might be—"

"What, because I'm twice your age it might be a little too sensitive to say that to me?"

"Well, here I was, involved with a man old enough to be my father." The first time she'd ever said that to me. "A man who was well educated. Well rounded in every way, and who, I must say, could very well get any woman he wanted, and the first time we make love, I'm going to say, 'You're the most passionate and sensitive man I've ever been with, and you make love like a girl.' I thought I'd be questioning your manhood. And I loved you so much I didn't want to do anything to ruin it. But you were doing everything right. Everything I wanted, so why say anything?"

I put my arms around her shoulders and kissed her on the top of her head. "But we've been together so long, and we've come to know each other so well—why didn't you tell me? You know how turned on I am when you talk to me when we're making love. What if I wasn't doing something right?"

"Look at it this way: you were."

"But how does a woman really know what a woman likes without ever having been with another woman?"

"Because I'm a woman, and I know where I want to be touched, and I know where I'd touch a woman if I was making love to a woman—and let's face it, unlike men, we women admire another woman's body, but that doesn't mean we want to make love to her. So Connie may not necessarily have been to bed with another woman, but as a feminine woman, she would know what another woman wants. I grew up with girls who you couldn't pay them to look at a dick, and I have heard them talk. Connie may have never been with a woman, yet"—she stressed the *yet*—"but if Gloria is a committed lesbian, and she stayed at her house since Thursday, she either fucked her or is setting it up. Trust me, it won't be long."

"That's what I'm worried about."

She released her hold on my waist. "Why should that worry you?"

"Because I think she'll get hurt."

"Or she might fall in love. Either way, she's a big girl."

"You're right," I said, only to get off the subject.

To say life was wonderful, that it was great, that I was having the greatest time of my life would be an understatement. At my age, I had had a full life. More than many men dreamed of. Or would ever hope to have. I had had everything going right in my life. Wonderful and supportive parents and extended family. A great and rewarding career. Money having never been a problem. Great friends and coworkers. And I had seen a great deal of the world—at least those that interested me. And now, when most men my age would have, and should have been—at least the forty-something men that I knew who were single and without children—looking to just enjoy the rest of their lives in the most carefree way, I was getting ready to turn my life around by getting married and being a father. Until this happened, I'd thought life couldn't have gotten any better. Boy, was I wrong.

Liseth and I fell asleep holding each other that afternoon. I wasn't keeping track of the time. I only knew that when I woke up, I was alone in the bed and it was dark outside, and a delicious aroma was coming from downstairs. The smell of food had nothing to do with it, but I felt as though I had a hole in my stomach. It was the hungriest I'd ever felt in my life. I felt as though I was being punished by being kept away from food deliberately. And that aroma, whatever Liseth was cooking, was only making it worse.

At the top of the stairs, I shouted and asked her if it was OK to come down.

"Of course it is," she said.

It wasn't until I approached the kitchen that I was able to identify what she was cooking. Chicken soup. Chicken soup? *Does she know how to cook chicken soup?* It certainly smelled good. The kitchen didn't look the way it would have looked if I was cooking. I could tell every vegetable that was in the soup from all the peelings on the counter. But she was trying her best. Either our impending nuptial and motherhood had transformed her into domestication, or Yale had taught her a lot more than the law in her first semester. But whatever had befallen her, I was not about to tinker with it.

"You read my mind." I walked over and kissed her on the cheek. "That's just what I need to bring my stomach back to normal."

"I thought some soup would be the best thing to put back some of what you may have lost last night." She added some spice to the pot. "Have a seat. It should be ready in a few minutes."

"I was gonna go in the living room and watch some TV."

"No, sit here with me. Turn this TV on."

I sat at the kitchen counter and watched as she cleaned up the carrot, potato, and peelings of some vegetable I was not familiar with from the counter. She stirred the pot with the large wooden spoon. Then she asked me to taste it. She blew on the liquid before I took it in my mouth. The soup was delicious. It was good. If I'd just come home and she'd had that waiting, I'd have sworn she had somebody cook it for her. There was no cookbook in the house on soup cooking. There were some books on how to cook other things, but none on soups. OK, so you called your mother or mine, and they walked you through the process. But you know what, baby?

You cared. And that's the most important thing. The soup was fucking good. Perfect. And I was not about to say a word. I was just going to enjoy the goddamn food.

"You think it needs anything?" she asked.

"This is great, baby."

"Good." She turned the heat down under the pot and took two soup bowls from the cupboard and set them on the counter.

I sat there, enthralled. I felt married already. She had her hair up, held together by some painted chopsticks. She had on jeans and a T-shirt under her apron and no makeup. She looked more at home in the kitchen than she may ever look behind a desk. She busied herself, finishing the cleanup of the kitchen before she served the soup. I loved what I was seeing. If she'd decided there and then that she was not going back to Yale, she would not get an argument out of me. But as much as it would give me great joy to have a full-time mother at home, I had to agree with Esmeralda. Get the degree first.

I turned the TV on and turned to the BBC Channel. She served the soup. The steam hit me in the face, and I dug into it without regard for the heat. Scorched tongue didn't stop me.

"God, you were hungry." She joined me at the counter. "Would you like some bread with it?"

"Nah. Not with all these vegetables in it." I continued eating. "What is this thing in the soup?" I asked, referring to a yellow chunk of semihard vegetable in my bowl. I must admit, it tasted very good. And I took another bite of it.

"That's yam. You never had it before? I'm sure Aunt B must have cooked it at your mother's."

"Maybe when I was younger, but I really can't remember."

"But it tastes good, doesn't it?"

"Yes, it does." I was almost finished. I asked for more. "Where did you learn to cook chicken soup like this? What else can you cook that you're not telling me about? I thought you could only cook salmon and eggs."

"You know that girl that came home with me from school?"

"Who, Claire?"

"I thought you'd remember her." She gave me a dirty look. "She's not the kind of girl a man easily forgets. And it's not just because she looks good. Well, she—"

"Well, she's kind of—"

"I know, Delroy. You don't have to tell me. You can tell your friends. As I was saying, she used to come over to my house and cook for everybody. On weekends, we'd have this big cookout. We'd just sit around after studying and eat and talk. Well, Claire, more than anyone else, was, as you can tell, is different. She's the only one I talked to about you, and told that I hoped you'd asked me to marry you."

"Was this before you knew you were pregnant?"

"Yes. As a matter of fact, she was the only one I told of our problems. And she was, maybe it's because of who she is, but she was supportive and considerate and understanding. I remember her saying to me that life is not like in the movies, that love is not love unless it's tested. And when it's tested, that's when you know if you really love someone. That's when I realized that I was not going to let Connie ruin what we had."

"So what are you saying, up until that moment you weren't sure if it was over?"

"She helped me to decide."

"Maybe I should thank her personally."

"That's all right. I'll thank her for us." She got up and went over to the stove and put a little more soup in her bowl. "You want some more?"

"I think I'm OK. You're not worried about me meeting Claire again, are you?"

"Well, let me put it this way: I talked about you with her like Ebony talked about you with me, and she is just as fascinated with you like I was before meeting you."

"But at that time, I was not involved with anyone. So it's different."

"You bet your ass it's different. There are two things you'll have to understand." She let the words linger for a moment before she continued. "I love my mother tremendously, but I'm nothing like her. Suffering in the name of love is not something I believe in. Loyalty is something I'm prepared to give one hundred percent of, and what I'll demand. One indiscretion is enough. One. There'll be no divided loyalty in my marriage." I couldn't wait to hear what the other one was, even though the angst of knowing did not fill me with the least bit of comfort. "I'd hate to see this child grow up an orphan."

It was the most unemotional I'd ever seen Liseth. The words came out with the most callous of intents. And yet her demeanor was calm.

"You have any idea when you want to get married? Or what kind of wedding you want? I can get married right now—today, if you want."

"Thanks, baby." She walked around the counter and hugged me. "But I think I'll maybe wait until I come back from school. We'll set a date before the start of the next semester. I'd like to have as many of my family there. Not that I have to have one of those big crazy weddings, but I most definitely have to—no, I insist on having—have the most exciting and fabulous wedding dress. And you in your tuxedo. I don't care what the others are wearing."

For a moment, I thought of asking her if she would think of inviting her father and his other children to the wedding, but I didn't. I knew the answer to the question.

"So we'd be getting married before your aunt. Isn't that something? You will invite her, won't you?"

"She'd kill me if I didn't."

"This way, she'll have to invite me to her wedding."

"Listen, my aunt didn't really believe I'd come to her wedding without you, so we won't even worry about what she feels."

"What if—" I knew I'd be entering dangerous waters and I should be careful in asking what I was about to ask, even though I earlier told myself I shouldn't. "What if—"

"What if what? My father shows up at our wedding uninvited? I would hope, for once in his life, he would have enough good manners and at least some respect for me not to. I'm sure all this might be too much for him to do, but I'd hope for the first time in his life he'd find it necessary to do something to make me happy. And that is, no matter how much he thinks he'd like to dance at my wedding, to just stay away. I don't even want a card or a gift from him. It's too late for any sentiments from him."

"How did you know that's what I was going to ask you?"

"Delroy, I'm a woman. I know how men think, and somehow I just had a feeling you'd have to have that question settled. So now you know." She gathered the dirty dishes and put them in the dishwasher. "And I hope you're not thinking of inviting him? Please don't do that. Do not disrespect me like that."

"The thought never crossed my mind." It really never did, even though I'd have loved to meet him.

"Promise me you won't. I'm sure you may think you're doing the right thing, but just don't."

I looked up at her, and I could tell she was serious about her request. I promised her and was tempted to raise my right hand. "I have an idea," I said, excitement in my voice.

"I don't want to hear anything that has to do with my father." Her voice was stern, but she referred to him as her father and not her mother's ex-husband. That was the first time, since I had known her, I'd heard her say that. It may have been the start of a crack in whatever armor she'd worn all those years.

"No, no, baby. This has nothing to do with your father. Nothing at all to do with him."

"Good. And the less we talk about my mother's ex-husband, the better, for me, at least. What's your great idea?"

Without giving it a second thought, and before I lost the thought completely, I said, "I was thinking maybe we could get married on New Year's Eve. You know, start the new year new. But only if you want to. What do you think? We could start working on it right away."

It would be the first marriage for the two of us. At my age, and my way of looking at things, I'd take my vows before anybody who was authorized to perform it. I'd even go to City Hall. Or a priest. What was important was that it was legal. But Liseth was young, and as much as she'd said she was not hung up on big weddings, all young girls would like to have a wedding they can remember. I was sure she would like something more than the big fancy dress.

I had a feeling she would say yes to New Year's Eve. We would have the ceremony at my parents'. They could easily get one of their friends, a judge, to perform the ceremony. We'd have the reception right there. My parents could erect a tent on the back lawn, next to the pool. We could seat enough of both our families and a few friends. It would be a great way to ring in the new year. And then we could leave the next day for our honeymoon and be back in time for her to make school. "It's a great idea to me, Liseth. What do you say, baby? Let's do it."

I didn't have to wait long for an answer. "Sounds like a great idea, baby." She threw her arms around me. "I couldn't have thought of a better time to get married. Where would we do it? I know, at your parents'. It's so exciting. I'll start making plans right away. Let me see," she said and reached for a legal pad and a pen and started to write things down. "It would've been nice if we could do it right here, with the ocean in our backyard and everything." She continued making notes on the legal pad. "But your parents have more yard space—plus, it would be easier for everybody to get to their place. This is great, Delroy. Us getting married on New Year's Eve. I can't wait to tell my mother."

Now why didn't I think of that? Maybe at least she'd let me chose the honeymoon location.

"We could leave the next day for our honeymoon," she continued. I'd never, for good reason, seen her this excited. "Where would you like to go? We won't have more than a week. Would you like me to choose somewhere?"

Of course I'm going to let you choose. This is the time in a man's life when he should know when to give in to his woman. If he doesn't know anything else, he should know that this is her moment. This is special to her, and the thing to do is give her the plastics and get the hell out of her way.

Chapter 18

·•⊷⊷•⧼⧽♥⧼⧽•⊶⊶•·

$\mathcal{I}$ was joining an elite club. Some of the members were men of renown: Sidney Poitier, Cary Grant, and Tony Randall were some, just to name a few. We're all men over forty-five, who had either become first-time fathers or had fathered children with women who were much younger. Mr. Grant and Mr. Randall had become first-time fathers at sixty-two and seventy-seven, respectively. Mr. Grant's wife, Dyan Cannon, was in her early twenties, and Mr. Randall's wife, who was an intern in his acting workshop, was also in her early twenties. Sidney Poitier's wife was not in her twenties, and it was not Mr. Poitier's first time being a father, but he was over fifty, which put him in that elite club.

According to all the so-called experts, men who become first-time fathers in the second half of their lives were more inclined to be better fathers. After his daughter's birth, Cary Grant had decided to retire from acting to spend more time with her. I could retire at fifty, or even now, and still maintain my present lifestyle for the rest of my life without lifting a finger. And Liseth, who had the thinking of a modern woman, I was sure, would like to work for a while and establish herself as a lawyer in her own right. I would encourage it. And on the other hand, if the both of us stayed at home, we would only get on each other's nerves. She could get a job in any of the major law firms and work for as many years as she wanted. But what would I do with all that time on my hands? I was a more successful trial lawyer than most of the lawyers who turned writers, so a second career was there for the asking.

I fell asleep, leaving Liseth downstairs on the phone, calling everybody she could get a hold of, telling them of our New Year's Eve wedding. Of course, my mother was the first one she called. And of course, my mother was just as excited as Liseth was. Mom thought New Year's Eve, starting the new millennium, was a perfect time; and her house was the ideal place. And into action they sprang. After finalizing their plans, Liseth called her mother. I had no idea when she came up to bed, and I vaguely remembered some foreplay, but I must be honest, I don't remember if we did anything else. Only that the next morning, we were both naked in bed. And since I was not drunk, then I must be getting old, not remembering if we'd made love. But what I couldn't remember doing the night before, I certainly made up for that day.

Getting married made me suddenly afraid of two things. One was what every man could live with. The other would scare any man my age. What scared me most was that I may be on the verge of getting lazy and then start to get fat. Oh my God. Now, I don't know about the other forty-something guys, but the thought of myself with a potbelly, me taking off my shirt and a piece of flesh hanging over my pants would be enough for me to embrace a religion or give up sex. Two things that anybody who knew me would find hard to believe.

But there I was, having not run since Liseth came home; and she, for whatever reason, may suddenly have me eating three square meals a day. Now the paradox, and what I supposed every man could live with but sort of scared me was that Liseth was becoming a domestic goddess.

Having woken up with a hangover on Monday, going running was out of the question. Tuesday I got up early enough, and with enough energy to go, but the both of us, naked in bed and she initiating sex was enough to change my mind. We went at it for pretty much the whole morning. It left me too exhausted to lift my eyebrows, let alone my feet to run. But whatever energy I'd used up was replenished by the huge brunch Liseth made me. Salmon eggs, buttermilk biscuits, orange juice, and tea. Then right after that, she brought me a piece of cheesecake. After that, I was too tired to do anything except sleep. And sleep I did.

I awoke sometime in the afternoon, about three thirty. I was alone in the bed. It was a wonderful day. The sun was out. The sun came in from the direction of the ocean. It skipped over the water, and the rays landed in the bedroom, transforming it into something even the greatest writer of fiction could not have thought of. Looking out on the ocean, I had to shield my eyes with my hands from the sun. But what a beauty the sun and the ocean created.

I stood at the window and looked out as far as I could see, where the sky and the ocean met. The majesty and the mystery surrounding what I was looking at made me realize why some people believed there had to be a god. It's hard for some people to accept this great beauty without giving some credit to some mysterious figure that they can't even explain what or who he or she is.

I stood there naked, unconcerned about who was responsible for what I was enjoying. Nor did I care. Whoever or whatever was responsible did not negate my appreciation for beauty. Especially great beauty. I was also unconcerned about anybody from the ocean seeing me standing there naked. If anyone could see me, it would have to be someone in a boat with a high-powered glass. Or someone in a low-flying plane.

I didn't hear Liseth come up behind me. She put her arms around me and hugged me from behind. We stood there awhile before either one of us said anything. I turned around and faced her.

"You'll have to learn to keep that thing under control," she said, referring to my erect penis.

"It's got a mind of its own," I said.

"Is that so?" she said, stroking it. We kissed. And I could smell food in her hair.

"You're cooking?"

"I'm making you dinner."

"You're making a habit of this, aren't you?"

"I'm home for a week, and I'm going to take care of my man. Something wrong with that?"

"That's what I'm worried about."

"Me taking care of you?"

"Believe me, don't think I don't appreciate it. Don't think I'm not enjoying having you home and putting some life into this house." I patted my belly as I spoke. "But you're going to make me fat. You know, I haven't run since you've been home."

"I noticed that, but you'll get back into it as soon as I leave. But on the other hand, look at all the exercise you're getting from all that lovemaking."

I asked what she was cooking. Roasted chicken, baked sweet potato, boiled cabbage, and a salad of lettuce, cucumber, and tomatoes.

"I know how much you want to stay slim," she said, pinching my belly, "and I don't want this getting in the way, so I'm cooking healthy food for you."

"Where did you learn to cook like this?" She handed me my sweat pants. "I didn't know you could cook anything other than eggs. Here I am, thinking that when we got married, I'd either have to get us a maid or buy you all the cookbooks in the world." She handed me the sweatshirt.

"I never said I couldn't cook. I just never had a reason to cook, so I didn't."

"But you're cooking all this food like an expert. You're becoming a domestic goddess. Don't tell me you learned all of this at Yale?"

"Some. But cooking a good meal is not difficult. Plus, according to Claire, a man in love won't know the difference between a good cooked meal and swill. And even if he did, he wouldn't complain. To a man in love, the fact that his woman is making an attempt to cook for him is enough. A man of class would compliment her, not criticize her."

"Claire said all that?"

"Hey, Claire is not only pretty, she's extremely smart too. And can cook on top of it."

"You and her seem to have a lot in common?."

"We're both from rough neighborhoods and grew up with certain disadvantages, but unlike her, I took a different direction early. She had to go through what she went through before she found that education was the answer. In a way, I'm kind of glad she experienced what she experienced."

"So all she needs now is a good man in her life. How come she doesn't have a man?"

"You'd have no way of knowing, but she can be very intimidating. Plus, she thinks the right man hasn't come her way yet."

"What's her idea of the right man?"

She looked at me, with a *Do you have to ask?* look. I went into the bathroom and emptied my bladder and put some toothpaste on my brush.

"I'm sure she'll find her ideal man at Yale," I said with the brush in my mouth.

She was saying something, but I couldn't hear her clearly. Not with the water running. "I can't hear you," I said with the toothbrush still in my mouth. I rinsed out my mouth and turned the water off. Then I emerged from the bathroom. "I couldn't hear a word you were saying."

"She thinks you're the ideal man."

"Most women do. But I'm taken, and unfortunately for her, I'm an only child."

"At what point in your life did you become so cocky? So sure of yourself? I meant to ask you that a long time ago."

"I was born this way, baby. This is something you just can't develop. And you did ask me this question the first time we met. If I'm not mistaken, I think that was what attracted me to you."

"The things some girls will do when they're young." We both laughed and headed downstairs.

***

I take back everything I ever said about Liseth. She can make more than a great salad. The chicken soup was not just a fluke. Her mother had nothing to fear from her cooking. But she could cook. Not that putting the proper seasoning on a chicken and putting it in a preheated oven at 350 degrees for two hours needed any culinary skills, and as she said, "cooking a good meal is not difficult." But dinner was delicious. The cabbage was a little overcooked—I liked my vegetables with a little crunch in them— but continued effort like that and my tailor might see an increase in his business.

Liseth ignored the phone while we had dinner. I loved that. It showed the kind of wife she would be. Whoever it was could either leave a message or call back, but at dinnertime, she was not going to be interrupted.

I sat in the living room and put my feet up. She brought me an after-dinner brandy. My first drink since Sunday. And only because she brought it. My sweat suit was one of those fancy sweat suits with a buttoned waist and zipper fly. I undid the waist of the pants, giving my waist room to breathe a little. I could tell already that this kind of eating would take no time for my waistline to get out of shape. I was beginning to love not only her cooking but also the way she was pampering me. I was sure somewhere down the line she'd be trying out new dishes, but I'd have to exercise some discipline.

I made myself comfortable on the sofa and took a sip of the brandy. "Come here," I said before she walked away.

She sat down beside me and put her arms around me. She looked at me. She didn't say anything. She didn't have to. If there was anybody in the world happier than she was, it would have been hard for me to imagine. She put her head on my chest. I stroked her long blonde mane, and she dug her head deeper in my chest.

"Thanks for everything, baby," I said as she tightened her arms around me. "You're spoiling me. You know that, don't you?"

"You deserve to be spoiled." The phone rang. "Sometimes," she said as she got up to answer it, laughing.

"Sometimes? What do you mean sometimes? I thought I deserved to be spoiled all the time. What do you mean sometimes?"

"Nobody deserves to be spoiled all the time. It will go to their head."

"Hey, I spoil you all the time. Does it go to your head?"

"But I'm different. I deserve to be spoiled, and to be kept that way. I'm a woman. And it already went to my head. It's been there so long there is nothing we can do about it anymore. For you, it has to be sometimes. You know what they say about men?"

"No, I don't. What do they say about men?"

"Your heads swell easily. That's why you have to be spoiled only sometimes."

"I'll sometimes your ass later," I said as I watched her tight ass exit the room. She mooned me. She was right. She deserved to be spoiled, every day.

Chapter 19

———◦❤◦———

*L*iseth left my parents' house for Yale on Sunday. Claire
and Toni were meeting her there. The Spanish virgin
had returned on Friday after having lunch with me,
Liseth, Claire, Toni, Ebony, and Roscoe Webb, a retired pro
basketball player who was a third year associate in my firm's
corporate department. Lunch was more than just a few friends, old
and new, getting together. It was a celebration. It was Ebony's treat.
Dalton couldn't be there; he had to be at the hospital. That's the life
of a doctor.

Ebony and Toni hit it off immediately. They exchanged numbers
and everything. Claire was another story. Ebony thought she was
smart, but abrasive. And that if she wanted to work in a major law
firm, she would have to tone down plenty. I agreed. But somehow I
had a feeling Claire wouldn't have a problem adjusting herself.

The girls' enthusiasm was overwhelming. They were noisy and
caused people in the restaurant to stare at us with mixed reactions.
Not that they cared. Nor did Roscoe or I. Carla did congratulate
us and gave us her best wishes and all, but she was not as emotional
as the others.

After lunch, and Carla's apology for leaving that afternoon, I
took Claire and Toni on a tour of my office and introduced them

to some people. Liseth and Toni were sorry to see Carla go, but Claire couldn't care less. I can't say I disagreed with her. I wouldn't want to spend that much time on the road with her, unless she was sitting on my dick all the way without her panties on. But seriously, all I had to do was meet that girl once to know she had serious problems. And until she got fucked, or grew up and accepted the fact that some people were not about to wait until their wedding night, she'd remain a head case.

There was a raw sexuality about Claire that would make men do illegal things. She and Toni were already at my parents' house when Liseth and I arrived. I'd called my mother to let her know they were coming.

As abrasive and as street smart as Claire was, she never dressed tartly or common. Though she didn't wear expensive clothes. Jeans and modest-length skirts with sweaters or tops that were not revealing were her choice of clothes. That Sunday, she had on a pair of tight faded jeans and a black turtleneck sweater, with her hair pulled back. She was also not big on makeup, but damn, did she look good. If I'd met her and Liseth the same night, I couldn't say who my choice would be. And even if I'd chosen Liseth over her, I'd feel cheated if I didn't at least fuck her. I still felt cheated, as it was, but I was getting married in less than three months, and having a baby in eight, so I was not going to jeopardize everything for some cheap thrill. But I was entitled to my fantasies. I would have loved for Roscoe to fuck her and tell me what I was missing, but he was interested in Toni, and she in him.

What a week it was. I proposed to my girlfriend. I found out I was going to be a father. We set a date for the wedding. I found out my girlfriend who couldn't cook, could cook. And if I was not careful, although I was loving every minute of it, I could get fat. For the first time, I had considered the thought of retiring. In four or five years, I'd quit the legal profession completely, maybe become a writer, stay at home and be a house husband. Seeing my son or daughter off to school while my wife went off to work. I wasn't sure I'd cook and bake and keep a neat house, waiting for my wife to come home from work. I'd get us a housekeeper. I'm sure Liseth would insist she be the grandmother type. But I'd certainly want one of us to be home when our child came home from school.

It was indeed a wonderful week. By Wednesday, I'd started running again. Thursday, I'd not only run ten miles with Charles and Mildred, but Liseth and I had marathon sex, as if we were trying to prove something. We took Friday off, but Saturday, after Charles, Mildred, and I went running and we'd all had lunch, we resumed the marathon. Or as Liseth would describe it, "the sex that would hold over till Thanksgiving." That was when she would be home again. She was always naming one of our sexual moments. And despite what Connie had said, I was beginning to accept that one woman could satisfy me. I could wait until Thanksgiving. Sunday morning we made love again. In the bed. In the shower. And again in the bed. What kind of animal were we?

Mom and Liseth didn't let me in on too much of their plans, only that we would be taking our vows at midnight on New Year's Eve. And that her old friend, Judge Constance Baker Motley, of the federal court, would perform the ceremony. The rest of the wedding plans—not that I needed to know, but they didn't tell me. Of course, I had my choice of people outside the family I could invite. And there were a few people from my office I wanted to invite. My best man, of course, would be my father.

I had to go to work the next day, so I didn't stay too late at my parents'. I said my good-byes after Liseth and her friends left and I hit the road. The first thing I did as I got on the highway was call Connie. The phone rang constantly, without any answer. Her answering machine picked it up. I didn't leave a message. I tried about ten minutes later. Same result. I still didn't leave a message. After the toll bridge, I tried her again. The result was the same, but this time, I left a message. "Connie, Delroy. Call me."

"So you really are getting married?" was the first thing out of the caller's mouth. I didn't even get a chance to get undressed. The caller didn't have to say another word. I knew it was Connie. "Is it because she's pregnant?"

"Suppose she'd answered the phone? What then? Aren't you taking a big chance on calling my house?"

"Your message was 'Call me.'"

"Yeah, but I didn't say at home."

"But you didn't say where. And I knew she wouldn't be home. Plus, I'm your client."

"Yeah, but what if she'd decided to leave tomorrow instead?"

"So I'm right she's not there. I figured she'd either leave yesterday or today."

"But what if she hadn't?"

"But this conversation proved she did."

I had to concede she was right. And carrying on this slapstick was getting neither one of us anywhere. "You did sleep with that woman, didn't you?"

"You didn't answer my question. Are you really going to marry her?"

"Yes. And her name is Liseth."

"Why, because she's pregnant?"

"No, because I love her."

"A lot of people are in love, and they don't get married. I loved you, but I didn't want to marry you."

"People also have children, but don't get married. I decided I wanted to get married before I knew Liseth was pregnant. For your information, I didn't know she was pregnant until after I proposed. Why am I justifying my reason for getting married to you anyway?"

"And why should I justify who I sleep with to you?"

"I'm not asking you to justify who you sleep with. I'm just trying to stop you from—"

"From doing what? Making a fool of myself? From getting hurt? If this was with a man, you wouldn't think so, would you?" Her voice raised as she spoke. And the contempt for what I was implying was evident.

I had to admit she was right. I did think she was making a fool of herself, and that she'd only get hurt in the long run. But was it my place to judge? Did I have that right?

"You men are all alike. You all think a woman's salvation is hanging between your legs. Well, I've been married to two, and they both fucked up my life. So now you know why I didn't want to marry you. I hope Liseth's luckier than I am." And she hung up on me.

I sat there in my bedroom, in my bed with the phone in my hand, wondering what the fuck was wrong with this woman. Was she fucking nuts? Was she totally fucking crazy? She certainly wasn't drinking this time. So why was she behaving like this? The answer was all too obvious, but somehow I didn't grasp it. I felt bad. I was insensitive. The woman could very well go to jail for who knew how long. And who knew how she'd handle it. I could have been a little bit more sensitive. I decided to call her back. Her phone was busy. I hung up. Then my phone rang.

Again, before I could say hello, the voice said, "All you're fuckin' concerned about is if I let some fuckin' woman suck my pussy. It doesn't bother you that I may go to fuckin' prison. That my daughter, after doing—after seeing what she saw, may never be the same again. You're not concerned about those things. You're not concerned about those things. You're only concerned about if I slept with some woman. Why is that important?"

But it's important to me. I should just sit back and let some dike fuck you and maybe fuck up your life, and say nothing about it. If she could see the look on my face, she'd know how I felt. "Connie," I said, "you know I'm deeply concerned and worried about the outcome of this case. You know the last thing I'd want to see is you going to prison. And you won't go to prison. Not with the new evidence we have. You also know I'm deeply concerned about Nicole's health. You know all these things. You have to. You know me well enough. The fact that I'm marrying someone else doesn't stop me from caring about you. We'll always be friends. I'll always care about you."

"But you can't guarantee that I won't go to prison, can you?"

"As a matter of fact, I can. The worst that can happen is you getting probation."

"Is that a guarantee, or is that what you hope will happen?"

"No, I'm guaranteeing that you won't go to prison. I'm betting everything on this."

"You're putting yourself out on a limb, aren't you?"

It may seem to her that I was putting myself out on a limb. And maybe I was, but I was convinced that even if she was found guilty, she wouldn't go to jail. And the chances of her being found guilty, in my opinion, were very slim. "Connie, you're not a criminal, and Kevin had serious baggage. We'll push for all the charges dropped, but if all else fails, we'll cut a deal. But that's a last resort. But I'm willing to bet everything you won't go to jail. And that I can guarantee you. And you know what else? As a matter of fact, I'm convinced that if we go to trial, no jury in the world would convict you."

She became a little subdued. She was calm, and her voice was soft and alluring. "Delroy, I don't want to go to prison. I'm so afraid." I could sense vulnerability in her voice. And I could imagine how she felt and how at that moment she wanted to be held. Not just by anybody but by me. I had seen her in that state before, when she lost total control of herself. When she wanted me to just hold her. She always felt stronger, even in the worst condition, when I was around. In all my life, I'd never met a woman who depended on me as much as Connie had come to depend on me. Despite her ability to take care of herself financially. I must say it made me felt good. "You know all my life, I did the right thing. I . . . I . . . ." She paused. She was definitely crying. "I try to live right. All I wanted was a man to love me and respect me. Where did I go wrong?"

Not marrying me, I wanted to say, but that would be rubbing salt in the proverbial wound. "Now stop blaming yourself. You didn't do anything wrong. You had no way of knowing Kevin was who he was. You know, Connie, we all take a chance when we marry someone. There are no guarantees how it will work out. No matter how much we know that person, or think we know them."

She apologized for coughing and blowing her nose. It was evident she was crying, and that she was drinking. I asked her if she was drinking.

"Some run and coke," she said. "Are you, Delroy, taking a chance in marrying Liseth?"

I wished I hadn't said that. With her state of mind, she was inclined to believe I may be having second thoughts.

"Everything we do in life is part of taking chances."

"You're not answering my question. Are you taking a chance in marrying Liseth?"

"Connie, life is full of possibilities, not predictabilities."

"Sometime I just wish you'd stop being a fuckin' lawyer for a minute."

"You said earlier when you were talking about Nicole, that after doing, and then you said, after seeing, . . . what—"

She cut me off before I could finish. "I said many things. I can't remember everything I said." Her tone was sharp and defensive.

"We both said a lot of things. We're both tired." I was appeasing her. I wanted to end the conversation anyhow. I wanted to sleep. "Can I say one thing before I go to bed?"

"We're not going back to Gloria again, are we?"

"Should I? As a matter of fact—"

Again she cut me off. "It's really none of your business."

I ignored her advice. "Where do you think this will go? And how long you think this will last? What happens when Nicole comes home—you're gonna what, sneak around and lie to her about where you're going just to see her? Is that the way you want to lead your life? How about the rest of your family? How do you think they'll handle it? Do you really know what you're getting into? Listen, Connie, Gloria has been at this for a long time. She's not going to be broken up if you end it. I'm sure she has had many lovers. Plus, do you really think she's faithful to you?"

She didn't hang up, but it sounded as though no one was on the other end. I couldn't even hear her breathe. "Hello . . . hello. Are you there?" The silence on the other end lasted for close to a minute. I called her name twice. Then she answered.

"Why are you doing this to me? Why are you trying to . . . why are you being so mean? So unkind? So cruel? Why?"

"I'm not being mean, unkind, or even cruel. I care about you. Because I don't want to see you do something that will only hurt you in the long run. Because I . . ." I was going to say *I love you.*

And I did, but she would only have misinterpreted it. "Because you're important to me," I said instead. "You're my friend. I'm your friend. And friends look out for friends."

"But not enough to be with me tonight, though."

"Ah, Connie, let's not start that again. You know I can't do that."

"No, you don't want to do it. See, that's where you and I differ. I'm an adult, and I can do whatever I want with whomever I want. I'm sure you have to go to work tomorrow. Why don't you try to get some sleep. You've more important things to do this week, like keeping me out of jail." She said good night and hung up before I could say anything.

***

Elizabeth stood in the frame of the bathroom door. Water dripped off her. Her strong athletic body of olive complexion glistened with the combination of the water and the light on her. The room was well lit. She walked over to the bed and got in on the left side, sandwiching me between her and Shawn. I'd heard of an actress named Shawn Young, but I'd never met any woman named Shawn. The name may sound masculine, but I assure you, there was everything feminine about Shawn Sinclair. Her father, she said, wanted a son.

I'd known Shawn since the start of the spring semester of my second year at Columbia. We bumped into each other, and I mean bumped into each other, in the bookstore. I knocked her books out of her hands. The largest one, a medical book, landed on her foot. A terrible way to start her first year at college, with a sprained foot. And an even stranger way to get acquainted with someone.

Elizabeth was a different story. I'd wanted to screw her the very first time I set eyes on her in the library earlier that same spring semester. She had a strong athletic, sculptured body, derived from her years of devotion to track and field. It was the kind of body that made you just want to see her naked, or in a thong before you fucked her. It was a new semester, and new girls were to be added to the list. Elizabeth and I were introduced by a mutual friend. I had a feeling she was attracted to me too. It didn't take me too long to add her to my list. She was easy. Shawn took a little longer. She had never slept with a black man before. But spring break would change that.

There was much more to Shawn than I'd imagined. An attractive skinny girl with a smile that made anyone, male or female, more than willing to just give in to her every demand, but who, despite her enormous appetite, always looked as though she was in great need of something to eat. Shawn could also appear to be shy. But that was if she didn't know you. *Shy* was not a word that could fairly apply to her. Shawn loved girls with equal passion as she loved men. She had been bisexual since she was fifteen, and although she'd never been with a black man, black girls were her favorite. Elizabeth was not a shy person and was one who was not afraid to try new things. She took to us, Shawn in particular, with an approach that exhibited such skills that would question any claim to have never done it before.

For me, it was my first time with two women, but it was an experience I'd long awaited. I'd dreamt of the moment. I had heard that a man hasn't lived until he'd been to bed with two women. And I had heard that on spring break, just about anything can happen. That's when the great majority of students drop or totally lose their inhibitions. On spring break, every student indulges in their fantasies. Some under the influence of some substance. Some with a clear head. And that night in the Bahamas, I realized what they were talking about. I defy any red-blooded heterosexual male to tell me they wouldn't enjoy making love to two women. Or anyone to tell me after trying it the first time they wouldn't want to do it again.

What we started in the Bahamas didn't end there, although it didn't go on for too long. And they were not the only girls I'd had a threesome with. And Elizabeth and Shawn went on without me and made no secret of it. And although it had been a while, a long while, since I'd been with two women, I don't mind saying that it was an experience I savored with extreme delight. But saying it would be an understatement.

Interesting how time changes all of us. There was a time when the idea of Connie making love with another woman would have intrigued me enough to want to get involved. Although I could hardly ever envision Gloria wanting a man in bed with her and another girl. Gloria had too much of a penis envy to want a man there. It would be too much of a challenge for her. The closest Gloria would probably let a man get to her was on a crowded train.

I always said that if my woman had to cheat on me, I'd rather she did it with a woman. With a man, there is one of two things you can do. You can either break it off and you both go your separate ways, or you can forgive her and put it behind you. But then something will always happen that will let you question her actions. But there is no way you're going to want to share her with another man. At least I wouldn't. With a woman, it is different. If she decides she doesn't want to break it off, the worst that could happen is that you could wind up with two lovers. Which wouldn't be all that bad. At least not for me.

***

I lay on my back, with my hand under my head, looking up at the ceiling. I tried not to think of anything. I was drifting in and out of sleep. As much as I tried not to think of anything, the thought of Connie making love to Gloria was as clear as a picture in my mind. As if they were there in the bed beside me. During our relationship, Connie had never talked about women in any way that led me to believe she found them attractive enough. Sure, she'd mentioned how good a particular girl in a particular outfit looked. Or comment on the body of another, but men sometimes comment on how well dressed another man is, and that does not mean a sexual attraction.

I yawned twice in succession. My eyes became watery from yawning. I yawned again. And in that moment before I fell asleep, I admitted to myself that I more than just cared for Connie. I admitted to myself that I was jealous of her sleeping with someone else. Even if it was a woman. Even though I didn't know that for a fact. I admitted to myself that I more than just loved her. For the first time, I admitted that I was still in love with her. There was something still there. I thought about what I'd do if Liseth was not pregnant. If she wasn't pregnant, I could do one of two things: I could stay with her. Marry her and carry on an affair with Connie. Or I could break off the engagement and be with Connie. I'd have to do the latter, because it would only be a matter of time before Liseth found out, and when she did, she would leave me, for sure. But Liseth was carrying my baby. My parents' first grandchild. In my family, honor superseded emotion. In time, I would get over Connie, but I'd always think of her with deep affection. I'd always love her. And I knew too that she would always feel the same.

Anyone who says one can't be in love with two women at the same time has never known true love. And if they are a man, they have never met anyone like Liseth and Connie. I yawned again. Then sleep overcame me.

The first thing I did the next morning was call Liseth, and before I could say hello, she answered with, "I'm sorry I didn't call you last night before I went to bed." She was apologetic. "I was so tired from the whole weekend, the trip and everything. I just fell asleep as soon as I got here. As a matter of fact, Claire did most of the driving."

"Are you OK?"

"I'm fine. I just miss you."

"I miss you too," I said as I lay there with a fistful of hard-on. "I was tired too. I fell asleep as soon as I got home. I could hardly keep my eyes open on the drive back home."

"Did you stop on the way?"

"Actually, I didn't."

"You know what I always tell you."

"I know, to pull over and rest. But I stopped only to get some tea, and made it home safe."

"Good. I don't want anything happening to you. You're all I've got."

"Thanks, baby."

"Did you get a good night's sleep?"

"Too good. If you hadn't called, I might be still sleeping."

"Luckily, I called, huh? Are you going running this morning?"

"No. But I promise I'll start tomorrow. I have a lot to work off."

"Will you stop. You didn't gain that much weight. As a matter of fact, I don't think you gained any at all. I didn't feel any."

"Would you be able to tell?"

"I'd be able to tell. I've been with you long enough."

"I can't tell you enough how much I miss you."

"I miss you just as much. Even more. You know what?"

"What?"

"We should have gotten married before I left."

"You wouldn't have gotten an argument out of me on that. But you're worth the wait."

"Thanks, baby. I'm going to be late for my class. I'll talk to you soon. Love you."

"And I gotta go to work. Take care of my son. I love you too."

***

Something that Connie said the night before came to me as I took my shower. I kept remembering what she said about her daughter. It could have been a slip of the tongue. It was subtle, and maybe really meant nothing, but I just couldn't shake it. Did she really mean to say what Nicole saw, instead of what she did? It was far-fetched, and it could be my deep-rooted pursuit of a viable defense, but what if it was Nicole who really killed Kevin? I could picture it: Kevin was downstairs beating the living daylights out of Connie. Nicole was asleep upstairs and was awakened by her mother's screams. She came downstairs, a little frantic and dazed from being awakened from a deep sleep. She had seen Kevin beat up her mother before. But this time it was different. He was no longer living there.

In a state of natural suspended consciousness, she asked Kevin to leave her mother alone. And then tried to pull him away from Connie. He wouldn't stop, and he pushed her away. She took a knife from the set on the counter. It was her first instinct. She hoped it would scare him off. He turned around, came at the kid, and she either stabbed him intentionally or he lunged at her, slipped, and fell on the knife. Either way, it was a kid who, seeing her mother being beaten up, and with every reason to believe both their lives were in danger, acted in self-defense. Self-defense, or accidental death, and with the history of abuses, no jury would convict a thirteen-year-old girl for coming to her mother's defense. The thing was to prove it.

We could make the argument, easily, that they were afraid to report the abuses because of fear for their safety. We could line up an array of experts to testify about the suppressive behavior of abused women. We could also get a whole host of abused women to testify to the reason why they were afraid to tell anyone of their abuses. We could even get some men to tell of how they instilled fear in their victims. That was the easy part.

The hard part would be getting Connie to admit it was Nicole and not her who killed Kevin. Without her admitting that it was Nicole and not her, it would be very difficult to prove otherwise. And with Nicole not responding to treatment, the cynics could very well claim she, or we, her defense team, were exploiting the sick child to get Connie off. It was a delicate path to take. It could backfire on us. I doubted it. But if it was the truth, we would have no choice but to pursue it. We would have to get a psychologist to evaluate her condition and determine if she could be questioned. And if she was too ill to be questioned, we could be stuck with only a theory. We must not forget that the prosecutor might want to get their own psychologist to evaluate her too. Connie was a nurse. She was familiar with and understood what Nicole could be subjected to. So I could understand why she would want to take the rap for her daughter. Who could blame a mother for wanting to protect her daughter in a case like this? The child was going through enough as it was.

What the fuck was I doing? I was thinking as though it was a foregone conclusion. As though I had the facts in front of me. And even if it was not Nicole, there was no doubt we could very easily get Connie off without using the "daughter did it" defense. The next thing we would have to keep in mind was that, depending on Kevin's estate—and from all indications he had a great portfolio, not including his life insurance—the prosecutor could try to bolster their case by using greed as a motive. If we were successful in proving that Nicole was the killer, they wouldn't be able to use greed as a motive. But even if we couldn't prove it was Nicole, our greatest advantage was playing up the suffering, depressed, abused wife and daughter. It was not easy, but it was doable.

I finished my breakfast—raisin bran cereal, orange juice, and tea—and was heading out the door when the phone rang. Connie again. A good night's sleep usually put everyone in a better mood. I hoped it did for her.

"We both said some harsh things to each other last night," she said. "I was a little drunk—"

"A little?" I laughed.

"I had a drink or two."

"Or three." We both laughed. I was glad we both could see things in a different light. A good night's sleep sure made a difference.

"I just want you to know I wouldn't have called if I thought for a minute she—I'm sorry, Liseth—was there last night." She was obviously sincere. "I wouldn't disrespect you that way."

"Thank you. Connie, can I ask you how Nicole is doing? We haven't talked about her as much as we should. You know how fond we used to be of each other. Have you visited her recently?"

She paused before she answered. "She's . . . she's OK, considering the circumstances." She paused again. Maybe I shouldn't have asked.

"Are you OK?" I asked. She said she was. "What are the doctors saying?"

She was evasive. And it was obvious she didn't want to talk too much about Nicole, and I didn't want to press the point this early in the morning. "She's responding slowly. But they're hopeful."

"Did the doctors say exactly what her problems are?"

"Something about a psychological block. And suppressed memory."

I could tell this was making her uneasy. And like all good lawyers, I knew when to change the subject. "How is work?"

"I had a lot of time saved up, so I'm taking some time off. And under the circumstances, the hospital understood. But right now, I'm not sure when I'll be going back to work. But I'll be going back."

"How are you for money?"

"As a matter of fact, it's not bad, for now. Everything is taken care of. Kevin had all the bills taken care of through auto payment. The mortgage and the car and all the other important payments. Despite everything, he'd never stopped making payments on anything. He'd never used money as a means to punish me or anything like that. So for now, I can afford to live here. In the next months, I don't know if I'll be living here, or where I'll be living."

I thought she was exaggerating on the uncertainty of her living condition in the months ahead.

"I might wind up in prison and my daughter in a mental hospital, and my sons"—she started to cry—"at least my parents will take care of them."

"You have to believe in me, Connie. That won't happen."

"I don't know what to believe anymore." The crying continued, and I tried to console her the best I could. She got a hold of herself long enough to say she did believe in me. That was after I told her I'd handle the case personally. And that if I was unable to get her off, I'd give up being a lawyer. Handling her case I'd may be able to do. There wasn't much of a problem with that. If the litigation team thought I was the best hope of getting her off, they'd agree. Anything that served the client's need. Give up being a lawyer, I didn't think so. But making her feel that I'd make the ultimate sacrifice for her made her feel good.

Chapter 20

—◦◦◦❤◦◦◦—

O h, the joy of getting married and being a father. What a feeling. What a rush it gave me. My head was four times larger than its usual size. And I was walking on air. My well-being and good spirits was obvious to everyone I came in contact with. I couldn't hide it even if I wanted to. As if I wanted to hide it anyway. I might as well have hung a sign on me saying I was an expectant father, and that the wedding date was less than three months away. Everybody I knew would ask me why I was so happy. And even those who didn't ask, and it was only because I'd tell them first that they didn't..

The trains were ten minutes late getting into Bay Shore that morning. Late trains were not an unusual occurrence. And ten minutes, when you're dealing with the New York Metropolitan Transport Authority, was not a strange occurrence once a month. And in the winters, with heavy snow, it was unpredictable. More often than most of us cared to remember, there would be an announcement over the PA system telling us that the trains would be ten minutes late. Only to be told, fifteen minutes later, that the trains would be half an hour late. Only to be told half an hour later that the trains were canceled, and that there would be buses to take us to Babylon.

Although a majority of the commuters found living on Long Island preferable to living in the city, half of them at that moment were evaluating the cost of their monthly ride into the city. Half of the other half were wondering if the risk of living in the city wasn't worth it. The rest of us, and I do say us because I was in that category, couldn't care less, because we knew as soon as the trains were back to normal, nobody would remember the last delay. But once the trains were delayed, the $200.00 a month for the unlimited ride into New York City was being looked at as being overpriced. Between the first announcement and the time the buses arrived, everybody would be on their cell phone calling their offices or whoever they had to call. Some were calling to say they'd be late for work. Others were using that sick day they'd set aside for just this occasion. Some were pooling for a ride to the Ronkonkoma line, assuming they were running on time. And they would if the problem was confined to our line and not in Jamaica or Penn station, which would throw the whole system in chaos and have several hundred thousand people mad at them. Others were calling their spouses to tell them they were coming back home. Others would just show up unannounced, to their spouses' dismay. For gardeners and handymen, it could be a very bad day.

The trains were ten minutes late, as promised. I'd gathered with some of the regulars and was explaining my state of transformation to them. Unlike the subways in the city, when you travel on the Long Island Railway on a regular basis, you tend to stake out your seats and sit with the same people every morning. The evenings were different. Although we'd catch the same trains in the mornings, most of us very seldom caught the same train in the evenings. Lawyers, in particular, didn't keep nine-to-five. And some of the others, some secretaries, would have to work late if their lawyer bosses asked them to.

The topic each morning could be varied. As you can imagine, my upcoming marriage and expected fatherhood were the topic that morning. Everybody was giving me their heartfelt congratulations. A slap on the back. And many "It's about time, you old dog you." Not to mention the usual "What took you so long?" I felt like the ballplayer who had just made the winning home run and was being mobbed in the dugout. But I could understand. Very few of them were not married. And although many were lawyers and you'd think they'd know better, some were on their second marriage. A few were even on their third. Didn't they ever hear that if at first you don't succeed, not to try again but to give up? I had every reason to believe that my marriage to Liseth would be my only one, and a happy one. But if for some reason it didn't work out, I would never, under any circumstances, get married again.

By the time the train pulled into Penn Station, I doubted there was anyone on the train who didn't know I was getting married, and that Liseth and I were expecting a baby in the summer. One man came up to me to tell me how much hope I'd given to men over fifty. I thanked him, avoided telling him that I still had five more years to go before I was worthy of his praises. Mr. O'Hare, who must have been the conductor on the Montauk line before there ever was a Long Island Rail Road, stopped me on the platform to tell me of his almost-fifty years of marriage and seven children and to give me his best wishes. I was not adverse to seven children, although I really had my mind on three; but fifty years of marriage meant I'd be ninety-five. Not that it was impossible. People lived long in my family. Something to look forward to.

The first thing I did when I got to the office was set up a meeting with Brian and Gloria. I asked Gloria to come see me, alone, before Brian arrived. His secretary said he'd be in late. Gloria didn't try to hide her curiosity, even though I tried to assure her it was strictly business. She asked if she could come up right away. Telling her the sooner the better didn't do anything to dampen her curiosity. She wanted me to give her an idea of what was on my mind. Just for the fun of it, I said, "Connie." And left it at that.

In the past week, my secretary had to deal with a deluge of congratulations coming in. She had a great deal of work to do, but she found the time to take all the calls and open all the mails. They came in from just about everybody, and from all our offices. And were still coming in by card and by phone. Some of the people I'd never talked to before. Others I'd only said hello to in the elevator, the dining room, or at the Christmas party. The news got around fast.

Besides my meeting with Brian and Gloria, the day had shaped up to be a busy one. The phone hadn't stopped ringing since I came in, and the visitors stopped by in a steady stream. Among my visitors was Roscoe Webb. For some strange reason, I had a feeling I knew why Roscoe was stopping by. He was smitten by Toni.

Roscoe and I were friends who shared a lot in common. Commitment to bachelorhood, among other things. And we were both workaholics. He was a guy who took his work as seriously as I did mine. He was the kind of person who would eat lunch at his desk. He was the kind of person who would work till nine, ten at night, and weekends. He took everything in life seriously. Even when he played basketball. He was a very good basketball player. He was drafted out of Georgetown, where he played forward and led the team to two championships. In the NBA, he played the same position for five seasons for the Knicks, before a second injury to his right knee brought his career to an end.

Roscoe came to the New York Knicks with great fanfare. He was hailed as a savior. Every player since the glory days of Reed, Frazier, Monroe, and the team of the 1971 and 1973 championship seasons had been hailed as saviors. Not only was he hailed as a savior, but he was hailed as the player who would do for New York what Magic Johnson did for the Lakers, Larry Bird for the Celtics, and Michael Jordan for the Bulls. The Knicks signed him to a ten-year $50 million dollar contract in 1987. It was a huge sum of money at the time. A record for the Knicks, and rivaled the $30 million dollars for ten years that Patrick Ewing signed for several years earlier. But New York needed a championship bad enough.

In his first year, the Knicks seemed as though they were about to get their money's worth. They made the playoffs for the first time in seven years, but they got swept in the first round. The second and third years, they went to the finals. The second year, the Lakers beat them in five. And the third year, they went to game 7 with Boston, and lost in overtime.

Roscoe had injured his right knee in his first year in college, but had recovered and had been injury free until his fourth year with the Knicks. Halfway in the fourth season, he injured the knee again and missed the rest of the season. The team never made the playoffs that year. After surgery and rehabilitation, he came back in the fifth season and was doing well, taking the team to the payoffs. Unfortunately, he injured the knee again, and the Knicks got swept in the second round. This time the knee was shattered so bad the doctors advised against him ever playing ball again.

After recuperating over the summer, and hoping to prove the doctors wrong, he made an attempt at working out with the team in training camp. A move that proved the doctors right. The knee swelled to three times its size, and further x-rays showed the damage that was done to it. He was advised that if he hoped to ever walk again, he should give up any desire to play ball again. It was a painful decision, but one that Roscoe realized he had to make. He took a year off to get his body and mind in shape. And after deciding what he wanted to do, secured by his wise investments and a guarantee contract that paid him majority of his salary for the remainder of his ten-year contract, at thirty, he decided to go to law school. After three years at New York University Law School and several summers at the firm, he was taken on as an associate. What Roscoe really wanted to be was a sports attorney.

As I suspected, what brought Roscoe to my office that morning was his attraction to Toni. And it must have been a serious attraction, because he was there trying to know as much as he could about her. Not that I could tell more than he knew. The way he and Toni were looking at each other was enough for me to know that whatever was going on was not going to stop there.

"Roscoe, what brought you here this early in the morning?"

"Listen, when you go up to visit Liseth, I'd like to come with you. You don't mind, do you?"

"Not at all. Does Toni know you'll be coming, or will this be a surprise?"

"It will be sort of a surprise."

"Either it is or it isn't. Which is it?"

"Well, I told her I'd like to come up one weekend, but I didn't say when. But I figured if I go up there with you—"

"Your motives won't look as obvious as they are," I interjected, cutting him off in midsentence. "Roscoe, you're a very assertive guy. Why is it I have this feeling that you're a little nervous with this girl? Are you?"

"Of course not, but she's different from most girls I'd been out with—"

"Roscoe, you haven't been out with her. You met her at lunch with us and exchanged phone numbers."

"I know, but I like her. And I'd like to get to know her better. And I think she likes me too."

Roscoe was acting like a man in love. It was written all over his face. Plus, he was acting like a schoolboy. Not that there was anything wrong with that. We all, given time, fall in love sooner or later. Why should he be any different? But for a guy who'll be negotiating million-dollar deals with some of the meanest ball club owners and who have bedded some famous women, supermodels among them, he was acting out of character when he was talking about Toni. *She might be a law student, Roscoe, but she was still a woman. Don't get clammy palms over her.*

"I thought you and Veronica Jenkins were a serious item? What's going on between you and her?"

"What made you think there was something serious going on between us? We're just fuckin', that's all. Plus, we work together. I see her every fuckin' day. It's hard to get serious with a girl you're seeing every day, especially the day after she'd just given you the best blowjob you'd ever had."

"Does she think there is more to it than that?"

Roscoe laughed and stretched his six-feet-nine-inch frame with extra-long legs out. He massaged his damaged knee without looking at it. He kept talking to me while he massaged the knee. His fingers worked it as though they were speaking to the knee. He didn't show any sign of discomfort when he walked, but the knee was a constant reminder that he'd never play ball or go jogging again. To keep his weight down, he worked out five days a week and stuck to a strict diet.

"I've never lied to her about my feelings. And we've never talked about anything that would lead her to believe that this was going anywhere beyond where it is."

"As long as she understands that. Plus, you and I may be friends, but as member of the firm, I shouldn't be having this conversation with you, in the office of all places. Just in case it gets nasty. And you've to admit that if you break it off, it could get nasty. I don't want to be dragged into it as somebody who knew what was going on. Plus, you know how the firm feels about inter-office dating. Not that they can stop it. And not that they don't know it's going on. It's only when it blows up that they act as if it's new news."

"I'm sure she wouldn't care if I broke it off." He stood up and stretched his long limbs. His arms outstretched almost covered the width of my office. He could sit in the driver's seat of a Cadillac and open and close the passenger side door without leaning over. "I really would like to go up with you when you do."

"Are we going to use the Rolls?" I told him I was kidding before he could answer. But I wouldn't have minded. He hardly drove the darn thing anyway.

"I don't know. Toni might think it's a little extravagant."

"Hey, a Rolls. A Jag. A Range Rover. What's the difference? Plus, it's not like we're poor people trying to impress someone. We're who we are." He laughed and exited my office, passing Gloria on his way out. They exchanged pleasantries.

If I should have ever grown to dislike Gloria, her penchant for the finer things in men's clothes wouldn't be one of the reasons why. As usual, her suits were well tailored. And the fabrics were of the finest quality. Her shirts were also well selected. Custom made from the best shirt maker in the city. Today she had on a gray double-breasted gabardine-and-wool suit with a light-gray shirt. French cuffs, of course. This time she had gold cuff links instead of the silk knots. Say whatever you want about Gloria, but don't ever say she didn't know how to dress. If she was a heterosexual, she would have been one of the best-dressed heterosexuals around. Which had me wondering at what age she decided she wanted to give up men.

Gloria entered my office with confidence in her steps, but her face gave away the apprehension she was harboring. It was not like Gloria to fear anyone. That much I knew about her. But I had a feeling she thought I'd asked her there for personal reasons. Especially when I said it was about Connie. She sat down before I could ask her to take a seat. She sat across from my desk. Her hair looked longer on the sides. It was hiding the top of her ears and fell farther down over her eyes than I'd seen it before. Even with no makeup and the man's outfit, she still couldn't look like the man I was sure she wanted to look like. All the time spent in the gym might have given her a knockout body, but it was not going to decrease her femininity. She brushed the hair away from her eyes. I had seen white men brush their hair from off their faces, and their actions were generally different. They did it with an unmistakable masculine touch. Women did it differently. And the way Gloria brushed her hair from off her face was definitely with a feminine touch. Once a woman, always a woman. It really made me wonder at what age and what caused her to give up men.

"How is Liseth?" she asked awkwardly. And if I had any doubt as to her apprehension of being there, her voice gave it away.

"Liseth is fine. Thanks for asking."

"Congratulations to both of you. And I really—"

I am sure you really mean it, but I didn't call you in here to talk about my personal life. "Thanks again. Gloria, I need to talk to you about something that has been bothering me for the past two days. It has been on my mind, and somehow, and maybe I'm wrong, but I have a feeling you can shed more light on this." I pulled a legal pad from out of my briefcase. There were some notes on it I wanted to refresh myself on. The expression on her face changed. It was defensive.

I studied my notes before looking up at her. She looked uncomfortable but was obviously ready to defend herself if she had to. I was having fun with this: watching her sitting there uncomfortable. I could just imagine what was going through her mind. I was mentally tormenting her. And maybe if I continued, she would confess she'd slept with Connie. I doubted it. And even if she did, it wouldn't be out of weakness of any kind but out of some pleasure of knowing that she was pushing my button.

Pushing her mentally was risky. She could claim harassment and discrimination. And with the power of the gay community, win or lose, it would be an embarrassment, not only for me personally but to the firm. And most of all, I'd be hurting my client's interest. As much as I would like to know if she'd fucked Connie, the price of knowing was too high. All I could do was sit there and hate her for seducing my ex-girlfriend. For taking advantage of Connie's weakened state.

I would have loved to keep this up all day—watching her being uncomfortable, but what would this prove? At some point, even if I didn't say why she was really there, she would have to ask why she was there. Awkward as it might be, I was sure she was ready, in the most polite way, to tell me that it was none of my business. And she would be right. And if I did raise the subject, I'd be super stupid. But as much as I had not asked her about what went on between her and Connie, she had answered my unasked questions. *You bitch.*

Her voice may have given away what she was concealing, but her body was rigid. She didn't shift her position. But she spoke with caution. "I . . . I'm . . . I'm not sure what you mean." She brushed her hair away from her eyes again. "What has been on your mind?"

"You've been spending some time with Connie, since—"

Her interruption was abrupt, with a slight raise in her voice. "With all due respect, Mr. Bradshaw . . ." The fact that she was addressing me as "Mr." showed her displeasure with what she perceived to be an encroachment in her private life. "I'm not sure if—"

It was my turn to interrupt her. I had to put to rest the apprehension she was harboring.

"Hold on, Gloria. Hold on a minute. Please. Let me explain why I asked you here. I wanted to talk to you and Brian about this, but I figured I'd get your perspective on it first." Her face relaxed. And I told her about my conversation with Connie, and of my theory. And asked her what she might think of it. She sat up even straighter, and her demeanor changed completely. The lawyer in her went to work.

It didn't take her long to run it through her head. At least I was not the only one thinking of that possibility. "It did accord to me, and I did bring it up with her, but she brushed it aside."

Yeah, I can just imagine the position you both were in when you brought it up. "I think there might be a definite possibility that Nicole might be the one who did it. As a matter of fact, I strongly believe she did it. But you can understand a mother's need to protect her daughter. In her position, I'd do the same. No doubt about it. What I want to know is, what do you think? Because what you think is important to our approach to this case."

"Thanks. I have to agree with you. My hunch is that Nicole did it. But I think it was an accident. I don't think it was deliberate. But it's a very delicate subject. We have to tread lightly on this one."

"I agree. That's where you come in."

"What do you mean?" Again, that look on her face. That look that said everything I was thinking.

"Well, you have been spending a lot of time with her lately. Which is good. Because I know her very well. She needs a friend at a time like this. And you know the position I'm in. It would not be appropriate for me to render anything other than professional advice. So I'd like you to use"—I looked straight at her, and we locked eyes for a minute before she looked away, brushing her hair from off her face as she looked away—"your friendship to find out as much as you can." There was a look on her face. A sentimental look. A look of deep caring, "If we're right and you and I seem to agree on this, we have to find a way to get her to corporate. We've to put all personal feelings aside and think of our client." That sort of slipped out. I didn't mean to say that. But it was already said. And Gloria was far from being a fool. That remark, if it didn't do anything else, had just told her how I felt about Connie. I wanted to tell her I didn't mean it the way it came out, but it would only do the opposite.

The more we talked about Connie and what was facing her, the more Gloria became sentimental, though she tried to hide it and was doing a good job of it—only, I knew who we were talking about and who I was talking to. My goodness, she was in love with Connie. I couldn't believe it. I thought all she would want, like all lesbians—because that was how we were conditioned to look at homosexuals: incapable of falling in love and having a long-lasting relationship—was to fuck her and move on. The bitch was in love. That was the thing about Connie: everybody who made love to her fell in love with her. Man or woman.

I thought of using Gloria's emotional state to our case's advantage. If she loved Connie as I thought she did, she would want to do anything to get her off.

"Listen," I said, "you and Connie are adults. The kind of friendship you share is your business. And I'm not implying that your relationship is anything other than you being good friends, but I care about her, and I want to get her off by any means necessary." She nodded in agreement with everything I said. "If you can find out more to what we just talked about, by any means necessary, then you have to get it."

What I was asking her to do, if she hadn't done so already, was to fuck Connie if she had to. As long as she got the information we needed. I was asking her to prostitute herself for the sake of our client. Except it was with our client. But on the other hand, if she was already sleeping with her, what difference would it make? And all the better—she'd be saving her lover from going to prison, because chances were, if she went to prison for a long time, she might wind up being somebody's girl anyway.

"Brian will be joining us shortly. As the lead attorney, I'd like to hear his opinion on this. But I wanted to talk to you about certain things before he sits in. You understand, don't you?"

"I do. And I'm glad you mentioned it. After I raised the subject with Connie that night, I never brought it up again, and it sort of just disappeared from my mind." Again she brushed her hair from her face.

"Are you letting your hair grow? Going for the long look? It looks good," I said, trying to add some levity to the mood. And it worked. She smiled for the first time since she entered my office.

"Actually, a friend of mine said I would look better with long hair." Her face took on a definitely different mood when she said it. And I could only assume it was Connie she was talking about. Connie was always partial to long hair. I always loved her with long hair. Maybe she was telling Gloria what I used to tell her.

"Listen, Gloria, Nicole is in the hospital, and you may know more than I do how sick she might be. Connie going to prison is not going to help her. Connie already admitted to the police she killed her husband. Although we know he used to beat her, it will be a hard defense. Not impossible, but hard. That is, if the DA decides they want to go to trial. But if we can prove that Nicole came to her mother's rescue, and by accident killed Kevin, our case would be much easier. If we can convince the prosecutors that this was purely an accident, we might not even have to go to trial."

"I'll do everything I can." I could hear the confidence in her voice; she didn't have to assure me. I thanked her and commented on her suit. She said thanks and flashed me a smile that was unquestionably genuine. The chauvinist in me couldn't help but feel that this fine female specimen was being lost on the opposite sex. I was sure a night with Roscoe or me would change her mind.

***

Brian was not only one of the best litigators I'd ever worked with, but he was a thorough and thoughtful person who was always well prepared in his approach to any case he took on. Like all good lawyers, the last thing he wanted was to be blindsided at trial. Information, and good, reliable information, was of uttermost importance. No lawyer wants to get the information they need at the last moment. They liked to have it in their hand with enough time to study it and check the reliability.

The thought of Nicole killing her stepfather was not farfetched, from Brian's point of view. He agreed with me and Gloria. All the elements were there. Nicole being traumatized by what she did. And Connie trying to spare her daughter from being further traumatized by taking the blame. She may be even, in some way, blocking out the idea of her daughter doing it. Psychologically, she could be blaming herself for what her daughter did. Feeling that if she hadn't married such a dreadful man, and stayed in the marriage, exposing her daughter to all the abuses she suffered, the kid wouldn't have to come to her rescue. Deep down, she may be feeling that since she didn't have the courage to leave Kevin, then Nicole felt that the only way to free her mother, and them for that purpose, from what she perceived to be a prison was to kill him. And that night was the opportunity Nicole was waiting for all along. The mind can play terrible games on us. In the normal course of life, it dictates what we do, but when it starts to lead us to believe in things that are not real, this is when we need help. Connie may be in that stage. She may be under some delusion that it was her who really did it. Because to think otherwise would be too much for her to live with.

There were two things Brian insisted we do. We should get Connie to reenact the whole incident exactly as it happened that night. That way, we would get a good idea of what really happened. And get him our findings as soon as possible. Gloria and I looked at each other. We agreed with him, but we knew without saying that it would be her who would be doing it.

We ended the meeting agreeing on one thing. Regardless of who killed Kevin, Connie was not going to jail. Even if we couldn't convince the DA it was Nicole who did the killing and they were foolish enough to go to trial, our biggest weapon was sympathy.

The rest of the week saw me getting back to my regular routine, and working hard and late. With Liseth away and all the wedding plans in the works, I worked late every night, had dinner in my office, caught the late train home, and was up at dawn every morning. By Wednesday, I'd caught up with all my paperwork. Thursday I had a meeting with one of my older clients. Older in the sense of him being my client for many, many years. He wanted me to meet a potential new client, who was an important man from an important family, whose business was importing wine. The family business was having problems with some business they had in an Eastern European country and wanted someone to straighten it out. My old friend and client, Cyrus, thought I'd be the right person to do just that for him, because of my success several years before in handling a delicate matter in the former Soviet Union. I was grateful to Cyrus. Over the years, he'd referred some very important and wealthy clients to me. I was sure I'd take on this new client, but as was the firm's policy, I had to present it to the committee to screen for any conflict of interest. So we set up a private meeting for the following Wednesday, when he'd be back from a trip to California that evening.

Gloria worked fast, or was it because she just couldn't wait to get in bed with Connie? Whatever the reason, she had the report on her findings by that Thursday; but with the meeting with Cyrus and the new client, I waited until that evening to be briefed.

According to Gloria's report, there was no way Connie could have killed her husband, although Connie was insisting she did it, not Nicole. Gloria drew me a layout of the kitchen. A very good one, I must admit. From what I was seeing, and based upon what Connie told her, I had to agree with her.

Kevin was indeed beating her to a pulp. The extent of her injuries was indisputable. The doctor's report spoke for itself. Which made her findings even more interesting. According to Gloria and the evidence she was presenting, Kevin had her pinned into one corner of the kitchen. She was helpless. And the wood block with the set of knives was behind Kevin. That would make it impossible for her to get to the knife and stab Kevin. She couldn't have moved that fast around him before he'd grabbed her. It would not have been impossible for her to reach for the knife if the wood block was on her side. She could have reached out for it in a last-ditch attempt. Or she could have fallen back on it. So it meant only one thing: Nicole came downstairs, took the knife out of the wood block, asked him to leave her mother, and he either lunged at her, lost his balance, and fell on the knife, or she deliberately stabbed him. It was either an unfortunate accident or an act of self-defense.

It was clear to Gloria and me, but our problem was Connie. She was adamant in insisting that she was the one who killed Kevin.

Did Connie have any idea what could possibly happen to her if we went to trial under these circumstances? Of course, we were confident we could win an acquittal; but if we went into court with her insisting that it was her who killed Kevin, it could very well, despite our best effort, go against her. A good lawyer should never lose hope. But a good lawyer should also be pragmatic. We must be mindful that events can change during the course of any trial. As hard as we were working to win our case, the prosecutors were working just as hard to win theirs. And even if we prevailed on the criminal charges, we couldn't rule out the possibility of Kevin's family bringing a civil suit against her for wrongful death. Winning that case would prove a harder task than the criminal case. The burden of proof in a civil case is much different than in the criminal case. And we had to bear in mind that the cost of mounting a defense in both cases would be significant. And should Kevin's family prevail, the damages would be enormous. They would go after everything their son owned. Everything they thought Connie would stand to gain from their son's death. By the time the dust was cleared, the only winners would be the lawyers on both sides. We would have to convince Connie to think as we were.

At the end of my first full week back at work, I had not only met a potentially new client, but I'd also gotten new information that would make a great difference in Connie's case. I was also back to working long hours, even though Liseth had asked me to be moderate in my hours. She'd called me several nights at the office and reminded me of what she'd asked me to do—go home early. I in turn told her that at least she knew where I was. "If you go home early, I know where you are," she said. We would laugh about it, and I'd tell her I was on my way. Only to stay a little longer. Most evenings, I'd take a car service home.

Chapter 21

—◦•◦❤◦•◦—

"On a day like this, I wish I was waking up next to you. With my legs wrapped around your sexy body and yours around mine."

"I must tell you I'll be a married man by the end of the year and a father by next summer. You can't talk to me like that. I'll have to tell my fiancée."

"You tell her everything?"

"I'm going to marry her, so I'll have to."

"That's good. You must love her a lot."

"I do."

"That's good to hear too. You think you deserve her?"

"I'm so fortunate. I can't believe she has agreed to marry me. And you know what?"

"No. What?"

"As a man who is getting married soon, I shouldn't be talking to you like this at six thirty in the morning."

"It's ten to seven."

"It was six thirty when you called me."

"So you weren't sleeping when I called then?"

"Of course I was."

"Liar."

"I was."

"Liar."

"I was dreaming about my very lovely, gorgeous, and very pregnant girlfriend."

"That's the one you're getting married to?"

"Yes, and you interrupted me."

"I miss you. You know that, don't you?"

"I miss you too, Liseth."

"Maybe I should let you get back to dreaming about me."

"It's too late. I'll never get it back."

"The dream or the hard-on?"

"The hard-on, of course."

"Good, save it for Thanksgiving."

"Ha ha ha. I've to get out of bed now."

"Are you going running?"

"Yeah, me and Charles and Mildred."

"Give them a little more time. It's Saturday. They have to work on their baby. Especially now that I'm pregnant."

Two beeps in the phone told me another call was coming in. I asked Liseth to wait while I see who it was. It was Charles.

"Kind of early for you on a Saturday morning?" I said to him.

"We went to bed early last night. I thought you might want to go early this morning," he said.

"As a matter of fact, I would. Liseth is on the other line. Let me let her go."

"We'll meet you out front."

"Speak of the devil," I said when I returned to Liseth.

"That was Charles?"

"Yeah. I guess they worked on the baby early."

"When they least expect it, it will happen."

"Like us."

"Yeah, like us. What are your plans today?"

"A bunch of things. Having lunch with Charles and Mildred. Going to my tailor. Getting my hair cut. Stopping by my parents'. Among other things."

"Well, you have a good day. I'll call you tonight."

"I love you. Bye."

"Love you too."

In some ways, I was kind of glad Charles called. For a while, I thought it would have gone on with me and Liseth all day. I missed her so much I wouldn't have known how to say good-bye. And I'm sure she wouldn't have known how to either.

I got to the barbershop much later than my usual hours. As a matter of fact, I didn't get there until close to six. I spent more time with my tailor than I'd planned, and the news of me getting married was welcomed, but I was subjected to a course of hilarious bantering from the guys. I was, according to Clive, a traitor to the cause of bachelorhood. Everyone was taking bets that I would be the last soldier standing on the field, firing the last shot and waving the flag as the rest of the troops went down defending bachelors all over the world. Of course, having gone through a messy divorce and losing his house to his wife of fifteen years in the process would explain why Clive had sworn allegiance to bachelorhood. Maybe I would too.

Of the three men working for Clive, the only married man in the shop was Jack, who had been married for forty years and had seven children. He was one of those old-time Jamaicans. He believed in a large family. He was in his late sixties, been a tailor all his life, and differed with Clive on the old ways of making clothes versus Clive's new ways. Clive used a pattern for cutting his suits. Jack used what he called scale. That's sketching and cutting. The rest of the guys, who were in their twenties, seemed to think that there were too many women out there to commit to anyone.

I chose some material for some new suits. I ordered six including a tuxedo for my wedding. The tuxedo I had was three years old and fit well, but I was not about to get married in a tux that I'd worn to other occasions.

The reception at the barbershop was more festive. A tide of celebration swept me up as I entered the shop. The crew and the regulars gave me a standing ovation. I felt like a major celebrity. But I was sure their enthusiasm was more for who I was marrying than for me getting married. They had all tripped over themselves when in the presence of Liseth.

I was the last person whose hair Victor cut. When the crowd thinned out a bit, he locked the doors and opened a bottle of champagne, and with some of the guys and his wife, we had a mini bachelor party. Some good married stories were traded. And out of respect for Victor's wife, the jokes were kept clean. Not that Greta was immune to risqué jokes. I'd been out with her, and Connie and had heard her talk. The contrast between the tailor shop and the barbershop couldn't have been more different. They were all West Indians, mostly Jamaicans, but while the guys at the barbershop looked at marriage in a more positive light. The guys at the tailor shop were not necessarily against it, but they saw themselves as upholding the honor of mankind by remaining single. As a matter of fact, one guy saw marriage as something one does when one gets old and wants a woman to take care of him.

I'd intended on stopping by my parents'. I didn't tell them or anything. Not that I had to, but by the time I left the barbershop, it was late. It was after eleven, so I decided not to stop. Even thought I'd drive by the house. The lights were on in the living room. Someone was watching the TV or had left it on.

I pointed the Jag toward the Hutch and headed home. The highway was clear all the way to the Whitestone Bridge. Except when I got up to the bridge, I found myself not going over it but swinging over to the service road and heading back north. Somehow I didn't feel like going home. And I wasn't sure where I was going, but as if guided by some unknown force, I was driving north and entering the Cross County Parkway, heading west toward Sawmill River Drive. Before I knew it, I was entering the village of Dobbs Ferry.

Dobbs Ferry was not a large village, neither by size or population. Neither are most of the villages in Westchester. But Dobbs Ferry was a nice place to live. Nestled on the banks of the Hudson River, it was hilly, and you could see money and tradition emanating from most parts of it. It occurred to me where I was and what I was doing, and I admitted to myself that just being there was the most stupid thing I'd ever done. I drove down Ashford Avenue and headed toward the riverbanks, ending up at the train station. I sat there for a while and contemplated my actions. The temperature was cool. Not cold for that time of the year. I took in the sights of the Hudson and gazed over into New Jersey. Beautiful place, I said to myself, but I wouldn't want to live there. Nothing personal. I knew a lot of people who lived in New Jersey. Some of them my friends, but I still wouldn't want to live there.

A train coming in from the city pulled into the station, and as if I was waiting for someone to get off, I scanned the passengers coming off. I watched them as they walked toward their cars, and the parking lot came to life. Then it emptied, and I felt as if the person I was waiting for had missed the train. The next one would not be until another hour.

I pulled out of the parking lot and headed up the hill away from the train station. Back toward Ashford Avenue. Several blocks up, I stopped and asked a young man where Cricket Lane was. The direction he gave was precise. It was not difficult to find.

Cricket Lane was a short lane. It was two streets off the main street. And yes, you guessed it. It went uphill. There were no more than four houses on each side of the lane. All huge houses of distinction. Connie's house was set apart from the rest. There were no cars parked on the road. Entering Cricket Lane would be for one of two reasons: either you lived there, or you were visiting someone. Oh, or you were lost.

Driving around the block a couple of times was out of the question. It was a dead-end street. Going up to the end once without being noticed was enough. If I was lucky, I might get away with doing it twice, but after that, I had the feeling someone would jot down my license plate number and call the police, even if I was driving a late-model Jaguar.

I drove up the hill, slowly, as if I was looking for an address. In a way, I was. I'd never been in Dobbs Ferry before. And technically, I was really looking for Connie's house. My client, if for some reason I had to explain to anybody. At the end of the lane, like most dead-end streets, there was a semicircle, which meant I didn't have to pull into somebody's drive to turn around.

Connie had often described her house to me, and since the death of her husband, it had been shown on the news a couple of times. I'd become familiar with it. I'd come to know the place without ever having set a foot in it.

As I slowly rolled down the hill, I paused to see if there were any signs of life inside. There were lights on in an upstairs room, but there was no sign of anyone. At after midnight, chances were Connie and whoever was there with her were sleeping. Maybe her sister or her mother was staying over for the weekend. I drove back down to the main street and pulled into the parking lot of an all-night convenience store. I bought a beer and drank it sitting in the car. Maybe Gloria was there with her, I thought. That bitch.

I reached for my cell phone and punched in Connie's number. She answered on the second ring. "What're you doing up at this time of night?" I asked.

"You sound as if you were expecting someone else to answer the phone," she responded.

"Of course not," I lied.

"What're you doing calling me this time of night? Not that I mind." She paused for a second.

"Are you alone?"

"Of course I am. Shouldn't I be?"

"Just asking."

"Why?"

"No special reason."

"There must be a reason why you're calling me at"—she paused and must have been looking at a clock or her watch to verify the time—"five minutes after one."

"Well . . .," I said.

"Well what? You tell me. You're calling me this late just to find out if I'm alone? Why? Are you in Dobbs Ferry?" She laughed.

"That would be crazy, wouldn't it?"

"What, being in Dobbs Ferry? What's so crazy about that?"

"Just say for the sake of argument I was, what would you say?"

"Then I'd have to say either you go home to Long Island or ring my bell. If you drive around here long enough, somebody will call the police, and then you'd really have to ring my bell." She laughed again.

"Sorry to disappoint you, but I'm . . ." I was about to say I was home, but instead, I said, "I'm on Long Island. Let me ask you, Connie. If I was in Dobbs Ferry, are you saying I could have come over?"

"If you wanted to, you'd be welcome."

"You're sure about that?"

"Well, you're not in Dobbs Ferry, so you'll never know."

Yeah. Right. I could just see me pulling up in her driveway at this god-awful time of the morning and saying, *Sorry, but I was just in the neighborhood. Can I come in?*

We ended the call, and I went back into the store and got another beer. A police car pulled up beside me. The cop got out of the car, and it made you wonder how in the fucking world he got in there in the first place. When most people stood on the other side of a car, you could only see from their shoulder up. You could see this guy from half his chest up. He had to be at least seven fucking feet or close to it. And he was wider than the car from bumper to bumper. He was somewhere in his midforties. And you just knew that if that motherfucka told you you were under arrest, there was no way you were going to disobey him, because he'd shoot your ass if you tried to run. Just walking up to the store was taxing on him as it was. There was no way he could run after anybody. *Slob* was written all over him. And there was not enough sun in the world to tan that fucking hulk.

I slid my beer between my legs and started the car. He looked over at me with that look that told me he knew I'd either had to go the fuck home to Long Island or ring Connie's bell. There was no way he'd run into me again that night and not pull me over. I backed out of the parking lot, slowly. Keeping an eye on the pale hulk, I headed toward the highway, but changed my mind before I took the exit. I passed it. Drove up about four blocks. Then turned around and headed in the direction I was coming from. I had every intention of turning around again and taking the exit to the highway had I not passed the pale-skinned hulk. I was not sure he looked in my direction. And for all I knew, the only thing he might have been able to remember was the black man driving the green Jaguar. Yeah. Right. Hulk was so dedicated to his job that I was sure he took pride in memorizing a person's description down to the gold in their tooth if they ever opened their mouth.

I watched his car in my rearview mirror until his taillights faded. Without hesitating, I turned off the main street and toward Cricket Lane. I pulled into Connie's driveway, as if I'd done it many times before. I cut the engine and walked up to her door. If Hulk had, for some reason, doubled back after me, the only thing that might tell him I hadn't been there before was me not putting a key in the door. Still holding the half-emptied bottle of beer, I rang the bell.

The first ring was without confidence. And without any thought of what I was really doing, of what this would do to my relationship with Liseth if she knew where I was and what I was doing. I wasn't really sure anyone was home, although lights were on upstairs. A part of me was hoping a voice other than Connie's would tell me to go away, that I was at the wrong house. The second ring had some muscle behind it, and before I could ring a third time, the lights went on downstairs; and through the heavy frosted glass in the door, I could see a shadow moving across the room. The lock on the other side of the door was being undone. My heart raced, and my hands felt clammy. I felt like a kid calling on his first date, fearing that her overprotective father might open the door with shotgun in hand.

The door opened slowly. But not fully. The figure standing in the doorway blocked most of the view inside the house. I couldn't see much of the interior, but little difference it would have made. The person standing in the doorway had on only her panties and a white T-shirt. Of course it was Connie, but it was almost two in the morning, and to be confronted with a woman standing in next to nothing was enough to obscure my vision. Connie's hair was down to her shoulders. She looked as though she'd just stepped out of the showers and was getting ready to go out on the town. Except for what she was wearing. A glass of something in one hand. The other hand held the door so I couldn't see fully inside. I stood there for what seemed like an hour, looking at her without saying a word.

"Are you going to come in, or you gonna just stand there looking at me?" she said, letting go of the door so I could pass.

I entered without saying anything. I didn't have to say why I was there. What explanation could I have given? *Oh, I just happened to be in the neighborhood. I took a wrong turn and ended up on your doorstep.* I don't think so. It was silly enough, me being there at that time of the morning—why make myself look sillier?

I couldn't help noticing that she'd lost some weight. Maybe ten pounds. Fifteen maybe. It didn't take away anything from her. As matter of fact, she looked great. Better than when we last made love.

"Do you always answer your door like that at two in the morning? Not knowing who's ringing your bell?" The T-shirt fell far enough to cover her breasts. No bra underneath. It was tight enough to show her nipples pushing out. And her underwear, although it was not a thong, was skimpy enough to give my member a rise.

"This is how I sleep," she said. "You should know that I sometimes sleep naked."

"Yes, but coming to answer your door, shouldn't you at least have put something on?"

"I saw your car pull into the driveway."

"You just happened to be looking out the window at this time of the morning?"

"No. You'd have no way of knowing, and you wouldn't see it anyway, which is the whole idea, but over a year ago, we had a break-in. We knew who it was, but we couldn't prove it. So Kevin had a camera installed."

"You knew who did the break-in?"

"Some kids from the neighborhood," she said, waving it off with her hand. "But they didn't take anything."

She closed the door and moved toward the kitchen. I stood where I was. In the foyer. My eyes scanned the house. The lights in the living room were off, but if the rest of the house lived up to the presence of the foyer, I'd say it was a grand place. A magnificent chandelier hung from the ceiling of the foyer. A Persian rug graced the floor, and a pair of Chinese Ming chairs were on opposite sides.

"Well, you've come this far. You might at least come in," she said, beckoning me into the kitchen.

I stepped into the doorway of the kitchen, and I couldn't help but envision Kevin lying there on the floor. Connie poured herself a drink and asked me if I wanted one. At first I said no, but I changed my mind. She was having rum and coke. At least there was a bottle of Coke on the kitchen counter. But it didn't seem as though she poured any Coke in her glass. The last time we were together, she was drinking the same thing. She didn't look drunk, but I was certain she was not having her second drink. She took out another glass and put some ice in it.

"On the other hand, maybe I'll take a beer," I said as I moved some more into the kitchen. My eyes scanned the place like a detective looking for clues. I moved up behind her and around her. I was facing her and standing next to the wood block. One of the knives was missing from the set. I was sure it was the murder weapon, and that it was with the DA. "I've had two beers tonight, and I have a long way to drive, so maybe I shouldn't mix my drinks."

She looked at me. She seemed puzzled by my statement. She looked in the fridge and then the cupboard. "I'm sorry I'm outta beers."

"I'll just have some Coke instead. With some ice and a piece of lemon."

"We wouldn't want you to fall asleep behind the wheel now, would we? The next thing we know, some cop comes over, taps on your window, asks you if you're all right, smell the rum on your breath, and, well, you know . . ." She laughed. I laughed too.

"This is a strange time of night to make a surprise visit." She sipped her drink as she put the ice in the other glass and took the huge knife from the wood block and sliced through one of the lemons in a nearby bowl. "Not that I'm complaining or anything. It's just that I'm very surprised. Sort of out of your way, isn't it?" She took another sip of her drink and poured the Coke in the glass.

"You're drinking straight rum?" I said incredulously.

"There's some Coke in it."

"Can't be much."

"You drove all the way up here to discuss my drinking habits?"

I raised the glass to my mouth and took a mouthful of the Coke. It was a little flat. The wedge of lemon gave it some flavor. My eyes danced around the room, and I tried not to make it obvious when I looked down on the spot that Kevin had supposedly fallen. Was I standing exactly where he fell? How much did he bleed? Was there a lot of blood? My eyes came up and met hers, and I could tell she knew what I was thinking.

"Why are you really here, Delroy?" she said.

I took a gulp of the flat Coke, and didn't respond to her question. She poured some more rum in her glass and repeated the question as she raised the glass to her lips. I still didn't respond to her question. I didn't have a rational answer. I was not sure myself. I was beginning to feel foolish. I would have kept on feeling foolish, and maybe possibly starting to look like a fool, if she hadn't put me at ease with what she said next. "Whatever your reasons for being here, I must say I'm not disappointed that you are. Curious, maybe. But not disappointed." She took a sip of her drink.

"Connie, I really can't give you a good reason why I'm here. And I'm sorry I dropped in like this." I took one of the napkins out of the holder and wiped my mouth. "I really am sorry. I think I should leave."

"You know, when I talked to you earlier, I had no reason in the world to think you were really in Dobbs Ferry. It just sort of came out when I asked you if you were in Dobbs." She finished the rest of her drink and poured herself another. I supposed it didn't matter how many drinks she had. She was at home. "You sure you won't join me?" she asked, holding out the bottle to me.

"I'd rather not. Really. Maybe I should leave."

"Is that what you really want to do?"

"I have no right to drop in on you like this."

"Like what?"

"Uninvited. I have no right. Maybe I should leave."

"So why don't you?" She looked at me with that look that said *You know you don't want to leave.* And she was right. I didn't want to leave. And she was not going to ask me to. So I quit repeating myself.

Dropping in on a woman at two in the morning, especially one who had just killed her husband, and particularly when you were a man who was engaged to be married on the coming New Year's Eve to another woman who was carrying your baby, could by no means be considered anything less than serious. But a certain seriousness engulfed the room as if to remind us that we were about to enter into something that neither one of us could retreat from. Silence descended on us, and nothing else had to be said. We moved closer to each other, and our raw animal instinct took over.

We were locked in each other's arms, and our mouth found each other's. We breathed in each other's mouth. And our saliva mixed. I could feel her nipples getting harder, and I was sure she could feel my erect penis trying to break out of my pants. I held her body closer to me. I wanted to pull her inside of me. For us to be one. I could feel saliva running down the side of my mouth. And I could also feel her tongue exploring the inside of my mouth.

We broke free, and she led me by the hand out of the kitchen and up the stairs. Nothing was said between us. She just led me up the stairs. Halfway up the stairs, she stopped, and we kissed again. A wet, passionate kiss, and then she took my hand again and led me into her bedroom. I started to unbutton my shirt, but she stopped me and did it instead. Except for two buttons. Pulling my shirt down to my elbow. She undid my pants and pulled it down far enough so it could fall to the floor by itself. I stepped out of my pants and stood there in my boxers and with my shirt halfway off, hanging off my back and down to my elbows, held by the two buttons in the front that restricted my hand movements. I eased back onto the bed as she peeled off her T-shirt and got on top of me in just her underwear. Unable to freely use my hands, I just lay there. But what did I need hands for when she was doing all the work? I was her captive and had no intention of putting up any resistance. Her tongue worked its way all over my upper body and down to my navel. She pulled my boxers off and took me in her mouth long enough for me to let out a slow moan. I don't remember when she took off her underwear, only that she was on top of me, guiding my penis into her. I didn't remember her putting a condom on either, and I should have protested. But with the rapturous state of my mind, I was hardly in a condition to protest.

She rode that dick like a cowboy trying to break a wild horse. Except I was not trying to throw her. I was as passive as if there was a bit in my mouth. The ride lasted for more than forty minutes, but it seemed like forever. We both were saying things. Nothing I could remember. And I certainly didn't care what was said by either one of us. I could only remember us both moaning together and moving in a rapid pace, and she collapsing on top of me.

I have heard many of my friends talk of a woman slipping on a condom when she takes the dick in her mouth. I'd never had it done to me, and I'd often thought only a prostitute would do something like that. Most of the women I knew enjoyed putting the condom on with their hands. After all, it was part of the foreplay. But when I got up to take a leak, there it was, a condom on my dick. So Connie must have slipped it on when she took me in her mouth. Where the fuck did she pick that up? Who cared? I loved it. It was the sort of sex that seemed cheap and dirty. The sort of sex that one had in the backseat of a car, on a dark street, with someone you met for the first time, but I loved it.

The bathroom was large, with two washbasins. Besides the toilet, there was one of those things that were made for feminine hygiene. Few young women have one in their bathrooms. There was a shower stall separate from the bath. That would figure. Connie was a person who loved to take baths. The bathtub was bigger than usual, and had a whirlpool. The place was done in a soft shade of pink, with lots of dishes with soaps in them. There were candle holders all over the bathroom. It was definitely a woman's bathroom.

There was a rack with a stack of towels in a corner of the room. I took one and dried the sweat off my body. I flushed the toilet

357

and watched the condom spin around with the water before it disappeared.

Connie was sitting on the edge of the bed when I came out of the bathroom. Her body glistened from the perspiration. I walked over and stood in front of her. My dick almost poked her in the eye as she took it in her mouth. As she sucked on it, I filled one hand with her long mane and the other held on to the shaft of my dick. No condom this time.

There is a tremendous amount of benefits for keeping oneself in shape. Exercise, eating right, keeping your weight under control, not smoking or drinking—well, skip the drinking part. But taking care of oneself has a great deal of advantages. Especially when you're forty-five and have to fuck women ten and twenty-five years younger. Now I don't want to insult all the women over forty. Some of them, I'm sure, are great fucks, but you ask any man over forty, given the choice, who would they choose, a young girl with a tight body and firm breasts or a forty-something with sagging breasts, and guess who they'd choose?

She brought me to a climax in her mouth, and I was still hard. She reached over to the night table for another condom. She ripped the package open with her teeth and slipped it on me. With her hands. Then she turned around, kneeling on the edge of the bed, her ass sticking up, and said, "Fuck me, Delroy."

I entered her from behind, both feet firmly planted on the floor and both hands grabbing her by the hips, and I sank deep into her. She let out a loud moan as I pulled her back and moved my hips forward. Her pussy felt as if it was tightening around my dick. I was still amazed that after three kids, a set of twins nonetheless, her pussy was still tight. I'd fucked girls in college, girls in their teens, whose pussies were so big you could run a truck through it. Connie not only had a tight pussy, but at close to her midthirties, her body was that of a woman ten years younger. And the weight she'd lost recently definitely contradicted her birth certificate.

"This pussy is yours," she said as she forced her ass back on me. I wet my index and middle fingers and reached around and massaged her clit. I could tell it was making her crazy. I need not tell you what it was doing to me either. But let's just say that if she'd asked me right then to call off the wedding to Liseth, I'd have said I would. I would have admitted to being the shooter on the grassy knoll. I'd have agreed to and admitted to doing anything she wanted. Whoever said money was the root of all evil had never had some good pussy. Samson didn't cut his hair for money. He did it because Delilah had some good pussy. King David once sent a man into battle, and to his certain death, because he coveted the man's wife. Again, it was good pussy that motivated the king to send that man to his death.

The king of England gave up his throne for the woman he loved. And he was not only the king of England but the emperor of half the world, with all the fucking money he could spend. This was before the war, when Britannia ruled the way. On top of not hurting for money, the king, as a bachelor, could get all the pussy in the world he wanted. Instead he gave up his empire for Wallis Simpson, an American. You know this bitch had to have had some good fucking pussy, because she was ugly. With a capital *U*.

Men doing silly things for a woman who can fuck them good is nothing new. It's as old as time. Remember Adam and Eve? That's how it all started. It had nothing to do with an apple. It's man's unaltered weakness. Very few—no, I take that back. No man is immune to it. Us men are not motivated by money and power, although it would seem that way. We are motivated by women. OK, so some of you will disagree with me, but let's face it, why do we seek money and power? To attract beautiful women. We don't seek women to attract money and power. And as we get older, our women get younger. Why does a middle-aged man divorce his wife of twenty or thirty years and give her five, ten, twenty, and in some cases even a hundred, million dollars to marry a woman young enough to be his daughter? Because after a while, a man wants to fuck a tight pussy on a firm body. All of us want it. And any one of us who says otherwise is either fucking lying or is already fucking one while staying married to his old wife, because it's cheaper to keep her. All the money in the world without some good pussy is a boring life.

Complaining about too much sex is the last thing anyone would ever hear from me. I wasn't complaining, but Connie wanted so much that night—or rather that morning—that I was beginning to question myself. Was stopping by her house the wisest thing I'd ever done? What had I intended to prove by doing it? And where would it lead to? So now you're thinking, eh? Which is what anybody would say to me. And which was what I should have done before I rang her bell.

I couldn't find anything inside of me that disagreed with my decision in coming to Connie's house. I guess deep down inside of me, I was trying to rationalize what I was doing. By then, I didn't think it had made any difference.

I went down to the kitchen to get something to drink. I didn't bother to put anything on. I took the orange juice container out of the fridge and put it to my head and drank a great deal of the contents. I shook the container before I returned it. Not much was left. I belched and wiped my mouth with the back of my hand.

I went into the living room to look around. I was part curious, but more nosy. The place was expensively furnished. You could see Connie's hands in the details and choice of every piece of furniture. I remember when we were talking about living together, she'd say, "Don't buy me a house without me going to see it first." Not that she didn't trust my judgment, but any house she was going to live in, she wanted to at least see it before she moved in. And after we moved in, in terms of furnishing the place, all I'd had to do was give her the money she needed and step aside. I could see I wouldn't have been disappointed.

The hardwood floor was a deep brown. It glazed under the plush imported rug in the center of the room. There was nothing I could have added or subtracted from the room. Nothing. The place put me at home. And anybody who could see me standing in the living room stark naked with my dick swinging would have believed it was my house.

Over the light-beige sofa, there was a painting that looked as though it had set them back much more than a few dollars. It looked like one of the old masters. If it wasn't an original, it was a damn good copy. But what did I know about artwork? I knew as much as what anybody told me. On the opposite wall, over an antique stand with a vase of three-day-old roses in it (must have been sent by Gloria), was picture of Kevin. Next to it was one with him and the children. He was not a bad-looking man. As a matter of fact, you could say he was handsome.

To look at Kevin in the pictures, you couldn't help but see quite a gentleman. A man who looked like he couldn't hurt a moth, let alone abuse a woman. But if looks was all it took, many men in prison wouldn't be there.

Just for the heck of it, I flicked on the wide-screen TV before I went back upstairs and slid back into bed and snuggled up to Connie. She pushed her body back to me as I got a handful of her breast. "Where were you?" she said as I gently squeezed.

"I was getting something to drink."

"I thought you'd left."

I didn't say anything. I just squeezed her breast some more and snuggled up some more.

Chapter 22

———◦◦◦✦◦◦◦———

ain fell heavily that Sunday morning. It fell heavily, but not for long. The downpour lasted for about forty-five minutes. It woke me up. It was sometime after ten o'clock. Connie was in the bathroom, and the TV, another large-screen TV—sixty inches; they seemed to love large-screen TVs—was on. It wasn't on the night before, but who really had time to watch TV anyway?

There was nothing important on the television, at least to me there wasn't. It was one of those televangelist programs, one of those hustlers who somewhere into the program would be telling the suckers watching where to send their money. As if he heard me, the address of where to send donations scrolled along the bottom of the screen.

As usual, the guy was sartorially resplendent. Light-blue suit, matching tie over a well-starched white French-cuffed shirt, with what I was sure was solid gold cuff links. What self-respecting televangelist would be caught dead with cuff links that were not real? Are you kidding? And I was sure it was one from his collection. The motherfucka, I was also sure, had a fleet of cars. No doubt Mercedes Benzes. Although, I was equally sure, not as many as Reverend Ike's twenty-four Rolls-Royces. Reverend Ike may be the most flamboyant of them, but I'm not sure he was the number one Mack around. The pope is the biggest pimp of all. He even owned his own fucking country. In another life, I'm going to theology school. Fuck that lawyering shit. I wouldn't have to be licensed by the state or pay taxes.

Connie came out of the bathroom just as it was healing time. The suckers were lining up to be touched by this con artist. His minions guided them up onto the stage to meet the man who could talk to God. They were being told to come forward. To walk by faith and not by sight. That without faith they couldn't be healed. And to transfer that faith into trusting him. That he would, through his unique powers that God bestowed on him, heal them. They were on crutches. In wheelchairs. And limping and dragging themselves up to be healed. What a scam. It's like a pimp telling his bitch that getting fucked for money is not sex. "Listen, baby," he says, "when you give those tricks some pussy, that's not sex. It's just business. It's only sex when I fuck you." He'd also tell her that he was the one person who could save her. Who could make her life better. Who could give her self-esteem. He was her daddy. Her mother. Her god. And all she had to do to be worthy of all this is to sell some pussy and give him the money. And you know the sad thing about all this? The bitch believes it. Just like the suckers going up to be healed. They believed, through the pimp in the double-breasted suit, that god would heal them. And you know the sad thing about all this? When they were not healed, they blamed themselves for not having enough faith. Was it too late for me to switch professions? For the time being, I'd wait until one of these pimps got in trouble, which they all did, and needed a good lawyer.

I still didn't have anything on when Connie got into the bed. She didn't have anything on either.

"This one of your favorite Sunday morning shows?" I asked her as she lay her head in the crook of my arm.

"I watch him sometimes." She turned on her side facing me and put one leg over me, then moved her hair from out of my face.

"As long as you don't send him any money."

"That's exactly what Kevin used to say."

"He was not a religious man?"

"He was, in terms of believing there is a God, but he believed they were playing on people's fear and weaknesses. He believed they should stick to saving souls and leave the healing to doctors and scientists."

I never thought I'd have anything in common with this guy.

She moved her body into mine, running her fingers down my chest, then gently over my dick, which by now was starting to come to life. I raised my head a bit and looked over on the night table. She realized what I was doing and said, "I have more." She gave a slight laugh as she reached into the drawer and pulled out three condoms joined together.

"Where did you learn to put a condom on with your mouth? You know, most people would think that only certain types of women know how to do that."

"One of my friends told me how to do it. And no, she is not a prostitute,"

"I didn't say it was a prostitute who was that certain type of people." I twisted a bunch of her locks around my fingers.

"You didn't have to," she said, definitely amused. "We know you men. You all fantasize about dirty sex, but when you get it, you start wondering where the hell we learned these things. Hey, we fantasize too. That's why some of us turn to other women. Because only other women know what we want."

"Oh," I said, tempted to ask her about Gloria. "What we want? We?" I emphasized the *we*.

"I know what you're thinking, but I love men. Doing it with a girl once in a while is OK, even though I hadn't done it for ages. But let's face it, no matter how good a man is, he can't eat pussy like a girl. But I love to be fucked hard, and Kevin wasn't doing either to my satisfaction. Of course if I'd loved him, it wouldn't have mattered."

What a sad life, to be married to somebody not in love with you. Especially when it was evident. And more so when the person told you she was not in love with you. Why would Kevin want to stay in a marriage when his wife didn't love him? He must have loved his children very much. Why else would he stay in the marriage, especially when he himself was not faithful to Connie? Why we men do some of the things we do is beyond me. I could only speak for myself, but I would never stay with anyone who told me, in no uncertain terms, she was not in love with him, and that she was in love with someone else. All the kids in the world could never make me compromise my principles, or abandon my self-respect. As Karl Marx said, "To love somebody who doesn't love you is a wasted love."

Connie and I went over each other's body like depraved animals. We licked each other like cats licking newborn kittens, but with more intensity, and certainly with more passion. Cats licked their kittens to show only love. We were licking each other, not only to show love, but to arouse certain passions and to excite each other. And excite we did. She grabbed on to the back of my head and raised her ass off the bed, one leg over my shoulder, as my mouth fully covered her clitoris. I could feel it swelling in my mouth, and I knew she was about to explode when her body started to tighten and she started to moan. And moan she did. She let out a wail like a person who was freed from years of confinement. As if that orgasm was not only pleasurable but liberating. The last time we made love, it was good, but I was, although willing, apprehensive. There was a lot of guilt on my part then. This time I felt no guilt. And there were no apprehensions. I wanted one of those marathon fuck sessions we used to have when we were younger. And in a way, I wanted to erase the Gloria factor.

I got up in the bed to face her as she was tearing one of the condoms open. She let the wrapper drop in the bed, and I didn't see anything in her hands. She spun me over on my back as she moved down to my crotch. She took my dick in one hand and then in her mouth. This time I was expecting it, and I couldn't feel when she did it, but I could tell she had slipped the condom on when she took me in her mouth. It must be one of those ultra-thin condoms, because I could feel her breath on my dick as if I had nothing on. My body went flaccid as my dick grew in her mouth, and right as I felt as I was about to come, she got on top of me and guided me in her, delaying my climax for another twenty-five minutes. Then we took a shower together, and fucked again in the shower. And then to help us regain our strength, she made us something to eat, and then we fucked some more.

I hadn't fucked that much in twenty-four hours for a long time. We did recapture our marathon fuck session, except I had to leave soon. At least by nightfall.

Back in the days when I didn't have to worry about a third person, and obviously before she was married with twins, she would leave Nicole with her sister and come over to my place. I was living in the city then, and we'd fuck all weekend. Those were the days. To be young, carefree, and able to live on sex. Not that we didn't eat. We would cook. Connie having only an apron on, running around in the kitchen, making a mess of the place. Then we'd eat, make love; then we'd sleep, and clean up afterward. Then we'd eat cheesecake with ice cream on top, washed down with champagne, while we lay in bed watching old movies. Then we'd make love some more. The whole weekend would be one big fuckfest. On Monday morning, I'd leave for work, and she'd go home and then go to work. Most of her shifts were usually in the evenings or afternoons. Sometimes we would meet up during the week; she only worked three, sometimes four, days a week, twelve hours a day. She'd stay over at my place, and we'd make love two or three times for the night.

Before I left Connie's house that evening, she gave me a tour of her house. The house had four bedrooms and two-and-a-half baths. It was built about thirty years ago, and except for the basement, which was Kevin's private sanctuary, they didn't change anything about the house. Well, the master bathroom was expanded and new things, like the oversize bath with the whirlpool, the shower stall, and that feminine thing that I couldn't remember the name of were added. Outside of that, everything else remained the same. The rooms were huge before they bought the place. It was one of the reasons they did. Connie loved that place. She would hate to have to move.

Connie had taken the phone off the hook the night before. It was the reason why it didn't ring all day. I was starting to wonder why, until she told me. It was just that it struck me strange that nobody was calling all day to check up on her. It gave us a chance to talk undisturbed. We had a lot to talk about.

"I'm going to marry Liseth, you know." I looked as deep into her eyes as I could, trying to see something other than what I would be hearing. "I just want you to know this is not going to change anything. I'm going to marry her."

Calmly, and without any hint of emotion, and except for running her fingers through her hair, with a voice that left no doubt that she meant what she was saying, she said, "And you should. There is no reason why you shouldn't. Your first child? You better."

We were seated in her living room. The sofa and love seat faced each other. We were dressed, and she sat on her crossed legs facing me. "I'm glad you understand," I said.

"What's not to understand?" She took a sip from the mug of tea she had made. Mine was too hot, so I let it cool. "Your girlfriend is pregnant with your first child, and you want to marry her. What's not to understand? I'd say it's not only the right thing to do, but the decent thing to do. I know you well enough, Delroy, and I wouldn't expect anything less from you."

"Thank you," I said as I reached for my mug. The tea had cooled enough.

"Listen, I suppose I should be a little more optimistic than I am, and some days I am. I really am. Right now, at this moment, I'm in between. The last thing I want right now is to complicate your life, to come between you and Liseth. I don't want that. You don't want that. And neither of us needs it." She took another sip of her tea. I had some of mine also. "God knows I love you, Delroy. I love you with all my heart. I love you to no ends, and I know you love me too. You always love me. And you'll always love me, no matter who you're with. That much I know. If I'm not sure of anything, I'm sure of that. But I'm not going to be selfish. I have learned so much from you over the years, Delroy. I've learned that to act selfishly is generally counterproductive. That it will only hurt me in the long run. Sometimes in life, we can't always get what we want. You taught me that. I want you to marry Liseth. I want you to love her, and to be respectful to her. I'll be respectful to her and your marriage. I want you to be kind to her." She paused, ran her fingers through her hair, and took another sip of her tea.

"You know what I'd like, Delroy?" She took another sip of her tea and scratched her crotch. Somehow I had a feeling that she wished there was something stronger in that mug. "You know what I'd really like?"

No, but you're going to tell me, aren't you?

"I'd like us to always have nights or weekends like this. Even after you're married, I'd like us to continue this way. I'd like you to come to my bed when it's convenient for you. All this might sound contradictory to a lot of people, but not to me. I'm willing to see you once a week. Once a month, or once a year. If that's what it takes. If I can't see you when I want, I'll see you when I can. If that's what it takes. I may not see you every day, Delroy, but I'll have you every day. I'm not going to be selfish and lose our love. And lose the one man I love more than anything in the world."

I was absolutely sure she needed something stronger than what was in that mug, if that was really tea in it after all. I reached for my mug and took a sip. Definitely tea in mine. She took another sip of hers. I was in the kitchen when she made both mugs. I saw her put the tea bags in them, put the sugar, and then pour the water and stir. She was sober. Drunk last night, but definitely sober today. "After this shit is over, I don't want another man but you."

What else could I say after that? She was pretty much set on being the other woman without making waves. Not many women would be willing to do that. But Connie recognized the facts. I was not about to leave Liseth for her. And why should she want me to? In the next several months, even though she was at times pessimistic about it, she'd be a free woman in more ways than one. She'd be free from the charge of killing her husband. The prosecutors would recognize they had no case, even if they think otherwise. Then she'd be a single woman again, with a lot of fucking money on top of that. At thirty-two, single, with a million dollars or so, a rich lawyer boyfriend to fuck maybe once or twice a month, and a female lover to eat her pussy anytime she wanted, who would want a permanent relationship? Could life be any better? Talk about having your cake. She wanted the bakery and the baker too. And who could blame her?

Maybe Connie was hedging her bets. Maybe she was betting on the future. Maybe deep down she was betting that Liseth and I wouldn't last. Maybe that was why she was willing to stay out of the way. To be discreet. That way, when we got a divorce, as she hoped we would, she'd be there for me.

Would that be so wrong of her to think that? Would it be impractical? Of course not. I had taught her well over the years. To be realistic and, most of all, to be pragmatic. Nothing lasts forever. Some of the best relationships ended in divorce. Speaking of pragmatic: I was forty-five. Liseth was twenty-two; when I was sixty-five, she would be forty-two. If we lasted that long, by then she may be more attracted to someone her age, if she hadn't done so at thirty-two, or thirty-five. Connie would only be thirteen years younger than I was. When I would be sixty-five, she would be fifty-two, more in my age group. And more compatible with my way of thinking. But then again, she too may have found a new interest, and like Liseth, she would have moved on. Maybe at age sixty-five I'd be with someone totally different. Who knew? But for now, I would play it as it was.

The problem was not on Connie's side. It was on mine. Granted that I'd made the biggest blunder in going over to her house. And like an arrow already in flight, I couldn't do anything about that weekend. But also, just like the archer who can refuse to pull another arrow from his quiver, I could. I could put an end to her fantasies. Not by telling her I couldn't go on—I had done that before, and it didn't live up to my word. No, she'd only think I was talking out of my ass. I'd have to do more than talk. I'd have to act.

"Assume for the moment, and I'm not saying I will, but let's assume for the moment that I agree with this plan of yours. I mean, let's say we have this affair after I'm married to Liseth and she has my baby. What about Gloria? Because you ought to know she's in love with you. You do know that, don't you?"

I anticipated her answer. My guess was that she would say Gloria was not important, and that with me in her life, Gloria would be pushed into the past. At least that was what I wanted hear.

"Don't be so obsessed with Gloria. You're making her out to be too important. She's not. And on the other hand, I can handle her." She ran a hand over my face.

"You think I'm obsessed with her?" I held her hand to my face and pressed it closer.

"She thinks you might use your position at work to harm her. I told her you wouldn't. And yes, I know she's in love with me." She moved her body closer.

"Of course I wouldn't do such a thing. You think I'm stupid? You know the kind of scandal a lawsuit would bring if I did that and she sued? And the fact that she even thinks that makes it dangerous. You know, if you break it off for any reason at all, who will she blame? How the fuck did you ever got involved with her in the first place? She is your lawyer, for God's sake."

She moved her hand from my face. Her action conveyed a certain displeasure with my last statement. "You're my lawyer too." Her face comported with her action. My foot didn't feel too good. "Anyhow, she was here as a friend. I didn't throw myself at her, if that's what you think."

"Of course that's not what I think." I reached for her hand and held it in both of mine. Her hand was stiff.

"The way you talk, you make it sound like I couldn't wait to throw myself at her." I was about to say something, but she cut me off. "Besides being my lawyer, which, I should point out to you, that you're the one who insisted that she handle the case. I wanted you to handle it. Besides being my lawyer, she was here also as a friend. I was at a low point, and when I needed a friend, and she was here. One night we were here together. I was in a bad mood. I was drinking—we were drinking, and we were talking, and I started to cry. I got drunk, we got drunk, except I was more drunk. She tried to sober me up. She suggested I take a shower while she made some coffee. She brought the coffee up, and I was sitting in the shower, without the water running, undressed, kind of passed out. She turned the water and pretty much held me in the shower, except she didn't take her clothes off. Not that I wanted her to." I looked at her and gave her that *Yeah, right* look.

I was still holding her hand. It had relaxed a little. "You may not have wanted her to take her clothes off, but I'm sure that was her intention."

"I swear to you, Delroy, and on the soul of my children, I didn't want her to—"

"But you let it happen. You didn't stop her."

"I haven't done anything like this since college, and when she kissed me, everything came rushing back. I remembered how good it was, and I didn't stop her, and I didn't want her to. The next thing I knew, she was on her knees and one of my legs was hiked up over her shoulder. I couldn't remember the last time I had my pussy eaten like that. And she sent me into orbit. I suppose the rum and Coke played a part, but I didn't have to be drunk to know that it was the best I have had in, well, since college. Her tongue and fingers made me come like a broken pipe."

"I can imagine. Considering before I came along you were starved for affection." She moved her hand back up to my face, and I held on to it, pressing it against my face.

"I didn't remember I could have orgasm like that before. She made me, no offense, feel like a woman again. She made me feel loved. She was gentle. She was tender. Not that I would give up men, no way, but, she made me feel special that night. She was what I wanted, at least at that moment."

I wanted to take her right there and show her that I had as good a tongue as any woman. But I had to face it, even if I wouldn't tell her, that on average, no man could eat pussy as good as another woman. "And she kept coming back for more, and you never tell her not to. Why didn't you tell her the first time was a mistake? That it was only because you were drunk?"

"I should have, but honestly, you wanna know the truth?"

"The truth. You were enjoying it," we said, except for her using the words "I was," almost the same thing. Word for word. And we laughed together.

"Oh, Delroy, you'd have to be a woman to understand. You know how sensitive and affectionate I am."

I did understand. More than she'd imagined. I just wished it had been with someone else. Anyone but Gloria. For two reasons: she worked for me, and there was no way we could ever wound up being a threesome.

"Are you against Gloria because you know she wouldn't want you in bed with us?" I did tell her once that if it was the last thing a heterosexual male did, it should be in bed with two women at the same time. And I admitted to her I'd done it more than once. "Because, let me tell you," she continued, "she is a good lover, with a fuckin' gorgeous body, and a pussy that would drive any heterosexual man wild, but she is definitely into girls only. Strictly girls only for her."

I hated that bulldogging bitch.

Connie said, "We could see each other when it's convenient for me, without any strings attached. Then that would be fine. If she would definitely accept her status as "the other woman," without conditions, and not start to bitch later, when I couldn't see her when she wanted me, then I supposed I could live with that. But we all know things don't usually work out the way they're planned. Why didn't I just tell her right there that I couldn't do it? Yeah, why didn't I?

We got off the subject of her love life, and although it was not the real reason why I came to her house, I brought up the subject of Nicole's condition and my and Gloria's theory that we strongly believed that Nicole was the one who really killed Kevin. It was not a topic that she wanted to engage in, but one she realized that couldn't be avoided. The idea that Gloria and I would even think such a thing was ridiculous, she said. And then she went on to reenact what happened that night. It sounded so rehearsed.

I told her the problem with her story was that the only one who would believe her was the prosecutor, and the only way I could prove she was not telling the truth was to put her on the stand and cross-examined her. Then the prosecutor would, rightly so, point out that I was badgering my own witness. I'd have to declare her a hostile witness, which would not be helpful to our case. And then, on the other hand, as she well knew, it was her constitutional right not to take the stand, and we couldn't force her. Which would leave us with the only other choice: raise the theory, without calling her to the stand, and create reasonable doubt in the minds of the jury. She may not like it, but it was our best defense, if we ever went to trial. Something deep inside of me was telling me that when everything was presented to the prosecutors, they too would be convinced that going to trial with this case was not worth it.

Connie was as stubborn as they came. I had experienced her stubbornness firsthand. Even when the facts were presented to her, she could still be adamant in refusing to accept it. I tried to tell her that if she lost the case, she could also lose everything. The house. The money. Kevin's life insurance. Everything. As a convicted murderer of her husband, she couldn't gain anything from his estate. And even if we won in court on the criminal trial, Kevin's parents could go after her in a civil court for wrongful death of their son, where the burden of proof would be narrower. I asked her to think it over.

"You're asking me to brand my daughter a murderer. You're asking me to tell the world my little girl killed her stepfather." The look in her eyes was enough for me to give in. The pain etched on her face was too much for me to insist. But it would only be too much for Delroy the man. Her lover. Not for Delroy the lawyer. As a lawyer, I was supposed to be dispassionate. I was supposed to see things only in terms of the law. Emotion was supposed to go out the window.

"Connie," I said, trying to be as sensitive as I could, "Nicole would never be looked at as a murderer. She acted in self-defense. She acted to save your life. She did what any child would have done if their mother was in danger. You would have done the same, wouldn't you?"

She paused for a moment, wiped the tears from her eyes, bowed her head in her hands, and said, "Do you have any idea what this would do to my baby? This could scar her for the rest of her life."

I put my arms around her and tried to console her the best I could. I knew just how she felt, and I didn't envy her.

"Connie, if we try to deny it, it won't do any better. At some point in Nicole's life, she'll know what she did, and it won't make her better. If we try to hide the truth, it will only do her more harm when it eventually comes out. And it will, Connie. You know that? It's better if we deal with it up front. This way, she won't have to think of herself as a murderer, which is what she'll think if we try to hide it. Think about it, Connie."

Part of me was convinced that I got through to her. That what I said made sense to her. She sniffled and then took a deep breath. I held her in my embrace. She didn't resist me. She wanted to be held. That was the one thing about Connie: she was affectionate, and very emotional. Whenever she was in a bad mood, she loved to be held and treated like a baby. She loved to be pampered. That was where Kevin went wrong. He didn't really know her. All that macho shit and trying to control her never worked. You couldn't control her. You could pamper her, but don't crowd her. The other thing about Connie was that she loved to think she was getting her way. That was the only way a man could win her over.

She raised her head and wiped her face with the end of her T-shirt. Then she blew her nose.

"Trust me, Connie, it's right thing to do."

I released her and stood up in front of her. She put her arms around my waist. Her chin rested in my belly button. Despite all of this, she still made me horny. I pulled away from her.

"I'm not sure . . . I'm not sure what is right, Delroy. I'm just not sure." She blew her nose again. I went into the kitchen and got her some napkins.

"I know, baby. I know. It's not easy. I'm not going to tell you it is. It isn't. But I'll tell you this much: prosecutors don't like to lose. They're not after the truth. They don't give a fuck. The truth is a by-product to them. Your daughter's medical condition is of least importance to them. They have to get something. They don't like to walk away empty-handed from a case, unless they're forced to. They have to have something. Anything. If not a short jail time, then probation. I suppose if they are willing to offer probation, then we could look at it as a sign of their case being weak, but, Connie, if you have to do any jail time, no matter how short, it won't do Nicole any good. And probation would play right into the hands of Kevin's parents for a civil suit. As your friend and lawyer, I'm giving you the best advice. You have to let us do it our way. If, God forbid, you have to do any jail time . . . Connie, listen to me. You can help Nicole more if you're out here. Trust me on this one, baby. I wouldn't do anything that would hurt you."

"I'm going to have to talk to my parents. My father in particular. I have to bring the whole family in on this." She used up the napkins I brought her.

That was good, because if I knew her father well, he was a reasonable man. He was a man who would do anything to protect his family. I was sure he would agree with me.

Chapter 23

———◦❤◦———

*I*t was after eight when I got home. I would be understating it if I said I was tired. All I wanted to do was take a long hot shower, climb into bed with a mug of hot chocolate, and just sleep undisturbed.

There were two calls from Liseth. The first one was at about five that evening. The second about a half hour before I got home. Nothing urgent, she said. Just calling to see how I was doing. Good, I thought, she didn't call that morning, or during the day. But why didn't she call my cell phone? And as if by some weird coincidence, or telepathy, the cell phone rang. The number displayed was hers. "I'm home," I told her. "Call me on the home phone." I'd get a better reception on the home phone anyhow. For some reason down by the beach where I lived, the reception on a cell phone was never that good.

Before I could put the cell phone down, the house phone rang. Before she could say or ask me anything, I told her I ran into an old friend I hadn't seen in quite some time, and we wound up talking. "Why didn't you call me on my cell phone?" I asked, even though I knew it was turned off from the minute I'd walked into Connie's house. Had she called, I would have used the dead or low battery excuse. "Are you OK?" I asked, anxiety and deep concern in my voice.

"Calm down, I'm fine," she said. "Everything is all right. I just felt like talking to you. That's all."

"Good." My voice returned to its normal tone.

"I'm taking it easy. You'd be proud of me. I haven't had a cigarette since I came back. Isn't that good?"

"That's very good."

"I'm also trying not to gain too much weight with this baby. Our good friend, you know who, is taking care of me like a big sister."

"I'm glad Claire is there for you. Thank her for me."

"What did you have for dinner?"

"Some leftover Chinese food." I knew what was coming next.

I was right. She asked, "Hasn't that been in the fridge awhile? You didn't wanna cook?"

"I didn't feel up to it."

"Try not to eat Chinese food too often. And don't cut back on your running. There's no reason the two of us should get fat."

"OK, mother. I promise I'll take care of myself."

"You better. I need you to be there when our kid graduate law school."

"I'll be there, if it's the last thing I do." I wanted to end the conversation. If I didn't, there was no telling how long I'd be up. "Shouldn't you and my son get some sleep?"

"As a matter of fact, I gotta be up early tomorrow. I've an early class. But I have to tell you before I go that everyone up here, including all my professors, are treating me so kind, you'd think I was the first pregnant person ever been at Yale."

"You're loved, Liseth. Not just by me, but by everyone."

"I know. I love everyone for being so kind to me."

I let out a loud yawn. I was really tired. I was not as young as I used to be. I couldn't do this shit on a regular basis. I yawned again. "Listen, baby, I need to get some sleep. I've an early day too."

"OK, sleep well. I love you."

"I love you too. I miss you."

"I miss you too."

I finally took that hot shower and made that mug of hot chocolate. But sleep didn't come as quickly as I'd hoped. And Connie calling didn't help either. She couldn't sleep either, and of course, the only one she could find to talk to was me. The question was, why me? What the fuck did I get myself into? I was beginning to sound like some of the people I'd defended over the years. Most criminals are not really stupid; on the contrary, most of them are extremely bright people. Certainly, nobody would think Michael Milken and Ivan Boskey were stupid. The fact that they got caught was not because they were stupid. It was their egos that got the best of them.

Most criminals know exactly what they are doing and the consequences of their actions. The career criminals, in particular, are, unlike what most people might think. They are one of the smartest. They're smart because they know the system. They know how it works. Majority of them could argue their case effectively. The reason why they hire us is that they see us—the legal system, that is—as one big club. From their point of view, we're all a bunch of crooks working together, and when we get together at our clubs to drink whiskey and smoke cigars, we make deals and decide how to dispose of the various cases. They truly believe this, and no one can tell them otherwise.

It makes no difference that we work our asses off. That we fight the states and the judges. That we defend their rights under the Constitution. That at times we succeed in keeping them out of jail. All this is a sham. All of what we do in the courtroom is putting on a show. We have to make it look good. We're nothing but a group of crooks who use the legal system to cover us up. All we do is use them by cutting them loose every now and then so they can go back out to commit more crimes, get caught, and hire us again. We're just shaking them down, and if you think they think badly of us on the whole, try being a Jew and a lawyer. To most criminals, Jewish lawyers are supersmart lawyers. I once heard a defendant reject a black lawyer and ask to be represented by a Jewish lawyer. And God knows it doesn't help our profession when some of us are arrested for stealing from our clients.

Like the criminal who should not only have considered the consequences of his actions before he committed a crime, but also refrained from breaking the law and not later on ask, "Why me?" Not later on ask, what the fuck did he get himself into? Like the criminal, I was beginning to think I could get away with what I was embarking on. I still had enough time to get out of what I was getting into, but I considered myself too smart for Liseth to ever find out. It didn't matter that I'd been warned. It didn't matter that my own father made the same mistake and almost lost his family. Nor did it matter that Liseth was from a broken home and was scarred for the rest of her life by her father leaving her mother for another woman. All of that didn't matter, because my self-justification was that I was not going to have kids with Connie, neither of us wanted any, and I was not going to leave Liseth for Connie. Neither Connie nor I want that either. My ego overruled any good judgment I had and should have used.

"I just want you to know," she said, "that I've considered what you said. I've given it serious consideration, and I'm not saying I've made up my mind on it, but I want you to know anything I decide it will have to be in my daughter's best interest. Even after I talk to my parents."

"I agree with you." I agreed with her, of course. But I was going to present my argument to the DA anyway.

Love is painful. It always is. Whoever said it's a bunch of roses or eternal bliss has never experienced true love. True love can indeed be a bunch of roses, but one has to be aware of the thorns. It can be blissful, but one has to watch out for pitfalls. Love does not always smell like a bouquet. At times love stinks. And it can be mean and cruel. Men have killed for love. Have betrayed their country for love. Have lied and stolen and suffered embarrassment and humiliation all in the name of love. Love's a fool's game. But what a miserable life it would be if we didn't participate in it. To live life and never experience love is a worse tragedy than to love and have your heart broken.

I had to be in court that Monday. I had a conference in the Southern District of New York. The federal court at 500 Pearl

Street. The conference was before Judge Harold Fairchild, Jr., an old-time liberal and son of the late Harold Fairchild, Sr., who, like his son, was a State Supreme Court judge, and also a liberal. As a matter of fact, the senior Fairchild was not just a liberal, but a New Deal liberal. He was from the inner circles of President Franklin D. Roosevelt.

Judge Harold Fairchild, Jr., was appointed to the federal court by President Clinton, and prior to his appointment, he had presided over some cases of notoriety that earned him, along with Judge Bruce Wright, the reputation as the most liberal judges in not only the Supreme Court of New York, but the state. Prosecutors feared them. They hated to go up before them, especially with weak cases. Defense attorneys loved them. Their clients always got bail, and usually had their rights protected when they were before theses judges.

Judge Fairchild didn't shed his liberal robe when he took the federal bench. As a matter of fact, unlike the state court, where he was subjected to the will of the mayor who had the power to reappoint him if he chose, the federal bench was a lifetime appointment.

One of his most famous cases after his appointment to the federal court was a drug case where the defendant, a Dominican woman living in Boston and visiting New York was observed one morning, at five thirty, loading several duffel bags in her car in Washington Heights, a community in Upper Manhattan that is known as a drug neighborhood.

Four undercover cops who were staking out the neighborhood approached the car that had Massachusetts plates, and the three men who were with the woman ran, leaving her holding the bags, so to speak. After identifying themselves, and the police searched the car and uncovered several tons of cocaine with a street value of several million dollars. The woman confessed and admitted she had made the trip from Boston for the sole purpose of buying the drug and taking it back to Boston.

"Good bust," ran the headlines of all the local newspapers. The local TV stations also ran the story, with the mayor and the US attorney being pictured with the bags of drugs, lauding the cops for the great job they did. End of story. The woman was looking at twenty-five to life in prison for being a major distributor of cocaine. That is, until they came before Judge Harold Fairchild, Jr. The woman's attorney moved to suppress the evidence and asked the judge to throw out the whole case on the grounds that the search was illegal. The police had no probable cause to search her car, and the only reason they suspected her and her friends was because they were Hispanic, and in Washington Heights.

The prosecutors countered that Washington Heights was a known drug neighborhood and the undercover officers had watched them load four duffel bags into the car, and that when the officers approached the car and identified themselves, the men ran, giving the officers probable causes to search the car.

No, said Judge Fairchild. There were no probable causes. These people, like anybody in any neighborhood, had a right to put bags in their car at any hour of the morning without being suspected of being drug dealers. The fact that the men ran, even after the police identified themselves, was typical of the mistrust the people in that neighborhood had for the police who treated them with disrespect. Had these people been in Scarsdale, a wealthy white suburb north of New York City, and were loading their car at three, four, or five in the morning, in a car with out-of-state license plates, it would have been naturally assumed they were honest people preparing to go on a well-deserved trip. Nobody, he went on, would assume that the people in Scarsdale were loading bags of cocaine in their cars. He threw the whole case out and ordered the woman to go free.

This set off a storm of protests from New York to Washington, DC. Congress and Senate, which were Republican controlled at the time and was waging a war on the people's president, Bill Clinton, called for his impeachment. The governor of New York, George Pataki, and the mayor of New York City, Rudolph Giuliani, also declared war on Judge Fairchild, calling for his removal. Calling for him to resign. The independence of the federal courts, of all courts—a court that was supposed to protect the rights of the people under the Constitution—was being attacked.

The prosecutor asked him to reconsider his decision. Something they could ask for but not one he had to entertain. But the pressure was too huge, and he caved in and gave the prosecutor ten days to come up with new evidence for reconsideration. What a load of shit. Everybody knew that the police would come back with the right type of evidence to make their case. The point was that they got an opportunity to take a bite at the same cake twice. And the second time, they knew just where to bite. But the judge caved in and sought a way to redeem himself.

The so-called new evidence, which wasn't there in the first place, was enough for the judge to reverse his decision.

Oh, he was still a liberal, all right. Still supported all the liberal causes, and rode the subways to and from work, unlike the rest of the federal judges; but except for making several rulings on prisoner's rights, including a controversial ruling on the amount of space each prisoner should have between their beds, nothing of that magnitude had come before him again to test him.

As a federal judge, he was appointed for life. He would leave the bench only if he died, quit, or was impeached. He didn't have to give in to the pressure. Cases are not assigned to federal judges by a chief judge who may like you. Cases are assigned by blind, random selection; and once assigned, the judge can recuse himself if he sees a conflict of interest. Judge Fairchild could have told them to go fuck themselves. In plain or simple words, there was nothing anyone, including Congress or the president, could have done about it.

Making unpopular ruling, which judges do every day, is not an impeachable offense. A federal judge can only be impeached if he made a ruling that he profited from.

Despite his caving in on the ruling, he was still one of the smartest and one of the best judges on the bench. But as the saying goes, "Each man has his limitations."

My conference was scheduled for nine thirty, but like all conferences, although all parties are usually on time, they never start on time. Most judges, even if they are at the courthouse early, would take their time—reading the morning papers, having their coffee, and doing a few things that could run maybe half an hour to an hour. For some reason, which I could never figure out, the women judges are usually more punctual.

My conference was to work out the fine points of a settlement that my adversary and I couldn't or were unable to work out. Sometimes what negotiating parties need is a third party to push them in the right direction. In this case, it was the judge.

My client was on time. So was my adversary and his client. The purpose of our conference was to avoid a protracted and costly trial, which we agreed on, and also to work out who would bear the cost to each other. My opponent's client admitted wrongdoing; and although he agreed to compensate my client, he was not amenable to our request to pay my client's legal bill. In England, it's much simpler. If you lose in court or admitted wrongdoings, it's a standard practice that you pay your opponent's legal bill. My client, the plaintiff, stood to gain $3.5 million, which the defendant agreed to pay in one lump sum, so what was another $25,000, plus disbursement? Had we gone to trial, we would have stood a very good chance of getting the whole $25 million we were suing for. Plus, it would have cost him an enormous amount of money in attorney's fees. The judge agreed, and he reluctantly agreed. The conference took less than forty-five minutes.

I don't get down to the federal court as often as I used to in my younger days and before I made partner. That was one of the advantages. Unless it's absolutely important, partners usually let the associates go to court. Although I didn't get down to court very often, I still had friends down there. One in particular was the judgment and order clerk, James Finneman.

Jim and I went way back to the days when I first got out of law school and clerked for the late Judge Jerome Wells, an old friend of the family's. Judge Wells died about ten years ago. He was in his nineties. He was considered to be, and I would differ with anybody who says otherwise, one of the most learned of all the judges in the district, if not the country. He was also touted as a candidate for the US Supreme Court, but with no vacancies during the Carter presidency and twelve years of Reagan/Bush, there was no way

Judge Wells was going to make it to the top court. Some say age was a factor, but those who knew better knew he was too liberal for Reagan or Bush.

Jim and I were the same age. Jim had been married to the same woman for over twenty years. Twenty-seven, to be exact. They had three daughters. The youngest was about eighteen years old, and his second daughter was the same age as Liseth.

The last time we saw each other, we were talking about old times; and as usual, he would ask me when, and if even, I was going to get married. It was then I told him about Liseth.

At first Jim didn't believe me, but when I showed him pictures of me and Liseth, he believed me and told me I was living every middle-aged man's dream. Had he been single, he said, there was no way he would go out with a woman his age. I had become his hero.

Jim was sitting behind his desk when I walked into his office. A wide grin dominated his beet-red face as I approached him. He still had a head full of hair, but the grays were outnumbering the blacks. Not a man who subscribed to any athletic pursuit, his midsection had expanded, putting his pants to rest below his waist. He might be overweight and drank a little too much, but all you had to do was take one look at James Finneman and you were looking at a happy and contented man.

"How is your daughter—I mean your girlfriend?" he said as we shook hands. He was cracking up with laughter as he said it. Wait until I told him she was pregnant.

"Get the fuck outta here," he said. "No fuckin' way. You got her pregnant? When is the wedding?"

I told him, and also told him he was invited. He said he wouldn't miss it for the world. "You're definitely my hero now. Do you know how many men our age envy you?" I could imagine. We spent about half an hour together. I took his address for mailing the invitation, gave him my card, and then said good-bye.

As I rode the subway back to my office, I could still see the grin on Jim's face. I could see him telling everyone who knew me about me and Liseth. I should stop by to see Jim more often. Just for the laughs, if nothing else.

I called Gloria to my office and told her about my discussion with Connie. Of course, I left out the part about sleeping at Connie's house. No need to mention that. I outlined my plans and how we were going to go about it. She agreed with me. I would make the call myself and then follow it up with a letter. I asked Gloria to draft the letter and, of course, asked her to run it by Brian and then me. That is, if the DA was amenable to our discussion. We couldn't see why she wouldn't.

Before Gloria left my office, she asked me if I'd seen Connie and how she was doing. I was sure that was not what she wanted to ask me, and she was sure I wouldn't give her the answer she was looking for.

I could have easily told her I'd only talked to Connie on the phone, but I told her we met at her brother-in-law's barbershop, and that Connie and I went to dinner. Of course, I just knew the jealous bitch was going to ask Connie if we really had dinner Saturday, and if I knew Connie well enough—and I did know her—she would just, for the fuck of it, tell Gloria what really happened over the weekend. God, I hoped she wouldn't.

As much as I doubted, even though I couldn't be sure, Gloria would not outright say anything to me about Connie. And Connie would tell her it was none of her fucking business, and to take it or leave it. What the fuck would she do, dump Connie? It was the best goddamn pussy she'd ever eaten. I doubted she'd want to give that up.

I guess Gloria's way of reminding me that I was about to be a father and was getting married on New Year's Eve was to ask me about Liseth. "How is Liseth handling being back at school and pregnancy?"

Well, she'd have to be stupid, which was the one thing nobody could accuse her of, to think I didn't know what she was getting at. OK, *I'll play your little game and be cordial.* "Well, it's kind of too early to say."

As calm as she'd asked the first question, she followed it up with, "I'm sure if she faces any difficulties, you'll bring her home. Most women with their first pregnancy usually go through a lot of morning sickness, and being a first-year law student won't help."

I wanted to ask her, how would you know? Ever been pregnant? You son of a bitch, you'd love that, wouldn't you? Instead, "We hope it doesn't get to that." She wasn't looking directly at me, or she might have known what I was thinking.

"I hope so too," she responded.

Sure you would.

She said she had to start working on that letter. I told her to ask Brian to stop by my office.

Brian and I made the call. It was not an easy sell. As a matter of fact, it was going to take a meeting at their office with Connie there. Why? We were a bit puzzled why the DA would want to play hardball on this one, but it was an election year.

We could produce a doctor's report that the possibility of Nicole being the one who did the killing was what caused her to withdraw. The doctor could further prove that under extensive treatment and certain drugs, she could remember the events of that night. All of this treatment could, of course, be done in the presence of a state appointed doctor, who would evaluate her and arrive at his or her opinion and report back to the DA. But the whole ordeal could push Nicole into a deeper depression. Which was what Connie was trying to avoid.

As much as we were assured by the doctors that the drug would have no adverse effects on Nicole, Connie was worried about the child reliving the event. We could all understand why. Since none of this couldn't be done without Connie's written consent, we wanted to reason with the DA and hoped they would understand. But they wanted a meeting anyhow. The meeting was set up for the following Monday, and Gloria didn't have to write the letter.

I called Connie and told her of our discussion with the DA. I can't say how she took it, but she was not exactly happy, although I told her that the fact that they were willing to talk was a positive sign. We set up a meeting for me and her that Wednesday evening.

It was not supposed to be a date. We were supposed to meet for dinner and talk about what to expect at the meeting. Dinner would be at an out-of-the-way place in the Village.

Gloria had wanted to call Connie to tell her of the discussion with the DA, and of the upcoming meeting. It was, I was sure, for her own selfish reasons. It would let the bitch feel better, so why not let her?

At dinner, Connie wanted to know why less than half an hour after I called Gloria called to tell her the same thing. She found it amusing when I told her why. And she was, to some extent—and to my surprise—flattered. Despite her explanation, I couldn't see why. This woman, she said, who was in a long-term relationship with a very successful artist who had had exhibitions all over the country, was crazy about her. Gloria and her companion had been together for close to ten years, and although she'd had many flings during those ten years, and her companion had always known about them and never felt threatened, with Connie it was different. Gloria wanted to leave her companion for Connie, but Connie, despite their tryst, was a heterosexual.

After dinner, Connie and I went to that new hotel on West Broadway. She had reserved a room in advance. I wondered what she would have done with the room had I said no. But I was sure she knew I wouldn't have said no.

Connie was in a very good mood that evening. It had nothing to do with the very likelihood that the DA might drop the charges. For once in her life, at least since the unfortunate death of her husband, she said, she was going to enjoy an evening as though it was her last day on earth. She would put aside everything that could cause her to worry and have the most enjoyable evening with the man she loved the most. It was my time to be flattered.

We lay in bed naked, watching TV for a while. We only made love once. A fulfilling, satisfying sex. And yes, she did put the condom on with her mouth. We showered together, and then we left. We would meet again that weekend at her house, and twice every week right up until Thanksgiving when Liseth came home.

Connie had wanted us to meet more often. If she had her way, it would have been every night. After all, she said, when Liseth got home, she'd be lucky if she would see me once a month.

"What will you do for the first three months after the baby's born?" she asked as we got dressed.

Oh, I knew what she was implying. And it was one of those questions you just hated to be asked. "I'm sure you have the answer to that question." Although I was not amused by the question, I was also not angry with her. I tried not to react in any way. She jokingly elbowed me in the right side.

"You're not angry, are you?"

I wasn't. "You don't expect me to sneak out to be with you during those times, do you?"

"I told you I expect you to show your wife respect. I wasn't implying that you should sneak out to be with me."

"We'll be doing that, in a matter of speaking. In case you forgot."

"I'm sorry I said what I said. Please forget that I said it. It was insensitive of me. I'm sorry."

She really was. I couldn't see why. I wasn't making a big deal out of it. I knew what she meant. I tried to assure her as we left the hotel that I was not angry in any way. And as much as she said she understood, and that she was all right, I couldn't help feeling, after we said good night, that she was hoping that nothing she said would ruin our relationship, and that we would meet again the following Wednesday night.

The last thing she said before we parted was that I was the most important person in her life, and that she didn't want to ruin it in any way. And she whined about her luck with men, going back as far as when she was a teenager. It seemed, she said, that she must be destined to fuck up all relationships she got into, even if she decided to share one. "What's wrong with me, Delroy?" she said. "Is there something about me that . . . why can't I develop and keep a relationship with any man? Not even the good ones? Because, Delroy, you're a good man." She paused for a few seconds.

"And I can't even share you without fucking it up. What's wrong with me?"

She had taken the train into the city that day. I'd walked her back to Grand Central Station. She wasn't crying or anything, but I didn't want her to get on the train looking upset or noticeably distraught in any way. I told her not to be so hard on herself and reminded her that there were no guarantees in life.

"I just don't want to hurt you or do anything to ruin your life," she said.

I told her I wouldn't let her. We kissed good-bye, and I watched her as she boarded the train.

Whether we want to believe it or not, many of the things we get into are caused by our own bad judgments and our refusal to heed our own warnings.

Chapter 24

‌‌‌⊷⊷❤⊶⊶

The table was set for two. Dinner plates, salad plates, wineglasses, water glasses, and all the proper silverware to go with them. There were even flowers in the center of the table. It was a big table. It could seat twelve. It sat on a Persian rug. I hated to think what it cost, but it certainly wasn't cheap. Neither was the chandelier over the dining table. A table for six with only two people eating at it was a disservice to its grandeur. I was sure she wouldn't mind if I fucked her on it. Chances were she never did.

I sipped the wine she'd greeted me at the door with as she busied herself in the kitchen. Whatever she was cooking smelled good. I was hungry too. It had to be chicken. Fish would have smelled. The last time Connie cooked for me was when I lived in the city. It was long ago, and since after I got married the chances of her cooking for me would be slim to none, she insisted that I came over for dinner that Friday evening after work. And since it would be easier for me to tell Liseth I was working late on a Friday night, I said yes. I would spend the night and leave sometime the next day.

Dinner was chicken, wild rice, baby carrots, and spinach salad. She also had cheesecake, ice cream, and champagne. What an evening it was. Everything went perfectly. Dinner was delicious. Then Gloria called. She wanted to know if she could see Connie that night, and I was sure Gloria would not have minded being told she couldn't, except that Connie told her she had company. Now bear in mind that company could have meant anybody. Anybody from her parents to her sister, to a friend just dropping by. It could have been anybody, but the fact that Gloria asked and Connie refused to say who it was irritated her. And prompted Gloria to ask if it was me, and Connie retorted by asking, what if it was?

I sat there and listened to Connie and Gloria going at it, and Connie reminding Gloria that, unlike her, she was not a lesbian. That she hadn't given up men. Then, in what I supposed was an answer to Gloria's question, she angrily asked, "What if he's getting married? I will always love him. And as long as he comes to me, I'll have him."

I looked at her, and the look on my face said what I was thinking. With the phone still at her ear, she mouthed the words, "What? Don't worry about it."

I shook my head and poured some more wine. I wished she hadn't said it, but the die had been cast. And I supposed at some point Gloria would have to know. After this, what was new? I asked myself.

"You're always welcome here," Connie told her, "but only when I want you to be here." Then she said good-bye, under what seemed like strong protestation from Gloria, and hung up.

"I wish you hadn't done that," I said after she got off the phone. She started to put the dirty dishes in the dishwasher. She was upset but was trying not to make it too obvious.

"Somebody had to tell her. What did she think, that I was gonna give up men?"

I laughed, only because I didn't know what else to say. It was not like having a man as a rival. That I knew how to handle. I'd been there before, and I'd either offered to step aside for the other guy who was obviously in love and was threatening to do something foolish, or I would just leave and let the girl figure out whom she wanted or what she wanted to do. But having a girl as a rival was something entirely new.

When I was younger, I met this girl, Cupid. It was not her real name, but it was what everybody called her. I think her real name was Nadine. I liked that name, but *Cupid* was cute. And it wasn't because of anything overly sexy or provocative why she was called Cupid, although she certainly was very good-looking. Anyway, Cupid was a hot tamale. Tall, skinny, loved to drink Guinness stout, and loved to fuck. Back then, that was the only thing I wanted from a woman. She couldn't be a prude. And any girl I went out with and didn't get to bed with within the second or third date, I'd drop her like bad news.

When I met Cupid, she had a boyfriend. She was, she said, in love with him. I couldn't see how, considering I was screwing her more often than he did. And short of seeing us in action, he had to know I was doing it. Come on now, the guy was in love, but he was not that dumb. Far from it.

Eventually, when he did open his eyes, she threatened to leave him; and for a time, she did. Even after I told her not to. I wasn't in love with her. It was strictly for the sex. Anyway, after she left him, one night I was at her apartment, and he came over. He rang the buzzer, and I told her to let him in. It was in the middle of winter; I didn't want the poor guy to freeze his ass off.

He came into the apartment, and after they exchanged a few words, I offered to leave so they could have some privacy. That was when the guy started to make all kinds of promises about what he would do if she took him back. Not wanting to see a grown man humiliate himself much more, I got up and left. Cupid came after me and begged me to stay, even though I told her she would be better off with him. But she wouldn't hear it.

What I really wanted Cupid to do was to keep her boyfriend and sneak off to see me when I wanted her to. And for a while, that worked, until Cupid came to her senses and realized she wouldn't get anywhere with me. She went back to her boyfriend, and the only thing I could say was I hoped they lived happily ever after.

Guys can, and will, do anything for a girl. Guys will also do crazy things to keep a girl. I have never gotten to that point, but I wasn't like most guys, and I supposed if Liseth threatened to leave me, from a rational point of view, I'd say it would be fine and that I wished her the best of luck, which would be how I'd feel at the moment; but who knew how I might really react in the real situation?

"You think this is funny?" Connie remarked. "What if this bitch decides she wants to make trouble for the both of us?"

"Like what?" I asked.

"Like find a way to let Liseth know. Like try to sabotage the case out of spite." She put some detergent in the dishwasher and said she'd turn it on before we went upstairs.

Gloria was a professional, and she had an ethical responsibility to serve her client's best interest, but jealousy can drive the most professional person to behave unprofessionally. But finding a way to let Liseth know wouldn't be hard. Gloria could send her letters without saying who she was. I'd know who sent it but would be helpless to do anything, knowing that to do anything would be to admit guilt.

Putting on my best *Who me, worried?* face, I said, "I don't think she'd do either one. I wouldn't worry about her. She'll go away quietly." At least that's what I hoped.

As usual, sex that night was great. I got home by six the next day, and Liseth hadn't called.

Chapter 25

—•⊷⟨◦◯♥◯◦⟩⊶•—

Our meeting at the Westchester County District Attorney's Office was for eleven that morning. Connie was not required to be there, but we wanted her there. It was a strategic move on our part. We felt that our client should be there so that whomever we were negotiating with would be able to see her demeanor. It couldn't hurt.

Like in most cases, the DA herself doesn't personally get involved. Most DAs usually stay behind the scene, doing more administrative business, and only come forward when they have to face the press and take the credit. Whatever makes them look good for reelection. So we weren't disappointed when a low-level bureaucrat and his assistant held the meeting with us. It was me, Brian, and Gloria. I went along because I was confident of the result and wanted to be there to give Connie any support she needed. Gloria and Brian would do all the talking.

Gloria and Brian came up together. I told them I would meet them there, since I stayed at my parents' the night before. Gloria called me early Monday morning to tell me she was meeting Brian at the office, as if I needed to know that. At six thirty in the morning? Yeah, Gloria.

Connie had wanted me to stay over at her place and leave with her to court that morning; but for personal and professional reasons, I told her I couldn't. Plus, Sunday before I left her house, Lorna, one of her best friends of many years, dropped by unannounced. They hadn't seen much of each other since the whole incident, and Lorna was worried to death and wanted to know how her old friend, whom she'd known since high school, was doing. Thank God for the security camera that Kevin had installed, we were able to tell who it was before Connie answered the door. It would have been difficult to ignore her at the door, or for Lorna to believe there was no one at home when there were two cars in the driveway.

Lorna came right in as soon as Connie opened the door, as if she'd lost her keys, and just went into "Hey girl, what'a goin' on? I can't tell you enough how sorry I am to hear about what happened. How you holdin' up? How is my goddaughter?" she asked, referring to Nicole.

There I was, standing in the middle of the kitchen, without a chance to get upstairs and put on some clothes, with only a towel between her and my member. She looked at me, and before introducing herself, she said, "Great legs." And I, as if I hadn't seen them before, looked down at them. "You must be Delroy," she said, extending her hand. I switched the orange juice from my right hand to the left to take hers. "I've heard a lot about you," she added.

"And you must be Lorna." She needed no introduction. Connie had talked about her so often I felt as though I had known her, but she was one of the few friends Connie had whom I had never met. Lorna was married and lived with her husband and four children in Boston. She was also a nurse and was visiting her parents who still lived in New York.

Connie and Lorna embraced and smooched each other on the cheek. They held each other and giggled like schoolgirls, and it was evident that they had a lot to catch up on, and that no amount of time would be ample enough to bridge the eight years they hadn't seen each other. My leaving sooner would not give them enough time, but it would help if I was not there.

There was no need for Connie and me to hide anything, even if we had wanted to. Standing in the kitchen with only a towel on, and Connie with a short silk robe on and nothing else underneath told Lorna more than we could ever have told her. But Lorna had already known about us.

I remarked on how late it was, looking up at the kitchen clock. Lorna looked at her wristwatch. It was close to one. I excused myself and went up to get dressed. They were still deep in whatever they were talking about when I came back down. We said our good-byes and that it was nice to meet each other.

For the meeting with the DA, everybody had dressed their best. I'd asked Connie to wear something, preferably a dress, that would portray sincerity. Not to look too much as though she was mourning but at the same time something that said she missed the children's father. No black, purple, or red. No brown either.

She wore a medium-blue dress with three-quarter-length sleeves and a high neck. She topped it off with a string of pearls and diamond studs in her ears, and with her hair pinned up. Her makeup was low key. She looked like a widow, but not like a person who was grieving or falling apart at the loss of her husband. She looked radiant.

In all honesty, Connie did miss her husband. After all, he was the father of her children, and he was a good father. But he was a brutal man.

After we passed up on coffee and bagel, the prosecutors got straight down to business. They were a man and a woman. The woman, black and in her mid to late thirties, was in charge. The man, older, would do less talking and more note taking, but would break in at what seemed to us to be rehearsed intervals that he thought was important to get his point through.

Cordiality ended at the offer of coffee and bagels. We were sure they knew their case was weak, but it also seemed, and we were equally sure that this was for public relation purposes, they were not about to acquiesce to our demands.

Gloria was magnificent. She was a first-rate litigator. Brian and I could have stayed at home. She laid it all out to them. She had floor plans of the whole house. And her minute-by-minute timeline of the incident, plus the doctor's report, convinced them that we would win if we went to trial. Not to mention the marriage certificate from Kevin's first marriage, the birth certificate of his son, and an affidavit from his first wife stating that she had never filed for a divorce in the United States or anywhere else. We also had affidavits from investigators of their search of every state he might have lived in that there were no records of Kevin ever having filed for or being granted a divorce.

"With all due respect, Ms."—then Gloria remembered the cluster of rings on the prosecutor's finger and changed the address—"Mrs. Gaynor, does your office really want to go to trial for political purposes with a case like this? We could go to trial. We're prepared. But do you really want us to present this to a jury? The only thing you'd gain is publicity, and need I tell you it wouldn't be good?"

Janet Gaynor pondered the facts that were just presented to her, and she looked at her partner, who, after careful examination, turned out to be not as old as he looked. Nigel Hawthorn was about fifty-five, but too much exposure to the sun, trying to maintain that tan he had in the middle of October, had damaged his skin and added at least fifteen years to his age.

Before Janet and Nigel could say anything, Gloria interjected, "I know the position you're in. And believe me, I understand. I used to be a prosecutor too. I had cases like this, and there was always someone in the office who wanted to take it to trial. There was always someone who'd say, 'Let the jury decide,' but you know what? The result was always the same, and the taxpayers are the only losers. They're the ones who lose. Because they're the ones who have to pay the bill no matter what." Then she looked over at Connie, who was sitting between me and her father, and said, "Any way this trial ends up, even after my client is acquitted, she will still lose, because in spite of who Mr. Minto was, she will have lost not only her husband, but also the father of her children.

So you see, not only will she lose her husband, but she will also lose the children, two infant boys"—emphasis was added to *infant boys*—"and her daughter. Do you know how ill this little girl is? She too will have lost a father. Because Nicole looked to him as a father figure."

Gloria went on nonstop. She didn't even take a deep breath or sip the water she'd asked for instead of coffee, tea, or orange juice. "I need not tell you that Nicole, only twelve, may never be the same again." Nicole was closer to fourteen, but why correct her when she was doing fine. I would have hated to break her rhythm. Then she acknowledged the loss of Kevin to his parents. "Nobody, no parents should lose a child. No parents should have to bury a child, no matter how old he is. It's usually the other way around. I'm sure Mr. and Mrs. Minto will forever mourn the loss of their son. He was a brilliant doctor, and I'm sure a good son. I can't imagine what their loss is."

Aggressive advocacy aside, she had me believing every word she said, until, "But we have to look at the facts. It was an accident, if nothing else. Tragic as it may be, it was an accident nonetheless. She only wanted him to stop hitting her mommy, and she thought she could scare him off with the knife. He also thought he could have taken it away from her, but whether he slipped and fell on the knife, or she did plunge it into him, and we think it was the former and not the latter, there is no case here. Try as we might, we can't make something out of nothing.

"Take it from a person who has been in this position before, and I'm sure I'm telling you nothing new. After all, you're seasoned lawyers. There is no case."

I could see the face of the jury. They were all shaking their heads in agreement. They were spellbound by her argument. They didn't even have to retire. They asked the judge if they had to retire to return a verdict. The judge said they didn't. They all said in unison, "Not guilty." Then stood up and applauded Gloria. The judge rapped his gavel repeatedly for order in the court. It took the court at least five minutes to be brought under control. The only thing the judge could say was, "Case dismissed. Mrs. Minto, you're free to go."

That was how I envisioned it, and barring the applause by the jury, I was sure that was how it would go.

Gloria was beyond magnificent. She was brilliant, way beyond anything I could have imagined. Brian and I had come along just for the ride. But I guess a partner had to be there.

When Gloria was finished, she looked around again in our direction. She didn't smile or anything, I suppose not wanting to rub Janet's and Nigel's faces in it, but I could see through her. I could read her mind. And she was, in her silence, sticking it to me. Because before Janet or Nigel could say a word, she knew she had just closed the case.

Janet was the first one to speak. "Will you excuse us, please? My colleague and I would like to discuss this for a moment. We won't be more than a minute or so." They both got up and exited through the same door they came in through.

Bill was the first one to congratulate Gloria. He was convinced, as we were, that they would drop the case. Then Brian too added his congratulations. "I could have stayed at home a little later this morning and spent a few more hours with my kids. You didn't need me." We all laughed. I told her how masterful I thought she was. I told her I couldn't have done better. She insisted I could. She was right, but I said no. She said I could. And in the midst of the mutual admiration dialogue Janet and Nigel came back into the conference room. The room went silent. You could have heard a feather drop.

The look on Janet's face was hard to read. She had on her poker face, although she wouldn't know the difference between an ace and a joker. If you mentioned a deck to her, she'd probably think you were talking about a ship. Janet was more the garden club, run-the-food-drive-at-church type. She was the type who would organize the fish fry at her annual church event. She was the type who would have everybody coming to her before they made a decision, and even if they did make a decision without her, they'd still come to her for confirmation.

"We feel we have a case. We feel we could convince a jury that she is guilty," Janet said as soon as we sat down. The expression on Connie's face changed. She looked as though someone had hit her in the stomach. I held her hand and squeezed it. She reciprocated. Bill started to say something, but I stopped him.

"First," Janet continued, "Mrs. Minto claimed that her husband beat her repeatedly, but she never confided any of this to anyone, not even to her sister, who, we understand, she told everything else." Bill was steaming. At any minute, the old cop was about to be unleashed. "The fact that Mr. Minto was—and we have no proof of that, only his wife's word, that he cheated on her repeatedly, that in and of itself doesn't make him a wife beater. Even the fact that he may have been married when he married the defendant"—now it was no longer *Mrs. Minto*, but *the defendant*—"would only make him a bigamist, not a wife beater. We feel—"

"I'm not going to sit here and listen to you do this to my little girl," Bill interrupted. He knew better. He'd been to conferences like this before. He'd seen the prosecutors at work. Their job was to play hardball and then negotiate. But Bill was not a cop that day. He was a father. "My little girl didn't tell anyone because she knew that had I known, I'd have killed the son of a bitch myself."

I was sure right after he said those words that he knew he had said the wrong thing. But again, he was acting as a father. Nigel, as an older man, thinking he had more in common with Bill as a father, interjected, "I know exactly how you feel."

"No, you don't," Bill shot back. "The son of a bitch was a woman beater. He beat every woman he had a relationship with. He's a bigamist, and God knows what else, and you want to send my little girl to jail for doing women and the world a favor. My poor granddaughter had to live with seeing her mother get beaten every day. And what about my granddaughter? What about her? Do you people really care? You're supposed to protect the innocent. You're supposed to seek the truth. What about her?"

Gloria and I tried to calm him down. It took some effort, but he finally calmed down.

Janet continued. She apologized for upsetting Bill, but she didn't say she knew how he felt. Had she done so, I would have told her to go "stuff it, and let's go to trial." I knew, though, that somewhere in the next few words she was going to offer us a deal on a lesser charge, and I was right.

"Let's get to the point," Janet said. "Here is what we can do. We will drop it to man two, and since she hadn't been in trouble before and is from a good family, and I'm also sure there is no risk of her ever getting in trouble again. That we don't have to worry about. We're also taking into consideration her daughter's medical condition and the twins. For that we are willing to recommend no jail time. With man one she could be looking at a steep jail time." She looked over at Bill when she mentioned Nicole and the steep jail time.

If that was supposed to scare us, it failed. Without skipping a beat, Gloria said, "We'll go to trial. We'll roll the dice."

It wasn't her decision to make, but she was making it, and I was sure Brian agreed with her. I did.

"Man two?" Brian said. "Are you kidding? I have to agree with my colleague. We can win at trial. No deal."

Janet and Nigel flashed a look at each other. Why? I didn't know. They knew we wouldn't go for it. "A doctor of distinction was killed," Nigel said. "Let's not forget that."

"By a kid who was saving her mother from being killed," Brian said. "Do you want a jury to look at the kid in her state?"

Janet and Nigel looked at each other again.

Janet put her pen down. She removed her glasses, wiped her face, and put her glasses back on. In that brief moment without her glasses, I saw a woman who was constrained by the duty of her office. I saw a woman who was ready to meet our demands. "What do you suggest?" she asked.

"Accept it for what it is—an accidental killing. Kevin charged at Nicole with the knife in her hand, lost his balance, and fell on Nicole holding the knife. That is the truth," said Brian.

"How about if we reduce it to aggravated assault? She still wouldn't do any jail time. It's the best we can do."

"Then we'll see you in court." Brian started to put his papers in his briefcase and stood up.

"Aggravated assault is not bad, considering the circumstances," said Nigel.

"You can't reduce man one to aggravated assault. This was not a barroom brawl, where any of a number of fifty people may have killed him, and so you just charge anyone you get your hands on, and with shaky evidence, you decide to reduce the charges even though the suspect is an ex-con. It just doesn't go that way. This was a husband beating his wife and got killed by either his wife, who did it in self-defense, or by his wife's daughter, who was trying to save her mother from what she perceived to be grave danger."

Janet and Nigel sat silent for a few minutes. It seemed longer. Then Janet said, "I'll have to talk to the DA about this." She moved her glasses again and wiped her eyes this time. If it was tears, then we definitely had her where we wanted her. At least that was what I thought, but I doubted it. "Can I get back to you in few days, Wednesday the latest? The DA has a busy day tomorrow."

"That would be fine," Brian said. We all got up. We shook hands all around and then left.

As agitated as Bill was, his optimism never waned. As a matter of fact, it was more on the rise as we rode the elevator down. From his years of experience as a cop, he knew when the other side had a weak case; but as a father and also an ex-cop, he figured from the start that Connie should not have been arrested in the first place. And even so, that the charges should have been thrown out at the preliminary hearing. "The goddamn case is so weak it has no legs," he said. "I've seen people with criminal records walk outta jail with more charges and stronger evidence." He put his arms around Connie as a sign of protection, as if to assure her that Daddy would always be there. "It's all political, baby," he said to her. "In a few days, they'll call and make a deal. They'll drop the charges. You'll see."

Bill was right. Later in the evening on Wednesday, Janet called. Brian delayed her until Gloria and I came to his office. She was put on the speaker. She put on a speech before she got to the point. "I just want you to know," she said, "that we still think we have a strong case." The *but* was coming. "But we also feel that in the interest of justice, we wouldn't be doing our office and the taxpayers any good by taking this case to trial.

"Even by proving our case, we still couldn't get a jury to convict her. It would be hard to find twelve jurors who wouldn't sympathize with her, particularly with her daughter. The DA thinks justice would be served better if we pass on this one." All three of us looked at each other. We wanted to burst out laughing, but we controlled ourselves. Gloria pumped the air with her clenched fist.

"We'll recommend to the judge our desire to have the charges dropped. Based upon the evidence, we'll ask the judge to rule the case an accidental death at the hands of a minor. We would just like to say that we think your client got away with murder."

Gloria mouthed the words "You had no case."

"We'll do the paperwork and send you over a copy. At her next court appearance, the judge will mark the case closed, and she'll be freed."

Protocol dictated that we act cordial. We thanked her and her office for the professional way in which they handled the matter and wished her luck.

There was some bitterness in her voice as she ended the conversation. It didn't surprise me. At our meeting Monday, she struck me as being a sensitive and caring person. I guess I was wrong, but like all good attorneys, she knew when she had a weak case.

I have to admit Gloria was right about her, even though I thought she was being the usual bitch; but she did say Janet was mean. Even though I think she went too far in saying that Janet was taking it personal. She thought Janet had subtly injected race into the case, even though I didn't see it. She thought that Janet was taking it personal because one of the brightest in the African American community, who had married a white woman, was killed in the prime of his life.

I told her I didn't think race had anything to do with it, but she thought that was how Janet saw it. I disagreed with her but didn't belabor the point. Brain agreed with me, but he also didn't belabor the point.

We congratulated each other on a job well done, but I insisted, rightly so, that the good work was done by Gloria, that she had worked hard and tirelessly on the case. She had followed every lead and checked every scrap of evidence, no matter how small, from New York to the Caribbean. She followed through, and followed through. That's the mark of a good attorney. I was happy for the ending, but I'd have loved to see her at work in the courtroom. She deserved every credit.

"I'd have loved to square off with that bitch in court," Gloria said. "I'd tear her to pieces."

"I'm sure you would," Brian said. "You'll get your chances on other cases." He leaned back in his chair and clasped his hands behind his head. "Which of you gonna call Connie and break the news to her?"

Gloria and I looked at each other. As subtle as we tried to make it, I was sure Brian read us.

"I think Gloria should do it. They're both the victors in this one." I was being my diplomatic best.

"Fine," said Brian. "Delroy, there is something I'd like to run by you. Will you stay a minute?"

Gloria said her good-byes and closed the door on her way out as Brian asked.

"This may be none of my business," were the first words out of his mouth, "but I'm going to ask anyway. Are you sleeping with Connie? Is Gloria sleeping with her too? I wouldn't ask Gloria this, you know the reason why, but you I can ask. We're friends. We go way back. We share a lot of things. So, are you?"

Before I could answer, he cut me off by telling me how unethical and inappropriate it was to sleep with a client, and that he didn't want to know. "So why did you ask?" My question was rhetorical.

"As I said, I'm more than just your partner. I'm your friend. And a very good friend. I'm a person who care a great deal about you. You have a young and beautiful woman who is carrying your child. Don't do anything to blow it. You know I can't have this talk with Gloria, without it being construed as something else. But you I can talk to."

"Listen, Brian, it's not what you think. I can't say more, but it's not what you think."

"What do you mean it's not what I think? Only a fool would be around the three of you and not know that something is going on between you guys. I don't know how her father doesn't see it."

"Listen, Connie and I have an understanding. That's all I can say."

"What kind of understanding? What, she agreed to be the other woman and be discreet about it? She agreed to not make waves? She agreed to have you once a month? Twice a month? Every other month or something like that? It may start that way. Take it from me, quit while you're ahead."

Brian nailed the matter right on the head. And after he told me that Gloria was in love and could pose a problem for me, and that the problem would be anonymous, I promised him that it was over now that the case was over.

Chapter 26

*I*t was not the kind of victory that Connie felt overjoyed
about. She was happy over the news that jail no longer
hung over her head, but her daughter was still in the
hospital, although her condition had improved. But she would have
had more of a reason to celebrate if Nicole and the twins were
home. She told Gloria that she wanted to spend the night alone.
Gloria said she understood, and that if Connie wanted to talk, she
could call her any hour of the night. Connie said she would, even
though she had no intention to.

It was after eleven that Friday evening when I pulled into
Connie's driveway. There were two cars in the driveway. I didn't
notice the MD license plates on the BMW parked beside her Benz.
It wasn't until I asked that she told me it was Kevin's car. She had
moved his car out of the garage so I could park mine in it. I wished
she hadn't done that, but she did.

That evening, before I left the office, I called Liseth first to tell
her the news, and that I was going by Connie's sister's house, where
their family would be gathering. I told Liseth of the excellent job
Gloria had done, I suppose as some sort of protection—from what I
didn't know. I told her that Connie and Gloria were having a torrid
affair, and that Connie had said that with her luck with men, she

was turning to women. Liseth laughed and said that it was because she couldn't have me. We both laughed at that.

I called my mother next and also gave her the news. Mom was happy for the outcome but was concerned about Nicole. I told her that Nicole was improving. Mom said she was glad to hear it. Then I called Ebony, and she was not only happy for Connie but she also cried. Ebony and Connie were very close when Connie and I were going out. And they had remained friends even after I broke up with Connie. They didn't see much of each other, but they did talk from time to time; and as with most friends who didn't see each other often enough, the talking became less over the years.

Ebony said she would call Connie. I told her that it would be nice, and that I was meeting at her at Greta's house with the rest of her family. And as some sort of corroboration, I told Ebony that Connie and Gloria were in a relationship. "Get the fuck outta here," Ebony exclaimed. "You're kidding, aren't you?"

"It's supposed to be a secret, so don't go saying anything to anybody," I admonished her.

Despite her reaction, Ebony was not totally surprised. Connie had confided in Ebony that in college, she had slept with more than one girl.

"I wouldn't worry too much about her and that girl," Ebony said. She laughed, and then as if it was more of a joke than anything else, she added, "You know why she's doing this, don't you?"

"Why? Because she can't have me?"

"Of course that's the reason. Why else would she do a thing like that?"

"That's exactly what Liseth said."

"You told Liseth that?"

"It sort of slipped out."

"It sort of slipped out, or you wanted her to know that?"

"Well, I told her that I was going to Greta's, and in the course of the conversation, I sort of told her about Connie and Gloria."

"That girl will never get over you, you know that, don't you? By the way, you're not encouraging her, are you?"

"What a silly question to ask." I rolled my eyes. "Of course not. I'm in love with Liseth."

"Just thought I'd ask, because if you're foolish enough to go there, your child might grow up not knowing a father."

"Funny."

"Just letting you know the facts. That Liseth wouldn't think it was funny."

***

"I lied to Liseth again today," I said to Connie as I uncorked the bottle of white wine in her kitchen.

"What did you lie to her about today?" There was a little sarcasm evident in her voice.

"That I am going to your sister's house where the rest of your family are meeting."

"Oh, that. I thought it was about something else." She was definitely being sarcastic.

"That's not enough?"

"The very fact that you're cheating on her means you're lying to her. But"—and she looked at me out of the corner of her eyes—"you could always tell her the truth and risk losing her. Then we can . . . then we wouldn't have to hide our relationship anymore." I poured the wine in the glasses. I took a sip of mine. She drank half the content of her glass and then held it out to me for a refill.

"You'd love that, wouldn't you?" I fixed my eyes on her, looking for a reaction. There weren't any.

"I'm willing to be the other woman in the background, the one you'll never talk about. The one you'll always love to make love to, not that you're not having a great sex life with Liseth, because I know you. But I'm the one you can, you'll always be able to call up at any hour, day, or night, and unless my kids need me at that moment, I'll drop everything for you. I'm the one you can have sex with anytime you want. And even if I'm having my period, I would come just to suck your dick. So, Delroy, what—if you want to ruin things between you and Liseth, don't blame me, because

I'm willing to stay as far in the background as you want me to. And you know what, I'm tired of us having this conversation, because we both know where we stand."

Connie was right. I either had to put up or shut the fuck up. We said nothing more about my guilty feelings that evening. We had great sex and continued seeing each other twice a week until Liseth came home.

***

There were a lot to give thanks for that Thanksgiving. Liseth was home. Mom and Liseth had communicated and finalized their plans for the wedding. As much as Mom was paying for everything, she didn't do anything that Liseth didn't agree with.

Mom had wanted Liseth's family to have dinner at her house, but Esmeralda had her own tradition that she didn't want to break; plus, her son had gone on a drug binge and had gotten himself in trouble with the police. To come to Mom's house would mean she'd have to bring him, which she didn't want to do, or leave him, which she certainly wouldn't want to do either. So even if there was no tradition to uphold, she had to be with her son.

Notwithstanding that, I had a lot to be thankful for in my family, but I had to be thankful as well for Connie. The Monday of the week of Thanksgiving, the judge officially dropped the charges. The court ruled Kevin's death as an accident caused by his own belligerent behavior. The official record stated that he was an abusive husband, and that evening, while beating his wife again, his young stepdaughter, who had suffered with her mother in silence over the years, tried to defend her mother, and he accidentally fell on the knife she picked up, hoping it would have scared him off her mother.

"Kevin Minto, MD, thirty-seven, died by accident caused by his own belligerent behavior." That was how the record read. He was the cause of his own death. No other party was responsible or contributed to the cause. There would be no civil suit, and Liseth would inherit the bulk of his estate. What a waste. A young and brilliant doctor. One of the most eminent heart surgeons, black or white, throwing away his life.

Except for his life insurance, 20 percent of which went to his parents, and which, because it was an accidental death, doubled the death benefit to $4 million. After the 20 percent, the rest was divided up between Connie and the children. The house and all his investments and savings, of course, went to his widow. After the estate was settled, Connie would be a very rich woman.

Connie too had a lot, in her own way, to be thankful for. More than just the ruling on her husband's death, she would have Nicole home for Thanksgiving. The doctors suggested that Nicole being home with her family would be helpful to her progress. Dinner would be at Connie's parents' house. I couldn't spend the weekend before Thanksgiving with Connie, since Liseth was coming home; but that Thursday, I took the day off and spent it with her.

***

Liseth was generally a thin person. Some people would even go as far as calling her skinny. I always told her that she was somewhere in between. But honestly, if you asked me, I'd have to admit she was skinny. But you didn't hear it from me.

Liseth was the type of woman who could eat anything and not have to worry about gaining even an ounce. Her friends hated her. All her life, she always said she wouldn't mind an extra five or ten pounds, and I'd say, "You'll just have to stop cutting your hair." And she would say, "But I don't even cut my hair. You don't want me to."

Pregnancy had solved Liseth's weight, or lack of weight, problem. It was not that obvious, but those who knew her could tell that she had gained some weight. It was somewhere between that five and ten pounds she had yearned for. Her belly was not sticking out in front of her yet. As a matter of fact, she was not really ready for maternity clothes yet, but she definitely needed new clothes. Her face was rounder, and her overall body had changed. The weight, instead of going to her belly, was evenly distributed.

Even her legs, still the most beautiful legs in the world, had gotten fatter. And her ankles were fat. If this was any indication of what to expect during the rest of her pregnancy, we could be looking at a forty-pound gain. At least.

It's not unusual for women who have been skinny all their lives, and have been unsuccessful in gaining weight, to gain a ton of weight and keep most of it after giving birth, never returning to being thin again. It wouldn't matter to me if Liseth was fat or skinny. And since I intended to get her pregnant at least three more times in rapid succession, her not going back to her pre-pregnant weight would not bother me in the least.

Despite the potential for possible huge weight gain, Liseth was in good health. And despite both our parents' and my objection to it, Liseth had decided she would go back to school to finish the fall semester and enroll for the spring. All the arguments we made could not persuade her to at least not go for the spring semester. She compromised on our insisting that should anything happen, she should call us immediately and we would come get her. She agreed. All she wanted, she said, was to complete her first year of law school. Reluctantly, we all agreed.

Getting that one year in was important to her, and we, who were lawyers, could understand. Her mother was very concerned, as much as we all were, about her and the baby's health. Liseth assured us she'd be all right.

***

Roscoe and I went up in his Rolls-Royce. I drove halfway up. I'd driven a Rolls before, and had always dreamed of owning one. You don't see many lawyers on the East Coast driving Rolls-Royces, but maybe when I retired and bought a bigger house for all the kids I had in mind of having with Liseth, I would buy one. Out west, in LA, lawyers driving Rolls were not unusual. Roscoe had his from his playing days in the NBA, which was not unusual.

Roscoe wanted to see Toni. And she was coming back to New York with him to spend Thanksgiving. From everything I heard and saw, it looked like the relationship was advancing to new heights. I was happy for both of them, but most of all, for Roscoe. He'd waited a long time to commit himself to someone.

Except for the prim little Puerto Rican, we saw everybody, including Claire, who was going home to Detroit for Thanksgiving.

Liseth had a lot to talk about, but she was tired and slept most of the way home. The one thing she said was that she couldn't wait to get home. To take a bath in her bathtub and snuggle up in her own bed next to her man. It was the farthest I'd driven a manual transmission vehicle.

That Saturday, we slept late. As much as I'd wanted to, we didn't make love. She was tired, and I could certainly use the rest. We didn't take the phone off the hook, but we'd told our families and friends, Charles and Mildred in particular, to not call us. That we'd call them as soon as we got up. It was after two when we finally got up.

I, of course, got up earlier. Charles, Mildred, and I went running. I came back, took my shower, had some orange juice, toast, and tea, and then got back in bed with the morning paper, and fell asleep again.

"You guys both slept like babies," I said to Liseth when she woke up.

"I was so fuckin' tired. I couldn't believe it." She sat up in bed and stretched those long arms and ruffled her own hair. "I don't have to tell you how fuckin' hard the first semester of law school is."

"No, you don't have to tell me," I said as she got up and went into the bathroom. "Thinking of quitting?"

"Is that what you want me to do? I hope not."

"Of course not."

She sounded as though she was throwing up, and I walked over to the door. Her head was in the toilet bowl.

"Are you OK? Can I get you anything?" Her head still in the bowl, she waved her hand. I took that to mean she was all right. She flushed the toilet and stood up. Before she said anything, she rinsed her mouth out with some water and then put some toothpaste on her toothbrush.

"I'm all right," she said. "Just felt nauseous for a minute. I'll be all right."

"Are you sure?" She shook her head in the affirmative as she put the toothbrush in her mouth.

"I'll get you some coffee," I said.

"No. Get me some ginger ale first," she said as she spat in the sink.

"Ginger ale? Are you sure? Does that work?"

"It's the only thing. Don't worry." She rinsed her mouth out with some water and went back in the bedroom.

I brought her the ginger ale, a large glass, but she drank only half of it. "I'm going to finish law school if it kills me. If I'm going to be a full-time mother, I'm going to be one with a law degree."

"I wasn't suggesting that you should quit. But please don't let law school kill you. I want more kids, at least two more, with you." She flashed that smile, that had I lost it, my confidence would have been restored.

"Come 'ere," she said. We wrapped our arms around each other and kissed. A long, passionate kiss. "Did I ever tell you, you're the most wonderful man in the world?"

"Only a million times, or two. But don't let me stop you from saying it again." We kissed again.

"Well, you are. And I just want you to know that I love you."

"Loving you, Liseth, is the one thing—if I've only done one thing right in my life—is the one thing I've done right."

"I'm flattered, but, Delroy, you have a perfect life. Everything in your life has been going right. You're—"

"You make my life complete, baby. And I want to thank you for that."

She put her arms around me and held me tight. I felt her heart beat. I felt it beating next to mine. It felt more like it was beating in mine. Like it was one heartbeat. We kissed again. I kissed her cheek and nibbled on her ear. She wrapped her legs around me and ran her fingers down my back.

"I want you to make love to me. Ravish me," she said. "Fuck me. Fuck the shit outta me, and don't worry, you won't hurt the baby. As a matter of fact, it's good for the baby. I've heard that the more sex a pregnant woman has, the easier the delivery. Then I want you to make me the biggest meal I've ever had, and then I want to go shopping for new clothes. Precisely in that order." Then she pulled her T-shirt off and lay back in bed. In only her black thong. She had definitely gained at least ten pounds. The thong stuck to her like it was painted on. It would leave an impression when I removed it. I rubbed my hand over her belly and put my head on it, pressing my ears closer.

"You won't hear anything," she said. Her fingers massaged my head. "She's not moving right now. She's asleep."

"She? Oh, so you're sure we're gonna have a girl, are you?"

"Would you be disappointed if we had a girl first?"

I liked the idea that she said "a girl first." I liked that. "I don't care, just as long as we have a healthy baby that looks like you. But if the next one is a girl, we'll just have to keep trying until we get a boy."

"We better get the boy on the second or third time. Four times is the limit. I don't want to keep doing this forever, or—"

"Or we'll what? You know I just have to have a son. We'll just keep trying till I have a son."

"That's what you think."

"Four, eh? Hmm. I guess I have a lot of work ahead of me." I kissed her navel and worked my way down. I pulled the thong off and moved down closer. It was good to have her home again, but I was at home. I was in heaven.

She'd shaved all the hair off her pubic area. It was completely bald. Only once before had she done that. As pretty as any girl is, the ugliest thing you ever wanted to see is a bald pussy. But eating a shaved pussy is one of the biggest turn-ons, and it made getting to the clit easier. And this time, with Liseth ten pounds heavier, the pussy was not only fatter, but the clit was much easier to find. Heaven was an understatement.

I showed no mercy and did as she asked. I fucked her with depraved abandonment. The first time for fifteen minutes. The second for close to half an hour. I would have gone for a triple had the phone not rung. I should have ignored it, but I didn't. It was my mother.

My breathing was not heavy, but it was enough for my mother to remark, "Did I interrupt something?"

"I thought we said we'd call you?" Even though I was in my own home, I was not comfortable talking to my mother on the phone stark naked, with my woman beside me, both of us all sweaty and me breathing irregular.

"You did, but I have to go see someone on short notice, and I wanted to catch you before I leave. What time are you kids coming over?"

I looked at the clock and said seven. Liseth nodded her head in agreement. Mom apologized and said she'd see us later. Then we hung up.

Liseth and I started to laugh. We remembered the number of times we had sex at my parents' house. And how Mom would never come up to my room when we were there. She wouldn't even call on the private line. She would just wait until we came down. Even on Sundays when we'd all have breakfast together. We laughed about Mom's timing this time. We laughed because I told Liseth that when I was younger, Mom literally walked in on me and this girl. It was the middle of the day, and we weren't expecting her home. But ever since, Mom would never come up to my room unannounced. And even though I never made a habit of having girls, except Connie, sleeping over, she would always let me get up when I was ready.

***

I made Liseth the usual. Her favorite: salmon and eggs. Four eggs. Lots of salmon. Two bagels with cream cheese, and a large mug of coffee. I brought it to her in bed and watched her eat the whole thing as though she hadn't eaten for days.

"This is what I miss most about being home. You making love to me and then making me breakfast at almost three in the afternoon, and serving it to me in bed and then sitting at the foot of the bed and watching me as I eat it."

I didn't say anything as she cleaned her plate and then pushed the tray away. She pushed her hair away from her face and held it back as she drank her coffee. I removed the tray and put it on the floor and got into bed next to her. "Thanks for everything, baby," she said. "Sex, breakfast—everything is good. I'm gonna miss all this when I leave."

"Imagine how I'll feel."

"Don't make me feel bad already."

"I'm sorry."

I lay beside her and put an arm around her, reaching around and feeling her nipple. She was still naked. I had on my underpants. She put her hand in my pants and wrapped her fist around my dick. It swelled in her fist. She kept drinking her coffee as she tightened her hold on it. I gently squeezed her nipple as she stroked me. We said nothing as we both did what we were doing. She looked down at me, smiled, finished her coffee, and then put the mug on the night table. Then she slid down beside me and took me in her mouth. There was coffee still in her mouth. I took a handful of her hair. We still said nothing even after she brought me to a climax. Then we snuggled up to each other. We just lay there in each other's arms and briefly dozed off, until the phone rang. It was a wrong number, but it got us out of bed and into the shower.

***

Liseth ate again before we left the house. She opened the last can of tuna and remarked about having to go food shopping as one the things she would have to do before she went back to school. Without barely moving my lips, I said, I was rarely ever home. I didn't think she heard me.

"That's no excuse," she said. "There should always be food in the house. You're starting to live like you were before I moved in. No food in the house.

"I'm going to leave a chart on the fridge door, and when something runs out, I want you to put a check mark beside it. That way you'll know what to buy. I don't want to come back and see this place so empty again. As a matter of fact, I'm gonna ask Mildred to check in on you and make sure there is always food in the house. Better still, I'll ask her to order the things that we needed. We have an account at the supermarket. So all she has to do is order it to this address."

"You make it sound as if I never go food shopping by myself."

She looked at me and smiled. "We know what you buy when you go food shopping."

"I'm getting better."

"That's true, but there's still room for improvement. Mildred goes shopping every week. I'll just ask her to buy what we need. She doesn't have to do it every week."

"I feel like a child having someone looking after me."

"That's your ego, Delroy. Mildred is a friend. And friends look after friends. Don't make a big deal out of it."

She had her sandwich and reminded me to make sure there was always ice cream in the house. I apologized as we got dressed. She said there was no need to, and that she wasn't angry. She could have fooled me.

"I know it will take some time for you to get used to the idea that you're living with someone permanently, but now that I'm pregnant, my appetite has grown. I'm sorry," she said and kissed me.

"That's all right," I responded.

"I'm eating like a sow, aren't I?"

"A little," I laughed. "But it's understandable. You're eating for two." I patted her belly as I said it.

"I seem to be more hungry and horny than usual now that I'm pregnant."

"You won't get an argument outta me on the second one."

"I didn't think I would."

We both laughed. Then we headed out the door. She said she'd like to drive. I gave her the keys to the Range Rover.

***

Mildred and Charles joined us shopping at Roosevelt Field. Mildred had some shopping of her own to do; plus, she wanted to catch up on what was going on in Liseth's life. School, the wedding, and all that they could find to talk about. I was glad they joined us. It gave me a chance to do some catching up of my own with them. Other than our occasional running together, I was beginning to feel as though I was ignoring two of our best friends.

Liseth did more than shop for herself. She bought a lot of stuff for the baby. Mostly things for the baby's room. Blankets, sheets, towels. She also bought some clothes—things that were gender neutral. Mostly whites.

Mildred reminded her of the baby shower that she was sure she would be having. Liseth said she knew, but she couldn't help buying some things she liked. It was her first child, after all. "You'll see what it's like when you get pregnant."

"We've been having sex so many times a day we lose track. We're not giving up, but sometimes I have to admit, I feel like it's not gonna happen." Mildred was clearly exasperated by her lack of success at conceiving. If there was any strain on Charles, it was not the performance, but the fact that he hadn't gotten his wife pregnant.

"Have you guys thought of working with a fertility specialist?" I asked.

"We're going to see one next week," Mildred answered. "For people like us who have just about everything, we need a kid. You don't know how bad we need a kid."

"We know," Liseth replied. "We really know. Hopefully, this doctor can help you."

"We hope so," Mildred said, looking at Charles, who agreed.

We finished our snacks, but not before Mildred remarked on how much Liseth had eaten. Three slices of pizza, two garlic bread knots, and a large soda. I told her of the large late breakfast I'd made Liseth.

"You'd think the way I'm eating I'd put on twenty pounds at least, but I've only gained ten pounds so far. And the other thing, I'm so fuckin' horny all the time." We all laughed.

"Neither one is unusual, but pretty soon, those Victoria's Secret thongs and those jeans won't fit you anymore," Mildred intoned.

"I'll work my ass off to get back into them. Delroy will have to put in a gym or something in that house. I'm not gonna be a fat housewife."

"Maybe you can start running with us?" Charles said.

"Maybe. I'm not sure about that. I was never one for the running thing, but maybe. We'll see."

"It's fun once you get into it," said Mildred.

"You tell her," I said.

"Maybe I'll try it," Liseth said as we got ready to leave. We had to be at my parents', and it was getting late.

Chapter 27

—•⊱❤⊰•—

I
t was sad to see Liseth leave again, but since she promised me that should any irregularities arise she would come home immediately, I didn't show any anxieties. Her Thanksgiving holiday was short, but it was one of the best times we had together. We talked about so much. I even got her to agree that we could have four kids. I didn't want any child of mine to grow up alone. Not that my childhood was a bad one. On the contrary, my childhood was fabulous. I wouldn't have changed it for the world, but I really regretted not having a brother or sister when I was growing up. And for that reason, I always said I didn't want to have just one child. She agreed.

At Thanksgiving dinner, Mom, in particular, noticed the increase in Liseth's appetite. Mom let us in on a secret of her own. When she was pregnant with me, her appetite had increased too. And as much as Mom and I talked about everything, she didn't go into details, but she told us that her appetite was not the only thing that had increased. We all laughed.

After dinner at my parents' house, we stopped at Liseth's mom's; and you guessed it, she ate again. I spent some time with them and then left Liseth there for the night. She wanted to spend some time with her mother and her brother, who was not doing too well.

I was sorry for the poor guy, not to mention their mother for what she was going through. The poor woman. She and Liseth stuck with him when everybody else turned their back. He kept getting on and off several methadone programs and kept getting in and out of trouble, mostly for petty larceny. But they were always there for him. Loyalty was something Liseth and her mother had in common, except when it came to infidelity. Esmeralda still loved her ex-husband and would have forgiven him and taken him back had he wanted to come back. But Liseth and her differed on that one. If we were married, there was no way Liseth would have taken me back if I cheated on her.

Mom, Liseth, and her mother were supposed to go look at the wedding dress the next day. Mom would pick them up at Esmeralda's. I wanted to stop by Roscoe's place and have a drink with him and Toni, but they had other plans. I could understand. There was so little time left before she went back to school.

The whole week Liseth was at home, she didn't mention Connie and her problem once. Not that she should, but the subject didn't come up. The closest we came to it was when we were at Ebony's, and it was only because Ebony and I were talking about Nicole's condition. And all Liseth did was listen. She said nothing. And Ebony and I made it brief.

***

The trauma Nicole suffered from having accidentally killed her stepfather was much more severe than we all imagined. The doctors and everybody had thought that being home for Thanksgiving would be helpful to her. They knew they were taking a risk. It could go either way, but it was a risk they thought was worth taking. It didn't help. It was a setback.

Nicole reacted adversely to her trip home, even though the doctors couldn't understand why. Just being home shouldn't have made her react the way she did. But since they could not think of another reason, they concluded that it must be the trip home. The thought on everyone's mind was that it was too soon bringing her back home. The poor kid. If the DA could only see her, they'd know that the decision they made was the right one.

Connie and I had kept up our same routine. Wednesdays and weekends. Fridays or Saturdays, depending on how busy I was at the office and how late I got out on Friday evenings. Our routine was safe, and Gloria was kept under control by Connie. Gloria was forced to accept the reality of life. Love was a powerful force. And when it's unleashed, nothing can hold it back. Those who oppose it will get run over if they stand in the way. Two people in love are like a bush fire. It's best to stand back and let it burn itself out.

Connie had wanted me to spend a whole weekend at her place. And I had wanted to too. So two weeks before Christmas, I told Liseth that I was going out of town to Los Angeles, to interview a client. I told her not to call me unless it was an emergency. And to call me only on my cell phone. She said she would call my mother. I told her she would get me no matter what, and that I'd catch the first plane out. We agreed.

I wanted to spend the whole weekend with Connie for two reasons: Christmas was coming, and Liseth would be home soon; and if for some reason she changed her mind about going back to school, the frequency of Connie and me seeing each other would reduce drastically.

That weekend, we decided to make it a complete weekend. We decided to go out. Something we hadn't done in a very long time. I left all the arrangements up to Connie, and she decided we would go out to dinner and then to a club. Dancing was something we had loved and had done often when we were dating. Connie was a good dancer, and especially when she drank. We would be on the dance floor for hours. It had been a long time. but even though Connie and I loved to dance, we would not stay on the dance floor for more than two tunes at the most. It may have been a while, but I hadn't lost my enthusiasm for dancing. And I could still keep up with Connie's marathon dancing.

We had to be selective in where we went, so she chose a restaurant and a club in New Jersey. Somewhere in East Orange. I'd never heard of either place, but it was somewhere she and her friends and sister had been to.

The evening was fabulous. We dined on lobster and drank champagne. And at the club, we danced as though we were teenagers. Nonstop. And drew everybody's attention. But we didn't care. We danced and drank more champagne. Between the restaurant and the club, we must have put away three or four bottles, even though I drank the most. All night I could feel people's eyes on us, even though I knew it was Connie they were looking at in that low-cut, tight black minidress.

It was one of the best nights out I'd had in a long time, and I made the most of it. The night was on Connie. She paid for everything and did the driving. So I didn't hold back on the drinking. I was as drunk as a sailor. Connie did her share, but she could always hold her liquor better than I could.

By the time we got to her place, I was too drunk to remember anything, but I vaguely remembered her giving me a blow job before I passed out.

***

The next day, I was planning on fucking the living daylights out of her. I figured that what alcohol robbed me of doing the night before I'd make up for the next day.

It was about two or three in the afternoon when I woke up. Connie was not beside me in bed. I went to the bathroom to take a leak. My head was spinning, so I just stumbled into the bathroom and deposited half the piss onto the floor. I was naked, so I didn't shake. The state I was in, it wouldn't have mattered had I had clothes on. I stumbled back into bed and lay crossways for about fifteen or twenty minutes. It could have been half an hour. I really didn't know. All I knew was that my head felt as though I'd fallen off the Empire State Building and landed on it. All that mix drinking at the club—at one point, we'd switched to shots. At the time, it felt good, but that day, I was paying for it. Big time. And Connie woke up at her usual hour as though nothing had happened the night before.

Not only was my head spinning, but I was incoherent, or still drunk. I couldn't be sure which one, but I must have thought I was at my house on Long Island, because I picked up the phone.

There were voices on the phone. Because I was still in that drunken, incoherent state, the voices startled me. But I didn't say anything. I just returned the phone to its cradle. Or at least that's what I thought I did.

I lay there in bed, totally out of it. Oblivious to my surroundings. The room felt like it was caving in on me. It was the worst hangover I'd ever had. The bed felt as though it was a raft going over a waterfall. And my stomach felt as if it was coming up through my mouth. And on top of everything, I was farting nonstop. And then I started to hear voices. Two women's voice. The same voices I heard earlier on the phone. "He's still asleep. I got him undressed and put him to bed. He'll be all right," one voice said. And I smiled, because this was part of a dream; and in my drunken, incoherent state, someone was looking after me. What the fuck was this, I got drunk and found religion?

"You can't let him know," the other voice said. I swore I smiled again. For what, I don't know. But I did.

"I promise you, he won't know," the first voice said.

"He'd better not, or we'll be in a lot of trouble." This sounded like a warning coming from the second voice. And at this point, I rolled over in bed and felt a hard object under me, squeezing me in my back. I reached under to move it. It was the phone. I hadn't put it back on the cradle as I thought.

"It was not supposed to be like this, Greta."

I assure you, I was still suffering from the effect of too much vodka and champagne from the night before, but when I heard Greta's name, somehow something inside my head turned off something. The phone was in my hand, and I was not dreaming. There was indeed a conversation on the phone. And I was curious.

"I didn't want it this way, either, but it worked out perfect, and you're a free woman now."

As much as I knew by now I was not dreaming, and I was sure of who were on the phone, I had no idea what they were talking about. But I knew I wanted to know, because they mentioned Nicole. And that, more than anything, piqued my interest.

"But what about Nicole?" Connie's voice started to crack when she mentioned her daughter. "She may never be the same again. And she's afraid to be around you. Look how she behaved on Thanksgiving. None of this . . ." She paused. "All the money in the world is not worth it . . ." She paused again. Her voice strained when she talked.

"Don't say that, Connie. You know this is not about money." I put my hand tight over the phone, held the receiver closer to my ear, and tried to hold my breath so not even air could get into the phone. Greta went on, "I didn't do it so you could get money, Connie. You ought to know that. This isn't about money. Somebody had to put a stop to him sooner or later. If not, you'd be the one who'd be dead."

I was shocked beyond comprehension at what I was hearing. It didn't take me too long, and I didn't have to hear any more, although I listened, to know that it was Greta who had killed Kevin. But how? And why?

"I couldn't just stay upstairs while he beat the shit outta you. I had to do something." Greta's voice was now beginning to crack. She was getting emotional, and I was sure she was about to cry. "I love you, Connie. You're my only sister. You don't deserve what you've been through. Nobody deserves it. I begged you for the longest time to leave him. You could have come to live with me and Victor. If this didn't happen, he would have killed you someday."

"We should have told the truth, Greta. We should have. Delroy would have taken care of everything. He's a good lawyer. Dad would have taken care of everything. He knows these things. He's—was—a policeman. God, we should have told the truth, Greta. We should have." Connie started to cry. I sat there and listened, still shocked, unable to understand what I was hearing.

Worst still, I was finding it hard to believe what I was hearing, but knowing that it was real.

Connie was still crying and pleading with her sister that the truth should have been told. Even at this point, she was telling Greta that it was not yet too late to tell the truth, but Greta responded icily, "You better pull your goddamn self together. You better get yourself in shape before Delroy hears you. It's too late now. It's over. We can't change anything. It's over, Connie. Are you listening to me? It's over." She raised her voice. Then she calmed down. "Connie, listen to me."

Connie was sniffling.

"Connie, are you listening to me? Nobody would have believed us. And I would have gone to prison. Plus, it was your beloved Delroy's brilliant idea. It was him and his legal mind that implicated Nicole. None of us would have implicated her. None of us would have even thought of saying it was her who did it. The idea was for you to plead self-defense. You were supposed to be the suppressed, battered spouse who couldn't take anymore. Nicole was the last person on our minds as a defense. It was his idea, but it worked out fine. You're free, and trust me, Nicole will be fine. She'll get better. Don't worry."

I certainly couldn't believe what I was hearing. And it disgusted me. I got up off the bed and reached for my clothes. I was sure the noise I was making would tell Connie I was awake. By now, my head was back to normal, but steam was coming out of my ears. She'd lied to me. She'd lied to all of us. But most of all, she'd manipulated our friendship.

"I think Delroy is up," Connie said. "I gotta go."

"Remember, don't say anything to him. It's better this way. Kevin was a piece of trash. He deserved what happened to him. Nicole will be all right. It will take some time, but she'll be all right."

"But—"

"But nothing, Connie." She never let Connie finish.

***

I was drunk last night. Drunker than I'd ever been in a long time, or that I could remember. That was what I was thinking as I got dressed. I was out with a woman whom I loved, and was putting everything on the line for her. Last night was a night that I enjoyed. A night that could compare with few nights in my life, although I couldn't remember everything or much of what went on after we got to her place, though I woke up naked today. Maybe that was it. I was suffering from the effects of too much vodka and champagne. Maybe the combination was playing tricks with my mind. Maybe it was a bad dream after all. Maybe I'll wake up and find Connie naked beside me. Then I'd tell her about my dream, and we'd laugh, then we'd make love, and it will all go away. But it was not a dream.

I was dressed and was halfway down the stairs when we met. The look on my face said it all. She asked what was wrong. I didn't tell her anything. She didn't buy it. I was dressed, and I was upset about something, she said. Something had to be wrong.

I wanted to storm out the door, get into my car, and just get the fuck out of there. That was what I wanted to do, but I also wanted to know the *how* and the *why*. I needed an explanation. She owed me one. She owed me that much, if nothing else.

I lingered in the kitchen. She walked in after me. "You hungry?" she asked. "Can I make you something to eat? Some scrambled eggs or something?"

My stomach felt like there was a hole in it. Whether the hole was from a bad hangover, or from being hungry, or from something else, I couldn't tell. But I knew no amount of food I ate could have filled that hole. And nothing I ate could have tasted any good.

I told Connie I wasn't hungry. She insisted that I should eat something. And that it wouldn't take her long to whip up something. I had the feeling she was trying to make small talk, and it tempted me to say something nasty, but I resisted it. I insisted I wasn't hungry. She asked me if I'd like for her to open a can of soup, or if I'd like some tea. I agreed to the tea. She filled the kettle and put it on the stove and took two cups out of the cupboard and put tea bags and sugar in them.

I leaned over the kitchen counter with my elbows supporting my head. She came up behind me and put her arms around my waist. I pulled myself away. "What's wrong with my baby?" she said.

Ah, come on now, bitch. You're not that dumb. And you're certainly not that smart. "Please, Connie, stop acting as if you don't know what's wrong. And stop calling me baby. I'm not your goddamn baby."

She stepped back from me and filled the cups with the boiling water. I didn't feel like having tea anymore, but I drank it anyway. There was a strange taste in my mouth. The tea made it worse. She moved in toward me. I moved away.

"Listen," she said, "there is something obviously bothering you, and I'm no fool. It has something to do with me. After the night we had last night, it must be something you think I did, or maybe you just feel like acting like a fuckin' prick. Maybe this is your way of breaking it off, because you're getting married. If that's the case, Delroy, you don't have to go through all this shit to break it off with me. You're better than that. But, whatever it is, at least tell me. I'm not going to stand here and watch you behave like you've just woke up with some girl you picked up in a bar the night before, and after sleepin' with her, you woke up and found your wallet missin'. If there is somethin' bothering you, say it."

At this point, I had no choice. I put the cup down and pushed it away. "That's rich, coming from you," I said, looking at her.

"What are you talking about?" There was no credibility in that question. And I was sure she knew that, and that she shouldn't have said it.

"You lied to me, Connie," I said indignantly, and without giving her a chance to ask me again what I was talking about, I said, "You used me. You manipulated me. You even used your own daughter. How could you do that to me? And to Nicole?"

She paused for a moment and then looked at me. The expression on her face had changed. That defiant, feisty facade was no longer there. She had realized that I'd just busted her. There wasn't much else to say. "It's not the way you think, Delroy. It's not like that. You have to believe me. I swear to you."

"Then you tell me what really happened. You tell me that what I heard earlier was a misunderstanding. Tell me that I didn't hear what I heard."

The feistiness returned. She got defensive and said, "You listened in on my call?"

"What fuckin' difference does it make?"

"You had no right to—"

I cut her off. "Come off it, Connie. We're not in a court of law. This is not inadmissible evidence. It doesn't matter how I heard it. The fact is I did. I heard what I heard, and you owe me a fuckin' explanation."

"Don't raise your voice at me in my house," she said, raising her own voice.

That remark was enough. Without another word, I headed toward the door. "Fuck you, bitch. I don't need you and this shit. Take your sorry-ass life and get the fuck away from me."

She caught up with me at the door and asked me not to leave, and that she would tell me what happened. That she would tell me the whole story, and that I should not form any judgment until I had heard everything. She asked me to come back into the house.

***

Connie and Greta were upstairs in her bedroom, talking. Nicole was in her room, the twins in theirs. Connie and Greta were talking about the divorce, and how the house might have to be sold, because she wouldn't be able to keep up the payment on her own. It was just as well, Connie said. It was too fuckin' big anyhow. And they both started to laugh.

Greta had told her that she and the kids could move in with her and Victor—at least until she found herself a place. They were laughing and talking. They were also drinking, but they were not drunk, even though Greta had drunk more than Connie. Greta was never as big a drinker as Connie, but it was all right, because she was staying over with Connie.

At some time after six, they weren't sure of the time, they saw Kevin's car pull up in the driveway. He got out and walked to the door. They watched him and were laughing at the fact that his keys wouldn't fit in the clocks. Connie had changed all the locks soon after he moved out.

Realizing that his keys didn't fit, Kevin decided to walk to the back of the house, but came back to the front door after none of his keys wouldn't fit any of the locks on the back or side doors either. He rang the bell, and after getting no response, he decided to bang on the door and call out to Connie. He knew she was in there. He didn't know Greta was there, because her husband dropped her off

The noise from the banging and shouting was enough to cause a disturbance in what could be considered a placid neighborhood. It didn't, however, stop him from carrying on. So Connie decided to let him in, even though Greta thought she shouldn't. He would eventually go away, Greta said. But he wouldn't have. And Connie knew that. So she let him in.

"You changed the lock on my fuckin' house," was the first thing out of his mouth. And in rapid succession, he accused her of one thing after another. Of even having a man upstairs. Telling him his accusation was ridiculous only inflamed him and made him more insistent on going upstairs. It certainly didn't help either that when she told him, he was not supposed to be there and that he should call next time before he came.

"To come to my house? I have to call before I come to my own house? Are you fuckin' kidding?" He advanced toward her. His face in her hers, Connie could smell the rum on his breath. And she further accused him of being a drunk and not being helpful.

A shouting match ensued, and Kevin's determination on going upstairs was hampered by Connie's feeble attempt to stop him. Shouting led to wrestling, which was then followed by him pushing her to the floor. In defense, she grabbed him, and that was followed by a succession of punches to her face. They came so fast she couldn't say how many there were.

The screaming brought Greta downstairs. Connie didn't see her, but she heard her say, "Don't you hit my sister again. I swear I'll kill you, motherfucka." Or something like that.

Greta had apparently took the knife from the butcher block, and just as she warned Kevin, she plunged the knife into Kevin's chest. It happened so fast, neither of them had time to think. And it was at that moment that Nicole came downstairs and witnessed what happened.

Nicole saw her aunt plunge the knife into her stepfather's chest, and she let out a scream. Kevin turned toward the child with the knife in his chest and staggered toward her. Frozen from what she had just witnessed, Nicole just stood there as Kevin staggered toward her and fell on her. That was why she was covered with all his blood.

It was the shock from seeing her aunt kill her stepfather that put her in her placid state. Not anything she did.

I asked what Greta did after that. Connie was crying, and Nicole was obviously crying and just kept murmuring, right up until the police came, "He's dead. He's dead."

I had known Greta for a long time. Longer than I'd known Connie. Greta was not a person without humor, and she was not one to not enjoy a good joke, but she was the one person you'd want on the deck of the Titanic. I suppose that was one of the qualities that kept her and Victor's marriage together. But the calmness she displayed after killing Kevin was without equal. She shouted for everybody to calm down. And as much as Connie too was hysterical, she obeyed. But Nicole just kept repeating over and over, "He's dead. He's dead."

As if rehearsed, and with a cold look in her eyes, and as if ice water was running through her veins, Greta calmly directed her sister on how to behave when the police came. She told Connie to give her twenty minutes before she called the police. And to tell them if they asked that she was too hysterical to call right away. No more than twenty minutes, she insisted. Then she further instructed Connie to call her at home when the police were there, and that she would call me.

Greta, Connie said, handled everything as though she had it all planned. And looking back at everything, and her feelings toward

Kevin, she very well could have had it planned, even though neither one of them knew Kevin was coming over that night.

"But according to you, no one, including Greta, knew that he was abusing you," I said to her.

"I lied to you," she said.

"No fuckin' kidding."

"She knew all along that Kevin had hit me several times. She knew every time he hit me. She was the only one I could talk to."

Then she went on to tell me in detail of how she and Greta would talk about what she was going through and how Greta had encouraged her to file for a divorce, but she wouldn't. At least not until she and I had that talk.

Greta was angry with her for staying in the relationship so long. The beating had started right after the twins were born, even though his temper had already been revealed before that.

The irony of the whole situation was that Greta thought Kevin would kill Connie if she didn't leave him. She had begged Connie to get out of that relationship no matter how hard it might be on her and the children. Connie started to cry when she talked about the ordeal. I felt sorry for her in one way, but on the other hand, I felt betrayed and used. Because she lied to me, and had I not picked up the phone in my delusional state, I would not have known the truth.

"I suppose it would be stupid of me to ask if you were ever going to tell me the truth?" If there was ever indeed a stupid question. This was it. "I guess not."

With her head bowed, she shook it from side to side and barely whispered, "No."

"No it was stupid of me to ask, or no, you weren't going to tell me the truth? Which is it?"

"I didn't see any sense in telling you."

At least she was honest enough to tell me the truth. "I didn't think so. Connie, you've betrayed our friendship. Not to mention our trust. What, you didn't think this was something you could tell me? You didn't think I could handle it? What the fuck were you and Greta thinking? Had you told me the truth from the beginning, I could have formulated a defense. There are defenses for everything. That's why we're lawyers. Do you realize the position you have put me in now?"

"I'm sorry. But I just didn't think . . ." She stopped for a minute. It was certainly not to think. "I didn't think . . . I don't know. It's just—"

"Of course you didn't think. That's why you need lawyers. We're trained to think. That's why people hire us. To think. That's what we're good at. To think. That's what we do best. Think. If half of you people could think, you wouldn't need us. Thank God. You were going to say something. Please finish."

She looked at me with some of the fire in her diminished. I felt no pity for her, because she was stupid. The one thing I don't do is have pity for stupid people.

"It's just that . . . well, Greta thought that if I said that, that I was the one who killed him, I could plead self defense and use the abused spouse as a defense."

There she was, thinking again. "You know, if your sister was really thinking, she would have told the truth. Ask your father. He'll tell you. The truth is important. Give us the truth. That's where we work from. You may have won the case, but look at the mess you've created. Look at Nicole."

"We just didn't think Nicole would be involved. We never, in a million years, considered blaming Nicole, and if you remember, I tried to resist your suggestion when you brought it up. We just couldn't tell you the truth." She wiped her eye. And if she hadn't told the truth in all the time we knew each other, that day she was telling me the truth. But I was in a difficult position.

As an officer of the court, I had an ethical obligation to uphold the integrity of the court. I'm also bound by ethical conduct to preserve and protect anything my client tells me. I'm not obligated to disclose anything my client tells me, but what I had just found out was not because my client confided it in me but because I listened, by accident, to a conversation between my client and her sister.

I'm not sure there were any ethical restrictions on me going to the DA and revealing what I heard; but the problem—and this could get me sanctioned, or even disbarred—was me sleeping with my client. I indeed had a problem, because even if by some miracle I escaped sanction or disbarment, which I doubted, I certainly could not escape Liseth leaving me. Or my partners asking me to leave the firm for bringing disgrace to them. I explained this to Connie.

"I'm sorry," was the only thing she could say.

"Don't worry, I won't go to the DA. I won't, because I have too much to lose. With my luck, the only thing would happen is that I'd get disbarred and lose my woman and child. Nothing bad would happen. Don't worry, Connie, your secret's safe with me. For some stupid reason, call it selfish, call it whatever you want, but I'm not going to ruin my career. Even though I came damn close to doing it. My parents would never speak to me again. That is, if they didn't kill me. I'd lose them too. And that, more than anything else, I couldn't live with. No, I couldn't live with that. But, Connie, here is what I'm going to do. And I mean this from the bottom of my heart."

Tears welled up in my eyes. This should have been easy, but I couldn't deny my heart wasn't broken. She had let me down. It was the hardest thing I'd ever done. "I'm going to walk out that door and get in my car. I'm going to drive away, and after today, you and I will never see or speak to each other again. I'm going to marry my woman and live happily ever after. You'll go on with your life. There are not many people to tell anything, but for those who ask about us, you can tell them anything you want. Tell them I'm a jerk, for all I care. It won't matter. If anybody asks me, I'll just tell them . . . I'll think of something. It doesn't matter, as long as I never see you or speak to you again."

She started to say something, but I stopped her. I held up my hand and said, "Don't." Then I walked out the door.

***

I should have been relieved. I should have been overjoyed. I should have been happy that the bitch did me a favor. But I was angry. Very, very angry. Had a cop been driving behind me, he would have pulled me over. My anger was showing in my driving, and I couldn't control it. The question was, who was I angry with? I was angry, for sure, but I wasn't sure who I was angry with. Maybe I was angry with myself more than anybody else. But why, I didn't know.

I should have been angry with Connie, but somehow I wasn't. Disappointed? Yes. But not anger. Pity? Yes. But not angry. With Greta? She was another story.

I always knew Greta was a smart girl. It was why Victor married her. She handled all his finances, and some said she wore the pants in the house. But killing someone? I'd never pegged her. A mild-mannered schoolteacher who loved kids and would go out of her way to help someone? Nah.

I punched in her number as I slowed down to go through the toll bridge. She answered on the first ring. As if she was waiting for me to call.

"You were listening, weren't you?" No "Hello." No "How are you doing?" She just went right into it. "He was a pig, Delroy. He deserved to die."

"Maybe so, Greta, but you just can't kill a person because he's a pig. And even pigs are covered by a city ordinance. You just can't kill one on your property. It's against the law. I feel no pity for him, but he was not attacking you, so it was not self defense. You should have told the truth."

She didn't miss a beat. "What's done is done. The question is what are you going to do now that you know the truth?"

"What do you think I should do?"

"Well, since you're an arbiter of the truth, you could start by telling the truth yourself. You could go to the DA and tell her that, hey, Ms. DA, I just happen to be fuckin' the suspect, who, by the way, I'm in love with, and one night, after both of us were drunk, I woke up in her house. In her bed. Picked up her phone and overheard her and her sister discussing how her sister murdered her husband. You could tell them that. It would be the truth. You could tell them how long you've been sleeping with my sister. It would be the truth. You could tell them how often and the different places you have been screwing her, while living with someone else. It would be the truth. I'm sure since you're an arbiter of the truth, you'd want to tell them everything. It would be the ethical thing to do now, wouldn't it? I'm sure you had told your fiancée all about what has been happening between you and Connie. I'm sure she has no problem with it. She's not adverse to open relationships, I'm sure. That's why she's marrying you."

I could see her giving me the finger. I could see her laughing in my face. She knew I couldn't do any of the things she mentioned without risking everything. If I told the truth, I would run the risk of losing everything. Greta knew that, and she knew I wouldn't risk it.

"Delroy, you're a good man. Kevin was a pig. Someday he would have killed my sister, and a smart lawyer like yourself would find a way to get him off. She's my only sister. She's my baby sister, and when we were younger, I swore I'd take care of her. I didn't know it would be like this."

There was no remorse in her voice, until she talked about Nicole. "The only thing I'm sorry about is . . ." She paused. "I'm sorry about what has happened to Nicole. I truly am sorry about that. Just like I didn't plan on killing that pig, but she'll get better, and we'll all go on with our lives. Just like you too will go on with your life. You will marry your girlfriend. You'll forget about Connie and let her put back the pieces of her life in place. She'll get over Gloria too. Oh yes, I know all about her and Gloria. You didn't think I knew? I knew Connie liked to sleep with girls every now and then. It's something she picked up in college. I'm sure she'll do it again with another girl, but like the others, she'll get this one out of her life too, and everything will get back to normal. Go on with your life, Delroy. There will be too many memories. There will be too much pain. It's best this way."

She hung up, and as I headed east on the Long Island Expressway, I thought about what she said, and I knew she was right. It would be best this way.